P9-CCO-997

A Mother's Promise

—— The ——
Women of Pinecraft

ANNA SCHMIDT

BARBOUR
PUBLISHING

© 2012 by Anna Schmidt

Print ISBN 978-1-61626-236-5

eBook Editions:
Adobe Digital Edition (.epub) 978-1-62029-634-9
Kindle and MobiPocket Edition (.prc) 978-1-62029-633-2

All rights reserved. No part of this publication may be reproduced or transmitted for commercial purposes, except for brief quotations in printed reviews, without written permission of the publisher.

All scripture quotations are taken from the King James Version of the Bible.

This book is a work of fiction. Names, characters, places, and incidents are either products of the author's imagination or used fictitiously. Any similarity to actual people, organizations, and/or events is purely coincidental.

For more information about Anna Schmidt, please access the author's website at the following Internet address: www.booksbyanna.com

Cover design: Kirk DouPonce, DogEared Design

Published by Barbour Publishing, Inc., P.O. Box 719, Uhrichsville, OH 44683, www.barbourbooks.com

Our mission is to publish and distribute inspirational products offering exceptional value and biblical encouragement to the masses.

Printed in the United States of America.

What People Are Saying About
The Women of Pinecraft Series:

"Amish fiction fans will be swept away by Schmidt's captivating story of love, the importance of dealing with grief and caring for others, and how God can help and guide even in the midst of life's storms."

—Christian Retailing

"A new series about Mennonite and Amish cultures with memorable characters who just want to help people. Schmidt is a wonderful storyteller. She invites readers into a world few outsides get the chance to experience."

—Romantic Times

"As a lover of contemporary rom-coms I don't often reach for books that straddle the fence of time, sticking buggies and horses next to modern convenience. Yes, I'm speaking of that great-selling, over-published subgenre of the inspirational market known as: Amish fiction.

"I'm not (usually) a fan.

"The new series by award-winning author Anna Schmidt, however, doesn't fall into the tidy Lancaster County box we've come to expect from cardboard-cutout Amish romances. In *A Stranger's Gift*, Book 1 in The Women of Pinecraft series, Schmidt has broken new ground by creating intelligent, original characters and setting her novel in Sarasota, Fla., within the Conservative Mennonite and Amish community of Pinecraft (yes, it is a real place!). Plain folk on the beach? I did not see that coming."

—USA Today

"A Stranger's Gift is an inspirational, uplifting romance that beautifully demonstrates both the strength and kindness of the Mennonite people. Even as a hurricane rages across Florida's Gulf Coast, even as her hometown faces destruction from the wind and water, the heroine works to help those in need. No matter what she must face in the aftermath of the hurricane and in her heart, the faith she has in God doesn't waver."

—Melanie Dobson, author of *Love Finds You in Amana, Iowa*

"This fast-paced novel (*A Stranger's Gift*) takes you on a journey into Florida's Mennonite community that you won't soon forget. Schmidt's characters come alive as their world crashes around them. You won't be able to stop turning pages until you reach the satisfying end. Can't wait until the next in the *Women of Pinecraft* series."

—Mary Ellis, author of *Abigail's New Hope*

"*A Stranger's Gift*, Book 1 of Anna Schmidt's Women of Pinecraft Mennonite series, is an engaging tale of loss and redemption, set against the background of hurricane season on Florida's Gulf Coast. Mennonite aid worker Hester Detweiler finds her courage and faith challenged by the devastating loss suffered by stubborn loner John Steiner. Schmidt crafts a fascinating picture of Mennonite life in an area that has been little explored in Plain fiction, and readers will be delighted with this new entrant in the popular genre."

—Marta Perry, author of *Vanish in Plain Sight* and *Katie's Way*

"Anna Schmidt takes us back to Pinecraft, Florida, and her Women of Pinecraft series with this compelling novel (*A Sister's Forgiveness*) set in this Mennonite community. It's a story about love of family, dealing with death and anger and finding forgiveness. It's about learning to seek forgiveness from others and to give forgiveness. In Tessa's journal she questions what mercy is and asks if that is what forgiveness is really all about. Your heart will be blessed by this story."

—Viki Ferrell of Fresh Fiction

"I do believe Anna Schmidt is one of my new favorite authors. Her books differ in style and content than most others in the Christian genre that I read. Redemption is a strong element and the characters dwell on things other than romance. These characters face real-life problems and struggles. I recommend this series, The Women of Pinecraft."

—Sally Riley, The Friendly Book Nook

Acknowledgments

Writing any story means finding "partners" to guide the process especially in those areas where the author is admittedly no expert. As with other books in this series I am deeply indebted to my Pinecraft/Sarasota friends Rosanna Bontrager, Doris Diener, and Tanya Kurtz Lehman. In addition I could not have brought the medical pieces of the story together without the assistance of Lois Pearson, Suzanne Berg, Barbara Oleksy, Jill Wiench, and Jim Greear. My thanks also go out to editors, Rebecca Germany and Traci DePree, as well as to my agent, Natasha Kern—a dear friend and unwavering cheerleader. Finally not one of the books I have written could ever have come to light without the constant love, support, and encouragement of my husband, best friend, and life partner, Larry.

Prologue

Ohio, Late Autumn, 2010

Rachel Kaufmann stood at the end of the lane that led to the farmhouse and waited for her husband to return from harvesting the last of the winter feed corn. It was coming on darkness and the wind that had come out of the southwest all day had shifted north.

She pulled her shawl over her white prayer covering and wrapped her hands in its folds. She had left her gloves back at the house, so anxious had she been to share her good news with James.

For several years she had helped supplement their farming income with private-duty nursing jobs, but now she'd been offered a full-time job as school nurse for their rural district. The nursing degree that she'd completed just before she and James married would finally be used to its full potential. She knew that her husband would be as pleased by the news as she was.

What could be keeping him?

She shivered a little and stamped her feet to offset the damp and cold as she peered into the lengthening shadows, listening carefully for the sound of the old tractor he would be riding back to the farm. It had rained steadily for days now, and the fields were awash with standing water. Twice that week the tractor had gotten stuck and James had had to abandon the work, but that morning he'd been confident that the strong overnight wind had done its job so he'd headed back to the fields.

She heard a car approach and knew it was a regular vehicle, not the tractor she longed to see coming around the sharp curve in the road. Headlights swept over her as the driver slowed and turned onto the lane.

Her sister-in-law, Rose, rolled down the passenger-side window. "Rachel? Is that you?"

"Of course it's her," James's brother Luke snapped irritably. "Who else would it be?"

"Just waiting for James," Rachel said. She drummed her fingernails on the back window, drawing the attention of the four children crowded on the backseat and waving to them.

"It's freezing," Rose protested as she wrapped a shawl more tightly around her shoulders. "Get in."

"No. I'm all right. I'll wait."

"Better you come on back with us and help Mom get supper on the table." Luke was not making conversation. He was—as usual—giving an order that he fully expected to be obeyed.

"James will be along soon." Rachel met her brother-in-law's eyes.

"Suit yourself," he said as he gunned the motor and sprayed gravel behind him on his way to his parents' farmhouse. Rachel saw Rose's hand waving at her as they sped away.

Perhaps it would have been best to stay in the house even though her mother-in-law, Grace, had smiled when she saw how Rachel kept glancing out the kitchen window watching for James. "Why don't you go on down there? Surprise him."

"Getting colder," James's father, Earl, had announced as he entered the house and hung his broad-brimmed black straw hat on its usual hook by the door. Next to it was the hook where James would hang his hat. "Just going to wash up," he'd added as he passed by his wife's rocker and leaned in to kiss her temple. "Take your shawl, Rachel. That wind is shifting."

Rachel loved her in-laws dearly. She just wished that she and James could have blessed them with more grandchildren. James's brothers all had large families, but James and Rachel had only one son, ten-year-old Justin.

"Can I come with you?" Justin had asked.

"No, finish your homework. We'll eat as soon as Dad gets home."

Now as she turned away from the tail lights of Luke's car and took up her vigil for the sound of James's tractor, she frowned. When she had told Justin that she had applied for the school nurse job, her son had asked a surprising question. "Dad will let you work there, right?"

"Of course. He'll be happy for me—for all of us. Why would you ask that?"

"Because Uncle Luke says that good Mennonite women shouldn't work outside the home," Justin had said. "He says that Aunt Rosie has plenty to keep her busy and then some."

"Aunt Rosie has four children all under the age of seven," Rachel had replied before she could censor herself.

But she knew that Luke would disapprove of her taking the job. In his view, if a woman wanted to take on the occasional cleaning job to earn what he called "pocket money," that was tolerable. But a job like this one, working for the county—outsiders—that would definitely not be to his liking. Even though Luke was the youngest of James's three brothers, he was the most conservative when it came to what he thought Mennonite women should and should not do. He was so strict that Rose always wore solid-colored caped dresses—never the occasional small floral print that other women of their faith wore. And the children—even though they were all well under the age when Mennonite boys and girls would be baptized, join the congregation, and start to follow the dress code and traditions of their elders, Luke insisted they be dressed in the homemade clothing that he and Rose wore.

Just then she heard the familiar sputter of the tractor, and all thoughts of her differences with her brother-in-law flew away on the wind that whipped at her skirt. James was coming. He would be as happy about this as she was. He would pull her up onto the tractor beside him, hold her tight, and kiss her. "That's my girl," he would say, and then he would kiss her again.

She stepped into the road as he came around the curve, the dim headlight of the battered tractor barely visible in the gathering dark. But she could see him waving, so she knew that he had spotted her, and she knew that he was smiling as he began steering the tractor into the left turn he needed to make to reach their lane.

Suddenly she heard another sound, much louder and far too close. Before she could cry out a warning to her husband, she was blinded by headlights that lit James from behind as if he were on a stage.

He motioned for Rachel to step back as he turned the tractor's steering wheel hard to the right.

In the chaos that followed, the screech of brakes applied too late, of metal hitting metal, the blaring of a car horn, Rachel stood frozen to the spot where she had last seen her husband.

And then she heard feet running toward her.

"Call 911, Grace," Earl shouted.

"Stay there, Justin," Luke ordered.

Rachel walked slowly toward the large modern car, its headlights now spotlighting a scene that she could not wholly comprehend. That vehicle showed no signs of damage other than a white airbag lying limply against the driver's seat. A young man was stumbling around next to it, making low keening sounds. On the far side of the car, the tractor lay on its side in the ditch. Pinned underneath it was the very still body of her beloved husband.

"James," she cried as she scrambled into the ditch, uncaring of the muddy water that soaked her skirt and apron. She knelt next to her husband, touching his cheeks and forehead, covering him with her shawl. "Lie still," she instructed. "Help is coming."

But she was a trained nurse. As she searched for a pulse and bent to administer CPR, she knew that the ambulance siren she could hear faintly through the fog of her shock would never arrive in time.

Part One

I will lift up mine eyes unto the hills,
from whence cometh my help.

PSALM 121:1

Chapter 1

Summer—Two Years Later

Rachel stood at the end of the lane waiting for the mail to be delivered. It wasn't that she was expecting anything. Her daily walk to the mailbox had become one way that she could find a few minutes respite from the way her life—and Justin's—had changed over the two years that had passed since that horrible night.

At first, as she had faced the hard grief besetting her following James's death, Rachel had asked God for many things—mostly for the strength to go on and for the wisdom to know how best to care for Justin. Certainly her strength to move forward without James's comforting presence had been tested many times and in many ways.

Earl had suffered a mild stroke, and the family had known that there was no way the elderly man could continue to manage the large farm with only some occasional help from his remaining sons. A week after that her brother-in-law Luke and his family had moved into the farmhouse.

Wanting to make them feel as welcome as possible, Rachel had immediately offered them the large upstairs bedroom that she and James had shared. Their boys had moved in with Justin while their girls took over the room once occupied by James's

13

parents. Grace and Earl moved out to the smaller cottage behind the main house.

Rachel had tried blaming their mutual grief for the tenseness that permeated the house. She told herself that everyone was feeling the loss of James in different ways. But as time passed she realized that the discord arose not because everyone was missing James so much but because Luke did not approve of her working.

"Your son needs you," he would tell her.

"Justin is in school during the hours I am at work," she pointed out. "When he is at home so am I."

"And leaving Rose to manage everything," he had continued as if Rachel hadn't spoken. "It's a large house."

Rachel did not point out that whenever she came to the kitchen and offered to help prepare their supper or feed the youngest children, Rose would shoo her away. "You go and rest now," she would chide. "You've been working all day."

Rachel had made the best of the situation and tried to encourage Justin to do so as well, promising that it would just take some time for them to all settle in. But after a year of Luke ordering Justin around and openly criticizing her failure to be the Mennonite woman he thought she should be, Rachel knew that there would be no *settling in*. This was their life.

A life without James.

And then one snowy afternoon just before Christmas break she had been called to her supervisor's office and told that her position as the school nurse was being eliminated due to budget cuts.

Without her job to fill her days, Rachel found herself spending more and more of her time out in the smaller cottage that James had built for his parents. She would sit at the kitchen table with her mother-in-law, rolling out dough or peeling apples for the pies that Grace made and sold at the local store. But after several weeks, she had to admit that there was little room for Justin and her in either house—physically there was, but they didn't fit in other ways. She considered moving down the road to the farm where she'd grown up, but her parents had died and the running of the farm was now shared by her two brothers, both of whom had large families of their own.

As the seasons passed, she watched helplessly as Justin became more withdrawn and somber. Now with no school in the summer he was even more at the mercy of his uncle's demands and criticisms.

"I can't do anything right," he'd muttered one evening as he stormed into the house and up to his room.

"Get back down here, Justin," Luke ordered.

"Let him be," Rachel said. "He's doing the best he can, Luke."

"No he is not and neither are you, Rachel. James was too soft on both of you—taken in by that pretty face and sweet smile of yours from the day you two met. Well, I'm not James, and I expect you and your son to do your part around here."

Rachel had walked away from him without another word. She'd gone up to Justin's room and tried to console him. But her attempts at comfort and reassurance fell on deaf ears—Justin's and her own.

Now as she waited for the mail to come she paced the side of the narrow country road as she tried to think of anything she could do to make things easier for Justin.

"Here you go," the postal worker called out as he leaned out the side of his vehicle and handed her a small stack of envelopes. "Have a good one, now," he added as he pulled away.

"And you," she called after him.

As she slowly walked back up the lane toward the house, she shuffled through the mail and paused when she reached a letter addressed to her—a letter from Florida.

She stopped walking and slid her thumbnail under the flap of the blue envelope. Inside she found a sympathy card and letter from her college friend Hester Steiner—a voice from her past that she found far more comforting than any of the voices surrounding her at the farm.

Dear Rachel,

Greetings from sunny Florida!

I have just heard the news of James's death. I am so sorry that I was not there with you during this terrible time.

I know we lost touch over the last several years, but I think
of you so often. Oh, how I miss you and our talks so much.

She wrote of her marriage and her work helping to manage
a nonprofit co-operative that employed homeless people to
distribute fresh fruit and homemade jams to food pantries.
Hester sounded so very happy that Rachel could not help but
feel a twinge of envy.

It took Rachel more than a week to write back. In her letter she
talked of the troubling aspects of her life in the same lighthearted
way the two friends had shared when they were roommates. She
made jokes about being banned from the kitchen, and rightly so,
since Hester would recall that Rachel was not much of a cook.

Hester's reply came within days. She had seen through
Rachel's poor attempts at humor and addressed the deep-seated
unhappiness that lay beneath. And true to form she had a solution.

Come to Florida, she wrote as if it were as simple as that.
Rachel snorted a wry laugh, remembering Hester always seemed
to think everything was possible.

There's an opening at a local hospital in the spiritual
care department. You'd be perfect for it. I've enclosed an
application form and the name and address of the senior
chaplain. He and his wife volunteer at the co-op, and we've
become friends. I've told him all about you and he's waiting
for your application so don't disappoint him—or me.

This too, was so like Hester, dishing out orders, expecting
Rachel would do her bidding simply because to her it was the
perfect solution to the problem at hand. Never mind that Rachel's
training was in nursing, not counseling.

Rachel put Hester's letter including the application in a
drawer of her bureau, and for the next three nights just before
she knelt next to her single bed for her nightly prayers, she read
through the form, mentally filling in each blank. Each night she
prayed for guidance, and on the fourth night she sat down and
completed the application. The following morning she waited by

the mailbox and personally handed the completed form to the mail carrier.

"Where is that boy?"

Justin cringed when his uncle Luke stormed into the kitchen. His aunt Rose murmured something. Aunt Rose always kind of whispered when she spoke to Uncle Luke, like she was afraid of him.

He was beginning to understand that fear because Uncle Luke seemed to be mad a lot about one thing or other. He wasn't anything like Justin's dad had been. But then nothing about his life now was like it had been before his dad got killed by a drunk driver.

At first it had seemed like things might get better. His grandpa had been sort of like his dad in those weeks right after the accident. His mom had started her job and his grandma had done what she'd always done—cooking, baking pies for a local store that he delivered with her after school and on weekends. His mom helped his grandma with the cleaning and cooking when she wasn't working. The way things went during that time, it had sometimes been easy to forget his dad was really never coming back. It had been almost normal, like Dad was just out planting a field or something.

But then Grandpa had had his stroke and after that it was like he was suddenly a whole lot older and weaker, and Gramma as well. It wasn't long after Grandpa got home from the hospital that Justin's uncles had this family meeting and decided that Uncle Luke and Aunt Rose should take over running the farm while his grandparents moved back out to the smaller cottage that Justin had helped his dad build for them in back of the main house.

His best buddy Harlan's grandparents lived in a house like theirs while Harlan and his parents and brothers and sisters lived in the main farmhouse. It was the way things were done in their world, although he'd met some kids who were not Mennonite who thought it was pretty weird the way Mennonite families all stayed together in one place. Well, Justin was pretty sure he wouldn't like living the way those kids did with their grandparents in some whole other state. He figured that those kids would be even lonelier than he was if their dad died.

"Justin!"

His uncle stood in the doorway of the small bedroom that Justin now shared with two of his cousins.

"Coming," he said automatically, although he had no idea if that was what his uncle wanted him to do.

"Don't give me that attitude," Luke said, his teeth and fists both clenched. "There's work to be done, boy. Now get to it."

Uncle Luke turned and walked back downstairs.

Justin wondered for a minute what his uncle might do if just this once Justin refused to follow his orders. But he already knew the answer to that one. Luke would take a willow switch to the backs of his bare legs, and his mom wouldn't be able to stop him. His dad could have because he was the eldest and as such Luke would have had to listen to him. But his dad was dead and his mom had no real power—none at all.

In early August, Rachel was hanging laundry on the line outside the kitchen of the main house when her mother-in-law called for her to come answer the telephone in the cottage. "Long distance," she added. Surely a long-distance call in the middle of the day meant bad news.

Rose came out onto the back porch of the main house, her lips pursed with curiosity.

Inside the cottage, where they kept the phone just in case Earl took a turn for the worse, Grace handed her the receiver before quietly returning to the kitchen.

"Hello?"

"Mrs. Kaufmann?"

"Yes?" Rachel's hand was shaking as she gripped the receiver of the old rotary dial telephone.

"This is Pastor Paul Cox, senior chaplain for Gulf Coast Medical Center."

"Oh, hello. How are you?" This was about the job—the Florida job. Her hand began to sweat, and her heart was beating so hard she thought that Pastor Cox must be able to hear it.

"I'm very well, thank you for asking. I have your application here. I am with our hospital administrator, Darcy Meekins, as well as a member of our board of directors, Malcolm Shepherd. Do you have a moment to talk?"

"Yes sir." Her reply was automatic. Her mind was busy trying to quell the hope she felt rising in her chest.

"Excellent. Let me put you on speakerphone." Rachel heard a rustling and crackling, and then Pastor Cox was back on the line, his voice now sounding amplified as if speaking from far away—which of course, he was. "Our time for filling this position is quite short, Mrs. Kaufmann. The hospital is set to open next week, and the truth is we had almost decided on another candidate when we received your application."

Rachel's heart sank. *Then, why call at all?*

As if she had spoken aloud, she heard a different male voice answer. "Mrs. Kaufmann? Malcolm Shepherd here. You see, this is a brand-new medical center. We're located a mile east of the Amish and Mennonite neighborhood here in Sarasota. We hope to serve the residents of that community as well as the growing communities that have sprung up over the years east of downtown Sarasota. One of our goals for the medical center is to offer a diversity of staffing in all departments. With that in mind we were understandably pleased to receive your application."

Malcolm Shepherd's calm explanation of the situation eased her concern that they had only called as a courtesy to say that her application had come too late. In her letters, Hester had mentioned the businessman who was also a large financial supporter of the fruit co-operative Hester and her husband had founded in Sarasota. Hester really admired him and the work he and his wife did in the community. Just hearing him on the phone, Rachel thought she understood why. He had a way of putting people at ease—at least he did that for her.

"Therefore," he continued, "we decided to extend the timeline in order to at least have the opportunity to interview you."

"I appreciate that," she said, her heart sinking once again. "But I cannot come to Florida for an interview."

"Rachel?" a clipped female voice interrupted. "Darcy Meekins, hospital administrator here. Assuming this time works for you, we are interviewing you now."

Rachel could not help being reminded of her brother-in-law when she heard the woman's clipped tone. Like Luke, Darcy Meekins seemed more inclined to giving orders than to being part of a general discussion. Rachel also could not help noticing that the woman had called her by her given name while both men had been more formal in addressing her. What did this mean? Was she supposed to call the woman *Darcy*?

"Is this a good time?" The woman sounded impatient.

"Yes, Miss Meekins. This is fine."

"I prefer *Ms.* Meekins."

Rachel barely heard the correction as Rose and three of her children entered the cottage. Rose shooed the children toward the kitchen. "Gramma has cookies," she promised in a whisper, and then she stood by the front door, her arms folded across the bibbed front of her dress, her eyebrows raised in question. "Is everything all right?" she mouthed.

Rachel nodded and covered the receiver with her palm. "It's. . . I'll tell you all about it after I get off." She met her sister-in-law's stare until Rose finally got the message and headed for the kitchen.

"Mrs. Kaufmann, are you still there?" Pastor Cox asked.

"Yes. I apologize. This is a family telephone and—"

"I see that you attended nursing school," the hospital administrator interrupted. "Please explain why you believe you are qualified to serve in our spiritual care department?"

"Well, I do have my degree in nursing, and as I mentioned on my application, I have additional course work in social work, plus certification in a special counseling program for victims of violent crimes and their offenders. I am a woman of deep faith and I believe I can. . ."

"The counseling needed here is hardly a match," Rachel heard the administrator say in a low voice obviously not intended for her ears. "I see that you are not currently employed. Why did you leave your last position?" Darcy continued.

Rachel's hand began to perspire as she clutched the receiver. All of a sudden she wanted this job and the opportunity it represented for her to start fresh, the possibility that she could provide for Justin. "The position was eliminated due to budget cuts," she replied, fighting to keep her voice calm and professional. "As I noted toward the back of the application, you may certainly contact my former employer for a reference."

One of the two men at the other end of the call cleared his throat, and then she heard Pastor Cox say, "Why don't I tell you a little more about the position?"

"I would appreciate that," Rachel said.

"We have a large children's wing here at Gulf Coast. You would be working primarily with children. Are you comfortable with that?"

Rachel could not control the smile that spread across her face and carried through to her voice. "That would be truly wonderful, Pastor. I love children."

"We are talking about children of all ages," Darcy cautioned. "Infants, toddlers, children in school, children with physical issues that have also, in some cases, exploded into serious emotional problems."

"That was the case when I worked as a school nurse. Well, not the infants and toddlers of course, but children of all ages from kindergarten through high school, and from all backgrounds."

"And faiths?" Darcy asked.

"Yes. All faiths. It was a county school system."

She heard what sounded like a door opening and closing and the rustle of papers as a man's muffled voice apologized for being late.

"Mrs. Kaufmann," Pastor Cox said, "Dr. Ben Booker has just joined us."

"Hello, Mrs. Kaufmann. I read your application. Impressive." The doctor's voice was kind, and she thought that he must've been very good at putting his patients at ease. She pictured a balding gray-haired man wearing a white coat with a stethoscope around his neck. The image made her smile.

"Thank you."

"So, do you think you're interested?"

Rachel hesitated. This doctor had just joined the interview, and this was his first question before he'd even asked one thing about her qualifications?

"I understand that there are other candidates," she said, choosing each word with care. "I certainly appreciate that you would consider my application at all."

There was a moment of such dead air that Rachel thought perhaps somehow they had been disconnected.

"That wasn't the question," the doctor said, breaking the silence.

"Yes. I would be very interested."

"You do understand that you would need to earn your certification as a spiritual counselor per Florida state regulations?" Darcy Meekins asked. "And you would need to do your course work on top of the hours spent at the position, hours that will include some nights and weekends. There's also some fieldwork included in the course."

"Yes. That was clear on the application."

"A formality," Pastor Cox added. "You can do the required field work right here."

"You would need to move here within a matter of a few weeks. Could you manage that should we offer you the position?" Ms. Meekins pressed.

"I could. Yes." Rachel had never felt more certain of anything—other than her decision to marry James—in her life. She wanted this job.

"You don't need time to consider?" the hospital administrator coached. "To speak with your family?" It was as if she was trying to remind Rachel of all the reasons why this was not a good idea.

"There's really just me and my twelve-year-old son, Ms. Meekins. My husband passed away nearly two years ago. My son understands that I make all decisions based on what's best for him."

She heard the woman blow out a puff of air. "Well, *we* need some time," she muttered, and Rachel realized that she had once again covered the receiver and said this to the others.

"Very well, then," Pastor Cox boomed. "We had narrowed the field of candidates to two and now with you we have three. Give us a few days to mull over the pros and cons and we'll be in touch. Is that all right?"

Rachel's heart sank. There was no way they were going to hire someone from over a thousand miles away for the position if they had two other qualified candidates right there. "That would be fine," Rachel said. "Is there anything else you need to know about me?" Now she just sounded desperate.

"As my brother might say, Mrs. Kaufmann," Malcolm Shepherd said in a tone that Rachel could only describe as kind, "no worries. We have already received electronic letters of reference from the superintendent of schools in your district there in Ohio as well as letters from three teachers that worked with you. Hester Steiner has given a verbal recommendation." He chuckled. "She's certainly been persistent in making sure we consider your application."

Rachel smiled. "Hester can be—"

"We'll call you," the hospital administrator interrupted. Rachel couldn't help wondering if the woman was perpetually impatient or maybe she just had a lot on her schedule and was anxious to get this meeting over with.

"Thank you again for considering me at all," Rachel said. "I'll look forward to your call."

"Three or four days," Pastor Cox promised. "We'll call either way. You enjoy your weekend now," he added, and after murmured good-byes all around the line went dead.

But the very next day—Friday—she had once again been called to the telephone.

"Mrs. Kaufmann? Pastor Cox here."

Her heart sank with disappointment. If they had made their choice so quickly then there was no chance that. . .

"How soon can you get here?"

Rachel was speechless. But that didn't seem to faze the chaplain, who continued talking as if the question had been purely rhetorical.

"Assuming you still want the job, we'd like you to get started as soon as possible. Now let me just put Mark from Human Resources on the line and he can give you the details of the offer, okay?"

"Yes, thank you."

The man from Human Resources took the phone and gave her information about salary, hours, benefits such as vacation and personal time, and insurance. "The search committee has approved a certification program for you so you'll work and attend classes, but they're available online so you fit it into your schedule however you like. All right?"

Her mind raced with the logistics of working and going to school even if it was online. And certainly there was the issue of being available for Justin as he got acclimated to his new surroundings. "Yes."

"There will be a probationary period of four months," Mark continued in a voice that told her this was hardly the first time he had delivered this information. "During that time others will be observing and assessing your work. If for any reason at the end of the probationary period, the members of the search committee—or you—decide this isn't working, the appointment can be terminated. Do you understand?"

"Yes."

"So how soon can you get here?" Mark's tone changed from official to casual.

Rachel couldn't help it. She laughed. This was the best news she'd had in months. For the first time since James's death she could actually see the possibility that God had a new plan for her life, one where she and Justin could start again and perhaps recover a measure of the joy they had known before. "I need two weeks if that's all right," she said.

"Suits me," Mark said. "Here's Pastor Cox."

"Let's make that Paul, okay?" the minister said as he took back the phone. "And may I call you Rachel?"

"That's fine. Oh, thank you so very much. You have no idea what this means to me. Please thank the others for me."

Paul laughed. "Happy to have you, Rachel. Now Mark will be

sending you some materials about the hospital, the certification program, and the general area to look over. It'll give you a head start before we see you in a couple of weeks. Until then, as Mark so aptly put it, welcome aboard."

Chapter 2

Just two days after the Kaufmann family celebrated Justin's twelfth birthday his mom gave him the news. Somehow he knew that what he would remember most about this birthday wouldn't be Gramma's spice cake with its caramel frosting—his favorite. Or the new clothes his aunts and uncles and cousins had given him. No, this was the birthday he would remember most because his world had just been turned upside down—again.

"Justin, I've been offered a job," she told him as the two of them sat on the wooden swing that hung from a large horizontal branch of the willow tree just outside the farmhouse kitchen.

He couldn't help but think about another day almost two years before when his mom had made a similar announcement just after Dad's funeral.

"The thing is," she continued as she pushed the swing into motion with her bare foot, "the job is in Florida."

Florida? Justin's mind raced as he tried to take in the idea of moving not just off the farm where his dad had grown up and he'd been born, but halfway across the whole country.

He didn't know a single person in Florida. Mom kept going on about her good friend, Hester. But Hester wasn't family. How could Mom even think of leaving Gramma and Gramps?

"We can start fresh there," he heard her say.

I don't want to start fresh, he thought, feeling a wave of the anger that was pretty much the way he felt most of the time these days. *I want our old life. The one where I helped Dad with the chores. The one where Dad and I fished in the pond in summer and went ice-skating in winter.*

"What do you think?" his mom asked him.

Justin mentally ran down the list of things that he'd learned about Florida from the books he'd read and stuff he'd learned at school.

"I know it's a big change," she continued when he didn't answer right away. She brought the swing to a halt so she could lean forward, her elbows resting on her knees as she stared out at the fields surrounding the farmhouse and its outbuildings. "But just think," Mom said, her voice high and nervous, "you can go swimming in the Gulf of Mexico."

"They have alligators," Justin said, as if that alone illustrated the scope of the change she was asking him to make.

"Alligators don't live in the Gulf," she replied.

"Sharks, then. And snakes—big poisonous ones, and what about how hot it is? Those skinny palm trees I've seen in pictures don't seem like they'd provide much shade." Justin was desperate to find something that would make his mother listen to reason. She didn't like hot weather all that much.

"They have seasons just like we do in Ohio, just no snow or hardly ever. And there are other trees besides palm trees."

"We don't know anybody there," he pointed out.

"I just told you, Justin. When we first get there, we'll stay with my college roommate, Hester, and her husband, John Steiner. When we were in college Hester and I were best friends."

Then why can't you understand that I'm not excited to leave my *best friend, Harlan?* Justin wondered, but his dad had taught him not to question his elders, especially his mom and grandparents. And now that his uncle Luke was in charge, Justin knew that he'd be risking a paddling if Luke heard him challenge his mother.

It had been a year, nine months and eight days since Justin's dad had died. Justin had heard people say that the force of the car's speed gave his dad no chance at all for survival. He'd died right there next to a stack of rocks that Justin and his cousins had pulled from the field earlier that year and piled by the roadside ditch. He died even though Mom had tried so hard to save him. The driver of the car had been drunk.

At first Justin had been so mad at that man for being drunk and driving his car, but his gramma had reminded him that as Mennonites they believed in forgiveness. He must not harbor hard feelings against the man. So Justin had tried to forgive—he really had. He and his mom had even gone to a kind of school to help people like them get past being so mad.

In the end Justin went along with the program mostly because it came up about the time his mom lost her job, and she was pretty excited about it. Afterward she even took some training so that she could help other people like them and the drunk man.

"It might lead to a paying job," she'd told him.

But it hadn't, and his dad was still dead.

He hated the way people at the funeral had kept clutching his shoulder—the men—or touching his cheek—the women—and saying that Justin was now the "man of this family." He wasn't sure what that meant. Was he supposed to get a job now? Or maybe they were saying that he needed to take on managing the farm like his dad had.

Justin pushed himself off the swing and walked a little ways from his mom, his back to her. He had to think. He had just turned twelve years old, and his world kept getting twisted inside out.

"What about school?" he asked, grasping for anything that might keep this from happening. He stopped short of reminding her that Dad had always talked about how important it was for him to keep up with his studies, especially math. The night his dad died he'd been working on his math assignment and he'd been excited about showing his dad how he'd solved every problem.

"There's a lot you have to figure in running a farm," Dad was always reminding him. "Not just what things might cost but how to know how many fence posts you need to fence in a certain field. Stuff like that."

And what about the fact that his dad had liked to read? Not just the scriptures or about farming but other stuff. Justin also liked to read, and he was good at it. And Dad was always real proud that Mom had gone to college even though as Mennonites, being proud about anything was considered a bad thing. But Dad was always teasing Mom about being the brains of the family. She would get all giggly like the girls at his school did and tell him to stop, but Justin could see that she liked it. Yes, school was important to both of his parents.

"Is there a school—one of *our* schools?" he asked again.

"Hester says that there's an entire Amish and Mennonite community right there with churches and a school and shops and everything." Her voice went all soft and dreamy. He turned around so he could see her face. She looked up at him with a smile and then bit her lower lip before adding, "We'll go to church there and shop and you'll meet people and—"

"Do the Steiners live near there?"

"Well, no. They live some distance away, but they shop there and attend church."

Justin frowned. Ever since his dad died school was his world—the one place where he could escape his uncle's constant criticism.

His mom sat back again. She wasn't looking directly at him—a sure sign that he wasn't going to like whatever she was about to say. "You see, when we first get there, we're going to need to be closer to everything—my work, your school. We won't have a car. There's public transportation of course—a bus line."

Justin's suspicions went on high alert. This was sounding like more change than he was ready to face. "But we'll be close to the school—the Mennonite school?" When his mom didn't answer immediately, he began guessing. "A Christian school? A church school?"

"A public school," she said, and then her words came out in a rush. "It's only for the first semester. Until after the first of the year. By that time we'll know for sure that my job is secure and we'll have had time to explore different neighborhoods and places to live. I'm in hopes that we can rent a little house in

Pinecraft near the church and the Mennonite school, but in the beginning—"

"Pinecraft? You said Sarasota."

"Pinecraft is what people call the Amish and Mennonite community right there in the middle of Sarasota, Justin," she explained. "From what Hester tells me it's more like a neighborhood than a separate town. But the hospital where I'll be working is some distance from there, and the public school is close to the hospital."

Public school. "I'm not dressing the way our people do in a public school," he said defiantly.

"No. I wouldn't ask that of you." She sighed as if she finally got it that he wasn't as excited about this as she was. "I know it's a big move, Justin," she said as she stood up. He was almost as tall as she was—something he wished that his dad could see.

"Justin!" His uncle was standing outside the barn, his hands on his hips. He looked mad. Of course, whenever he talked to Justin at all, he always seemed to be mad about something. "Chores?"

"He's coming," his mom called back. She sounded almost as mad as Uncle Luke did. His mom and uncle had never really gotten along, especially not since his dad had died.

"Justin," his mom said. "I promise you that it's all going to work out—for both of us. We'll come back for visits, and Gramps and Gramma will come see us in Florida. You can take Gramps fishing." She brushed his hair away from his forehead with two fingers the same way she'd done a million times before. "I need you to trust me, okay?"

Justin knew that she wasn't asking his permission. In their world the adults made the rules and the decisions.

"Yes ma'am," he murmured.

As he trudged off, he clung to the promise she had made—a promise he didn't see how she could keep, but one that he intended to hold her to.

As the bus half-filled with passengers sped along the highway connecting the life that Rachel and Justin were leaving behind to the one she prayed would not turn out to be a mistake of catastrophic proportions, she absently fingered the fine silky wisps of her son's hair. He was asleep now, his head on her lap, his lean, long body so like his father's folded into the bus seat beside her. He was tall for his age and looked older than his twelve years.

The growth spurt he had experienced this last year was not all that had changed about Justin. Ever since his father's death, he'd become more introverted. Before that, he had asked questions about everything from the weather to learning about the path the Kaufmann family had taken generations earlier in settling in Ohio. His insatiable curiosity was a source of gentle teasing from everyone in their large extended family. But after the funeral, and especially after Luke's family had moved into the farmhouse, Justin had taken to spending much of his time alone. When he was with family, he barely said two words. It was as if he had buried all of his questions and curiosity about life along with his father, and that worried Rachel.

She felt so uncertain of everything now that James was not with her to make the decisions for their family. It was the way of their people that the man of the house made all the major decisions while the woman cared for the children and managed the household. But James wasn't here. This was a decision she had made completely on her own. Maybe she was making a mistake. Maybe Justin would be better off living close to his cousins and grandparents even if Luke insisted on taking out his dislike of her on her son.

If she challenged him, Luke excused his strictness by telling her that Justin needed the strong hand of a man now that James was no longer around to guide him. He had actually laughed at her the first time she'd worked up the nerve to express her concern. "You and my brother have always been far too easy on the boy. He will not thank you for it when he is grown," he'd warned. "Do not question my authority here, Rachel. You are too much tied to the ways of those outsiders you work with."

As she stared out the tinted window of the bus, she could see little but the reflected lights of passing cars on the highway and the silhouettes of buildings in the distance. She searched the eastern sky for the first signs of the new day and saw only darkness. It was in these blackest hours before dawn that Rachel thought most often of James.

Of course, in the weeks that immediately followed his death, she had thought of little else. How could she possibly go on without him? They had known each other all their lives. Her parents had raised chickens just up the road from where James and his family had their dairy farm. She and her siblings had walked to school with James and his siblings. Her brother had married one of his sisters. The two families had joined forces numerous times to register the hallmarks of their lives—holidays, weddings, births, and deaths.

James had never been sick a day in his nearly forty years. Even the normal childhood illnesses like measles or mumps had passed him by. He had been a tall man with a kind of gauntness to his body and features. After they had married and he had let his beard grow out, more than one person had commented on his resemblance to Abraham Lincoln. It was a comparison that James found flattering in spite of the Mennonite call to avoid such compliments. More than once when he seemed to puff up a bit after someone made the comparison, Rachel had teased him that she might buy him a stovepipe hat like the one that President Lincoln had worn.

Oh, they had laughed together about so many things. And they had cried together as well. After she had miscarried four times, James had held her close, the tears leaking slowly down the burnished plains of his face. "God has a plan for us, darling girl."

And then their prayers had finally been answered with the arrival of Justin. "I'll never ask for anything again," Rachel had vowed.

But James had placed his fingers against her lips, shushing her. "That's a promise you cannot keep. God is with us," he told her. "You can ask."

She had prayed every day since the funeral for God's guidance. Then Hester's letter had arrived, and here they were less than two weeks later on their way to Florida. Of course, Hester was already way ahead of her.

"Malcolm and his wife have a guest cottage on their property that they never use," Hester had told Rachel when she called a week earlier. "They'd be willing to rent it to you. It's small but it's only half a mile from the hospital. As soon as you get here we can take a look at that, and I'll check on other possibilities as well."

"What about a school for Justin?"

"If you decide to rent the Shepherds' guesthouse, he can walk to the public school I told you about. The Shepherds' daughter, Sally, attends classes there, so that will give him someone to know right away. I know public school is not ideal, but the main thing is to get you both down here. Once you get into the routine of work and school and such, we can look at other options—hopefully something closer to Pinecraft."

"I don't know about this, Hester. Mr. Shepherd is on the hospital board and—"

Hester had laughed. "He's on half a dozen boards around Sarasota, including the one here at the co-op, but don't let that intimidate you. Malcolm and his wife, Sharon, are salt-of-the-earth people, Rachel. And as for Sally—I mean, you are going to love her. She'll introduce Justin to a host of friends in no time, so that's a plus."

"It would be nice for him to have a friend right away," Rachel had said.

Hester actually squealed with delight. Her obvious excitement was contagious. "Do you believe this? You are coming to Florida."

Rachel laughed. "You seem to have everything arranged."

"Just get here. We're going to have such fun getting you and Justin settled. Having you near will be like old times when we were back in college."

Except our lives have changed. We have changed, Rachel thought. But she'd been unwilling to dampen Hester's enthusiasm with her doubts. "We'll be there this time a week from tomorrow," Rachel had promised.

"John and I will meet the bus. I can't wait for the two of you to meet."

As the bus rolled on she caught sight of a sign welcoming them to Florida. She glanced down at her sleeping son. He had said little about the move, but she knew him so well. She understood that he was not happy about leaving his friends and the familiar routine of the farm and family—even his uncle—to strike out for the unknown. Truth be told, she had no idea if she had just made the best or worst decision of her life.

She wished James were there to reassure them both.

Chapter 3

Dr. Benjamin Booker stood outside the front entrance of Gulf Coast Medical Center, marveling at the twists and turns his life had taken to bring him to this moment. As the son of a small-town preacher, he'd been raised with the idea that he would follow in his father's footsteps into the ministry. But ironically it was his father's example that had made Ben run as far and as fast as he could from that career.

Instead Ben had excelled in the sciences, eventually earning a free ride to one of the best premed programs in the country. His goal had been simple. He would get his medical degree and then go overseas to bring his healing skills to the malnourished and suffering children he'd seen as a boy on the TV news. He was going to go out into the world and not mouth the words his father preached, but do his best to put his faith to the test by offering real solutions.

But then he'd gotten seduced by the opportunities that came his way after he'd completed his training. In those early days when he'd gone to work for Sarasota Memorial, the teaching hospital, he'd told himself that the post was temporary. That he needed to hone his skills, learn everything he could before he tried to save the world. But that year had lengthened into two, then four, then eight. . . .

Then a group of local civic leaders had seen the need for a hospital that placed a major focus on both treatment and research on the illnesses of children. His younger sister, Sharon, and his brother-in-law, Malcolm, had been the driving force behind the movement to get the hospital built. But it had been their freckle-faced daughter, Sally, who had persuaded Ben to make the change. "What if all those poor, sick, and injured children in faraway places could be brought here?" she'd asked. "You could treat them right here where you'd have everything you need."

Now as he watched the construction workers finish mounting the sign at the front of the hospital, he thought about Sally's powers of persuasion and smiled.

"Here's the way I see it, Uncle Ben," she had said one day two summers earlier as they tossed a ball back and forth on the lush front yard of Malcolm and Sharon's large home. "It's pretty clear that you're married to your work so I've given up all hope of helping you find romance. On top of that, Mom and Dad are determined to get this hospital built, and that means that once it's up and running with their name on little brass plates all over the place, they have no choice but to take me there for my medical stuff. You're my pediatrician, so you do the math."

Ben had laughed. "You're the healthiest kid I ever met, not to mention the most precocious." He'd crouched into a catcher's position and pounded his glove. "Now let me see if you've got anything resembling a decent curveball."

A week later Sally had come home complaining of pain in her leg. They'd been tossing the ball back and forth that day as well. When the pain hadn't gone away over the next few days, Ben had suggested that Sharon bring his niece to the hospital. "Routine blood tests," he had assured her. "I want to rule out anything more sinister than a strained muscle or torn ligament."

"I have a game on Tuesday," Sally had reminded him. "I'm pitching."

"Good thing it's not your pitching arm that's causing you trouble, then," Ben had teased. The two of them had bantered back and forth in this way from the time Sally had been six or seven. Ben had been the one Sally had come to when she needed to persuade her mother that playing on an all-boy baseball team was not going to be a problem.

"I'm eleven years old—not exactly a baby." She'd sighed, although at the time she'd been a couple of months shy of that birthday. Still she had a point. As the only child of two well-educated and superactive parents, Sally spent far more time in the company of adults than she did with kids her own age. Being on the baseball team around kids her own age would be good for her.

"Talk to her, please?" she had pleaded.

"I'll talk to your mom," Ben had promised. "But maybe your dad..."

Sally had rolled her eyes. "Ever so much more of a problem," she moaned.

The blood tests had come back with the worst possible news. Sally had leukemia and not the *good* kind, if there was such a thing. No, Sally did not have the strain that was 90 percent curable in children her age. Against all the prototypes for the disease, she had been diagnosed with AML—acute myelogenous leukemia. And so their journey had begun with all of its peaks and valleys.

So Sally was no longer the healthiest kid he knew. For more than a year she had spent most of her time in hospitals receiving treatments and living among other children battling childhood illnesses of varying degrees of seriousness. Once the standard treatment regimen of chemotherapy and radiation failed—not once but twice—their only option had been a bone marrow transplant. For the transplant she had gone to a clinic in Tampa that specialized in such procedures. To her credit her spirits had remained high, and she had stayed in touch with friends via Skype and of course, the cell phone that she used incessantly to text back and forth with her friends.

It had been six months now since the transplant and in a few days Sally would head back to school for the first time in over a year.

"I cannot wait to get back to school," she had announced a couple of days earlier when Ben had stopped at his sister's for lunch. "It seems like forever."

"You're sure you're ready for that?" Ben didn't need to remind her that for many transplant patients the recovery time was more like a year than the six months it would be for her by the time the school year started. But even he had to admit that her recovery had been remarkable and unquestionable. Her blood tests consistently came back in the normal range and showed that the graft was helping her to recover the healthy cells and immune system that had been so compromised by the disease.

Sally had rolled her eyes and glanced toward the kitchen where her mom was preparing lunch. "Please do not let Mom hear you asking that. If she had her way I'd be kept in isolation until I'm like twenty-five."

Ben laughed. "She's not that bad, and she worries about you."

"I know. But you cannot imagine how wonderful *normal* sounds to me right about now."

"Just don't push it, okay?"

In many ways Sally's illness had pushed them all to make building the new hospital a reality. Now, standing outside the front doors, Ben shook off the memory of that horrifying journey. The construction team hoisted and attached stainless steel letters that spelled out the new hospital's name. He closed his eyes. If he were a man given to prayer, this would no doubt be a good time to offer a silent one for the skill and wisdom to heal the patients—some of them like Sally—that he would treat here. Certainly his sister would encourage that. Her unwavering faith so like their father's had kept her amazingly calm in the face of Sally's diagnosis and everything that followed. But Ben did not share his sister's brand of blind faith.

As the crew secured the last letter into place, a city bus swung onto the circular drive, forcing Ben to take a step back. The first person off the bus was a woman he would guess to be in her mid-to-late thirties. She wore an ankle-length green print dress with three-quarter-length sleeves, the traditional white-starched prayer covering of the Mennonite faith, and in spite of the heat and humidity, a thin black sweater over her shoulders. She paused for a moment while the other passengers made their way around her and on into the hospital. She closed her eyes and bowed her head.

Assuming that she had come to visit a patient in the hospital, he moved a step closer and waited for her to finish. "May I help you?" he asked.

He saw her take in his white lab coat, his glasses perched on top of his thick black hair, and his stethoscope jammed in a pocket of the lab coat.

"*Nein, danke,*" she said then shook her head and smiled. "Sorry. No thank you, Doctor. It's pretty clear that I have come to the right place." She indicated the stainless steel letters of the sign glimmering in the sunlight. "If you would please excuse me, I don't want to be late for my first day."

He could not help noticing that while her smile was certainly sincere, there was something about the way it didn't quite light up her features that made him reluctant to let her go. He knew that look. He had seen it in the eyes of his sister and brother-in-law and countless others when he'd given them a difficult diagnosis and again over the long months as treatment after treatment had failed. It was a look of deep sadness.

"You work here?" he asked.

"I am to be part of the spiritual care department," she said. "I am Rachel Kaufmann."

Ben grinned, remembering the voice over the telephone, the way her speech had been slightly formal, her tone soft and yet confident. "We've met," he told her. He noted that her eyes were a remarkable shade of violet, like Elizabeth Taylor's. They widened in surprise.

"I believe you are mistaken," she said politely. "I just arrived in Sarasota on Friday."

"Ben Booker." Ben extended his hand and then wondered if her culture would permit her to shake it. He saw her hesitation and instead waved his hand toward the entrance. "I was part of the committee that interviewed you by phone."

"Oh, you were the late one," she blurted and then covered her mouth in embarrassment. "I am so sorry," she murmured.

"Never apologize for being right. I was running late that day as it appears you are today." He glanced at his watch. "How about I show you the way to the chaplain's office? You're going to enjoy working with Paul Cox—the man is quite something."

He started toward the entrance. After a few seconds she caught up to him. "I can ask for directions inside," she said. "You must be busy."

"I'm scheduled to start rounds with the pediatric residents in ten minutes. Come on. Pastor Cox's office is on my way." He waited for her to enter ahead of him and knew the exact moment when she realized that although they had moved inside she was standing in a tropical garden. She took a moment to appreciate the ferns and bromeliads and orchids surrounding the waterfall that cascaded over boulders and then settled into a calm pool featuring several large koi fish.

"Our design team may have gotten a little carried away," he said, aware that for a woman of her faith such opulence might be troubling

"Oh no," she said, her voice barely audible against the noise of the splashing water. "The children will love it. Are those real butterflies?"

"They are," Ben assured her, and this time when she smiled at him, that smile reached her eyes, softening them into violet pools. Flustered to have had such a poetic thought, he pretended interest in the design of the hospital's reception area. "It's pretty neat, isn't it?"

"It's wonderful," she replied. "And such a welcoming place for the children—and other patients—to begin their journey if they must travel this road." She smiled at him. "It's certainly going to be a pleasure coming to work every day."

"My feelings exactly. Now let's get you to Pastor Paul's office."

He led the way down a wide corridor, greeting other members of the staff and nodding to patients and their families along the way. Rachel matched him step for step, her sensible shoes a far cry from the platform heels or wedged sandals his sister wore. He was aware that those they passed were curious about this woman in her plain dress complete with the traditional prayer covering of her faith. But Rachel seemed not to notice, and he wondered if she had simply grown used to being stared at.

"Have you found a place to live yet?" he asked as they turned a corner and started down another long corridor.

"Right now we're staying with my friends Hester and John Steiner. After I finish work today Hester is going to take us to see the guesthouse on Mr. Shepherd's property. It would be convenient—an easy walk or bus ride to the hospital."

"Malcolm is married to my sister," Ben told her. "Want me to put in a good word for you?" He grinned to let her know he was teasing her and was charmed by the way her cheeks turned a shade rosier than their normal pink. But he also saw the shadow of a frown furrow her brow. "Hey, I was kidding."

"I know. It's just. . ." She shook off the thought. "You must have much better things to do than play the role of tour guide for me, Dr. Booker."

"Ben," he corrected. "We're a pretty casual group here. No standing on ceremony, at least behind the scenes."

"So it will be Dr. Booker when we're with patients and Ben when we're with other staff," she said. "Very well. And I am Rachel."

"Before when you mentioned my sister's guesthouse, you said 'we.' It's none of my business of course," he hurried to add.

"Not at all. I have a twelve-year-old son, Justin."

"That's right. You mentioned him on the phone." He recalled that she had also mentioned the death of her husband. "How's your son doing with this big change?"

The sad wariness he'd first noticed in her eyes was back. "He'll be fine. He needs some time." She glanced at the nameplate next to Paul Cox's closed door. "Ah, this must be the place. Thank you, Ben, for making me feel so welcome."

"My pleasure." He reached around to open the door for her. "Hello, Eileen," he said to the woman who looked up from her work as they entered. "Eileen, this is Rachel Kaufmann. Rachel, Eileen Walls."

"Oh, hello, dear," Eileen gushed as she came around the desk and took Rachel's hand between both of hers. She was shorter than Rachel and dressed in an orange knit pantsuit that strained across her ample bosom and hips. She had always reminded Ben of his grandmother. "We have so been looking forward to meeting you in person. Pastor Cox is especially delighted to have you on staff."

"Thank you," Rachel replied.

"Is Paul in?" Ben asked.

Eileen glanced at a large wall clock. "He should be completing his morning rounds." She turned her attention to Rachel. "He likes to see those patients facing surgery or procedures first thing."

She took hold of Rachel's hand and patted it. "Oh, it is going to be so nice having you here with us. You're going to fit in just fine."

Eileen had nothing to base that statement on, and yet Ben could see that Rachel understood that this sweet matronly woman was trying to put her at ease. "I hope so," Rachel replied.

"Well, I'll leave you in Eileen's capable hands," Ben said as he turned to go. "I'm looking forward to working with you, Rachel."

"Danke—I mean, thank you for everything."

Ben smiled. "You're welcome."

He had retraced his steps down the hall when he saw Darcy Meekins coming his way. She was walking fast in spite of her three-inch heels, her cell phone to her ear as she balanced a notebook filled with papers that she was shuffling through.

"Well, I don't have it, Mark," she said curtly. "Never mind." She pulled a single sheet from the stack. "Got it." She ended the call and glanced up. When she saw Ben, her demeanor changed. She smiled and slowed her pace, clutching her binder of papers to her chest. "Are you lost, Dr. Booker?" she teased.

Ben chuckled. "That wouldn't be hard in this place. How about you?"

"Oh, I'm running fifteen minutes behind schedule. Paul wanted me to come down so we could go over everything with the new hire."

"You're in luck. Paul's also running behind. I left Rachel with Eileen."

"So what did you think of her?"

Ben shrugged. "She's nice."

"Well, I mean, no one has actually seen her," Darcy said.

"Oh, you want to know what she *looks* like? Well, let's see, other than the two heads and the single eye in the center of her forehead. . ."

"You know what I mean."

"Not really. I'd say the adage 'what you see'—or in her case, 'heard over the phone'—is pretty much what you get."

Darcy frowned. Of everyone on the search committee she had been the only one to express strong doubts about hiring Rachel Kaufmann. Even when Paul Cox had pointed out that, of all the applicants they were considering, Rachel's background and years working as a nurse and even her limited counseling experience topped the other two candidates who were fresh out of college, Darcy had insisted they offer the position to another person. Only after that candidate had turned it down, citing the fact that he had already accepted another job, did Darcy agree to make the offer to Rachel.

"Hey, give her a chance. It's her first day and frankly—"

"She's different in so many ways. I mean she's not from here, and she's Mennonite—as in *serious* Mennonite. I looked it up—the different groups, and she's from what's called *Old Order*—very conservative and strict. We have to keep in mind that our patients run the gamut of the religious spectrum."

"Well, granted I was only with her a short time, but I have to say she doesn't strike me as someone on a mission to convert anyone." He touched Darcy's arm. "Look, you protected the hospital's interests when you insisted on a four-month probation while she gets her state certification. If she doesn't work out, you can let her go."

This reminder seemed to give Darcy some comfort. She lowered her voice. "Oh, don't mind me. The stress gets to me sometimes. I need to make sure that this place succeeds in a market already crowded with other facilities." She smiled apologetically. "You know what a worrier I am. How about meeting me after work for a pizza? We could decompress."

"I'll take a rain check," Ben said. "I promised Sally that I'd bring over Chinese. The kid is counting the days until she can be out in the world again."

"But until that day, you insist on bringing the world to her, right? You spoil that child shamelessly," Darcy said, but he understood that she was really praising him.

"Don't have kids of my own to spoil, and Sally's the only niece I've got."

"There's a remedy for that," Darcy teased. "You could settle down and get married, and have a house filled with kids."

"Like you, I'm already married to my work." He checked his watch. "Have to run. I'm holding you to that pizza," he called as he turned the corner.

Chapter 4

Darcy Meekins had fallen hard for Ben Booker the first time she met him. He wasn't like many of the other doctors she'd known over the course of her career as she worked her way up the administrative ladder of hospital management. All too often the medical degree seemed to come with an attitude of authority. Darcy thought of it as the I'm-the-doctor-and-you're-not syndrome.

But Ben Booker was different. He wore his medical expertise as a responsibility, not an entitlement. He respected the contributions that others could make. It didn't matter to him if he was dealing with the security guard on duty in the lobby after hours or one of the aides who provided more than half the actual hands-on care a patient received during a hospital stay. He showed them the same consideration as he did any of his professional colleagues. Ben was an equal-opportunity guy when it came to his curiosity about others. That only added to his appeal for Darcy. She wasn't used to being around men who cared what others thought—especially the women in their lives.

Her father had been a bully of the first order, always ordering others around, making fun of their failures, and taking personal credit for their successes.

But Ben was not anything like her father, and Darcy could only imagine how he must have charmed the Mennonite woman. In the course of a walk from the hospital entrance to the chaplain's office, he would have put her completely at ease. To that end, Darcy supposed that she owed him a debt of gratitude. Putting people at ease was not her strong suit.

As Ben had pointed out, they were both workaholics. They spent hours together in meetings when the hospital was being built. Before the hospital food service was up and running, they had shared meals and coffee at a local neighborhood café. They had never had an actual date, but Darcy had high hopes that now that the hospital was open and fully staffed, that would change. Her invitation for pizza had been her first step in a targeted campaign to take her business relationship with Ben to another—more personal—level.

The door to the office for spiritual care services was ajar. She could hear Paul Cox's assistant, Eileen Walls, laughing. She tapped on the door and then entered the reception area. "Hello, Eileen," she said before turning her attention to Rachel. "I'm Darcy Meekins, hospital administrator." She extended her hand to the woman dressed in the garb of her faith. "And you must be the newest member of our team."

"Yes. Rachel. Rachel Kaufmann. I'm so glad to meet you in person," the woman replied, pumping Darcy's hand once and then releasing it.

"I've been filling her in while we wait for Pastor Paul to get here," Eileen explained. "That man needs three clocks to keep him on schedule." She sighed.

"I'm here," a male voice boomed as Paul Cox came huffing his way through the door. He was a large man in both height and weight, and with his bushy gray hair and his pulpit voice, he had a way of filling up whatever space might be left in the small room of the outer office.

Eileen made the introductions, and Darcy saw by Rachel's broad smile that she was not any more immune to the minister's charisma than anyone she'd ever seen him meet had been.

"Now aren't you just a breath of sunshine," he exclaimed as

he smiled down at Rachel. "It's got to be ninety degrees out there and here you are looking fresh as a daisy."

Darcy stifled a groan. Paul Cox was given to clichés. It was part of the aw-shucks folksy persona that had made him so successful in his previous position at Sarasota Memorial Hospital before Ben persuaded him to jump ship and head up the team at Gulf Coast. Paul opened the door to his office and stepped aside to allow Rachel and her to enter ahead of him. "Hold any calls, Eileen," he said, "unless. . ."

"How many years have I been working for you, Pastor Paul?" Eileen said sweetly.

Paul chuckled and gently closed the door. "Have a seat, ladies. Can I get anyone anything? Glass of water? How about a peppermint candy?" He indicated a covered dish on his desk filled with individually wrapped candies.

Darcy was impatient to get down to business. She had another meeting in twenty minutes. She checked her watch and was a little annoyed that Rachel accepted the offer of water. But then Darcy glanced at her and realized the woman was nervous. And why not? Rachel Kaufmann had accepted a job by phone from over a thousand miles away and was only now facing the realities of that decision.

"So, Rachel, how was your flight?" Paul asked as he handed her the water then sat down in the swivel chair behind his desk.

"We did not make the trip on an airplane," Rachel said after swallowing a sip of the water. "We came on the bus."

"My goodness, that must have taken days," Paul exclaimed. "Have you had some time to rest up and get settled into—where are you living now?"

Rachel smiled. "My son and I arrived on Friday. We are staying with friends. We had the weekend to rest."

"That's right. Hester Steiner mentioned you were going to bunk in with her and John when I was there last week for the co-op board meeting. All settled in then?"

"Our stay with the Steiners is temporary. Tonight Hester is taking me to look at a cottage that Mr. Shepherd has for rent."

"Malcolm Shepherd?" Darcy asked, her attention now

riveted on this quiet-spoken woman, surprised that she had already connected with Ben Booker and Malcolm Shepherd. She felt a familiar tingle of alarm. Darcy had worked hard to establish herself in a career where she was in charge, where she reported only to the board of trustees. She was fiercely protective of that position. It had taken her some time to win the respect and support of Malcolm Shepherd, the president of the hospital's board of directors.

Now this woman was possibly going to be living next door to him? On his property?

"You've met Malcolm?" she asked while at the same time assuring herself that Rachel with her prayer cap and her hands now folded piously in her lap was of no possible threat to her.

Rachel smiled. "Only in the way I met both you and Dr. Booker before now. By the telephone interview. It is my friend Hester Steiner who has made the arrangements for me to see the guesthouse on Mr. Shepherd's property."

"Excellent," Paul boomed. "You'll be close to the hospital. We do have emergencies and as the new kid on the block, those will most likely come your way." He arched an eyebrow as if waiting to see how this bit of information would be received.

"That would be fine," Rachel replied and smiled. "What are my other duties?"

"As I mentioned on the phone I want you to focus on the cases that come through our pediatrics wing while I handle the adult cases," he said. "Right now we have more adult patients than children, so you'll have some time to get your bearings. Anyway, I'm taking you at your word."

Obviously confused, Rachel looked up at him and then at Darcy.

"You said on the phone that you liked working with children," Paul reminded her. "And now that I've met you in person I think you might be exactly the right person for the job."

Darcy opened her mouth to object. Paul was getting ahead of himself. He could not possibly know if this woman had the special skills necessary to minister to children and their parents without at least supervising her work initially. He was already handing Rachel a folder and a pager.

"You'll need to wear this pager or have it handy even when you aren't actually here at the hospital. If a kid comes in during the night or on the weekend, this thing will buzz." He pushed a button to demonstrate. "You'll see a number on the screen, and you'll need to call that as soon as possible."

"I believe you mentioned that you had a child, Rachel." Darcy felt the need to remind Paul that he should proceed more slowly here.

"Yes. Justin." Rachel's smile brightened in exactly the same way that practically every mother Darcy had ever met came alive at the mention of her child—every mother that was, except hers.

"And you are a single parent?"

The smile faltered. *"Ja."*

Darcy could feel Paul's eyes on her. "We are sorry for your loss, Rachel," he said. Then turning his full attention back to the business at hand, he indicated the folder he'd handed her. "I took the liberty of putting together some information I thought might be useful in helping you get up to speed. Well, actually, Eileen put the information together at my request," he admitted with a disarming chuckle. "That woman is my right arm. You need anything and can't find me? Ask Eileen."

Rachel opened the folder and removed the top item—a two-page stapled paper entitled "Role of a Spiritual Care Counselor at Gulf Coast Medical Center."

"Paul, I wonder if I might have a copy of that," Darcy asked, indicating the paper Rachel was scanning.

"Sure." He turned and shouted, "Eileen."

The door opened. "You have an intercom," his assistant reminded him.

"You know me and technical stuff," he said with a boyish grin. "Can you make Darcy a copy of that?"

Rachel quickly scanned the paper before handing it to Eileen and turning her attention back to Paul. "It all looks fine," she said. "I'm certain to have questions as we get started."

"Well, of course you will," Paul agreed. "And either Eileen or I will be right here to answer them. Maybe for the first few days we should plan to have lunch together."

"I'd like that—I would really appreciate it. Clearly I have a lot to learn."

"You'll do fine."

Darcy glanced between them, wondering for a moment if they thought she'd left the room. She stood up. "I have another appointment. It was nice meeting you in person, Rachel. Welcome to Gulf Coast."

Rachel stood as well. "Thank you," she said. "Thank you both so much for giving me this opportunity."

"Now, Rachel, it's you we should be thanking," Paul said. "Isn't that right, Darcy?" He walked her to the door.

Darcy shot him a look of warning. Rachel was a new employee on probation. Statements like that could make it harder down the road if they needed to let her go. "We'll talk later," she said.

But Paul just patted her shoulder in that paternal way he had. "She's going to do fine," he replied as he took the papers Eileen handed him. He gave the copy to Darcy and carried the original back inside his office to hand to Rachel.

Darcy felt dismissed as the office door closed behind him, and yet she had been the one to end the meeting. *No, it wasn't that I felt dismissed,* she thought as she hurried off to her next appointment. *Left out.* That was it. As if once more in her life she had done all the right things and still she did not feel part of the inner circle.

Rachel and Paul had connected almost on sight. Darcy had never in her life known that kind of instant connection—not with school friends, not with her college roommates, not with co-workers, not even with her own family.

Rachel's first day on the job was flying by. After her meeting with Darcy and Paul, Eileen had guided her to the Human Resources department where Mark Boynton had taken her through the details of being an employee at Gulf Coast.

"There's a dress code," he had said at one point, and then he'd looked up at her and his cheeks had turned a fiery red. "You'll be fine," he amended before turning his attention back to the employee handbook that he had insisted on going over page by page.

There were papers to sign followed by a tour of the entire facility that left her head spinning. So many corridors. So many people coming and going in all directions. So much suffering on the cancer wing and then utter joy when they walked through the maternity wing. There she witnessed a man in the midst of a throng of well-wishers in the waiting room as he held up his phone to show pictures of his newborn child. They passed two hospital rooms occupied by mothers nursing their babies.

"Children's wing is across this skywalk," Mark told her. "Patients who come here as well as friends and family have their own separate chapel." He opened the door to a small room that took her breath away.

The chapel he'd shown her in the main part of the hospital had been generic, with stained glass windows in a geometric design that lined the two side walls. The front of the room was furnished with a small lectern and a simple wooden table that held a vase of fresh flowers. The rest of the carpeted room had been furnished with three rows of chairs—four chairs per row to each side of a center aisle. The low-level lighting created an atmosphere of peace and quiet, a haven to escape the noise, bright lights, and fast-paced activity outside the double cypress doors.

But, although it was also a small room, the children's chapel was filled with natural light from a trio of frosted skylights above and windows that looked out onto the manicured grounds of the medical center's campus all around. The floor was tile interrupted by two circles of bright-colored square cushions.

"The children who are able to do so will sit on the cushions," Mark explained. "Those gaps in between are for children in wheelchairs. Those chairs against the walls are for times like Christmas when we might have a special program, or they could be used for a memorial service if necessary. The room will be used for multiple purposes." He pointed to a second door. "In there is a room where family and friends can get away if they need to cry or pray or simply escape the clamor," he explained.

"It's wonderful," Rachel told him. "Thank you so much for taking the time to show me around."

Mark smiled. "Hey, from what I hear this is where you're likely to spend a good amount of your time." He led the way back into the children's area and opened a narrow door concealed as part of the wall. "Locked storage for whatever you might want to keep here," he said, taking out a plastic bag that held a clown's red rubber nose and a chartreuse frizzy wig. "Pastor Paul's," he explained. "He sometimes wears them when he's on his rounds." He placed the items back in the closet and closed and locked the door before handing her the key.

On their way out, Rachel couldn't help but notice a small silver plaque that read CHAPEL OF HOPE: A GIFT OF MALCOLM, SHARON, AND SALLY SHEPHERD.

"There's an activity room across the hall here." Mark pointed to an open door, beyond which Rachel could see an area set up with a quartet of computers, an area for crafts, and some colorful plastic toys geared toward toddlers.

"And that's pretty much the grand tour," Mark said. He glanced at his watch. "Oops. I promised to have you back fifteen minutes ago. Eileen wants to get you set up in your office."

Mark made one more stop at the nurses' station and introduced Rachel to the staff on duty. Then as they retraced their steps back through the corridor lined with patients' rooms, they couldn't help noticing that most were empty. "They'll fill up," Mark said as if she had asked. They rounded a corner, and she glanced into a room where a child was watching cartoons. The boy, who could not have been more than seven, glanced over at her, and Rachel smiled and waved at him.

As they approached the entrance to the skywalk, they passed a room where the window blinds were closed. When she looked closer Rachel saw the silhouette of a small body lying in bed surrounded by a network of tubes. The child was linked to a series of machines blinking their neon signals and wheezing their rhythmic codes. She could barely make out the form of a woman sitting by the bedside, her head resting on her hand.

Rachel's longing to stop and offer the woman some comfort

was huge, but Mark was already several steps ahead of her. The one thing that Rachel had grasped after the two hours she had spent with this young man was that a hospital this large had rules and routines—*protocol*, Mark called it. It would not do to start following her instincts—at least not until she had learned those guidelines.

Back in the spiritual care department, Eileen showed her to a small cubicle next to the reception desk. There was already a nameplate on the cloth wall of the divider that read RACHEL KAUFMANN, CHILD LIFE SPECIALIST.

"That's your new title," Eileen explained when she saw that Rachel had paused to study the sign. "Human Resources seems to have this need to keep reinventing labels for what people do around here. Pay it no mind. When the rubber meets the road, you are a chaplain, just like Paul Cox is."

"But Pastor Cox is an ordained minister and board certified." Rachel remembered the neatly framed degrees and certification documents she'd noticed on the wall of Paul's office.

"Thus his position as senior chaplain. The bottom line is that we all work from the same basic creed—you, Paul, and even me." She pointed to a framed poster on the wall, entitled OUR MISSION.

Rachel stepped closer to read it.

The spiritual care services of Gulf Coast Medical Center provide support and comfort that respects the full diversity of spiritual values to our patients, the family and friends of those patients, and to members of our staff twenty-four hours a day, 365 days a year.

Eileen reached around her and picked up a laminated bookmark from a clear plastic holder on the counter. She handed the bookmark to Rachel, who saw that it repeated the mission statement and also included information for contacting members of their staff when needed.

"That's impressive," Rachel said.

"And ambitious, especially when it looked like maybe it

would be Paul doing all the work. But you're here now," she added brightly. "Come check out your cubicle and let me know if you need anything in the way of supplies or a different chair or more storage above the desk. Anything at all."

Rachel stepped into the small space and opened the top drawer of a two-drawer file cabinet. It had already been stocked with hanging file folders in a rainbow of colors. She opened one of the overhead bins above her desk. There she found legal pads, pens, a stapler and staple remover, scissors, paper clips, and notepads in a variety of sizes. There was a telephone with an intimidating row of buttons in addition to the usual numerical keypad. And all the while she tried to ignore the computer that dominated the corner where her built-in desk wrapped itself past the window and onto the solid wall. She knew the basics of how to use a computer. In the school system she had been responsible for inserting data, but beyond that she wasn't exactly computer savvy.

"Do not ask me to explain why they would situate your computer and chair so that you are looking out into daylight. Talk about a headache in the making." Eileen frowned, but then she took a step closer to the window and her features softened. "On the other hand, it is a lovely view with the serenity garden and all."

"It's very nice," Rachel assured her.

Eileen pulled her gaze away from the tropical scene outside and glanced around. "Well, I'll leave you to it. Paul wants to meet with you at noon. And then somebody from I.T. will be by at four to finish setting up your phone and computer."

"I.T.?"

"Information Technology. The computer and phone geeks."

"I see."

"There's coffee and tea behind the counter in my space. If you need anything, give me a shout." Her warm brown eyes sparkled with merriment as she indicated the open space above the cloth-covered divider separating them. "I'm right over the fence here."

"Thank you, Eileen. Thank you for everything."

For the next hour Rachel busied herself getting settled in.

She rearranged the supplies to her liking and could not help but wonder if she would ever have enough files to fill up even one, much less both of the file drawers. A volunteer from the hospital gift shop stopped by to deliver a dish garden filled with a variety of living plants. Rachel opened the florist's card and read the typed message: *From everyone at Gulf Coast Medical Center, WELCOME!*

As she worked, she was comforted by the sounds of Eileen attending to her duties. Paul's assistant answered phone calls, dealt with two or three people who came looking for Paul, and in between seemed to be constantly tapping away at the keyboard of her computer.

Rachel had started to read through the materials in the folder that Paul Cox had given her during their first meeting when Eileen said, "Call for you, Rachel. I'll send it over."

Rachel stared at the red light blinking on her phone. "What do I do?" she asked.

"Pick it up," Eileen instructed. "It looks complicated, but it's really just a telephone."

"Hello," Rachel said tentatively.

"Well, hello yourself." Her friend Hester chuckled. "Are you supposed to greet me with something official like 'This is Rachel Kaufmann, Hospital Chaplain' or whatever your title is?"

Rachel couldn't seem to stifle the kind of girlish giggle the two friends had exchanged when they'd been roommates. "My title, I'll have you know, is *child life specialist*," she said, keeping her voice down even though Eileen seemed to be completely occupied with her typing.

"Well, get you," Hester teased, then her tone shifted. "How's it really going?"

"Too fast. I mean the morning has flown by and it's been a whirlwind of meetings and touring the hospital and getting my office space set up." She turned to look out the window. "How's Justin doing? I wanted to call, but I'm not sure if I'm allowed to do that yet." She had lowered her voice to almost a whisper.

"Justin seems fine. John put him to work in the packinghouse getting everything cleaned up and ready for the new season. He's a quiet one, isn't he?"

He didn't used to be, Rachel thought. "He's been through a lot." She glanced at the wall clock and saw that she had only five minutes before her meeting with Paul Cox. "I have to go, Hester."

"Understood. How about I bring Justin and come by to pick you up at the front entrance at five so we can go meet Sharon Shepherd and see the cottage."

"Ja, and Hester?"

"Ja?"

"Thank you so much."

"You don't need to keep thanking me, Rachel," Hester told her. "It's the least I can do after everything you and Justin have been through. See you at five."

The line went dead at the same time that Rachel heard Paul Cox enter the office. "Is she in?" he asked even as he bypassed Eileen's desk and tapped on the metal edge of Rachel's cubicle. "We've got an emergency," he said. "Want to come along and see how this works?"

Paul did not wait for an answer as he headed back out the door and then down the corridor toward the skywalk that led to the children's wing. "I hope you don't get queasy at the sight of blood," he added grimly as he turned down a hallway then strode through a set of double doors that marked the entrance to the emergency room for the children's wing.

Chapter 5

Ben took one look at the boy's arm and knew it was going to take a miracle to save it. At least the arm had not been ripped entirely off. Shark attacks were extremely rare, but when one did strike, the outcome usually always favored the shark. In this case the amazing thing was that the kid still had his arm. Ben was grateful for the team of nurses and specialists surrounding him as he worked to get the boy stabilized so that they could move him on to surgery as soon as possible. Mercifully the kid was pretty much out of it and probably wouldn't remember all the blood loss and pain he was suffering.

A man and woman stood in the doorway as if frozen into a state of disbelief. *The parents.* It was hard to offer reassurance with the better part of his face covered by a surgical mask, but Ben felt the need to make an attempt. He glanced over at the couple, and the father met his look and nodded. Then the man murmured something to his wife. Her wails of panic and fear settled into shuddering sobs.

"Did somebody call for Paul Cox?" he asked the nurse working next to him.

"On his way."

Ben turned his attention back to his work. He gathered

information about vital signs and loss of blood even as he issued orders for what would be needed in surgery. When his colleague and the best orthopedic surgeon in southwest Florida, Jess Wilson, came through the double doors and scanned the chart an aide held for him, Ben let out a breath of relief.

The pneumatic doors swung closed behind Jess but not before Ben saw three other teens still wet, wearing their T-shirts and surfing shorts. They were sitting on the edge of a row of plastic chairs, their hands dangling helplessly between their knees, their gangly bodies seeming too large for the chairs.

"How could this happen?" the mother moaned, drawing Ben's attention back to the job of prepping the kid for surgery. "He was supposed to be at Todd's house," she added, her voice dropping until her tone was that of a lost little girl.

It didn't take much to put the pieces together, Ben thought as he and Jess worked together. Those boys—high school seniors given the age of the kid on the table—had decided to have one last fling before school started in a couple of days. The high, hot west wind that had been building all night would have been all anyone who loved surfing needed to know that the wave action off Lido Key was going to be great. Ben could almost visualize the four of them heading straight for the beach.

"Name?" he murmured to the ER nurse working next to him and nodding toward the boy.

"David Olson," she replied. "Paperwork is done," she added with a glance toward a young woman holding a clipboard out to the father.

Ben pulled down his mask and peeled off his gloves as he approached the parents. "Mr. and Mrs. Olson?"

They lifted dazed glances before Ben went on, "We're going to take David up to surgery," he said even as the medical team unlocked the wheels on the gurney and started rolling it down the corridor. "As soon as there's any news someone will be down to talk with you, okay?"

He really didn't expect an answer. Someone else would take charge of the parents and friends until Paul got there, lead them to the waiting room, offer them coffee, and volunteer to call other family for them. So when Mr. Olson clasped his shoulder, Ben wasn't sure how to react.

"Doc? Can you save his arm?" Olson was a large man, overweight in the way of a former athlete who hadn't kept up with his regimen of exercise. His eyes were full of tears he was fighting to hold at bay, and his voice shook. "See, he's on the basketball team and several colleges have been after him and..."

"We're going to do our best, Mr. Olson," Ben said as he gently patted the man's arm. "Just hang in there, okay?"

With relief he saw Paul Cox and the new chaplain enter the waiting area. Paul moved toward the parents, indicating with a nod that his cohort should check on the other teenagers. The gurney was already halfway on the elevator, and the surgeon was holding the door for Ben.

"Got this," Paul said as he stepped between Ben and Mr. Olson. "I'm Paul Cox, hospital chaplain," he said. "Let me show you folks to our family care area. You'll be more comfortable waiting there."

Rachel approached the other boys as Paul led the parents away. She bent down to their level as if she instinctively knew how best to connect with them. As the elevator doors slid shut she glanced up at Ben. For an instant it looked as if she was pleading with him to make things better—not for her but for those boys who had saved their friend. But he would not offer false hope, and he knew she had read the severity of the situation in his expression when she drew in a breath and briefly bowed her head before turning her attention back to the boys.

"I'm sure you did everything you could have done," Rachel said to the boy who had broken down completely and was sobbing into his hands.

"That sucker came out of nowhere," another boy said, shaking his head as if he still couldn't believe it. "I mean one minute we were catching a wave and the next the water was red with Dave's blood and his arm was..." He was pacing back and forth.

The third friend remained silent. He was the smallest of the three, and in a way his size made him appear more vulnerable. *Like Justin.* He sat quietly a little apart from his friends and stared at his hands.

"If Todd here hadn't hit that shark with his board," the second boy continued, wheeling around and coming up next to her as he continued his story. "That was amazing, dude. We all froze, but Todd handled it."

Rachel slid onto the empty chair that separated the boy— Todd—from his friends. She placed her hand on his bony shoulder. "You quite possibly saved your friend's life," she told him and silently prayed to God that his life would indeed be saved.

An aide carrying a cardboard tray with cups of orange juice came toward them. "Thank you," Rachel said as she stood up and distributed the juice. All three boys guzzled it down as if they hadn't had liquids in days. All three murmured their thanks as they placed the empty paper cups back on the tray.

"Pastor Paul asked that you bring them to the chapel," the aide told Rachel. "We've called their parents."

"Thank you. Come on, boys." Rachel guided them toward the corridor that led to the chapel and family waiting area. The emergency room was quiet now, and the only sounds were a nurse's rhythmic tapping on a computer keyboard and the squeak of the boys' rubber flip-flops on the polished tile floor.

When they reached the chapel, both Mr. and Mrs. Olson came forward and hugged each boy. Rachel breathed a sigh of relief. She had been afraid that the Olsons might release their own fear by chastising the boys. But when Todd finally broke down and let his tears come, it was Mr. Olson who took him under his wing. "Hey, what's this?" he said. "From what Brent and Jack told us, you saved the day."

"That shark was huge," Todd blubbered.

"You did good, Todd. Whatever happens, you saved our boy," Mr. Olson said as he hugged Todd again.

Over the next couple of hours the family waiting room gradually filled with other family and friends. The parents of the three friends arrived, as did David Olson's coach and the pastor of his church. Paul spoke at length with the minister, and the two men exchanged business cards. Then Paul crossed the room to where Rachel was setting up a makeshift buffet of the snacks, sandwiches, fresh fruit, and soft drinks that Eileen had ordered sent up from the hospital cafeteria.

"Okay," he said, glancing at a young man in scrubs who had come to the room, spoken with the Olsons and Paul and their minister, and was now leaving. "The good news is it looks like the boy's going to make it."

"But?" Rachel said.

"They're working on reattaching his arm and that could take eight to ten hours, assuming they can do it at all." He glanced over to where the Olsons and the boys were seated in the center of a circle of supportive friends and family. "I think things are pretty well in hand here. Why don't we go back to my office and have a late working lunch while we go over your new responsibilities?"

Rachel was reluctant to leave. The truth was she wanted to be there when Ben came from surgery to tell the Olsons how things had gone. Would the surgical team be able to save the boy's arm? Rachel recalled how the floor of the ER had been littered with bloody refuse when David was on his way to the elevator and the operating room. She had never seen so much blood in all her life. "Eight hours more?" she whispered as she looked at the clock in the hall ticking off the seconds.

Paul nodded and thrust his hands into the pockets of his trousers. "We'll check back," he told her. "This is the way it goes sometimes, Rachel. I assure you that the feeling of wanting to do more when there's no more to be done never goes away. But these folks clearly have a strong network of support. They're in good hands."

He waited for her to speak with the Olsons, and then the two of them walked side by side in silence across the skywalk on their way back to the spiritual care department. Rachel could not help noticing how blue the sky was, unmarked by a single cloud. She thought about David and his three friends surfing the waves on this perfect day, never guessing that danger lurked beneath the water's surface.

She thought about Justin. "There are sharks," he had argued when she'd told him about the move to Florida.

"What's a bull shark?" she asked, remembering that one of the nurses had mentioned that species.

"It's a big shark," Paul told her. "Adults average about seven feet long and can weigh close to three hundred pounds. But the real problem is that a bull shark has serrated teeth, and when it bites, it tears. That's what complicates David Olson's chances of coming out with a reattached arm. Hard to put that all back together."

Rachel took a moment to digest the bleak outlook for this boy and his family. "Why would the shark attack?"

Paul shrugged. "It's not done with malice. Usually the problem is that the water is churned up and sharks have poor eyesight. If they see something moving in the water that they can't identify as friend, foe, or food they strike first and ask questions later." He held the door to their offices open for her. "Either way that young man has got a long road ahead of him—physically, emotionally, and spiritually. Good that they are people of strong faith."

Eileen looked up as they entered, her snow-white eyebrows raised in question.

"No news yet," Paul said. "Rachel, call your son. I expect he's on your mind right about now." He walked into his office and closed the door.

"He needs a moment," Eileen explained. "The young ones always hit him hardest." She shook her head and fell silent for a long moment before going on in a quiet voice, "His daughter drowned in a freak swimming accident when she was ten. It's been twenty years, but he still grieves."

"And yet he does this kind of work?"

"Paul feels that it's his calling. In some ways he honors the memory of his daughter by offering comfort to others."

Rachel nodded, understanding all too well how the man felt. "Let me know when he's ready," she said as she sat down at her desk and dialed Hester's number. "Hester? Could I speak to Justin?"

Ben had to give Jess Wilson credit. The man was cocky and abrasive but he was the best surgeon Ben had ever worked with. After six and a half grueling hours, he had secured the final stitch to reattach David Olson's arm. Then he'd snapped off his gloves and pulled down his mask. "He may lose that arm yet, but tell them I've done my best," he said wearily and left the operating room, leaving it to someone else to go and talk with the parents.

The Olsons and their son's friends had been understandably relieved at the news, but it worried Ben that they had also been almost hysterically happy. Ben had tried to caution them that David had months of therapy ahead of him. He doubted that they had grasped what he'd tried to tell them about rehabilitation and the possibility that the boy would never have the full range of motion he had enjoyed before. At least the family's minister seemed to understand that this was only the beginning of a long journey for David and his family.

Due to the length of the surgery, Ben had had to cancel his plans with Sally. Still, he decided to stop by his sister's house. He was bone tired, but even the shower he'd taken in the doctors' locker room had done little to calm him. The intensity of the surgery had left him wired, and he doubted he would be able to settle down to sleep for several hours yet. It was a beautiful night, and sitting around the pool under his sister's screened lanai listening to Sally talk about the upcoming school year would be exactly what he needed.

But when he got to the impressive estate his brother-in-law and sister owned, the bright orange van with the logo for the fruit co-op that Malcolm and Sharon supported and the Steiners managed was parked on the circular drive. Ben wondered if perhaps Malcolm's brother, Zeke, had stopped by.

Zeke worked at the co-op—when he worked at all. He and Malcolm could not have been more different. While Malcolm had taken over the family's multiple business ventures, Zeke had served three tours of duty with the Marines in the Middle East. When he came back the third time, he'd abandoned the comforts of his family's wealth for life on the street. Ben knew that Malcolm had decided to fund the fruit co-op run by Hester and John Steiner in part because it was one way to get Zeke into a situation where he wasn't living hand-to-mouth. Frankly Ben didn't understand Zeke's nonchalance when it came to where he might sleep or get his next meal. Yet Ben couldn't help but admire Zeke—and sometimes he even envied him. After the day he'd had it would be nice to have "no worries," as Zeke was fond of saying.

"Hello?" Ben called as he walked into the front foyer and kicked off his shoes. His sister had white carpeting in the two main downstairs rooms, and she was adamant about the removal of shoes—especially his.

"I don't know what you've been standing in all day," she would say with a shudder. "All those germs."

He had tried pointing out that at the end of the day he always showered and switched to sandals but to no avail. Ever since Sally was first diagnosed with leukemia, his sister had become obsessed with protecting her only child from any danger of infection.

"Hello?" he called out again as he followed the sound of distant conversation through the formal living room with its high ceilings and wall of french doors that opened out onto the expansive deck. For all of Sharon's attempts to make the house and its furnishings formal, there was an open feeling to the place. A lightness that Ben had long ago decided was less about the trappings and more about the people who lived there. Malcolm and Sharon were people who appreciated the many blessings they had received—financially, from Malcolm's father and grandfather as well as his own business astuteness—and they lived by the dedication that with such riches came great responsibility to "share and care," as his sister said so often.

Ben stepped out onto the lanai that screened the large pool area. Across the yard at the end of the path that wound through Sharon's lush gardens stood a cluster of people—his sister, Malcolm, Hester Steiner—who, he decided, must have driven the van over—and the new chaplain. It was little wonder they had not heard his calls. The four of them were standing outside the guesthouse, deep in conversation.

"But that hardly seems fair," he heard Rachel Kaufmann say as he followed the path toward them.

Malcolm shrugged. "Take it or leave it," he said. "It's my final offer."

Hester Steiner sighed. "You may as well stop trying to bargain with him, Rachel. Once Malcolm makes up his mind, there's no changing it."

"Besides," Sharon added, "think of all we stand to gain by having you and your son living here. Justin, is it?"

Rachel nodded. "Ja, *aber*. . .I mean. . ."

"Hester's right," Ben said as he joined the group. "Might as well save yourself some time and give in to whatever they're pushing. My sister and brother-in-law can be two of the most stubborn people I know when it comes to having their way." He grinned at Sharon. "I should know. I grew up with this one and never could win a debate with her once she'd made up her mind."

"But for free? No rent?"

"Just for your probationary period," Malcolm said. "That way if you decide this isn't working out, you and Justin can go back home without obligations tying you down here. And in the meantime, you can check out other possibilities perhaps over in Pinecraft if you think you would be more at home living there. Besides, rules in the neighborhood prohibit us taking in a tenant, so you're saving me some hassle once the neighbors find out you're staying here."

Ben saw Rachel glance back toward the main house where every room was lit up as if to emphasize its sprawling luxury. He thought he saw a hint of a smile play across her lips—a smile that she suppressed as she turned her attention back to Malcolm.

"Very well," she said. "But I insist that Justin and I will tend the gardens."

"Oh Rachel, we have help for that, and you're going to have so much on your plate—work, classes, getting Justin settled." Sharon looked to Hester for support. "You agree, right?"

Now Rachel's smile blossomed in full. "Those are *my* terms," she said.

Malcolm laughed and held out his hand for her to shake, sealing the bargain. "Welcome, Rachel," he said.

"Well, please understand that if things become too difficult, we're right here to help," Sharon added.

"See what I mean?" Ben grinned and wrapped his arm around his sister. "She always has to have the final word."

"Stop that," Sharon said when Ben rubbed her head with his knuckles. "Come on up to the house, Rachel. I have ice cream cake, and I want you to meet our daughter, Sally."

Ben frowned as he followed the others through the garden. He had assumed that his niece was outside with the others, but Sharon's comment made him realize that Sally had been in the house all along. The fact that she had not come running at the sound of his call raised an alarm for him, and he had to wonder if any of them would ever get past that knee-jerk instinct to imagine the worst when it came to Sally's health.

He fell into step with Malcolm as the women went on ahead of them. "How's Sally doing?"

Malcolm glanced toward the house. "Better every day. She's upstairs now—something about needing to get ready for school." He paused for a moment and gazed across the yard at the inviting golden light spilling from the house onto the lawn streaked with the shadows of twilight. "Do you think it's a good idea to send her back to school? I mean, maybe we should wait until second semester—give her a few more months."

Sally's worst fear was that her parents would do exactly what Malcolm was suggesting. "I just want a little normal," she'd moaned one day. "After everything I've been through, is that too much to ask?"

"You can always take her out of school if necessary," Ben reminded Malcolm. "Right now I think it's really important to let her start the school year, be back with her friends and teachers, let others see how well she's doing."

"I know you're right." Malcolm drew in a long breath, and Ben realized that his brother-in-law had been fighting his emotions. "We've operated so long in what Sally calls *sick mode* that it's hard to believe things are better."

"Now that the new hospital is up and running, what are your plans for her medical needs?"

"Well of course, she'll continue to go back to Tampa for anything connected to her bone marrow transplant."

Ben nodded. "I can understand that, but I'll be finishing up at Memorial by the end of the month and well, selfishly I'd like to keep an eye on things where Sally is concerned."

"You mean once you move over to Gulf Coast full-time? Let me talk to Sharon," Malcolm said.

"Ask Sally," Ben added. "It should be her choice."

"We'll go where she can get whatever it takes to keep her healthy, Ben."

"Of course." They had reached the house. The women were already inside. Ben could hear Sharon conducting the grand tour. He noticed that his sister had not asked Rachel or Hester to remove their shoes.

"Uncle Ben!"

Ben turned toward the foyer and saw his niece coming quickly down the stairs. He couldn't help remembering all the weeks and months when merely walking across her hospital room had been exhausting for the child. Now her blue eyes sparkled with delight as she effortlessly descended the curved staircase. She was wearing shorts and a T-shirt with a baseball cap covering her short hair. After the chemo, her hair had grown back in brown tufts highlighted with red instead of the honey blond it had been before she got sick.

"Is it true? Did that boy really get attacked by a shark? It's all over the news. They interviewed Dr. Wilson on national television."

"First, a hug for your weary uncle, then we can talk shark attacks." Ben held out his arms to her.

She threw her arms around his neck and held on. As he released her he fingered the earplugs from her MP3 player dangling around her neck. "So this is why you didn't hear me call out when I first got here. You are going to seriously damage your hearing, turning that stuff you think passes for music up so loud."

"I'll have you know I was listening to a book," she replied, with a quirk in her smile.

Ben tousled her short hair. "Well. . . ," he said, "there may be hope for you yet."

The phone rang, and Malcolm went to answer it. Sally squeezed Ben's hand and lowered her voice, her eyes darting toward the kitchen. "Did you hear? We're taking in boarders," she whispered.

"I heard."

"They're Amish," Sally whispered.

"Mennonite like Mr. and Mrs. Steiner," Ben corrected. "Problem?"

Sally looked doubtful. "I don't know. Do you think Dad's got money problems? I mean my friend down the block? They're selling their house because her dad—"

Ben gave her another hug. "Nothing's wrong. It's your mom and dad doing what they always do—helping others. Ms. Kaufmann started a job at the new hospital today. She needs a place to stay until she can get settled." He released her and added, "She's got a son—Justin. I think he's around your age."

She smiled, her eyes dancing with excitement. "Does he play baseball?"

"I don't know. How about we check with his mom?"

Chapter 6

By the time Rachel returned to Hester's house, she was bone weary. Justin was waiting for her, his blue eyes so like his father's mirroring a dozen unspoken questions. And yet when Rachel had climbed into the paneled orange van after completing her first full day of work, Justin had not been in the backseat as she had expected.

"John took him fishing," Hester explained. Then she sighed. "It was pretty obvious that he didn't want to come see the cottage," she admitted quietly, "and it seemed like maybe..."

"It's all right," Rachel assured her. "I've asked a lot of him, and he's still struggling with everything—and there's more he has yet to face."

In two days he would start classes at the public middle school near the hospital, the same school that Sally Shepherd attended. And even though they had talked about all the reasons why this was the best choice at least for the time being, Rachel knew that Justin was extremely nervous. And why not? It was a large school with children he did not know. These children lived in ways that would be so very different for Justin.

"What was it like?" Justin asked when the two of them were alone in the room they were sharing at the Steiners'. Rachel saw his curiosity as the opening she'd been looking for to begin to help him adjust to their new life.

"I think you might like it, Justin," she said as she busied herself turning down the twin beds while he got into his pajamas. "There's a park nearby and the Shepherds have a swimming pool and—"

"Why can't we stay here? I could help John at the packinghouse."

He sat down by the window, his arms folded tightly across his thin chest. He was not looking at her.

"I explained why." She sat on the other bed, across from him. "Until I've had a chance to settle into my new job, this is the best plan. We'll be living close to my work and your school."

Justin said nothing.

"The Shepherds have a daughter about your age. She asked me tonight if you played baseball." She saw a flicker of interest cross his features, but he continued looking out the window. "She goes to the same school you'll be attending. I asked her to look for you."

This, at last, got his attention. "You didn't," he moaned. "Mom, it's bad enough that I'm starting a school where nobody is—you know—like us."

"There will be lots of children who are different from you and from each other. They'll come from all sorts of backgrounds like the people I'll be working with at the hospital do. And besides, you won't be the only new student there."

"You don't know that for sure."

"No, I don't, Justin." She felt so inadequate to calm her son's fears. "I know that tonight it all seems overwhelming," she said. "That's the way I felt last night knowing this morning I would be starting a new job where I knew no one. But I got there and right away someone welcomed me and made sure I got to the right place. And throughout the day I met other people—good, caring people. Some of them needed my help, and before I knew what was happening, all of that nervousness seemed to disappear."

"Kids aren't like grown-ups," he muttered.

Rachel resisted the urge to put her arms around him. "It's

not forever, Justin," she said.

"Promise?"

"Yes, now go brush your teeth."

Later after they'd said their prayers and Rachel had read a passage from the Bible, they lay in their separate beds in the dark. She was aware that Justin was not sleeping. Finally he flipped over onto his side facing her.

"Mom?"

"Ja?"

"Will I have my own room?"

"Ja."

"When are we moving?"

"On Saturday. The cottage is furnished already, but Hester and John will help us move the boxes that Gramma sent from the farm. We'll make the place our own, Justin—just like home."

Her son did not reply, and she thought perhaps he had finally dozed off. But after a moment he said, "Not just like home—we never had a swimming pool." This was followed by a snort of laughter muffled by his pillow.

"That's true," Rachel agreed. "Oh, and I forgot to tell you. In place of paying rent, you and I will be tending the garden."

There was a pause while he digested this news. "How big is this garden?"

"Big."

Justin groaned, and this time it was Rachel who smothered a laugh.

Rachel's second day at work was every bit as busy as her first, and she began to accept that the pace for this job would be double what it had been back in Ohio in her role as school nurse. Thankfully there were no emergencies like the Olson boy's encounter with the shark, but there was plenty to fill the hours, including visiting David and his parents as well as meeting the young mother she'd seen sitting by her child's bedside that first day.

In between she attended a training session on using the computer, accepted Eileen's invitation to join her and other hospital staff members for lunch, and accompanied Pastor Paul on rounds. In the hours she spent at her desk she worked on the assignment that Paul had given her to develop a draft for a training manual for volunteers working in the children's wing.

When she returned to Hester's that evening, she was relieved to see that Justin seemed resigned to the idea that they were in Florida to stay—at least for now. And the following morning—Justin's first day of school—she was not surprised to open her eyes and see Justin already dressed and standing at the window.

Sometime in the night it had started to rain, and it didn't appear that it would let up any time soon. "Well, this rain should cool things off a bit," she said, making conversation as the two of them sat at breakfast with Hester and some of the women who worked at the co-op. She could see by the slight tremor of his hands when he picked up his glass of juice and drained it without pausing for a breath that he was nervous.

"I'd better go help John," he said. "Danke," he added with a nod to Hester as he wiped his mouth on his forearm and bolted out the back door. He was wearing jeans, a solid blue T-shirt, and a pair of running shoes that Hester had insisted on taking him to buy at the thrift store in Pinecraft. Earlier Justin had asked Hester if she thought he looked okay.

"Like any other Sarasota seventh grader," Hester had assured him. Justin had grinned with obvious relief.

Now Rachel stood at the kitchen window of the farm-house that served as both headquarters for the fruit co-op and home to the Steiner family. Behind her Hester was giving the women their assignments for the day before they too headed off to the packinghouse. Outside Justin ran through the steady rain to where John Steiner was directing a team of men as they unloaded a truckload of empty crates.

"How's Justin doing?" Hester asked, coming to stand next to her.

"He's nervous."

"About school?"

Rachel thought about the way his hands had actually trembled. "About everything," she admitted.

"Well, that's to be expected. He'll be fine, Rachel."

Rachel turned her attention to washing the dishes. "He's changed so much since James died. He's so quiet and reserved when he used to be—"

Hester laughed. "He's twelve. Neither fish nor fowl in the world of boys—too young to count as a teenager but too old to be one of the kids. Give him some time."

"Ja." But in her heart, Rachel wasn't so certain that this was simply a phase. She had asked a lot of Justin since his father died. "Perhaps once we move on Saturday and he's settled in one place, some of the old Justin will return. He'll have his own room there and he seems excited about the swimming pool," she added more to herself than to Hester.

"Did he not have a room of his own in Ohio?"

"He did until James's brother and his family moved into the farmhouse. His uncle was hard on him, far stricter than James ever was. And then I lost my job, and now I've brought him here. Everything is so new for him."

"And for you," Hester reminded her. "You can always go back home if things don't work out here."

"Maybe." But what Hester did not know was that Luke had made it plain that he thought she was making a huge mistake.

"You only think of yourself, Rachel," he had said. "What about my folks? James's folks? Who is supposed to watch over them? Rosie has her hands full with the house and the little ones. I thought with all your nursing training and college at least we might be able to count on you for that. I'm telling you right now that James would be—"

"Do not tell me what James would or would not do," she had told her brother-in-law. Rachel had never come so close to losing her temper with him.

"Suit yourself," Luke had replied. "You always have, but know this—if things don't work out we'll take the boy in, but as for you. . ."

Rachel shook off the unpleasant memory.

"Hey," Hester said as she glanced out the window at the rain now coming down in sheets, "you okay?"

Rachel inhaled, glancing at her friend. "I'm fine," she finally whispered.

"Well, here's a good thing." She motioned toward the window. "At least you aren't moving today in this rain."

Both women laughed, and Hester folded the dish towel and hung it over the edge of the sink. "Tonight we should make a list of things you'll need, and tomorrow we can go shopping."

"Oh, I don't think there's anything," Rachel replied. "I mean every cabinet that Sharon opened was filled—dishes, pots and pans, even the basic foodstuffs like flour and sugar and such. And did you see the refrigerator and freezer?"

Hester nodded. "It's the way she is. Generous almost to a fault."

Rachel accepted the refilled mug of coffee that Hester handed her. She had some time before Justin was due at school and she needed to be at the hospital. Today John would drive them each to their destinations. "Ja. Justin will like having his own room again," she said as if they were still on that topic. "Sharing a room is hard. If James and I had been able to have more—to give him brothers and sisters. . ."

"It'll do you both good to be settled in one place, to know that at least for now, that's home," Hester assured her. "And wait until he meets Sally Shepherd. I know she's a girl but that kid is a guy's girl if ever I met one."

"She seems very nice," Rachel agreed, remembering the effervescent girl they had shared ice cream cake with the evening before. "I didn't want to pry last night, but what kind of cancer does she have?"

"Acute myelogenous leukemia—AML for short."

"We studied that in nursing school, but I thought it affected mostly older people."

"That's right. Less than 10 percent are children. Go figure how a healthy active kid like Sally ends up getting it."

"She's such a lovely child. So that form of leukemia is really fast growing?"

"Ja. It's pretty aggressive."

"When did Sally have her transplant?"

Hester nodded. "Last February. Neither Sharon nor Malcolm was a match and of course, she has no siblings so they had to wait for a donor."

"They must have considered using her own blood cells?"

Hester nodded. "The medical team thought it was too risky in her case."

Rachel was well aware that using the patient's own blood increased the risk of a relapse since that blood could still carry some of the abnormal cells. "But an unrelated donor match is also risky."

"True, but with a lower risk of relapse down the road. The reality is that there are downsides to both options."

The two of them were silent for a moment as they continued to watch the rain.

"Will you listen to us—talking shop like we used to when we were in nursing school?" Hester said, shaking her head at the memory.

Rachel smiled, but she couldn't seem to get Sally Shepherd out of her mind. "She seems to be doing well now," she ventured.

"Remarkably well." Hester started folding clothes from an overflowing basket of laundry. "Can you imagine? One day your child is healthy and whole, and the next. . ." She held on to one of John's shirts, clutching it to her as she stared off into space imagining the impossible.

"She was very sick, then?" Rachel asked.

"Ja."

Rachel thought about Ben and the way he and Sally had laughed together when they shared the ice cream cake. It had been clear that they adored each other. She remembered the watchful way that he studied Sally as the girl gobbled down a large piece of ice cream cake and quizzed Rachel about Justin. She had thought that she understood his concern for his niece. How often over these long months had she watched Justin as he struggled with coming to terms with his father's death? Ben wanting to make sure Sally was truly better was very similar to how Rachel felt whenever she was forced to face the fact that James was gone and there was nothing she could do to change that—for her son or herself.

"Mom? John says it's time," Justin called out to her from the porch. "Bring my backpack, okay?" His voice quavered, and Rachel wasn't sure whether or not that was the result of excitement or nerves or more likely a combination of the two.

"Coming," she called as she picked up her rain slicker and Justin's backpack. She hooked an arm through the straps of the nylon satchel that Hester had bought for her. She'd insisted that Rachel would need something for transporting books and papers for her certification studies from work to class to home and back again. She stepped outside she covered herself as well as Justin with the rain slicker as they ran down the steps to John's truck.

"It's all going to be fine," she told her son as he waited for her to slide in next to John before climbing in beside her and wordlessly closing the door.

Chapter 7

Ben was on his way to Sarasota Memorial Hospital when he heard the ambulances behind him. He pulled to one side of the road to let them weave their way through traffic and across a busy four-lane road. There were two of them—one following less than a minute behind the other. If Ben had to guess he would assume car accident. He just hoped no one was seriously injured and that whatever had happened didn't involve kids on their way to their first day of school.

He was starting his last two weeks at this hospital before moving permanently to Gulf Coast. Selfishly he thought about how difficult it would be for him to leave behind a juvenile patient that he might be able to treat in the short term but not follow up on once he left Memorial for good. And then for one horrible instant as he eased his way back into the flow of traffic, he pictured Sally lying in the back of one of those ambulances.

As hard as it had been for Sharon and Malcolm to come to terms with the idea that their only child had contracted a form of cancer rare in children her age, it had been impossible for Ben to wrap his head around the prospect that he might not be able to find the medical professionals and science it would take to save her life. He was a doctor and dedicated to healing.

Failure was simply not an option.

"Lighten up," Sally had demanded after they had gotten the news that her first round of therapy had not eradicated the disease. "We're only in the bottom of the first inning here," she'd announced with a great deal more certainty than either he or her parents had been able to muster. That was when they had first begun to consider the possibility of a bone marrow transplant.

Sharon and Malcolm had been tested and proved not to be a match, and then everyone in their extended families had been tested with the same results. Understanding that they needed a stranger to be a match for Sally and that finding that perfect stranger could take months, they had launched the search.

Ben's pager buzzed as he pulled into a space reserved for physicians and staff, jarring him back to the present and the reality of the day ahead of him. He glanced at the screen and saw the number for the ER. "And so it begins," he whispered aloud as he dashed through the pouring rain to the hospital's side entrance.

As the morning developed he learned that his concern for the occupants of the ambulances had not been misplaced. A teenage girl on her way to pick up her friend for the first day of school had lost control of the car and struck the other student. Both girls as well as the boy riding with the driver had been brought to the ER.

The girl that had been struck was on her way to surgery so Ben went to check on the other two teens. He was surprised that the nurse indicated a room where a Mennonite couple dressed in traditional garb hovered near the patient. But before he could skim through the chart and enter the room, he was accosted by a man he recognized as a member of the hospital's board of trustees.

"Dr. Booker!"

"Hello, Mr. Kline," Ben replied, glancing into the exam room the man had just left. In an instant he grasped the situation. "Your son was the third victim in this accident?" he asked. He looked at his notes again and saw that of the two, the girl was the more seriously injured. "If you'll give me a moment to check on—"

Kline's eager smile faded. "My son is in pain," he announced, as if this proclamation should be enough for the entire staff to come running.

Ben saw that the hospitalist was already with the Kline boy. "I'll be there as soon as I've tended to the girl."

"Given the fortune I have donated to this institution over the years," Kline said through gritted teeth as he took hold of Ben's arm, "I think I have a right to—"

"—the same quality of care as every other patient we treat here," Ben replied quietly. He met the man's glare directly. "Dr. Thompson is with your son and your wife. I will be with you as soon as I can."

"Thompson is not our son's physician. You are."

"Dr. Thompson is an excellent physician." He looked pointedly at Kline's fingers that were still grasping his sleeve. "Sir, we're wasting time here."

The businessman released him and turned back to the room where his son could be heard anxiously asking the hospitalist if he would be able to play in that week's football game.

Ben turned his attention to the nurse at his side who was quickly filling him in on the girl's injuries. "It's her state of mind that seems to be the worst of it. She just lies there oblivious to everything and everyone around her."

"Well, let's get her lip stitched up and order a psych evaluation. She was the driver?"

The nurse nodded. "The girl in surgery is her cousin."

Ben nodded. "See if there's a bed available in case we want to keep her overnight for observation." He entered the exam room, and the parents glanced up at him with relief. "Hello, Sadie. I'm Dr. Booker. I need to take a look at you and ask you some questions. Would that be all right?"

The girl was sitting on the edge of a chair, her arms locked around her body as if she wore a straitjacket. She had no reaction to his presence as she stared at the wall and rocked slowly back and forth.

Ben took his time pulling on a pair of protective gloves and then walked around the bed to examine her lip. "That's going to need some stitches." The girl was sixteen, but he decided to try addressing her as if she were far younger. Either it would further calm her or it would make her annoyed enough to rouse her from her catatonic state. "I could use my special pink thread— or purple."

No response. The nurse was right. Her state of mind was far more worrisome than the split lip. He tried again as he gently checked for evidence of further injury.

"How about it, Sadie?" he asked, watching her face for any sign of pain as he performed his examination. "What's your favorite color? I'm partial to blue myself—or green. My mom used to say that's because I'm the outdoors type—I like nature— water, trees. . . ." Gradually Sadie's arms and legs started to relax.

As Ben continued his work he addressed his comments to the parents. "I'm going to suggest that Sadie be admitted at least overnight. Right now she's showing all the classic signs of shock, but I'd like to make certain there's nothing else going on."

"The officer. . . ," the father began, lowering his voice and glancing toward the corridor where a police officer was standing at the nurses' station.

"I'd like to get some X-rays—not that I suspect anything, but since she's not really responding to touch or perhaps pain, we want to be sure. And we should probably consider a psych consultation."

Both parents nodded. Ben clipped the thread with a small scissors and then pulled off his gloves. He offered the man a handshake while the nurse assured them that someone would be along soon to transport Sadie to radiology. Not knowing what he could possibly say that might bring this stoic couple a measure of reassurance, Ben simply nodded to the woman and left.

By the time he finished treating Sadie Keller, the Klines had arranged to have their son seen by another doctor—a specialist in sports medicine. They did not even glance at Ben as he passed, for which he was grateful. He stopped at the nurses' station and signed orders for X-rays and a bed for Sadie as well as the psych evaluation, then he headed off to make his rounds.

The rain was still coming down with no sign of letting up.

Ben decided to grab a salad to go from the hospital café before heading to his office in the physicians building across the skywalk where according to his schedule he would have a waiting room filled with patients. On his way out of the hospital he passed by the family waiting room. There he was surprised to see Hester Steiner hovering near a woman with flaming red curls. The woman was sobbing uncontrollably. Hester's husband, John, had his arm around a man who looked as distraught as the woman sounded. Sitting to either side of the woman were the parents of the girl he'd treated that morning.

Ben's heart went out to all three families, including the Klines.

Growing up in his father's house, any sign of emotion had been viewed as weakness. Ben was expected to accept everything that happened as God's will—not to be questioned. And he had quickly learned to bury his feelings and focus all of his energy on achievement—the one thing his father seemed to value. He had excelled in his studies and on the athletic field. He had been elected president of his high school's student council, and eventually he had been accepted into three of the nation's top premed programs. And his father took credit for all of it even as he preached humility on Sundays.

Ben had never understood his father. The man who stood in the pulpit Sunday after Sunday did not mesh with the man who sat at the head of the table in the house where Ben and Sharon had grown up. Somehow Sharon had never struggled with the duality that Ben found so utterly confusing.

Once he became a doctor, Ben had dedicated his life to one purpose—making sure he put his medical skills to work to heal every child that came to him if he could. But once Sally was diagnosed, Ben had found that he was suddenly engaged in a raging tug-of-war between his emotions and his determination not to allow himself to feel—anything.

All afternoon as he attended to his appointments the memory of those Mennonite parents and then the news that the child had died stayed with him. After he finished his last office appointment for the day, he went back to the hospital to check on Sadie Keller. Her father was sitting by her bed, and a boy a year or so younger than Sadie was curled into a chair, sleeping.

Ben checked the notes left by the psychologist.

"She'll be taken into custody as soon as we discharge her," the nurse on duty told him. "These kids today," she added, shaking her head, "they assume nothing like this can happen to them."

The same way Sharon and Malcolm could never imagine that a child as healthy and lively as Sally might be struck down by leukemia, Ben thought. "Let's try to keep her through tomorrow night," he said.

He did not miss the look of skepticism the nurse gave him. The chances that the hospital brass might let the girl stay beyond one night were slim to none, but right then Ben felt he had to bank on slim. If this were Gulf Coast Medical Center he could speak directly to Darcy, but here at Memorial it was common knowledge that he was leaving. Those in charge would hardly be inclined to stretch the rules for him.

On his way home to his condo overlooking Sarasota Bay, Ben suddenly decided to prescribe something for himself—a strong dose of family. His sister's home cooking, his brother-in-law's wry take on the news of the day and most of all, Sally's sunny smile.

Justin's first day of school was a nightmare. The place was an endless maze of hallways lined with lockers and classroom doors that all looked alike to him. At the end of a long assembly where all the students crowded into a large auditorium and paid little attention to the principal as he laid out his plans for the coming year, a jangling bell announced that Justin had less than three minutes to find his locker and get to his class.

So much noise and confusion. The hallways were filled with kids, all talking and laughing and all seeming to be pushing their way toward him. He felt like a fish trying to swim upstream. He saw kids looking at him and in spite of trying not to stand out, he was sure that they knew that he was different from them. They all seemed to know each other, and they all had cell phones that they stared at even as they wove their way through the crowded halls bumping into anyone in their way without so much as glancing up.

Justin found his locker and fumbled with the combination lock.

"Need some help?"

He looked up and saw a chubby-faced girl wearing a pink baseball cap. She was opening the locker next to his.

"No," he mumbled and turned his attention back to the dial.

"The key is to make sure you go a little past the second number before you go back to the third one," the girl said. She was busy storing a bunch of stuff from her backpack. "Are you in Mr. Mortimer's class?"

"Yeah." The lock finally gave, and Justin hurried to hang up the slicker his mom had insisted he take. The minute John had driven off with his mom after dropping him off, Justin had stuffed the slicker into the backpack that was still stiff with newness. He slammed his locker door the way he'd seen a guy do down the way and spun the dial on the lock. Without another glance at the girl, he headed for class.

"Hey," the girl said, catching up to him. "Mortimer's room is this way."

"I know," he lied. "I'll be there, okay?" His voice was practically a growl but at the moment, he would do anything to break this girl's connection. He was all too aware that every move he made in the first few hours would set the way others would look at him for weeks to come. That was the way it was with kids, and the last thing he needed was to be tagged as a guy who hung out with girls. She seemed nice enough, but she was a girl and well, he was pretty sure it would not be a good idea to be seen with her until he could figure out the way things worked around here.

"Well, all righty then," she huffed. "Just trying to help."

Justin kept walking away from her, his head down as he plowed his way through a group of kids.

"Well, will you look who's back? Yo, Fat Sally!" The boy he'd seen slamming his locker yelled, and the two boys standing near him snickered.

From behind him he heard the girl shout, "Shows what you

know about anything, Derek Piper. Maybe if you opened a book once in a while. . ."

The boys around the large muscular guy grinned, and one of them punched him in the arm. But Justin saw the boy roughly shrug him off as he started down the hall after the girl, his eyes ablaze. Then he spotted Justin and paused. "Hey newbie," he said with a grin.

Justin froze and tried to come up with something to say. "Hey," he finally managed as Derek and his friends passed him.

He breathed a sigh of relief, but then Derek turned around and stared at him. "You coming or not?"

And all of a sudden Justin found himself part of a quartet of boys headed for Mr. Mortimer's classroom where the boy called Derek slumped into a seat in the back row and continued to glare at the girl wearing the baseball cap. She ignored him until their teacher decided to rearrange students, and Justin found himself seated across from Derek Piper and just in front of the girl.

"Sally Shepherd," she whispered as if he might not have heard Mr. Mortimer call out each and every name.

"Got it," he muttered, mortified to realize that this was the girl his mom and Hester kept going on and on about. He saw Derek Piper glance his way and roll his eyes. "Sally Shepherd," Derek mimicked with an exaggerated grimace.

Justin couldn't hide his smile. Derek's antics were so over the top. Justin felt flattered that for whatever reason Derek had decided to include him in his group.

"Ah Mr. Piper," the teacher said in a voice that sounded a little like the pastor's voice at church. "So nice to have you back again this year."

Piper sat up to his full height—a good three or four inches taller than any other boy in the class—and grinned at Mr. Mortimer. "It was like I couldn't stay away," he said.

"Do try to move on with the rest of your class this year, won't you, Mr. Piper? I would not want to deny any one of the secondary institutions in the community the pleasure of teaching you next year."

"But Mr. Mortimer, I kind of like it here."

"And I would like to live in Hawaii, sir. Sadly, we cannot always have our way." Mr. Mortimer clapped his hands together, effectively ending the conversation, and instructed the class to open their textbooks.

Halfway through the class, the girl called Sally started to cough.

"Here we go again," Justin heard Derek mutter.

Mr. Mortimer stopped writing on the whiteboard and came down the aisle to stand next to the girl's desk. "Are you all right, Sally?" he asked quietly.

She nodded but continued to cough.

"Perhaps some water," she said.

To Justin's surprise, Derek was immediately on his feet. "I'll get it." He was out the door in a flash. Mr. Mortimer sighed and glanced around, his gaze falling on Justin.

"Mr. Kaufmann, would you be so kind as to take a paper cup from the stack on my desk and get Miss Shepherd some water?"

"But. . ." Justin glanced toward the door.

"Please do as I ask," the teacher said.

In the hallway, Justin saw Derek duck out a side door and take off across the schoolyard. He was actually leaving school in the middle of class.

"Mr. Kaufmann?" his teacher called.

Justin filled the paper cup and returned to the classroom, debating whether or not to tell Mr. Mortimer what he'd seen.

But there was no need. As he entered the room, one of the boys he'd seen hanging out with Derek at his locker glanced out the window. He pointed, and soon the entire class was straining to watch as Derek loped across the ball field. On his way he turned and made rude signs to the students watching him. Mr. Mortimer clapped his hands to get their attention.

"Desks, now, people," he announced and returned to the front of the classroom.

Behind him, Justin heard Sally Shepherd clear her throat. "Thanks for the water," she whispered.

Justin saw one of Derek's friends silently mimic her as he looked straight at Justin. Not knowing what else to do, Justin ignored Sally completely. The boy grinned, and for the second time that morning Justin felt like he might have connected with some of the other boys.

As the day went along, Justin realized that unlike his little Mennonite school in Ohio where he and his friends worked pretty much on their own and at their own speed, here he was going to be expected to deliver assignments daily and actively participate in class. Three times Mr. Mortimer called on him for answers. But that wasn't nearly as embarrassing as when the social studies teacher had him read a passage from their history book aloud and then asked, "And what do you think, Mr. Kaufmann?"

"About what?" Justin replied as he heard a rustle of giggles around him.

"About what you just read."

"I don't know," Justin hedged, trying to come up with the right answer.

"Was it right for America to go to war in this case?"

Justin breathed a sigh of relief. He knew this. He'd learned it from his parents and his pastors. "War is never the answer," he said, quoting them.

But the way the teacher's eyebrows shot up in surprise, Justin knew he'd gotten himself into a deeper hole.

"Why?"

"Because. . ." Justin prayed for deliverance. *Please. It's my first day. Please.*

The bell rang and immediately the other students were clamoring to leave the room. He was saved.

"We'll pick up here tomorrow," the teacher shouted above the noise. "Chapters one and two for tomorrow if you please—and be prepared for a pop quiz."

At the end of the day, Justin headed for his locker to pack his backpack before he went to the hospital where he would meet his mom. Sally Shepherd was waiting for him.

"I realized who you are," she said. "You're Justin Kaufmann—you and your mom are going to live with us in our guesthouse." She actually said this as if it were something that Justin should be really excited about. "Your mom is really nice. I like the way—"

"I gotta go," Justin said as he spotted Derek's friends watching him. He grabbed his backpack and ran down the hall and out the side door that he'd seen Derek use earlier.

Rachel first learned of the car accident involving the teens when she was making her morning rounds, visiting patients on the children's wing at Gulf Coast. Toward the end of her rounds, she stopped by a room where a mother was sitting alone watching the television mounted on one wall. The reporter was standing in front of another hospital.

"The girl died," the woman announced without preamble when Rachel knocked at the door and then entered the room. She must have noticed Rachel's confusion because she gestured toward the television before continuing, "Terrible thing. They were cousins—the girl driving and the one that died. First day of school. Can you imagine? My son goes to school with those kids. Maybe if they'd brought them here instead of to Memorial. . ." She shook her head and turned her attention back to the television.

"How old were they?" Rachel asked, not knowing how else to respond.

"Fifteen and sixteen. Mennonites from Pinecraft, according to the reports. My son's coach is the father of the girl that died."

Rachel couldn't help but wonder if she might have met them when she and Justin went to church with John and Hester that first Sunday. Her heart went out to these families, for she of all people knew at least some of the shock and grief they were facing right now. She closed her eyes and thought of that terrible night when James—

In the corridor behind, her someone slammed a door, and Rachel startled back to the reality of the news of the day. She forced her attention to the television and saw that the reporters had moved on to another more lighthearted story. "Is there anything you need, Mrs. Baker?" she asked the woman.

"No. Thank you for asking." She seemed to focus on Rachel for the first time, taking in her plain dress and prayer covering. "You're Amish?"

"Mennonite," Rachel said.

Mrs. Baker's eyes widened with sympathy. "Then you must know these poor people," she said, indicating the television. It was not unusual for outsiders to assume that people of her faith must all know one another.

"I'm new to this area," Rachel explained, "but we must all pray for them. They have many difficult days ahead."

Mrs. Baker sighed and stood up to straighten the covers on the rumpled hospital bed. "Don't I know it," she murmured. Suddenly her entire body started to shake, and Rachel went to her, placing a comforting hand on the woman's back. "It's so hard," Mrs. Baker sobbed.

"Would you like to talk about it?" Rachel asked.

"I don't want to trouble you. They should be bringing my son back soon."

"There's time. How about a change of scenery? I can let the nurse know where you are so she can send for you the minute he comes back." She gently guided the woman toward the door. "What's your son's name?" she asked.

Mrs. Baker smiled. "Alan—he hates the name—prefers to go by the nickname his friends gave him."

"And what's that?"

Mrs. Baker actually giggled. "Bubba. Can you imagine? He prefers Bubba to Alan."

Rachel smiled and guided the woman toward the chapel. She nodded to the nurse keying in data at the nurses' station and told her where Mrs. Baker would be.

"It'll be awhile yet. They're pretty backed up downstairs," the nurse assured her.

"Thank you," Mrs. Baker said.

They sat together for over an hour as Mrs. Baker poured out the story of her failed marriage, her three other children, her job that was in jeopardy because she was so preoccupied with her son's care, and her worries over the bills.

So engrossed was Rachel in listening to the woman that she barely noticed the time. Eileen had told her that Paul needed her to attend the weekly meeting for department heads—a working lunch, she had called it, her tone laced with sarcasm. "It never fails to amaze me how some folks assume that if there's food involved it can't really be called work."

Rachel was nearly half an hour late when she finally slipped into the single remaining chair surrounding the large conference table. Mark from Human Resources slid a box lunch over to her, and a woman she had not yet met poured her a glass of ice water.

"As I was saying,"—Darcy said even as she pinned Rachel with a look of displeasure—"each department and every individual in that department must understand the mission of that department and its priorities." She waited a beat for this to register and added, "So today I thought we would go around the table and have each department representative state the mission for your area."

There was a rustling of paper as others pulled out folders or notebooks.

"Rachel, why don't you lead the way?" Darcy said with a tight smile. "For those of you who have not had the pleasure—and since she did not arrive in time for our opening introductions—this is Rachel Kaufmann, Pastor Paul's assistant."

"Chaplain," Mark muttered under his breath.

"Did you have something to add, Mark?"

It was a little like being back in school, Rachel thought. She actually felt sorry for Mark as every eye focused on him. But he was undaunted.

"Eileen Walls is Pastor Paul's assistant. Ms. Kaufmann is his associate or child life specialist, to be exact."

"Ooh, my bad," Darcy said sarcastically with that same tight smile. Everyone around the table exchanged nervous glances. "So, specialist Kaufmann, the mission for spiritual care services?"

Rachel had studied the bookmark that Eileen had given her until she had memorized the words, so it wasn't difficult to recall. She said softly, "The spiritual care services of Gulf Coast Medical Center provide comfort and support—"

"If you could speak up for those of us at this end of the table," Darcy interrupted.

"I'm sorry." Rachel stood and delivered the rest of the

statement in a strong clear voice. ". . .comfort and support that respects the full diversity of spiritual values to our patients, the family and friends of those patients and to members of our staff twenty-four hours a day, 365 days a year."

She sat down and took a sip of her water.

"Thank you, Rachel." Darcy turned to a large whiteboard and uncapped a marking pen. "So let's pull out the key words here."

As each department representative stated their mission and Darcy led them in identifying the key words, Rachel saw that she was trying to lead them to come up with a universal mission statement for the entire hospital, one that would incorporate the goals of each department.

"In the end," Darcy said when the last report had been delivered, "we are all individual departments with our roles to play, but we are also a part of the whole." She turned to the whiteboard, covered now with words in many colors. "Where do our missions intersect?"

Over the next half hour the group worked together, and by meeting's end they had constructed a mission statement for the hospital. Rachel was very impressed, and as everyone gathered up their things and headed back to work, she stayed a moment, clearing away the last of the lunch items and wiping the table clean with the leftover unused napkins.

"We have a housekeeping department," Darcy said. She had turned away to take a phone call and seemed surprised to find Rachel still there.

"It's no bother," Rachel replied. "I wanted to apologize for being late. I was with—"

"The work that you and Paul do is very important to the overall work of this institution, Rachel. However, you are going to have to learn to prioritize."

It was the second time she had directed that exact comment to Rachel. "I thought I was—that is, I thought that spending time with Mrs. Baker was—"

"More important than this?" Darcy flung a hand toward the whiteboard. "Well, perhaps you have a point, but a hospital is a business, Rachel, and unless we are all on the same page all the time, then we have no chance if we are to make our mark against the more established hospitals in the area." She began erasing the whiteboard with brisk slashing motions. "I know this may seem trivial to you, but. . ."

"Not at all. I think it's very important. You're right. We must all work together."

But instead of calming Darcy, Rachel's words seemed to only upset her more. "It's more than that," she said. Her tone was argumentative. She set the eraser on the narrow tray at the base of the board and dusted off her hands as if she'd been erasing chalk instead of dry marker. "I don't expect you to appreciate the finer points of running a major business like this one, but make no mistake, our work here goes beyond simply ministering to our patients and their families. The board of trustees will expect results. There is a bottom line, and every department is expected to contribute to it."

Rachel studied the other woman's frown, her failure to look directly at Rachel. "It's obvious that you have been given a great deal of responsibility, but surely the board would not have chosen you as administrator if they did not have complete confidence in you."

Now Darcy looked directly at Rachel for a long moment. She did not smile or in any way acknowledge Rachel's attempt to set her mind at ease. Instead, she picked up the pile of papers and folders she'd brought with her to the meeting and left the room.

Rachel returned to her cubicle and spent the rest of the afternoon in another computer training session and then entering notes about her visits that day in preparation for filing the weekly report that Paul had requested. Meanwhile Eileen kept her up to date on the latest news about the car accident involving the two Mennonite teens.

"They took them to Memorial of course," she announced without preamble when she returned from her midafternoon break. "The younger one was in surgery for some time, but she didn't make it. I wonder if Dr. Booker was there when it happened. He said something yesterday about being over there today."

Just then Rachel saw Justin coming across the hospital grounds toward the entrance. He trudged along under the weight of a bulging backpack, and Rachel felt glad to see him. She was anxious to hear about his first day at school. Paul Cox had agreed that Justin could come to the office and start on his homework while he waited for Rachel to finish her day.

"It will only be until next week," Rachel had assured him. "Once we move into the Shepherds' guesthouse he can go straight home."

"Sally will take him in hand," Paul had told her with a chuckle. "That little girl is going to be president of these United States one of these days right after she retires from playing professional baseball. Never saw a kid more self-confident or capable than that one. She can make your boy feel right at home and before you know it—do you folks play baseball?"

Rachel had smiled. "We do."

But watching Justin now, she wasn't so sure that things would go as smoothly as Paul and Eileen promised. Her hopes for Justin had been so high as she'd watched him jump down from John's truck and head into the school without a backward look. She had prayed that this day would be as good for him as her first day at the hospital had been for her. But now as she watched him cross the parking lot on his way into the hospital, she realized that everything about her son's posture and stride shouted, *Misery.*

≈ *Chapter 8* *≈*

I was thinking," Rachel said later as she and Justin sat waiting for the bus. "Wouldn't you like to see where we're going to live? I already have the key, and the Shepherds said we should not stand on ceremony."

"What does that mean?" Justin mumbled, his eyes still focused on the ground as he sat on the edge of the park bench as if poised for flight.

"Stand on ceremony? Oh, it's an old saying. In this case it means that even though officially we aren't moving to the guesthouse until Saturday, we can go there whenever we like." She held up the key.

Justin showed no interest.

"I thought perhaps you'd like to see your room. I was going to make a list for shopping so that we would have everything we needed on Saturday when we move."

Justin shrugged. "Will they be there? The Shepherds?"

"Maybe, but we are not going for a visit, Justin. If we see them, then of course you must be polite and introduce yourself, but—"

"How far is this house from their house?"

"Not so far. There's the main house and then the swimming

93

pool and the gardens. The guesthouse is at the back of the gardens. Why?"

"No reason."

A city bus made the turn onto the circular driveway. "Do you want to go or not, Justin? If so, this is the bus we need."

Justin picked up his backpack and stood. He wore his unhappiness like a suit of heavy armor. Rachel had prayed for God's guidance to help her see her son through these difficult times and on to the better days she could only hope would be in his future. But in all the time that had passed since James's funeral, it seemed as if nothing she said or did gave her son any comfort. "Justin," she said quietly as she waited alongside him for the exiting passengers to get off the bus, "it will work out."

"You keep saying that," he said and met her eyes for the first time since they'd come out to wait for the bus. Her heart broke as she read in his expression his desperate need to believe her mingled with his doubt that she could ever deliver on her promise.

He turned away and boarded the bus ahead of her, flashing the driver the pass she had bought for him. Several other employees from the hospital stepped around her and boarded so that Rachel was the last to show her pass and look for a seat as the bus pulled away.

Justin was sitting near the back, his backpack between his feet, his head bowed. A man near the front stood and offered Rachel his seat and she accepted.

It was moments like these when she missed James's strength. He would never have allowed their son to show such disrespect for his mother. But what was she going to do? Cause a scene?

She glanced around, and a woman smiled at her over the top of the book she was reading. Next to her sat a young girl, reading a textbook that Rachel recognized as one she had seen Justin studying at the hospital. Perhaps the girl attended the same school, was even in his class. She closed her eyes and prayed silently that in time Justin would find friends at his new school.

As the bus approached the stop for the Shepherd house Rachel sat forward on the edge of her seat and glanced back at

Justin who was not looking at her. Because someone was waiting for the bus, she didn't see the need to signal her desire to get off. Instead when the bus stopped, she got up and moved to the rear exit. "This is our stop," she said when she reached Justin, but she did not wait to see if he would follow her.

Instead she got off the bus and started walking the half block to the Shepherds' driveway. And what if Justin didn't follow her? She had no idea what she would do if the bus continued on its way with Justin still on board.

As she hesitated, she heard Justin running to catch up. "I'm sorry, Mom," he murmured as he fell into step with her. "It's just so. . .hard."

She could point out that it was also hard for her, but she knew that it would be little comfort. "And what did your father teach us about weathering hard times?" she asked, forcing her voice to a lighthearted tone that she did not really feel. She was rewarded by the hint of a grin lifting the corners of Justin's mouth.

"As Thomas Jefferson once said,"—Justin intoned, mimicking his father's deep voice as in unison they chanted the saying that had been a favorite of Justin's father—" 'I'm a great believer in luck and I find the harder I work, the more I have of it.' "

And by the time they started up the service drive that led to the guesthouse, they were both laughing.

Ben was standing at the window in Malcolm's study when he saw the chaplain and her son pass the main house on their way to the guesthouse. They were laughing, and then the boy caught sight of the pool and stopped to take a closer look. Rachel Kaufmann waited on the path and when her son turned back to her, everything about his body language gave voice to his excitement. Rachel smiled, and then she led the way through the garden, gesturing to the plants as they walked.

He remembered how her eyes had finally lost their sadness her first day at the hospital when she had seen the atrium, and he remembered thinking how refreshing it was to see a woman who had no need to rely upon cosmetics or fashion for her loveliness.

There was beauty in the simple serenity of Rachel Kaufmann's smile.

"Oh, is that Rachel?" his sister asked as she set down a tray that held glasses, a pitcher of water, and a decanter of wine along with an assortment of cheese and crackers.

"Yeah." Ben turned away from the window and poured himself a glass of wine. "Have they moved in already?"

"Saturday. But I gave her a key and told her to stop by whenever she liked." She sank into one of two overstuffed chairs and propped her bare feet on an ottoman. "I'll go down there in a minute and invite them to supper, but first tell me about this terrible accident today. Were you at Memorial when they brought those children in?"

Ben nodded and took the chair opposite hers. "I don't know a lot—I heard that the one girl died in surgery."

"Well, it's all over the news, and it's why Malcolm is going to be late. He went out to the co-op after leaving his office today so he could make sure everything was locked up for the night. Hester and John are close friends with the families of both girls, and even if they weren't, you know how everyone in Pinecraft comes together whenever anything like this happens."

"They're going to need all the support they can get," Ben said, and then he realized that Sharon was crying. "Hey, what's this?"

She swiped at her tears. "Oh, don't mind me. Ever since. . . well, you know. . .since Sally. . ."

"This is different," Ben said, moving to sit on the ottoman to be closer to her.

"That girl was their only child," she whispered.

"I know, but she's not Sally." Ben spread cheese on a cracker and handed it to her before preparing another for himself. "Where is Sally, anyway?"

"She had a meeting of the student council—she's the secretary this year and then she and a couple of friends were going to the mall. If she'd known you were going to stop by I'm sure you would have been her first choice."

"Over shopping? I doubt that very much," Ben said.

They turned at the sound of a car on the driveway, followed

by the slam of the front door.

"Mom? I'm home," Sally called, her voice filling the large house with the sheer exuberance of youth. "I got a new hat."

"In here," Sharon called.

They heard the rattle of a plastic shopping bag, and a moment later Sally appeared in the doorway dressed in jeans and a T-shirt and the silliest little hat Ben had ever seen. "What is that thing on your head?" Ben asked, not sure whether to laugh or not. When it came to women's taste in fashion he was often mystified.

"It's called a 'fascinator.' It's all the rage right now ever since the wedding."

Ben must have had a blank expression because Sally placed her hands on her hips and added, "The *royal* wedding—Kate and Will?" Then she rolled her eyes as if he were hopeless. "Of course, it would help if I had a little more hair to anchor it to," she continued.

"How *did* you anchor it?" Sharon asked.

"Chewing gum," Sally said and giggled as she pulled the ridiculous hat away from her scalp, exposing the strings of pink gum with which she'd attached it to her forehead and temples.

"Sally!"

Ben made no attempt to cover his laughter.

"It's not funny," his sister fumed as she leaped up and began examining Sally's head, picking out bits of gum.

"Actually, Mom, it kind of is," Sally said and then grimaced as Sharon worked a blob of the gum free.

"What were you thinking?"

Sally shrugged. "It was a rough day at school. I needed a smile."

Sharon's touch gentled to a tender caress. "What happened?"

"Nothing I can't handle, but it's hard sometimes. Like I'm some kind of freak or something." She picked at the remnants of gum left on the hat then looked up, her eyes bright with excitement. "The new kid started today and guess what? His locker is right next to mine." She pulled away from her mother and flung herself into the chair that Sharon had vacated. "I think he's shy—he's very quiet." Again her eyes widened as an idea occurred to her. "I'll bet he was afraid I would let the other kids know that he's Mennonite. That explains why he took off after school the way he did."

"Wouldn't the other kids know anyway—I mean the dress and all?" Sharon asked.

"Apparently the kids have more freedom when it comes to that," Sally told her. "I looked it up. Kids don't officially get baptized or join the church until they're like practically grown up. That's when they put on the uniform. I'm getting some juice." Sally was up and moving to the kitchen as she continued to talk. "When they move in, we should take them some cookies or something," she called as they heard the slam of the refrigerator door.

"I made some today," Sharon called after her. "The boy and his mother are at the guesthouse now. Your dad is going to be late, so why don't you go invite them to stay for supper?"

"I'll go with you," Ben volunteered. Restless after the long and emotionally draining day he'd had, he too was anxious to be up and moving.

The truth was that in the wake of the accident that morning, he'd realized that he had some regrets about leaving Memorial for good. His time there had shaped the doctor he'd become, and he was grateful for that. In some ways he and Rachel Kaufmann were both starting out fresh at the new hospital. Of course, his was by choice while hers had been the result of a change in her life over which she'd had no control. Perhaps it would do him good to be around someone who might understand that sometimes change—even change by choice—could be hard.

Rachel heard voices from outside. She glanced out the open front door of the guesthouse to see Ben Booker and his niece, Sally, coming through the garden. The girl was carrying a platter of cookies. "We've got company," she called to Justin.

The minute she'd shown him the small bedroom he was to occupy, Justin had busied himself exploring the space, commenting on changes he'd like to make. "Can I take that picture down?" he'd asked, pointing to a painting of three girls looking for seashells at the beach.

"Ja. The Shepherds have given permission for us to arrange things to suit our ways. But you must wrap it carefully and store it in the closet, and when we move it must be put back as it is now."

"I'd like to move the desk over there," Justin said, more to himself than to her. She had left him to think about how best to make the room his while she started making a list of things she would need to purchase and bring with her on Saturday. As she had suspected, her list was short. Sharon Shepherd had truly anticipated their needs.

"It's Dr. Booker and his niece, Sally. Come say hello," she instructed as she nervously adjusted her prayer covering and pressed her hands over her skirt. She wasn't sure why she got so nervous around the doctor. Darcy Meekins was far more intimidating. Like everyone else that Rachel had met at the hospital, Ben Booker was friendly and had made her feel most welcomed.

"I met Sally at school," Justin said. "And Dr. Booker..."

"They are our guests," Rachel said firmly.

Justin frowned and then grinned. "Guests in the guesthouse?"

Relieved to see a glimpse of the more easygoing boy her son had been before his father's death, Rachel smiled. "Come," she said at the exact moment that she heard a knock on the screen door.

"Hi, Mrs. Kaufmann."

"Come in, Sally. Dr. Booker."

"It's Ben, remember?" he said as he followed Sally into the tiny living room.

Sally presented her with the cookies.

"Danke," she said. "Did you make these, Sally?"

"Mom did. Does *don-ka* mean 'thank you'?"

"It does, and you must forgive me. Sometimes I forget and slip into the ways of our people."

"I like learning about other people and their ways," Sally said. "Maybe after you and Justin move in I can learn more words?"

Rachel saw Justin hanging back in the shadows of the hallway that led to the two small bedrooms. "Justin can teach you," Rachel offered. She ignored the way her son's body stiffened in protest. "I understand that the two of you met at school today?"

"Yes ma'am. His locker is next to mine. Hi, Justin," she said with a self-conscious wave.

"Hi," he replied, his voice barely audible.

"Please come and sit," Rachel invited, indicating the small couch that dominated the room. "Perhaps a glass of water? It's so warm today."

"We came to say hi, bring the cookies, and invite you to come up to our house for supper," Sally said. "Mom's grilling chicken, and we'll eat as soon as Dad gets home from the co-op."

"Oh, thank you, Sally—and thank your mother for the kind invitation. Justin and I just stopped by to make a shopping list. The Steiners will be expecting us for supper."

Ben looked at her strangely. "I expect Hester and John may have had to make other plans," he said. "There was an accident this morning. Two of the victims were Mennonite. I saw Hester and John at the hospital with the parents."

Of course, Hester would have gone to the hospital to be with the parents—even if she only knew them slightly. In time Rachel knew that she and Justin would be part of the community of those who would gather for events both joyous and tragic in the lives of their neighbors. It was their way, and it was one of the traditions of their faith that Rachel held most dear. There were no strangers in a Mennonite community.

"You have to eat," Sally reasoned. "And my uncle can take you home, right? It's on your way, sort of."

Ben smiled. "Sort of is," he replied, his eyes on Rachel. "Come on—grilled chicken, potato salad, and the best pie you've ever tasted? You can't turn that down."

"All right."

"Don-ka," Sally said. "Hey Justin, want to catch for me? I've got an extra glove, and I need to practice before tomorrow's game."

Justin gave Rachel a pleading look that she decided to take

for him asking her permission to stay for supper and play the game with Sally. "Go ahead," she said.

It was the expression of horror that crossed her son's face that let her know she had said the exact opposite of what he'd wanted. But she'd made her decision. "Go," she said, and Justin reluctantly followed Sally out the door.

"I didn't want to say anything in front of the kids," Ben told her, "but you should know that one of the three teens injured in that accident died earlier today. I treated the other girl—her cousin—and from what I was able to gather, she played a part in causing the accident. It looks like she'll be arrested and charged as soon as she's released from the hospital."

"Oh Ben, no," Rachel said. "Arrested on top of everything those poor families have already suffered?"

"I made arrangements for her to be kept overnight at the hospital, but I'm pretty sure the powers that be will discharge her tomorrow. Poor kid."

"I need to call Hester," Rachel said, picking up her cell phone. "Maybe there's something I can do to help."

"But you'll stay for supper?"

"Ja—yes."

Ben grinned. "*Sehr gut,*" he said as he left her to make her call.

Chapter 9

Saturday dawned sunny and felt far less tropical than it had been over the last several days. "A perfect day for moving," Hester announced as she dished up breakfast. "Are you all packed?" she asked Justin, ignoring his failure to show any excitement at all as she placed three large pancakes on his plate.

"Not much to pack," he replied and reached for the pitcher of maple syrup.

Rachel cleared her throat and bowed her head as Hester sat down and John led them in prayer. She couldn't help but wonder if Justin remembered to say grace before eating his lunch at school. *Probably not,* she thought. Silently she vowed for what seemed like the thousandth time since they'd arrived in Sarasota that she would find them a home in Pinecraft as soon as her probationary period ended. At least in Pinecraft, Justin would be surrounded by others of their faith and tradition.

"Everything's loaded into the van," John said, glancing at Rachel and then Justin. "Zeke should be here soon. He's volunteered to drive you over and help with the heavy lifting."

"I'm sorry we can't help." Hester's eyes filled with tears as they had ever since her friends had lost their daughter in the accident.

"Zeke will be a great help," Rachel assured her, "and besides, there's not that much to be moved."

Malcolm Shepherd's younger brother could not be more different than Ben. The one thing they had in common was that they were both devoted to Sally.

"Yoo-hoo," a raspy female voice called from the back porch.

"Come on in, Margery," John called. "Have some breakfast."

"Already ate," Margery Barker announced. "But I could use a refill on my coffee." She helped herself, filling her travel mug from the pot Hester had left warming on the stove. Like Rachel, Margery was a widow, although she was at least a couple of decades older than Rachel and several more years down the path of her grief. She ran a marina and charter boat business not far from the co-op, and Hester said she stopped by often to visit. She loved to tease John and tell stories of the time when his property had been completely destroyed by a hurricane named Hester.

"And then he came face-to-face with the real deal," she would say as she patted Hester's hand, "and bingo-bongo his life was changed."

Being around Margery gave Rachel hope that one day she and Justin would find their place in a world without James.

"Busy week for you two." Margery pulled a chair closer to the table, next to Justin who was picking at his food. "You gonna eat those pancakes or let them drown in all that syrup?"

Rachel saw Justin flash Margery a hint of a smile as he stuffed a large piece of pancake into his mouth. She could see that he liked Margery, probably because she reminded him of his grandmother. James's mother, like Margery, was a no-nonsense woman with a soft side that she could bring out whenever the occasion seemed to warrant it. But she had little patience for what she called wallowing, and she'd made that clear to Justin the day they'd first met.

"Is Zeke here?" Justin asked, knowing that Zeke often caught a ride with Margery on the boat she used to ferry herself and the homeless people working at the co-op back and forth.

"He's around here somewhere. I saw his guitar leaning up against the porch, and you know Zeke, he and that guitar of his are joined at the hip most times." She took a sip of her coffee and turned her attention to Hester. "I was sorry to hear about the Messner girl." She shook her head. "How's Jeannie holding up?"

Hester shrugged. "It's so very hard, on all of them. Sadie has been arrested and taken to a detention center in Bradenton. Emma and Lars can only visit her for half an hour at a time and only on certain days."

Justin seemed to be following this conversation with interest. "Sadie is the girl who was driving the car that struck the girl who died," she explained.

"She's in jail?"

"Sounds like it," Margery said with a heavy sigh as she stood and headed for the door. "Well, got to go take care of my own business. Got two fishing charters going out today." Margery glanced outside. "Good day for fishing and a good day for moving," she announced. "See you folks later."

"Margery's right," John said, wiping his mouth. "I'll go get Zeke. And, Justin, you help your mother bring out the rest of your things."

"We're staying at the new place tonight?" Justin asked as if the idea had just struck him.

"Of course we are. We're moving there."

Her son glanced around the large kitchen. "But we'll come back here—I mean for visits and stuff?"

John laughed and ruffled Justin's sandy hair. "You're not getting out of working here that easy. I've gotten used to having you around, and soon we'll be getting into the busiest part of the season."

"But how will we get back and forth? It's a long way to the Shepherds' house."

"The boy's right, John," Hester said with a worried frown as she ran water over the dishes. "Wait a minute. What's that Zeke is working on out there?"

John carried his dishes to the sink and looked out the window. "Well, will you look at that? It's a bike," he said. "He's putting a bike together."

"For?" Hester coached as Justin ran to the open door to see for himself.

"For...me?" Justin looked from Hester to John and back for confirmation.

"It's a gift from your grandparents," Rachel told him, happy beyond words to see him finally excited about something. "You can ride it to the park and even to the hospital and out here when you come for visits and to help at the packinghouse."

"And to school?"

"You'll take the bus to and from school." She saw his disappointment, but Sharon Shepherd had advised, and she agreed, that riding the bus would provide more opportunities for Justin to make new friends. Besides, he had all those books to carry back and forth.

"Can I go help Zeke finish putting it together?"

Rachel nodded, and Justin bounded out of the kitchen, taking the porch steps in a single leap and running across the yard to where Zeke was working in the shade of the packinghouse.

Hester put her arm around Rachel's waist. "A new bicycle for Justin and a new home for you both."

"Well, good morning," Sharon said when she saw her brother having coffee with Malcolm. "You might as well move in—you're here more than at that mausoleum of a condo you bought. What's all this?"

Ben gathered up the papers spread across the glass-topped table and stuffed them into a manila folder. "And good morning to you, sleepyhead."

But Sharon was not to be pacified. "What's going on?" She indicated the papers.

"I asked Ben to get us copies of Sally's records from Memorial so when we transfer her care to Gulf Coast..."

"We haven't decided that for sure yet," Sharon reminded him.

"Just in case," Malcolm replied.

Ben fished a second set of papers out of his briefcase and handed them to her.

Sharon accepted the stack of papers and flipped through it without really pausing to read any of it. "So many medical people," she said.

"It takes a village," Ben said.

She looked at him for a moment then dropped the papers onto the table and sank into a chaise lounge next to them. As she looked out toward the gardens, her eyes welled with tears. "I can't seem to wrap my head around the fact that after everything we went through our Sally has come to a place where she can be in school instead of a hospital. Where she can go to the mall with her friends. That our lives can be normal again."

Malcolm reached over and held her hand. "Believe it, honey," he told her. "All the waiting for a donor, all the fear and sleepless nights, that's all in the past."

Sharon wove her fingers between his. A single tear leaked down her cheek. "I think about that girl killed in the car accident and her parents and what they must be going through. We're so very blessed."

The three of them sat quietly for several long minutes. What more was there to say? Getting Sally to the point where she was finally in remission—a remission that hopefully would last her the rest of her life—had been a journey riddled with medical land mines. Ben understood his sister's hesitancy to put her faith in the idea that Sally might finally be on her way toward a future free of hospitals and medical procedures.

No more false hopes that the second round of chemotherapy would work better than the first induction therapy had. That Sharon or Malcolm would be a match for a transplant. That someone from their extended family would match when Sharon and Malcolm had not. No more if onlys—"If only we had had more children" being Sharon's main regret.

"It's over, sis," Ben said. "Time to start living again."

Sharon brushed her tears away. "You're right. No more living in the past." She stretched her arms over her head and sighed as she looked up at the cloudless sky. "We are so very blessed," she repeated. Ben understood it for the prayer of gratitude that he knew it was.

From the front of the house they heard a vehicle turn onto the property, and a few seconds later the orange van from the co-op made its way past the garage and down the side lane to the guesthouse.

Sharon leaped to her feet. "It's moving day. I almost forgot." She bent and kissed Malcolm's forehead. "I should take them some snacks and lemonade." Then she pushed the papers Ben had shown her back across the table. "We don't need to decide this today. There's plenty of time."

Ben watched his sister walk back into the house. She had aged—Sally's illness had taken years off her life, and she was only in her midthirties.

"Did you and Sharon ever think of trying again, having another child?" he asked and then shook off the question that he couldn't believe he'd spoken aloud. "Don't answer that," he said. "I'm sorry. I just. . ."

Malcolm's expression was that of a man trying hard to control his temper. "We could never replace Sally, Ben." He stood up abruptly and followed his wife inside.

Having managed to upset his brother-in-law with his stupid question, Ben got up and wandered down the path that wound its way through the gardens. Through an arbor of wisteria vines he saw Justin pedaling a shiny new bike up and down the service road that ran behind the guesthouse. Ben paused to watch him for a moment, recalling the way he'd observed Sally on her bike a mere three months after her transplant, her head thrown back, her eyes closed and an aura of utter joy lighting her entire being in spite of the surgical mask that Sharon insisted she wear anytime she was outside the house. This boy rode with his head down, and his body tensed as if he could not possibly ride fast enough to escape whatever he imagined was chasing him.

Not wanting to startle the kid, Ben waited until he'd pedaled to the end of the drive and turned to come back before stepping out from the foliage of the garden and walking toward him. "Hey there," he called.

The boy looked up, and the bike's front wheel wobbled unsteadily for an instant. He squinted and held his position as if waiting for Ben's next move.

"Remember me? Sally's uncle?" Ben jerked his head in the general direction of the main house.

The boy continued to stare at him, offering nothing more than a slight nod.

"Is your mom here?"

Another nod. "She's inside," Justin said, his pubescent voice vacillating between the tenor of childhood and something deeper.

"I thought maybe I could lend a hand," Ben continued. "With the moving."

The boy shrugged. "It's mostly boxes and stuff."

"Boxes can be heavy," Ben said as he headed toward the open back of the van. "Give me a hand here, will you?"

"Mom wants us to wait. She wants to get things put away as she opens each box. There's not that much."

"So you're kind of on call?"

"Ja." He cleared his throat and tried again. "Yes sir. Mr. Shepherd's with her."

"That would be Zeke Shepherd?"

"Yes sir."

"I'll go see if I can be of any help." He paused as he passed by the boy still balancing his bike ready to take off again. "Maybe later if your mom says it's okay you'd like to come with us to watch Sally's baseball game over in the park?"

Justin stopped short of rolling his eyes, but Ben did not miss the expression of distaste the boy fought to control. Clearly Justin thought he was being asked to watch a girls' game and no self-respecting twelve-year-old boy would be caught dead at such an event. He grinned. "Sally's not playing today, but when she does she's the only girl on the team," he said and walked around the van toward the guesthouse. "I'll check with you later," he called and heard Justin take off on his bike in the opposite direction.

" 'Bout time you showed up." Zeke Shepherd greeted Ben with a grin. "Now that the work's half done." He was sitting at the bistro-style table in the small kitchen, sipping a cup of steaming coffee. The two men bumped fists in greeting.

"Yeah, I can see you're really working hard," Ben said. He

glanced around. The place was small but had an open feeling to it with a high white-beamed ceiling and lots of windows that looked out onto the garden. Sharon had chosen the cast-off furnishings with care—a mishmash of pieces, some of which he recognized from their childhood home, blended with new pieces like the bistro table and chairs that served as dining space.

Sharon regularly visited their father, especially now that their mom had died. Ben always begged off going with her to the family home in Tennessee, but he knew that Sharon saw through his excuse that he had too much work to do.

"You and Dad are the two most stubborn men I have ever known," she would say, but she never pressed him to do more.

Ben fingered the back of a rocking chair that he recognized as the one his mom used to sit in. From the end of the short hallway where he knew there were two small bedrooms and the cottage's only bathroom, he heard drawers opening and closing and the muted sound of singing.

"She's putting stuff away," Zeke reported. "Coffee?" He indicated the half-filled pot on the counter.

Ben filled a mug and took the chair opposite Zeke. He glanced around the kitchen. "How's she going to manage?" he asked. "I mean, electricity and telephone and all? Although the stove is gas. Can her people use gas for cooking?"

"*Her people*, as you so quaintly put it, use electricity, own cell phones, drive cars, even watch television. She's Mennonite—you're thinking Amish. No worries. It's a common mistake."

The two men drank their coffee in silence, each listening to the song coming from down the hall.

"Hester tells me that she's been through a lot, and her boy. . ." Zeke shook his head. "Trying to find his place in all of this. I know how that is."

Ben understood that Zeke was reflecting on his own life and the difficulties he'd had settling back into the routine he'd known before volunteering for the military. After each tour of duty it seemed as if he came back more lost than the time before and the only solution he saw was to sign up for yet another round of service. Ben didn't understand how trying to stay alive in a combat zone could possibly be preferable to the life of comfort he could have enjoyed. But he gave Zeke credit for understanding what Rachel Kaufmann was going through better than he could. "It can't be easy," Ben said.

"You've got no idea," Zeke replied and got up to refill his mug.

Rachel came down the hall and her eyes widened in surprise when she saw Ben, but her smile told him it was a pleasant surprise.

"Looks like we've got an extra pair of hands," Zeke said. Ben gave her a wave. She looked like she'd just stepped out of the shower. Her floral print dress—this one lavender—fell to well below her knees and was covered by a full apron. In place of her usual white starched prayer hat, she had covered her hair with a black scarf. She was wearing white tennis shoes that while still pristine had clearly seen miles of wear.

"How can I help?" Ben asked. "Perhaps with three strong men here you'd like to consider rearranging the furniture to better suit your style?"

"Three?" She blinked.

"Justin?" Ben nodded toward the window where the boy could be seen pedaling up and down the driveway with the same furious intent he'd demonstrated when Ben first arrived.

"Ja." She watched her son until he was once again out of sight, a wistful expression clouding those beautiful violet eyes. "Justin." It came out as a whisper, as if she had not intended to speak it aloud.

"So, what do you think?" Ben asked, moving to stand in the middle of the cottage's main room. "Sofa here or facing the fireplace? How about this chair?"

"I couldn't," Rachel exclaimed, clearly realizing what he was suggesting. "These are not my things."

"No worries," Zeke said. "Sharon said to make yourself at home, and if that means moving a chair or two, then so be it." He set down his mug and moved to the opposite end of the sofa from Ben. "Where do you want this?"

Still Rachel hesitated.

"It's your home," Ben reminded her. "Yours and Justin's, at least for now."

"Justin," Rachel called with a smile. "Come help."

An hour later, after Sharon had shown up with a pitcher of lemonade and a platter of fruit and cookies, they had completely transformed the space. The small flat-screened television that had been the focal point of the room, visible from everywhere including the kitchen, had been relocated to a corner. The sofa had been repositioned to take full advantage of the view of the gardens as well as a cozy fire on cool evenings. A handmade rag rug that Rachel told them had been a wedding present now covered the planks of the floor in front of the sofa.

"But your rug is lovely," Rachel assured Sharon as they rolled up the threadbare Oriental that had been there. Zeke carried it outside.

"This is better," Sharon said, her amateur designer's eye taking in the changes. "Do you have a patchwork quilt or perhaps an afghan you brought along?"

"I do."

"These beige slipcovers are so bland and now with the wonderful muted colors in your rug. . .shall we try it?"

Ben realized that his sister's involvement with the decorating had rekindled a hint of the enthusiasm and high spirits with which she had approached every new day before Sally's diagnosis. It occurred to him that Sharon and Rachel had a lot in common— they both had children they were concerned about. He watched as the two women draped a patchwork quilt first over the sofa and then moved it to the back of his mom's wicker rocking chair.

"You two make a good team," he said when they stood back to consider their handiwork.

"Oh, it's going to be such fun having you here, Rachel," Sharon gushed. "And, Justin," she added, turning to include the boy. "You and Sally are going to have such good times together."

Justin's smile was polite but definitely forced.

"That reminds me," Ben said. "I was telling Justin that Sally's team has a ball game this afternoon, Rachel. I was thinking perhaps Justin could come along with us, meet some of the other kids in the neighborhood. It's only a few blocks away in the park."

"Works for me," Zeke said before Rachel could reply. "Looks like everything's pretty well settled here. Mind if I come along?"

"Sounds like a plan," Ben said. "That is, if it's all right with Rachel."

He watched as Rachel looked first at Justin and then at everyone else. "You are all so kind. Danke. Justin, do you wish to see this ball game?"

Justin shrugged and studied the toe of his shoe. "I guess."

"Ah, the enthusiasm of youth," Zeke said, and all of the adults chuckled. Justin's cheeks flamed red. "Come on, sport," Zeke said as he wrapped his arm around the boy. "Let's you and me return the van and then we can bike back here for the game. Four o'clock, right?"

"See you there," Sharon replied. "Come up to the house before you leave. I have some clothes of your brother's that. . ."

Zeke rolled his eyes and grinned as he hugged Sharon and kissed the top of her head. "She fails to realize that my brother and I are not exactly the same size and that I travel light," he explained to Rachel. "But her heart is in the right place and I love her for it."

Sharon grimaced. "Traveling light for this one means a single change of clothing and his guitar. I will never understand that." She looked up at him and brushed his shoulder-length black hair away from his face. "Do you know how handsome you would be with a simple haircut?"

Zeke laughed. "I'd have to beat the ladies off with a stick, and I really am not up to that in this heat."

Ben heard a snicker and realized it had come from Justin. For the first time all morning the boy looked as if he might actually be enjoying himself. Maybe there was hope for him yet. Ben glanced at Rachel and saw by her smile that she was thinking exactly the same thing.

Chapter 10

Darcy had a plan. She knew that Ben attended his niece Sally's baseball game every Saturday afternoon. Since she lived near the park and often ran there in her off-hours, she had decided to time her run to coincide with the game. Then she would stop by to say hello to Ben and his sister—perfectly normal—and she would remind Ben of that rain check for pizza she'd offered.

Her experience in coming up with plans of action for business projects included making sure she considered all possible outcomes. In this case she believed that one of three things would happen. Ben would have already made plans for the evening. That was the worst outcome and one she could do little to change. Number two was the possibility that Sharon Shepherd would suggest that she join the family for a casual supper after the game. That outcome certainly had appeal. It would give her a chance to become closer to Ben's sister. On more than one occasion she had heard Ben moan that Sharon was a born matchmaker and her current project was finding someone for him. The best outcome of course, was that it would be just the two of them. Ben would be available and offer to pick her up at seven.

With her plan mapped out, she changed into her running clothes then changed again into the red stretch top with black shorts. The outfit flattered her figure, showed off her arms without an ounce of flab on them, and accented her platinum hair. She grabbed her water bottle and sunglasses and set out.

The asphalt track ran around the perimeter of the park's multiple sports fields. She was on her second lap and at the far side of the oval track when she saw Ben arrive with Malcolm and Sharon, their daughter, Sally—who immediately took off to join her teammates—and Malcolm's brother, Zeke. She frowned. Zeke made her uneasy. Not that she had had much contact with the homeless veteran. And it was precisely because seeing Zeke with the family gave her pause that it took a moment and another several yards along the track for her to realize that Rachel Kaufmann was taking a seat in the bleachers next to Ben. Trailing behind Rachel was a boy that looked to be about Sally's age. He sat next to Zeke in the row behind the others.

Darcy stumbled, found her footing, and then paused to take a long drink of her water while she considered the effects of these unexpected developments on her plan. Ben was talking to Rachel, and she was laughing. Darcy capped her water bottle and started to run again, her long, graceful strides bringing her closer and closer to the bleachers.

But Ben never looked up. His focus was on Rachel and then on the players as they took their places on the field. The only one who seemed even vaguely aware of her presence was Zeke Shepherd. He glanced at her as she reached the bleachers and passed behind them.

Say something, she silently coached him. *Ask Ben if that isn't his coworker running the track.*

But Zeke kept watching her, his head turning slowly as he followed her progress. She heard the tinny crack of an aluminum bat and the voices of the fielders calling to each other as the ball sailed high and long. She watched it arc, clear the fence, and land at her feet.

"Hey lady," a kid called out. "Little help?"

She picked up the ball and tossed it back over the fence to the kid and started to run again, but this time as she rounded the curve of the oval and approached the bleachers, she was smiling.

Ben Booker was looking straight at her. As she came closer he got up, eased past Rachel, and jumped down from the bleachers to wait for her.

"Darcy!" he called as she approached.

She waved and turned off the track onto the grass, covering the distance between them with ease. "Hi."

"Nice throw out there," he said.

Darcy tossed her blond ponytail and grinned as she wiped a bead of perspiration from her temple. "I have many talents, Dr. Booker. If you'd care to take me up on that rain check for pizza, perhaps we could talk about it."

Too pushy, she chastised herself silently. She had been determined to let him take the lead, but her need to take control had jinxed that.

"I'm free tonight," he said.

"Great." She smiled. "Seven?"

"I'll pick you up," Ben agreed.

Beside herself with the pure thrill of victory, Darcy took off running again. "I'll look forward to it," she called over her shoulder as she ran behind the bleachers. It was all she could do not to pump her fist in the air. She had a date with Ben Booker. A real honest-to-goodness date. Life was so sweet.

On Sunday, Justin and his mom rode their bicycles to the small church in Pinecraft that John and Hester had taken them to the weekend they arrived. Then, everything was so new that Justin had barely noticed other people filling the church's benches. Now as he parked his bike next to about a dozen others and looked around, it seemed to him that everyone waiting to go in for the service had one thing in common. They were old—as in his mom's age or, more likely, as old as his grandparents were. There was not a kid even close to his age in sight. And if there were no kids, then how could there be a school?

"Let's go in," his mom said, steering him toward the entrance.

He barely heard the sermon. All he knew was that it was hot and his good wool pants made him feel like he was boiling.

Once everyone was inside he did notice a few other kids, but they were either older by at least a year or so or much younger. Not that it mattered while he and his mom were living so far out of Pinecraft.

The way he saw it, this whole move-to-Florida adventure had been a big mistake. And now his mom seemed determined to have him be friends with Sally, but Justin was sure that Derek wouldn't like that—wouldn't like him. After the game the day before—a game where Sally had spent her time sitting on the bench and cheering on her teammates—his mom had urged him to go meet the boys on Sally's team.

Reluctantly he had climbed down from the bleachers and stood at the wire fence that marked the dugout. Sally and the rest of the team were laughing and talking all excited about winning the game and they sure didn't notice him, so he stood there a minute then turned away.

He'd rather spend his time with Zeke anyway. Zeke wasn't like other adults. He didn't talk about rules or manners, and he knew how to do just about everything—work with tools, fix a boat motor or the conveyor belt in the packinghouse, play the guitar. And he lived wherever he felt like living, did whatever he felt like doing when he felt like doing it.

"Hey," he'd heard Sally call out. "Hey Justin."

His mom had been watching him so, even though he had preferred to keep walking, he turned around. "Hey." He retraced his steps until he was once again at the fence. The rest of the team was walking away, and Sally had just picked up her glove and started around the end of the fence.

"Did you like the game?" she asked, like he was some foreigner and had never seen a ball game in his life.

Irritated, Justin frowned at her. "I do know how to play," he grumbled.

"I know. I just. . ." She heaved a heavy sigh. "Okay, let's try this one more time. Would you like to be on the team? I was telling the other guys about you. I saw you tossing the ball with those guys at school. You've got a good arm, and we could use another pitcher while I'm. . .until I can play for real."

"You had another pitcher today," Justin pointed out, still looking at the ground as they walked back toward their parents.

"Mickey? Oh, he was filling in. He plays for another team, the team we play next week. So what do you say? Want me to ask coach to give you a tryout?"

Justin thought then about the two days he'd spent at school—the way Derek Piper and his friends had watched him. The way Derek had asked casually on Friday if Justin wanted to go with them to the mall.

"Can't," Justin had told him.

Derek had smiled. "Oh, I suppose you have to walk your little girlfriend home." He'd nodded toward where Sally was loading her backpack with books.

"I have to be at the hospital."

Derek's eyes had widened. "You sick or something?"

"My mom works there, and we're staying with friends so we have to take a bus."

"Well, maybe next week," Derek had said, apparently satisfied that Justin had a good excuse.

Recalling that moment with Derek, he'd come up with an equally good excuse for turning down Sally's offer. "I can't try out. I have to work in the garden and help my mom," he told her.

"Oh, we can work around that," Sally said with such confidence that Justin got even more annoyed with her.

"Look, I don't want you to work around anything. I don't want to play, okay?" And he'd kept on walking while Sally stopped. He had felt her watching him as he sat down on the first row of the bleachers and waited for his mom to notice. But Mom had been talking to the doctor, laughing and smiling, her voice all high and excited the way it got when she was having fun.

Finally Sally had walked past him, punching her glove with her fist and not even glancing his way. "I'm tired," he'd heard her say to her parents. "Can we go?"

"Sure, honey." Her dad had bent down so he was eye level with her. "You okay?"

Justin remembered now how he had looked at Malcolm Shepherd. He'd seen something in the man's face that he hadn't thought about in a long time. Sally's dad had stopped thinking about the other adults around them. He was giving Sally what Justin's dad used to call his *undivided attention*. The sight of it made his heart ache.

So Sunday during church as he heard the minister droning on and on, Justin thought about those times when he and his dad had spent time together—fishing, working, talking. He could talk to his mom of course. But that was different. He missed his dad so much and there was nothing that would ever make that any better.

He thought about the promise his mom had made that life would be better here in Florida. How could she know that? How could she make that happen? Oh sure, it looked like things were better for her—she loved her job and she talked about friends she was making at the hospital and all. But what about him? Hadn't she promised him that *his* life would be better too?

He looked over at the boy whose sister was in jail. *Matthew*, he remembered Hester telling his mom. The guy looked as miserable as Justin felt. Maybe if his mom would agree to move to Pinecraft so he could attend the school there, he and Matthew could be friends. The hospital wasn't that far away, and there was a bus that went between there and Pinecraft. Hester had said so.

In Pinecraft they would be close to shopping and the church and everything and, most importantly, he could go to school right here with kids like him. It wouldn't be the same as living on the farm back in Ohio or having his friend Harlan close by and it certainly wouldn't make missing his dad any easier, but it would be a start.

He would talk to his mom as soon as they got back to the guesthouse. It was the perfect time. It would be the two of them because the Steiners were going straight to the home of the girl that had died in the car accident. Having made up his mind, Justin stood with everyone else for the singing of the final hymn.

But even after he'd told his mom all the reasons why it made sense for them to move to Pinecraft right away, she still didn't agree.

"I know it's hard right now, Justin. But we've barely been here a week. You have to give this a chance to work."

"I am. I will, but. . ."

"We took a big risk in deciding to move here," his mom told him, and the way she spoke he understood that she was struggling to find the right way to explain why his plan wouldn't work. "I have to prove myself in this job before we can be sure that we have enough of an income to support us."

"But what difference does it make where we live while you do that?"

"This place is free, Justin. If things don't work out we'll at least have some savings from my salary that we can use to live on. . . ."

"And then what?" he asked.

"If I can save most of the earnings I make at the hospital while I'm on probation, then we would be able to rent a little place and maybe I could work as a private nurse like I did before."

"But we'd stay here—in Florida?"

His mom looked at him, her lips moving but no sound coming out. Finally she sighed heavily and got up to get the pie she'd baked the day before. She set the pie on the table and cut a slice for him. "Justin, you're going to have to trust me that I am doing the best I can—for both of us."

After that they ate their dessert in silence; then he took his dishes to the sink and rinsed them. "I have homework."

She looked surprised. "I thought you finished at the hospital on Friday."

"I want to go over it again."

He wasn't exactly mad at his mom, just disappointed. It seemed she was making all the decisions now that they were in Florida. Actually, it had begun even before they'd left for Florida. She sure hadn't asked if he was okay with her taking the job or enrolling him in the public school or taking this place. These were all things he wanted to say to her, but he knew better. His dad would not like it if he questioned her.

"Okay?" he asked when she didn't say anything.

"Ja."

He was already inside the small bedroom when he heard her

call out, "Maybe this evening when it cools off we will go back to the park? I saw an ice cream shop near there."

"Okay." He heard the water running over the dishes and closed the door.

Outside, he heard Sally squealing as she and her dad played some stupid game in the yard. He stood at his window watching them. In spite of the heat she was wearing long pants and a long-sleeved top and a stupid-looking hat. His mom had explained about Sally needing to protect herself from the sun because of the medicine she had to take.

Justin closed his window to shut out the sound of Mr. Shepherd's deep voice. Then he flopped down onto the single bed and stared up at the ceiling. And not once did he move to wipe away the tears that ran down his face and onto the quilt his grandmother had made especially for him. They couldn't go back to the farm. His mom didn't know it, but he'd overheard Uncle Luke saying they would take him back but not her. He'd felt really good when his mom had told Uncle Luke that there was no way that would ever happen. But he knew what that meant— like it or not they would have to find a way to make this place work out.

Part Two

*In the multitude of my thoughts within me
thy comforts delight my soul.*

PSALM 94:19

Chapter 11

Paul Cox had explained to Rachel that in order to qualify for her position in the spiritual care department, she would need to become a certified pastoral counselor. "Here in Florida that means you hold either a license as an LPC—licensed professional counselor or LMFT—licensed marriage and family therapist," he explained.

"Do you have a preference?" Rachel asked.

Paul grinned. "Sure do. The one that gets you certified the quickest." He shuffled through a stack of papers on his desk. "Eileen!"

"You bellowed?" Eileen pushed open his half-closed office door with one hip while she rummaged through a thick folder in her hands. "Is this what you're looking for?"

"The woman is a mind reader." Paul grinned.

Eileen turned to go.

"And I do not bellow," Paul added as he perched reading glasses on the end of his nose and scanned the paper Eileen had given him.

"How about howl or roar or perhaps bark then?"

Paul peered at his assistant over the top of the glasses and grinned. "Bellow it is. Thanks, Eileen."

Rachel could not help smiling. She had come to enjoy the banter that flew back and forth between Paul and Eileen throughout the day.

"Now then," Paul said as he ran his finger down the page. "In your resume you show that you took some credits in social work. Is that right?"

"Ja. Yes."

He turned to another paper. "And in the transcript from the university I see that you completed the required hours of fieldwork."

"Yes, when I was a school nurse."

"Supervised? The fieldwork?"

"Yes."

He leaned back in his chair and grinned at her. "Comparing your transcript and credentials to the checklist of requirements for certification, it would appear that you've already fulfilled several of the requirements. We'll need to submit all of this to the powers that be in Tallahassee. They'll test you and evaluate you for competence to receive certification."

"I would have to go to Tallahassee?" Alarm bells went off as Rachel imagined how Justin might take the news of her having to leave.

"Just for the testing and evaluation." He frowned. "Can you folks ride on an airplane?"

"Yes."

"Then we can make arrangements for you to fly up there, go through the process, and be back the same day."

"And after this evaluation?"

"My guess is that they will require you to perform a certain number of hours of long-term as well as crisis therapy hopefully under my direct supervision, but barring that they will send someone to supervise and observe. There will no doubt be some classes, but I think we can arrange for you to do the course work online. You have a computer?"

"Only the laptop here."

"Fine. You can use that at home on your days off." He made some figures on a scratch pad and then beamed at her. "The way I see it, you will finish your probationary period at about the same time you become fully certified, right after the New Year. How does that sound?"

A little overwhelming, Rachel wanted to admit. "And what if the people in Tallahassee have other ideas? How do you know—?"

Paul chuckled. "Sometimes, Rachel, it's not how you know— it's *who* you know."

Within days Paul had arranged the trip to the state capital. Because she would not get back to Sarasota until well after dark, Justin would spend the night with Hester and John, but she had promised him that she would tell him all about the airplane ride no matter how late she got back.

On the return flight, Rachel could not help feeling hopeful. Her interview with the certification board had gone well. There were courses she would need to complete, but the good news was that she could do most of the work online or attend a class right in Sarasota. The person she had spoken to had indicated that he saw no problem with the state awarding her a provisional license. With that she could work—with supervision—while she completed the other requirements for certification.

"Paul Cox will be an excellent mentor for you during this time," the state employee had said.

Rachel held on to those words as the airplane engines droned and she marveled at the sensation of flying above a field of clouds that looked like marshmallows. Silently, she thanked God for the many blessings He had sent her way over this last month. Then remembering James counseling her that "it never hurts to ask" when she had hesitated to pray for another chance to bring a child to term, she decided to ask for one more blessing.

"Please guide me in the ways that will allow Justin to find his way in this new life we've started," she murmured, and then she closed her eyes as the airplane began its descent.

"Justin can't wait to hear all about your trip," Hester announced after she'd picked Rachel up at the airport. "I've got supper waiting. I'll bet you barely ate all day."

It was true. She'd been too nervous about the plane trip and the meetings in Tallahassee to take more than a couple of bites of toast for her breakfast. Lunch had been a sandwich from a vending machine in the state office building, and supper had been a tiny bag of miniature pretzels and a cup of hot tea on the plane.

"I am a little hungry," she admitted. "But it's not so late. Justin and I can go home after all and—"

"After you have a decent meal," Hester said as she waited for the traffic light to change.

Rachel knew better than to argue and, besides, it would be nice to talk about everything that had happened that day. "It feels like I've been gone for a week," she admitted.

Hester smiled and then focused all of her attention on the road. After they'd gone past the bridge that led to the islands that separated the bay from the Gulf of Mexico, they passed the gigantic statue of the sailor kissing the nurse based on the famous photograph from the victory celebration at the end of World War II.

"Still kissing," Hester murmured.

Rachel smiled. "Do you think the real sailor and nurse ever got together?"

"Oh, you are such a romantic," Hester teased, but then her smile faded. "Do you think you'll ever—I mean it's been what? Nearly two years?"

"Ja." In some ways the time seemed such a brief period, Justin aging from ten years old to twelve. On the other hand the almost two years that had passed since James's death seemed much longer. Rachel supposed that Hester's question was perfectly normal, but she wasn't ready to think about the idea that she might ever love another man the way she had loved James.

"How are your friends doing? The couple that lost their child?" she said instead.

Hester clutched the steering wheel a little tighter and shook her head. "It's a mess. Emma and Jeannie were never just sisters. They've always been best friends as well. But now with one child dead and the other in jail—now when they need each other the most, they barely speak."

"I'm so sorry for them and for you, having to struggle with how best to help them."

"You know me—Little Miss Fix-It, as John sometimes calls me. But this I can't fix. I can't even ease their pain a little bit." Her shoulders sagged with weariness. "I thought I understood grief. I mean, all those years watching my mother get sicker and sicker. . ."

Hester's mother had died of Lou Gehrig's disease a few years before she met John. Hester had been her mother's caregiver for five long years. Rachel could only imagine how awful it had been for her, a trained nurse, standing helplessly by and watching a loved one struggle without being able to offer any help beyond compassion and comfort.

But the car accident that had ripped apart the lives of Hester's friends was a very different kind of grieving. "I imagine that they are all struggling with the suddenness of their loss—and they are fighting their anger as well."

"That's it exactly. It was all so senseless, and yet it has happened and how are they supposed to get through it? Even if Emma's daughter doesn't go to jail, how is she going to live with what happened?" She glanced over at Rachel. "I mean, you must have felt some of that when James died—so sudden and senseless."

"Ja. We all struggled to find forgiveness. I think Justin may be struggling still. It's very hard for the children."

"So how did you get through it?"

"Just after I lost my job with the school system I heard about a program called VORP. It stands for Victim Offender Reconciliation Program. It was all about victims of a crime or accident finding a way to forgive the offender."

"I can't even think how you would begin to do that," Hester said.

"I'll admit that it took me awhile to come to the point where I wanted any part of facing the young man who was driving his car with a blood alcohol content three times the legal limit."

"You had to be so angry."

"I was furious," Rachel admitted. "In a blink of an eye that young man had changed our lives forever and all for what?

Because he didn't think? Because the last person to see him didn't take his car keys and prevent him from driving? It was done, and we had to find our way. Our way has always been forgiveness."

As they made the rest of the drive to Hester's place, Rachel told her about the program—how she and Justin and others from their extended family had met with the young man. How they had learned that he was a husband and father who had recently lost his job. "Something he and I had in common," Rachel said. And most of all she spoke of how with the help of a trained mediator they were able to create a sort of contract so the man could make amends. "Get help with his drinking problem. Go back to school. Speak out to other young people to help them see the consequences of his action."

"VORP," Hester said softly to herself as she turned onto the lane leading to the farmhouse. "Rachel, I hate to ask, but would you be willing to meet my friend Jeannie—she's the one whose daughter was killed—and tell her about this?"

"Of course. Anything I can do that might help." The lights from the farmhouse streaked the yard as Hester drove past the packinghouse and other outbuildings. She parked beside the main house and tooted the horn.

Rachel couldn't stifle a yelp of pure pleasure when she saw Justin come bounding down the porch steps. She got out of the car and held open her arms, and her son came to her.

"How was it?" he asked. "Were you scared? Was it bumpy and stuff?"

"It was like riding on a cloud," she told him as they walked back to the house arm in arm. "Did you miss me?"

Justin ducked his head. "I had school, and you were only gone for the day."

"So you didn't miss me?" she teased.

He looked up at her then and grinned. "Maybe a little," he admitted.

She ruffled his hair. "I don't know about you, but I am starving," she said.

"Zeke's here," Justin said. "He's been playing his guitar and showing me some chords."

Inside, Zeke Shepherd was sitting on the rag rug that lined the hardwood floor in the living room strumming his guitar.

Such a small thing, Rachel thought. *A little music always brings such pleasure.*

"Showtime," Zeke said and handed Justin the instrument.

"Supper time first," Hester instructed, "and then if you guys finish every bite of your vegetables, it will be showtime."

Justin grinned at Zeke, and Rachel couldn't help but think that the prayer she'd said on the plane had been answered. Maybe they were going to be all right—both of them.

It was the music that had attracted Darcy to the room in the first place. She'd been making her weekly tour of the building, checking to be sure that the housekeeping staff was doing their job to the standards she had set for them and that those on the nursing staff were tending to patients and staying on top of their reports.

Oh, she knew how the word of her tour spread from department to department and wing to wing as she made her rounds. Well, if people lived in fear of her visits, then they probably weren't doing their job. She had made it plain from day one that she would accept no excuses and that she expected people to take responsibility if anything was amiss—and fix it.

She had almost completed her tour and had a list of infractions that was disturbingly long when she heard the music. A couple of nursing assistants were standing in the doorway of the activity room. They scurried back to work when they saw Darcy coming.

She sighed. She wasn't a total ogre, after all. Needing a break, Darcy put her phone on vibrate and smiled as she heard the voices of the children raised in the ever-inspiring chorus of "This Land Is My Land."

But when she reached the entrance to the activity room she could not believe what she was seeing. Malcolm Shepherd's homeless brother was sitting in the middle of the floor with a dozen patients gathered around him. He was playing his guitar and appeared to be leading the children in a sing-along.

Beside him Rachel Kaufmann was nodding and smiling as she encouraged the children to clap their hands on cue and join in on the chorus.

He might be the brother of the president of the hospital's board—and technically Darcy's boss—but this was unconscionable. The man lived on the streets. She glanced from Zeke to Rachel and waited for Paul's assistant to meet her gaze.

When finally she did, Darcy motioned that she needed to speak with her right away.

"I'll be right back," Darcy heard Rachel tell Zeke and the children as soon as the song ended. There was a slight pause, and then Zeke started strumming a new tune.

"Who knows this one?" he asked.

Rachel was smiling when she reached the doorway.

Darcy was not.

"Was this your idea?" she demanded in a hushed tone meant for Rachel's ears only.

"You mean Zeke and the music?"

"Of course I mean Zeke. What were you thinking? The man is homeless. Do you have any idea what kind of disease and germs he could be carrying?"

"Zeke?" Rachel blinked as she looked back at Zeke, who caught her glance and raised a questioning eyebrow.

Darcy moved farther away from the doorway. She deliberately positioned herself so that Rachel's back was to Zeke. "Yes, *that* man in there with children, some of whom have compromised immune systems. This is exactly what I feared when we hired you, Rachel. You have never worked in a true hospital setting—oh, I know you were a school nurse in some little rural school system back in Ohio but that is not the same thing, not at all."

Rachel took all of this in her usual pious and serene way. She offered no apology or excuse, just waited there with her hands folded in front of her, her eyes meeting Darcy's without flinching. And that only irritated Darcy more.

"Did Paul Cox authorize this?"

"Pastor Paul and I discussed offering some outside entertainment for the children," Rachel said.

"But did he authorize *this*?" She pointed directly at Zeke.

"No. I invited Mr. Shepherd after observing him playing at a friend's house."

Darcy hesitated. Wondering if the friend had been Sharon and Malcolm Shepherd. "Well, I will be speaking to Paul Cox about this. Clearly he has overestimated your ability to choose appropriate avenues for working with the children." She glanced past Rachel to where Zeke was finishing another song. "Let him finish this song and then send him on his way."

"All right." Rachel turned and started back toward the activity room. Her refusal to debate the point with Darcy made it imperative that Darcy have the final word.

"And, Rachel?" The Mennonite woman turned to face her. "Understand that this incident will be part of your file and probationary review."

"I know." Once again she turned to go and then turned back. "You should know, then, that Zeke was quite adamant about being properly bathed and groomed before coming here. My friends, John and Hester Steiner, lent him their facilities as well as new clean clothes and shoes for him to wear. And at his request both he and the children—as you can see—are wearing masks."

"That's all well and good, but germs travel and germs thrive wherever they remain once the person carrying them leaves the premises," Darcy replied. She was pleased to see that this time Rachel Kaufmann kept walking.

Darcy watched her end the sing-along by asking the children to give Zeke a round of applause, and then the few parents and a couple of nursing assistants that Darcy had not noticed sitting in the back of the room slowly wheeled or walked the patients back to their rooms.

On the one hand, she could see that the escape from their treatment had done wonders for the children. They were talking excitedly and smiling as they left the activity room. But on the other, this was a hospital—*her* hospital in the sense that if anything went wrong she would be the one called upon to answer for it.

"Can I leave or did you want to call security and have me escorted out?"

Darcy wheeled around and found herself face-to-face with Zeke Shepherd. The mask was gone, and he was actually grinning at her. And she couldn't help but notice that it was not a smirk, but an honest-to-goodness and surprisingly good-looking grin at that. His smile made his deep-set dark eyes sparkle. Flustered that it was possible for her to feel any remote semblance of an attraction to this man, Darcy walked past him into the activity room where Rachel was putting away some supplies.

"I'll take that as no security necessary, then," Zeke called out to her after waiting a beat. Then she heard the man actually chuckling as he strolled down the hall, his guitar slung over his back.

Chapter 12

Ben had a problem, and it had nothing to do with his work. In the two weeks that had passed since their pizza date, he and Darcy Meekins had fallen into the habit of grabbing something to eat or reviewing their day with other singles from the hospital over a cold beer at the tiki bar by the bay. Afterward the two of them had twice gone back to his condo to watch a movie. When he'd mentioned that he planned to participate in a charity five-kilometer run, she had laughed and commented that he wasn't exactly prepared for that distance, especially in September when the humidity and temperature could still be real factors.

"I work out regularly," he'd protested.

"But you aren't a runner," she'd pointed out. "If you think you can keep up with me, I could get you ready in the next couple of weeks."

Never one to back down from a challenge, Ben had started meeting her at the park closer to her condo early in the mornings. They would run together and then go back to her place for breakfast. After they ate, he would head for the hospital and the doctors' lounge to shower and change, promising to see her later. On one of those mornings, after his sister had presented him with two tickets to a ball for one of the charities that she and

Malcolm supported, Ben had told Darcy about the tickets.

"Are you going?" Darcy asked as they jogged alongside each other for their cooldown lap.

"Do I have a choice?"

"Well, yeah. You're a big boy."

"I know. It's just that charity balls are not exactly my thing, but this event is very important to Sharon. Agreeing to co-chair was the first real sign that she was ready to start living *her* life instead of living only for Sally. So for no other reason than that it will please Sharon, I'll do it. Wanna come?"

"Gee. I don't know. You make it sound like the world's most boring evening."

"Come on. There'll be great food, dancing, a silent art auction—the usual stuff. If things get too unbearable one of us can fake a headache."

"That would be me, I presume?"

"Well, yeah. What kind of guy would I be if I let you go home alone?"

Darcy had laughed. "All right. I'll come, but you are going to owe me big-time, buster." She'd taken off then, running with those long graceful strides that Ben had come to admire.

"Pick anything you want from the auction," he'd called out as he ran to catch up to her. "My treat."

Darcy had grinned. "Okay, you're on."

She's a good friend, he had thought.

When he told Sharon that he was bringing Darcy, she had beamed her matchmaker smile. "I knew it. This whole 'we're just friends' thing has been a cover."

"We *are* just friends," Ben protested.

"Really? I've never known you to spend this much time with any other friend—drinks by the bay, movies at your place, breakfast at her place." She actually pinched his cheek. "Come on, big brother, admit it. Finally someone has found her way around that science experiment that passes for a heart in you."

Ben did not begin to know how to protest Sharon's multiple assumptions. "First of all, I am all heart and you know it. Did I not turn to absolute mush when Sally was born? And as for Darcy..."

"It's okay, Ben. If you're not ready to go public with this, I get it. But once the two of you show up together at that ball tongues will wag."

Later that night, after he and Darcy had shared a late supper at a restaurant near the hospital, he was walking her back to her car. He had been about to tell her of Sharon's ridiculous assumption when she'd said, "I bought a gown for the ball today."

Half a dozen responses shot through his mind, but what came out was a noncommittal, "Really?"

Apparently that was all the encouragement she needed to provide details. By the time they reached her car in the mostly deserted parking garage, she was twirling around as if modeling the gown for him and laughing like a schoolgirl.

"Oh Ben, this is going to be so much fun," she gushed and pirouetted straight into his arms.

Their faces were inches apart, and her expression turned from girlish exuberance to grown-up serious. She ran her fingers across his lips. In all the time they had spent together these past weeks, they had kissed only twice—a quick peck both times when she left his place after they'd watched the movies.

"Kiss me, Ben," she whispered now, and before he could find words to say. . .whatever he might come up with to explain that he didn't see her that way, she kissed him.

Darcy was one gorgeous woman. And there was no doubt that she was bright and funny and had all the qualities most men would find attractive. But for Ben something was missing. Still, she was a good kisser, and he ignored his feeling of guilt when his natural instincts to return her passionate kiss kicked in. After a moment he was the one to pull away.

And there was the problem. Her kiss told him that she was 100 percent on the same page as his sister was. For Darcy this was no casual friendship—she wanted more. No, she thought it already *was* more.

"Wow," he said for lack of anything else to offer to break the moment.

She grinned. "Yeah, wow indeed." She failed to notice his hesitation. Instead she spun out of his arms and got into her car.

"See you in the morning. I'll have the coffee ready."

The charity run was coming up on Saturday morning, the same day as the ball. He had two more days to train, and certainly he could use every lap he took around the track at the park. But the need to put the brakes on whatever this was with Darcy took priority.

"Can't tomorrow. I have an early meeting at Memorial, and Friday's my last day there before I move over to Gulf Coast full-time, so. . ."

"It's going to be so great working in the same hospital—seeing each other every day." She grinned. "All right, I guess you can miss two days of training. I'll pick you up on Saturday morning."

He'd begun to notice that Darcy spoke in declarative sentences, not questions. She simply assumed he would expect her to stop by his condo and they would go to the run together. And the reality was that there was no way around that. His place was less than a block from the starting line for the run. "Sounds like a plan."

She backed out of her parking space and waved as she drove away.

Wondering what on earth he had gotten himself into and how he was going to fix it, Ben stood rooted to the cement floor of the parking garage. It wasn't as if he could simply sit Darcy down and make it clear that they had a great friendship with lots of interests in common, but that was as far as it went. No, he had to work with this woman, serve on committees to make hospital policy with her, attend the same hospital functions as she did. And the main issue was that he didn't want to hurt her. "How come you've never married?" she'd asked him one night as she prepared a cold supper of sushi at his place before settling in to watch a movie.

He had shrugged. "Medical school took all my time."

"You've been out of med school for years."

"Married to my work, then. How about you?"

She'd been facing away from him when he'd asked it, but there was no question that she had gone very still. "I came close," she said after a moment and then turned to him with a smile. "I actually got left at the altar, or almost. Two days before the wedding the guy sent me a 'Dear Darcy' letter and left town."

Ben hadn't known what to say, but she had saved him by waving off his expression of sympathy. "Not a big deal. I realize now the jerk did me a real favor. The truth is that I think my mother was more upset than I was. She worried for weeks over how this would play with her friends—refused to leave the house for days because she was so mortified."

Again not knowing what to say, Ben had offered the first thing that came to mind. "Well, any guy who would leave you must be a jerk."

Now he realized how a woman who clearly had romantic feelings for him would have interpreted such a statement. He groaned, and the sound echoed in the deserted parking structure as he walked to his car. Saturday was going to be a long day.

Rachel carefully separated the herb seedlings that Hester had given her and knelt to plant them in the flower bed outside the cozy screened porch at the back of the guesthouse. It was hard to believe that they had lived in the cottage for almost a month now. It was even more impossible to believe that she was planting any spring or summer flower in October.

"Rachel?" Sharon Shepherd was knocking on the front screen door of the guesthouse.

"Out here." Rachel wiped her hands on a rag as she went to meet Sharon. The normally cheerful woman's face was lined with worry. "Is Sally all right?" It was the first question anyone asked if Sharon or Malcolm seemed upset.

"She's fine. Thank you for asking. It's this charity ball tonight." She heaved a sigh of pure frustration. "My co-chair called, and it seems that the pastry chef for the catering service we hired just walked off the job and his two helpers left with him."

"That's terrible."

"Fortunately he had already baked the key lime cakes that will form the foundation of our dessert. However, there are five hundred plates that need berries and a chocolate drizzle in the shape of a fiddlehead fern. I suppose we could serve the cake without the decoration, but the fiddlehead is the theme."

Sharon seemed close to tears, and Rachel realized that the woman had come to her not to relieve herself of her frustration but to ask for some concrete help.

"What can I do?" she asked although she could not imagine how she might solve Sharon's problem. Perhaps she could wash the berries?

"I called Hester thinking she might be able to recommend someone from Pinecraft—perhaps a baker from one of the restaurants there—Yoder's or Troyer's. But she's over at her friend Jeannie's and I don't want to bother her when they have far more serious problems than this."

"You could call the restaurants yourself or I could," Rachel offered.

"I already did. It's Saturday—their busiest day." She hesitated. "I really hate to ask, but do you think you might come with me? Perhaps together we could at least see what we could do about the desserts. We might as well forget about the fancy fern design." She sighed. "Although that was the point—it's the Fiddlehead Ball, after all."

"Of course, I can help," Rachel readily agreed. "And Justin can come as well."

Sharon's smile was radiant. "Thank you. Sally's already insisting on going so between the four of us maybe we can save the day. I'll go pack up my gown and shoes. I can change there. We can take my car. Malcolm can come in our other car so he can drive you and Justin and Sally home when we're done." She ticked each item off on her manicured fingernails. "Can you be ready in fifteen minutes?"

"Justin and I will be ready," Rachel assured her. As soon as Sharon left, Rachel called Justin in from his work weeding one of the flower beds and told him to wash up and change his clothes.

As she explained what was happening she changed into a fresh dress and put on a clean apron. She checked her hair, anchoring any stray wisps under her starched prayer covering and then knocked lightly on Justin's door.

"Coming." He had not questioned anything about this strange turn of events, and for that she was grateful since over the last couple of weeks he had become even more reclusive, rarely talking about what had happened at school and never mentioning any new friends.

He emerged from his room dressed in jeans and a short-sleeved shirt. His hair was wet where he had tried to tame the cowlick.

"You look nice," Rachel said.

Outside, a car horn tooted as Sharon pulled up in front of the guesthouse. Rachel saw Justin hesitate when he realized that Sally was seated in the backseat. "You ride up front," Rachel said quietly. "I'll sit in back with Sally." The look of pure relief and gratitude that Justin gave her was worth everything.

The ball was to take place at a large hall on the north end of town. When they entered the building, Rachel saw that the place had been transformed into a tropical garden. While Sharon and Sally went to speak with Sharon's co-chair who was clearly in charge of decorating the hall, Rachel waited patiently with Justin near the entrance.

"There must be a thousand candles," Justin said. "Do you think they plan to light them all?"

"Probably so."

"I could help with that," he offered, and Rachel understood that for a boy the attraction of matches and fire was far more interesting than the idea of working in a kitchen.

"We'll see." Sharon was crossing the room to where they waited. She looked even more stressed than she had when she'd first shown up at the guesthouse. "Is everything all right?"

"When it rains it pours," Sharon grumbled. "The caterer has informed my cochair that his people will not arrive until fifteen minutes before we need them to start circulating with the appetizers, and more to the point, they are *waitstaff*, not *kitchen staff*."

"What's the difference?" Justin asked.

"My point exactly," Sharon said. "But a contract is a contract, and everything was already spelled out there. These people consider themselves specialists. There are separate teams to prepare the appetizers, salad, and entree, a wine steward and bartender, waitstaff, and the pastry chef and his two helpers that walked off the job. The caterer will do what he can, but we really need him overseeing everything and. . ."

Sharon looked as if she might burst into tears. "I'm so sorry, Rachel. I thought that if we could come down here for an hour or so and you could help. . . But I can't possibly ask you and Justin to stay all evening." The lines around her eyes and mouth told Rachel that she was exhausted.

"Perhaps we could see the kitchen. After all, you don't have to replace all of those people you mentioned—just the three who left."

"Right, Mom," Sally said. "We have three people right here, so exactly what is the problem?"

Sharon looked skeptical, but she led the way to the large kitchen. On tables that ran the length of one long wall were stacks of green plates.

"As soon as the salads go out, you can start assembling the desserts here," the caterer told them. Rachel saw several flat trays with the undecorated key lime cakes waiting to be cut. At least the baking was already finished.

Sally peered at a pencil drawing taped to the wall. It was the design for the chocolate fern that the pastry chef had planned to decorate each plate with. She grinned and started rolling back the sleeves of her shirt. "I can do that."

Her mother was skeptical, as was the caterer. "Can't you make an exception and do this part?" she asked him.

"Not if you want everything else to come off smoothly. Have you seen the list of things we have yet to do?"

Sally nudged her mother's side. "Let me try, okay?"

The caterer filled a pastry bag with chocolate and handed it to Sally. Several of the kitchen staff stopped what they were doing and gathered around as she bent over the plate and began drawing the fern.

"Perfecto," one man whispered.

Sally grinned. "I'm going to be a famous artist one day."

"I thought you were going to be a baseball player," Justin said.

"That too," she told him. She glanced at her mother and Rachel. "Well, do you want me to get started on the other four hundred ninety-nine ferns or not?"

Sharon kissed Sally's forehead. "I do love you, kiddo," she murmured before turning her attention to Rachel. "Are you sure this isn't asking too much of you?"

"Not at all. We're happy to help, and one late night is not going to cause us any harm."

"Thank you so much." Sharon clapped her hands together to gain everyone's attention. "So, Rachel and her son, Justin, and my daughter, Sally, will manage the assembly of the desserts."

"If anybody wants to help. . ." Sally left the thought hanging as she grinned at the rest of the kitchen staff. They all chuckled and went back to work preparing trays of appetizers and putting the finishing touches on the other courses. "Guess we're on our own, then." Sally looked at Rachel and Justin. "Just give us the green light when you're ready," she told the caterer.

While Sharon went to change into her ball gown, Rachel, Justin, and Sally did whatever they could to help make sure everything was ready for receiving the guests. They helped prepare the appetizer trays, cleared away used skillets and other cooking utensils, and filled carafes with ice cubes, water, and thin slices of lemon. To Justin's delight, Sharon and her co-chair recruited him to assist with the job of lighting the small votive candles that formed a circle around centerpieces of a single orchid surrounded by ferns on each of the tables set for ten guests.

"Five hundred candles," he said when he came back to the kitchen. "And that doesn't count the ones that are on the stage."

He was excited—more like the boy he'd once been, and Rachel sent up a silent prayer of thanksgiving.

They were so busy that Rachel barely noticed the time passing. It was only after the last large oval tray had been loaded with the final plates of dessert that she accepted the plate of food the caterer handed her.

"Thank you," he said. "I quite literally could not have pulled this off without you and the children. Any time you might want a job. . ."

Rachel smiled. "I have a job, but I do appreciate the offer."

"Mrs. Kaufmann," Sally whispered from her place near the door that led to the ballroom, "come look. It's magical."

Now that the kitchen was quiet, Rachel could hear the music, the clink of flatware on china, and the laughter and conversation of people enjoying themselves.

"Follow me," Sally said with a twinkle in her eyes and a mischievous grin that made it impossible not to want to know what she was up to. Even Justin followed her through the hallway and up a narrow staircase to a balcony that overlooked the ballroom below.

It took a moment for Rachel to adjust her vision from the glaring fluorescent lighting of the kitchen to the shadows and candlelight of the ballroom—a different world where men in tuxedos and women in jewel-toned gowns seemed almost to be a part of the decoration. It was like looking at a painting, a moving painting, as the guests danced or sat enjoying their dessert and talking.

"There's Mom and Dad." Sally pointed toward the center of the dance floor. She sighed happily. "Isn't she beautiful?"

"She is," Rachel agreed.

"I'm glad that she's having a good time," Sally continued. "She's been through a lot, worrying about me and all."

Rachel could not help but marvel at the girl's perceptiveness and her kindness in taking joy from the fact that after all the weeks and months of worry her mother was carefree, at least for the moment.

"Ooh," Sally whispered, "there's Uncle Ben."

Rachel searched the dancers for a glimpse of the handsome doctor.

"He's with that lady from the hospital." For the first time that Rachel could recall, Sally sounded less than her usual upbeat self.

"Ms. Meekins looks lovely," Rachel said.

"Yeah." Sally's tone was grudging.

Darcy Meekins looked very different than she did at the

hospital. She was wearing a beautiful aqua-colored satin gown and her hair—usually caught up into a sophisticated twist at work—cascaded down her back in platinum waves. Rachel turned her attention from Darcy back to Ben. On those occasions when she happened to see him at the hospital, more often than not he was wearing scrubs or an ill-fitting lab coat. Even in such casual clothes, there was no denying how handsome he was. But seeing him in formal wear took her breath away.

Embarrassed and confused by her reaction, Rachel turned her attention back to Darcy who was laughing at something Ben had said. Rachel had to admit that they made a perfect couple. And she wondered why the idea of Ben with Darcy made her feel sad.

Chapter 13

I t had not taken long for Justin to realize that the reason Derek Piper had accepted him into his group of friends was that Justin was good at math. So he certainly did not need Sally Shepherd lecturing him on that subject.

"I'm helping him with math. So what?" They were waiting for the school bus together—a situation that Justin had tried his best to avoid without success.

"You are *doing* his math for him," Sally corrected him. As usual she wore clothes that covered her from head to foot and one of her collection of stupid hats. In Justin's view, the way she dressed was one more way she stood out in a crowd. "He won't thank you for it," she continued, "and if Mr. Mortimer catches on, it's for sure that Derek Piper won't take the blame."

"Are you gonna tell?"

The bus arrived at that moment, and without another word Sally mounted the steps, exchanged a cheery greeting with the bus driver—who like everyone else seemed to think the girl was some kind of angel or something—and took a seat next to one of her girlfriends.

Justin walked past her toward the back of the bus where the last two rows were empty and he could hold places for Derek and the other guys. He slouched down in one of the seats and stared at Sally. Like the bus driver and Mr. Mortimer and pretty much everybody else, his mom thought Sally could do no wrong. His mom had gone on and on one day about how very sick Sally had been and how brave she'd been through it all and stuff like that. She sure didn't look sick, and she had an appetite that was enormous.

And besides, what about *his* courage in the way he'd handled himself after his dad died and through this whole business of moving to Florida? What about the way *he* had to smile and act like it didn't matter that his mom had almost no time for him at all now that they were here. She was always studying for some test or course she had to take or she was at work or she got a call in the middle of the night and had to go back to the hospital. What about that?

The bus squealed to its final stop before they reached the school and Derek got on with his best buddies, Max and Connor. Derek was in the lead, and when the bus driver told him to keep his voice down, Derek started speaking in an exaggerated whisper that had everyone on the bus giggling.

Everyone except Sally. She simply ignored him.

Derek paused next to her seat. She was on the aisle, her back to him. She was talking to her friend, but her friend's eyes were on Derek. The bus made a wide turn, and Derek lost his balance and fell heavily against Sally. When he regained his footing, Justin saw that he was grinning and knew that he had lost his balance on purpose.

"Are you all right?" His voice dripped with false concern. "Good thing you've got all that extra padding or I might have really hurt you." He was still grinning as he continued on his way and flung himself into the seat next to Justin. "Hey J-man, got that math homework done?"

Justin saw Sally glance back at them. She was rubbing her shoulder, and she was looking directly at Justin. He felt bad about what Derek had said about her weight, but he also had no doubt that she had heard Derek's question about the math homework. It was all there in the way that she arched her eyebrows, questioning Justin's next move.

With deliberate slowness he pulled his math notebook out of his backpack and handed it over to Derek. He had stayed up late making notes he thought Derek could follow to help him find the answers. He called them *study sheets* and told himself that he was helping Derek understand the problem so that when he had to figure it out on his own on a test he would be able to do it.

So let her tell on him if she dared. He'd take that risk. If the cost of having Derek and the others as his friends—his only friends—was helping them out so they kept up in math, it was worth it. Besides, he was pretty sure Sally wouldn't tell. After all no matter how popular a kid was, nobody trusted a tattler.

When Ben had looked up while dancing with Darcy and seen Rachel peering over the auditorium's balcony, he had actually stumbled a little and narrowly missed stepping on Darcy's exposed toes.

Darcy had laughed. "Easy there. I'm going to need those toes later."

Ben had turned her so that his back was to the balcony. He realized that he was not only surprised to see Rachel standing there, her white prayer covering unmistakable even in the soft candlelight, but he also realized that the novelty of her in this setting had unnerved him. For the rest of that evening—although he did not see Rachel again—he could not seem to get her out of his mind. And in his dreams later that night it wasn't Darcy he was dancing with—he was holding Rachel in his arms.

In the days that followed, on those rare occasions when their paths crossed at the hospital, he tripped over his greeting as he had stumbled on the dance floor that evening. Rachel remained her usual serene self during these brief encounters, her smile warm and open, and, as Paul Cox was given to exclaiming, "a breath of pure fresh air in these sometimes difficult surroundings."

In the monthly meeting of department heads that Ben had just left, Paul had made it crystal clear that in his opinion they could not have chosen a better candidate for the spiritual counselor position. "The woman is a wonder," he declared in that voice that was better suited to the pulpit than the conference room. And Ben had seen Darcy wince as Paul went on to enumerate all the ways that in six short weeks Rachel Kaufmann had established herself as a "pure blessing to this place."

"Ben, wait up."

He turned at the sound of Darcy's heels on the tiled floor. Ever since the run followed by the charity ball he had worked hard at keeping his interactions with Darcy outside the hospital as casual as possible. And to his relief she seemed fine with that, to the point that he'd decided he must have misread their kiss in the parking lot.

"Going my way?" He grinned as he waited for her to catch up to him.

But Darcy was in full business mode—the thin line of her mouth told him as much.

"Hey, what's up?"

"Can we grab a cup of coffee? I need to talk to you about something—something I was reluctant to mention in the meeting."

"Sounds serious." They had reached the entrance to the small coffee bar in the lobby. It was fairly deserted at this time of day, and Ben indicated that Darcy should choose a table while he got their coffee. When he set the cup in front of her and pushed the dish containing packets of sweetener toward her, she was staring out the window.

"Thanks. I needed this." She laughed and added, "Intravenously would be even more helpful."

"Looks like what you need is a break. What's going on?"

She leaned closer, glancing around as if afraid of being overheard. "Houston, we have a problem," she murmured, "and her name is Rachel Kaufmann."

Ben could not have been more surprised if Darcy had suddenly spilled her hot coffee all over him. "Rachel? But Paul said..."

Darcy snorted and gave a dismissive wave of her hand. "Paul thinks the woman practically walks on water. That's part of the problem. He believes that her going through certification and getting her license is a mere formality. He can't seem to stop praising her."

"And *your* problem is. . . ?" Ben was surprised to realize that he was feeling a little defensive when the fact was that he knew next to nothing about how she was doing her job.

"I didn't want to mention it before—I mean she is living with your sister and Malcolm."

"But?"

Darcy took a deep breath and dived in. "A few weeks ago I was doing my weekly tour of the various departments. Imagine my shock to see Zeke Shepherd playing his guitar for the children on the children's ward—in the activity room."

"Okay, now you've lost me. What's that got to do with Rachel?"

"She invited him—without Paul's approval apparently. Oh, he approved the idea of musical entertainment for the children, but Zeke? No way would he ever have—"

"Why not?"

Her eyes bugged at this question. Her mouth worked, but no words came out. Finally she managed, "You are joking."

"Not so much." Ben took a sip of his coffee. "What's your problem with Zeke? I've heard him play and sing—he's talented and especially good with children."

"He is a street person, as in he lives on the street, takes his meals out of trash bins, sleeps on park benches or under bushes, and who knows how or where he manages to bathe or shower."

"Whoa!" Ben held up his hands to stop her tirade. "First of all, Zeke has a steady job at the fruit co-op that the Steiners run—and that my brother-in-law funds. Second, I'll grant you that he prefers sleeping out under the stars and I have no idea where he gets his meals or does his personal grooming, but the fact remains that any time I've seen him he is always clean-shaven and dressed in albeit ill-fitting but freshly laundered clothes."

He paused when he saw tears glistening on the rims of Darcy's eyes. "Hey, sorry." He lowered his voice. "Please explain to me why this has you so upset."

"I don't know. It's her. I have this uneasy feeling about her. I know that's totally unprofessional, but I'm usually right about these things. True there was no real harm, but when she goes out on her own and pulls a stunt like this she is not only putting the children in danger of picking up some germ or infection that man might be carrying but she's also endangering the entire hospital. What if a reporter had been here or a TV journalist?"

"You're talking in riddles, Darcy."

She cupped her hand as if holding a microphone. "We're here at the newly opened Gulf Coast Hospital where this reporter was stunned to see Sarasota's own well-known street musician and homeless veteran, Zeke Shepherd, entertaining the children. Given the outbreak of cryptosporidium that spread through the homeless population after last year's hurricane, this reporter had to question—"

"Okay, I get it. So talk to Rachel and help her to understand why—"

"I did."

"And?"

"Oh, you know how she is—all sweetness and light. She told me that Paul had given his permission but that it was her responsibility since Paul did not know that she was going to invite Zeke."

"Okay, so we're back to square one. What's the problem? Seems to me you handled it." Ben took another swallow of his coffee.

"But don't you think—I mean, she placed the hospital in danger."

Ben could see that what Darcy had really wanted was for him to be as incensed by Rachel's action as she was. But he really couldn't see the harm. There had to be more behind Darcy's fury.

"Hey, it's over," he said. "She didn't set the place on fire. There was no reporter or television camera. Zeke didn't infect the children, and you covered the chance for any liability by writing Rachel up for the infraction, right? It wasn't her best choice, but her heart was in the right place. I mean, we want an environment that brings the world to children isolated by their illness, don't we?"

"I suppose. But. . ."

Ben grinned at her, trying to lighten the moment. "Come on, admit it. You hate being wrong about somebody and from day one you were sure that Rachel was the wrong person for this job. Admit that she's good, Meekins, and move on." He reached across the small round table and patted her hand.

She let out a deep shuddering sigh and went so far as to give him a slight nod. "You're right. I worry so much about the hospital and getting our reputation solidly established. Rachel Kaufmann isn't the only one on probation here. I mean, this whole hospital has to shine."

"And that's exactly why the board hired you," Ben assured her. He glanced at his watch and stood up. "I have rounds. You okay?"

"Sure. Thanks for listening."

"What are friends for? Maybe I'll see you later, after work? Some of the other doctors plan to check out that new Italian place in the Rosemary District."

Her demeanor turned on a dime. She smiled up at him. "Why, Dr. Booker, are you asking me out?"

"Actually, maybe the best idea would be to ask Rachel to join us. If the two of you got better acquainted outside the hospital. . ."

Her eyes clouded over and her smile faded. "You know, I completely forgot. I have a previous engagement. Another time maybe."

Without another word she got up and went to refill her coffee mug before heading back to her office.

Rachel's mind was reeling with everything she had going on these days. Her course work was not especially difficult, but it took up a lot of her time. The same was true of her work at the hospital, especially when she had to return after hours to handle some emergency. Then there was the reprimand regarding Zeke that she had received from Darcy Meekins—a reprimand that was now a part of her employment record. Mark Boynton had explained to her that the hospital had a three-strikes-and-you're-out policy when it came to such things.

But uppermost in her thoughts was the feeling that she was not spending enough time with Justin. Not that he had said anything or given any indication that he was upset with her. To her relief he seemed to have connected with a group of boys from his school. One day she'd happened to be coming back to the guest cottage at the same time the school bus pulled up and Justin got off.

He hadn't seen her right away because his attention had been on a boy leaning out one of the windows of the bus, shouting something to Justin. Justin had been smiling and then laughing as the bus pulled away and the boy continued to hang out the window.

"Who was that?" she'd asked.

"Just somebody in my class," Justin replied.

"Does this person have a name?"

"Derek."

"He seems. . ."

Justin had shot her a look that warned her not to say anything derogatory about his friend so she changed tactics.

"Does he live nearby?"

Justin shrugged.

"Because maybe you'd like to invite him over for supper one day, or we could. . ."

"I see him at school. I've got homework," he added. "Math test tomorrow."

On the surface everything with Justin seemed to be going as well as could be expected. His grades were fine. He was making friends given the exchange with the boy on the bus and his occasional comment about a couple of other boys. He did his chores and did not complain when she had to go back to the hospital late at night. But there was something. . . .

"I can call Sally's parents and ask if you could stay with them until I get back, or you could come with me," she'd offered the first time she'd gotten a late-night call.

"I can stay on my own, Mom. I'm not a little kid anymore."

No, he wasn't. In the short time since they'd come to Florida it seemed to Rachel that he had grown taller and his body—always rail thin—had begun to fill out. And his voice was changing as well. It was rougher, and he had developed a tendency toward mumbling. But what worried her most was that his attitude had changed. He was quieter than ever—sometimes bordering on sullen.

She needed to speak to him about that. Sometimes when Sharon or Malcolm Shepherd walked over to the garden when he was out doing the weeding, he was not as polite as Rachel would like him to be. But the fact was that she had little enough time to spend with Justin these days and she was reluctant to use a minute of it to chastise him.

"It's a phase," Hester assured her one day when Rachel and Justin had gone over to the co-op so that Justin could help in the packinghouse and Rachel could help Hester label the jars of marmalade they would sell at the farmers' market.

Rachel wasn't so sure. As she made her way through the labyrinth of corridors that led from the children's wing to her office, she had one more worry on her mind. She simply could not afford to lose this job. She forced herself to take a deep, calming breath and silently sent God a plea to show her how best to earn Darcy's approval.

And then she turned the corner and bumped—quite literally—into Ben Booker.

Chapter 14

Hey there. I was hoping I might run into you," Ben said with a grin.

Rachel felt her cheeks flush. She lowered her eyelids, protecting herself from the effect that his smile had on her. Ever since seeing him at the charity ball she had been unable to get Ben Booker out of her mind. After Justin had gone to bed, when she would sit alone in the cottage's small kitchen studying, images of Ben dressed up for the ball would return. She was convinced that her thinking of the man at such times was nothing more than loneliness and fatigue.

"Rachel?"

"I wasn't paying attention," she admitted. "I'm so sorry."

"Not at all, and I meant what I said. It's been awhile since I checked up on you." He leaned against the wall, one ankle casually crossed over the other as if he had all the time in the world. "How are things going?"

For one fleeting moment she was tempted to confide in him, to tell him that she often felt overwhelmed by work and her studies for the certification examination and she was worried about Justin. Most of all she was tempted to seek his advice on how best to smooth things over with Darcy.

But then she remembered them dancing. Clearly, they had a relationship that went beyond work. If Rachel could believe Eileen, the two were *an item*.

"I believe that Pastor Paul is pleased with my work. At least. . ."

"I'm not asking about work, Rachel. How are *you* doing?"

She heard the genuine concern in his words, and she looked up at him. His eyes reflected his sincerity. This was no casual inquiry. He really wanted to know. Still, it was important for her to remember that in spite of the times they had been together when he visited his sister, theirs was a working relationship. "I am well. Thank you for asking," she said, and then with a smile she added, "And you? Have you completed your duties at Memorial yet?"

"I have. From now on I'm full-time here at Gulf Coast, but stop changing the subject. We were talking about you. How's Justin?"

"He is also well." She thought about the note her son had handed her that morning as he rushed off to catch the bus. It was from his teacher asking her to call to set up a meeting. Justin did not answer when she asked him to explain.

"I'm late," was all he'd shouted as he jogged down the lane.

Ben nodded. "Must be tough on a kid his age losing his dad and then moving to a place where he has no friends."

"He seems to have made friends at school—and of course, there is Sally."

"Sally tells me he's some kind of math whiz?"

Rachel fought the swell of pride that came from hearing Justin praised. "He is very good in that subject."

Ben pushed himself away from the wall. "Maybe come tax time I'll get his help. I am terrible at that subject." He hesitated as if not knowing what to say. "It's good to have you here, Rachel."

She did not miss the way his tone had changed from teasing to serious, and she paused, not sure how to answer him. "Danke," she murmured.

Ben seemed about to say something more, but then he cleared his throat. "Well, I have one more patient to see and you've probably got work to do." But he made no move to go. "Sharon tells me that you're always working—studying or cleaning or weeding the garden with Justin. Seems to me you could use a break. How about grabbing a quick bite to eat after work?"

Startled, she said the first thing that came to mind. "With you?"

He smiled and glanced around as if looking for someone else. "Why not? We work together. You live next door to my sister. My niece seems to think you are pretty special—all I hear lately is Rachel this and Rachel that. I thought that maybe we should get to know each other outside of this place."

She had often seen groups of coworkers leaving the hospital together, chatting about plans to share a meal or attend some event. Sometimes they had invited her to join them but she had always begged off, citing the need to go home to Justin.

"Rachel?" Ben was watching her now, waiting for her answer. "It's not a date or anything," he assured her.

She felt her cheeks grow hot with embarrassment. Was that why he thought she'd hesitated? Because she thought he was asking her for a date? Was he right? "Nein," she murmured. "I mean, no, I realize that. It's just that I have Justin and..."

"How about I get Sally and you get Justin and the four of us go out tomorrow after work? Do you like boats?"

The way this man's mind leaped from topic to topic was confusing to Rachel. "Boats?"

"I'll rent one from Margery Barker's marina. We could pack a picnic and take a ride around the bay—calm waters and all—and watch the sun set."

"Justin would love a boat ride." It might be the very thing to lift his spirits. He would not be quite as excited that the offer included Sally.

"Then it's a date—not a date—a boat ride with food," he said. "We'll have the kids meet us here after school and as soon as we've both finished for the day, we can go, okay?"

"Okay," she agreed, her head still spinning with the way this casual inquiry about how she was doing had turned into something much more complicated. "I will prepare some—"

"You will not. I'll take care of everything—boat, food, the works, okay?"

It was impossible to refuse him. "Okay."

When Rachel spoke to Hester about the teacher's note, her friend could come up with no ideas about why Mr. Mortimer would ask to meet with Rachel.

"I think it's kind of a normal thing in public schools," Hester had suggested, and that did make sense. After all, in their Mennonite school back in Ohio with its much smaller enrollment it was routine for the teacher to call upon a parent to talk about how a child was progressing—especially a child new to the community.

So Rachel called the school and left a message for Mr. Mortimer to contact her at work after asking Eileen if she thought it would be all right to receive the call there.

"Of course," Paul's assistant assured her. "Heavens, if you only knew how some people abuse the system with their personal calls. It's not like you're going to make a habit of this."

The teacher's call came the next afternoon, right before Justin was due to arrive at her office after school for their boat ride.

"Mrs. Kaufmann? This is Justin's teacher—Ralph Mortimer."

"Yes, hello." Rachel heard the nervousness in her voice and cleared her throat to cover it. "How are you?"

"Very well, thank you. I'm afraid that I have a concern, however, about Justin."

"He has shown me several papers with high marks," she ventured.

"Your son is a bright and industrious student, Mrs. Kaufmann. It is not his work ethic that concerns me. It is his choice in companions."

"I don't understand."

She heard the teacher sigh heavily. "That is why I think it would be good if we could meet in person."

Rachel's mind reeled with everything that she had to accomplish over the coming days. Pastor Paul was out of town attending a conference so she was filling in for him. On top of that she had sole responsibility for any on-call emergencies. In addition she had a paper due for one of her online classes and a supervisor from the certification board in Tallahassee was coming to observe her work.

"Mrs. Kaufmann?"

"I apologize. Is there no way you can simply tell me what the problem is now?"

"Well, I would prefer a face-to-face but it is Friday. Could I meet with you in person on Monday?"

"Of course." Rachel had no idea whether or not she could arrange such a thing, but when it came to Justin, she would move whatever mountain stood in the way of helping her child. "But please tell me exactly what this is about."

"Very well. Has Justin mentioned another student named Derek Piper?"

"Not exactly." Rachel thought about the boy on the bus, the rowdy boy shouting out the window at Justin as the bus pulled away. Was that Derek? She couldn't remember.

"I won't pull punches here, Mrs. Kaufmann. Derek is older—he was held back this year. He's a bright enough student but lazy."

"I don't understand what that has to do with—"

"I have evidence that Justin is providing Derek with answers to the math assignments."

"He wouldn't do that," Rachel protested. "We are a family of strong faith."

"Under normal circumstances I believe that Justin would follow the right path. But Derek can be a very persuasive young man and, as you must know, Justin is quite introverted. Since arriving here, he has struggled in connecting with other students. Derek seems to have taken your son under his wing, so to speak, and I don't think that Justin fully appreciates that there is a price for that friendship."

Rachel's mouth had gone dry, and she had to swallow several times before she could form her next words. "My son is an honest child, Mr. Mortimer. He would not. . ."

"Mrs. Kaufmann, from the brief conversation Justin and I had, I don't believe that he sees himself as breaking any rules. From what I have observed he sincerely believes that he is simply coaching Derek in math."

"I will discuss this matter with him, Mr. Mortimer. Thank you for bringing it to my attention."

"So I will see you on Monday?"

"Ja—yes. I will be there."

As she hung up the phone, she heard Eileen greet Justin. "Going on a little boat ride, I hear," she said in her trademark cheerful voice.

"Yes ma'am."

Not wanting to spoil the outing, Rachel greeted her son with a smile. "I have work to do in the children's wing so why don't you sit at my desk and work on your homework?"

"But you won't have to stay late, will you?" Justin said. "I mean, we'll still be able to go?"

"We certainly will," Rachel assured him. "Dr. Booker told me he might even let you drive the boat."

Justin's smile had none of the hesitation and uncertainty that Rachel had begun to fear was becoming his permanent reaction to anything she might say. "No way."

It was an expression he had picked up at school and she had decided to let it stand without comment. "That's what Dr. Booker told me. He said that Sally takes the helm whenever they go out."

At the mention of Sally, Justin's smile faded. "She's coming, then?"

"Well yes, that was always the plan, Justin."

Without further comment Justin edged past her and sat down at her desk. He bent to unzip his backpack and remove a stack of books.

Eileen's phone rang. "She's on her way." Paul's assistant gave her a sympathetic look and then reached into the small refrigerator by her desk and took out a soft drink. "Hey Justin, how about a soda?"

Justin glanced at Rachel and then swiveled the chair to face away from her. "No thanks. I'm good," he muttered and opened a fat oversized book and started to read.

Later, when they left the hospital, Ben was waiting for them. Rachel did not even hesitate when it came to the seating arrangements. She greeted Sally with a smile and climbed in back with her while Justin deposited his backpack in the trunk and then got into the front seat next to Ben. He was still brooding, but Ben seemed to be very good at finding his way through that.

"What's your mother feeding you, Justin? Looks to me like you've grown a couple of inches since you moved here."

Justin shot Ben a look and gave him a slow grin. "I'm taller than she is."

Ben laughed and glanced at her in the rearview mirror. "That's not saying much. Your mom is a bit of shrimp in the height department."

Justin snorted and Sally giggled.

"I beg your pardon. I will have you know, Dr. Booker, that I am easily the tallest one among my female relatives."

Ben rolled his eyes at her, and both kids exploded into laughter.

It occurred to her that he would make a very good father. But then she thought about him married to Darcy, and somehow she could not picture Darcy as anything other than an overprotective and controlling parent. Embarrassed at such an unkind thought, she turned her attention to Sally.

"I have a message for you from Caroline Royce," she said. "She wanted me to let you know that the group decided to go with lemon yellow."

"Finally," Sally sighed happily.

"Lemon yellow for what?" Ben asked.

"The theme color for our club," Sally said. "A bunch of the kids I got to know last year are forming a club—kind of a survivor support group. They wanted to go with blue—like heaven or something. I said we had made lemonade out of the lemons we'd been handed and therefore, yellow made more sense."

"These are all sick kids?" Justin asked, interested in spite of himself.

"Well, not anymore—or at least not all of us. I'm not sick," she said firmly then turned to Rachel. "When did you see Caroline?"

"Today."

"She's back in the hospital?"

Rachel heard the distress in Sally's voice, and she glanced at the mirror. Ben shot her a sympathetic look and nodded.

"Yes, Sally. She was admitted late last night. She had developed a high fever."

"It's not related to her cancer, honey," Ben assured her. "It's an infection she picked up while she was camping with her parents last week."

"Everything's related to cancer," Sally muttered, folding her arms across her chest and staring out the window. "Why do you think it's called the 'Big C'? Because it's always got to be in charge."

"Hey," Ben said soothingly. "Where's that lemonade spirit?"

Sally's fierce expression softened slightly. "She'll be okay?"

"She'll be okay," Ben assured her.

"I'm going to get her a bright yellow T-shirt. Will you be sure she gets it, Rachel?"

"I will."

Rachel turned her attention back to Justin, his light blond hair visible over the top of the headrest on his seat. How fortunate she was that he was so healthy. And Justin was a good child regardless of his teacher's obvious concern. Surely Mr. Mortimer had misread the situation. Justin would never cheat or help someone else do such a thing. On Monday she would make sure that Mr. Mortimer—and anyone else with questions—understood that.

Chapter 15

Darcy was on her way back to her office but her thoughts were on Ben. Something between them was different, and the shift had come even before she had told him about the incident with Rachel and Zeke. She thought back to the ball and realized that he'd acted differently even before then—at the run.

At first she hadn't noticed. Competitive by nature, she had been totally focused on recording her best time when she and Ben had joined hundreds of other runners at the starting line. And when she had crossed the finish line ahead of Ben she had teased him about how missing those last two days of training had cost him.

He had grinned and invited her to celebrate with breakfast at a popular restaurant on St. Armand's Circle. The restaurant had been full of other runners as well as volunteers from the race. The noisy conversation had made it impossible to share anything more intimate than a smile. Afterward they had walked back across the arching Ringling Bridge with its incredible views of the bay and the Gulf beyond to his condo where she had left her car.

Along the way, Ben had kept the conversation impersonal, talking about his final days at the teaching hospital, the party the staff there had thrown for him, and his relief to be able to concentrate fully on his role at the new hospital. When they reached the entrance to his condo he had walked her to her car, thanking her for helping him train and saying he would see her later.

At the time she had chastised herself for wanting to press for more—lunch by the bay perhaps. But she had sternly reminded herself that men did not like it when a woman was too pushy. If she had learned nothing else from her mother that lesson had been drummed into her head repeatedly. So she had gone home, done her laundry, cleaned her apartment, treated herself to a pedicure, and generally counted the minutes until she would see Ben again in a matter of a few hours.

So engrossed was Darcy with analyzing what might have gone wrong with her relationship with Ben that the very last person that she expected to find waiting for her outside her office was Zeke Shepherd.

"I thought I asked you to stay away from this hospital," she said.

"Actually you never really asked—just sort of implied that I was less than welcome here." He followed her into her office and sat down in one of two blue leather armchairs that faced her desk. "Nice digs," he added, glancing around.

"Thank you. What is it that you want, Mr. Shepherd?" Using his surname reminded her that he was the brother of the president of the hospital's board of directors—her boss. She stepped behind her desk and sat down, folding her hands on the large bare surface.

"I want to make sure that you have no worries about my performance for the children a few weeks ago. It's been eating at me that you might have gotten the wrong idea, so how can I reassure you?"

"Why do you think it's necessary to do this?"

He grinned, and Darcy was unnerved to realize that she found his smile—his white, even teeth, his wide mouth, his entire person now that she was really seeing him for any real length of time—charming.

"Because I upset you that day—rather, my presence here did." He leaned forward to look her in the eye. "Why is that?"

"I am responsible for—"

He got up then and started walking around, his hands locked behind his back as he studied the framed degrees on her wall and the few personal items she'd added to her office. "You see, one thing that I got to be very good at while I was in the service," he continued as if she had not spoken, "was reading other people. I was especially good at reading fear or distrust in others. It made me pretty valuable over in the desert where there are real language and cultural barriers."

"You think I distrust you?"

He shot her a look over his shoulder then continued his tour. "No ma'am. I think I scare the bejeebers out of you."

"Don't be ridiculous."

Zeke grinned, straightened her framed MBA degree, and sat down again. "But here's the thing," he said, leaning forward and pinning her with those deep-set black eyes, "I'm reflecting on my future these days."

He left the comment hanging as he studied his hands. Darcy couldn't help but notice that his nails were clean and neatly trimmed.

"And?" she asked, impatient with herself for being even the slightest bit interested.

"And I was thinking I ought to probably get on with it."

Darcy stood up. "If you're looking for a job, Mr. Shepherd, I'm afraid you've come—"

"It's Zeke, and I've got a good steady job over there at the co-op." He remained seated and continued to study his hands. "What I'm looking for, Darcy, is a mentor."

"A mentor? I'm afraid I don't understand." That was the understatement of the hour. She studied him closely, searching for any sign that he might be putting her on.

"My brother admires you," he continued. "Says you're the kind of self-made business person that he rarely encounters these days—male or female. He and Sharon—among others—have been pushing me to get back into the rat race for some time now." He grinned sheepishly. "But I find that I no longer understand the rules of the game."

Darcy moved to the door, intent on sending him the message that their meeting was over, a message that even he couldn't possibly misinterpret. "Mr. Shepherd—Zeke—if you need mentoring you won't find anyone better than your brother so I suggest—"

"Come on, Darcy. One piece of advice." He ambled toward the door.

"Get a haircut," she said. "Now if you'll excuse me, I have a hospital to run."

He fingered the glossy black ponytail that hung a little past his shoulders. "No worries. Thanks for your time." He walked into the outer office where, thankfully, Darcy's assistant was away from her desk. When he reached the elevators, he turned back. "Just one more—"

"Good day, Mr. Shepherd," Darcy said and closed her office door before he could complete his sentence.

Then, like someone hiding out, she hovered near the door listening for the elevator to arrive. Only after she heard the elevator doors open and close did she return to her desk.

Her hands were actually shaking. That was how much her up close and personal encounter with Zeke Shepherd had unnerved her.

The truth was that he was nothing like the man she had thought him to be—neither in looks nor conversation or attitude. Of course he was very different from Malcolm, and yet the similarities could not be missed. The eyes that probed and questioned. The smile—a little crooked and slow to come. The easy grace and confidence with which both men moved.

Certainly anyone who spent time in Sarasota knew Zeke on sight. He was a regular at the weekly farmers' market and almost as often could be seen on Main Street or near the bay strumming his guitar or sipping a coffee as he enjoyed the passing parade of people. But she had to wonder how many people would be surprised at the way his eyes flashed with curiosity and, yes, intelligence. She wondered how many people would look beyond the ill-fitting clothes and the long hair to see the man himself.

She rocked back in her chair, staring at the place where he had sat across from her, recalling his probing black eyes that had looked at her with amusement yet genuine interest as if he wanted to understand her. The smile that seemed forever lurking behind a mouth that was set at a slightly crooked angle in his sun-toasted face. She found herself imagining what he might look like with a proper haircut. She had never seen him other than clean-shaven and wondered why always if she considered him at all she had assumed he would have at least a scruffy sprout of whiskers.

She opened her eyes and tilted her chair upright, shaking off all thoughts of Zeke and his demeanor and his good looks. What could it possibly matter to her one way or another if the man shaved or not? And yet throughout the afternoon, every time she looked up from her work at the now vacant leather chair she remembered his smile. . .and those eyes. Eyes that challenged and questioned and, she had to admit, eyes that had completely changed the way she thought about Zeke Shepherd.

"You are simply associating him with his brother," she muttered to herself as she gathered the work she needed to carry home with her and prepared to leave for the day. Other than the similarities in looks and intelligence, Zeke was nothing like Malcolm.

She was on her way to the skywalk that led to the parking garage when she looked down and saw Ben with his niece, Sally. He was grinning and waving at someone as he waited by the open door of his car. She was about to continue on her way, assuming he was waiting for his sister when she saw the unmistakable starched white prayer covering the Mennonite woman wore.

Rachel Kaufmann and her son hurried toward Ben's car. The only good news as far as Darcy was concerned was that Rachel took a seat in back with Sally while her son climbed into the passenger seat up front.

So Ben was giving the woman and her son a lift. So what? He was a nice guy, always doing things for others. Still she could not seem to shake the envy that crawled over her like a bunch of pesky no-see-ums, the tiny bugs that attacked those silly enough to linger on the beach past sundown.

It was a perfect night for a boat ride on the bay. The water was calm, reflecting the surroundings like an enormous mirror. Ben set the motor on the small craft that he'd rented to the low speed required in these inland waters and steered along the shoreline of Sarasota. He first headed north, passing under the Ringling Bridge connecting the mainland to the string of barrier islands that gave the city protection from the worst of most hurricanes and tropical storms.

"What's that purple building?" Justin asked.

"It's called the Van Wezel Performing Arts Center," Sally replied before Ben could answer the boy. "They have all kinds of shows there—concerts and plays and everything."

"Why is it purple?" Justin asked and seemed pleased when Sally had no answer for that.

"I don't know. It always has been." Sally brightened. "Remember when we went to see *The Lion King* there, Uncle Ben?"

"Sure do."

"Did you see the movie, Justin?" Sally asked.

Justin's cheeks flushed with embarrassment.

"In our faith we do not go to movies or plays, Sally," Rachel said quietly.

"Oh."

Ben had rarely seen his niece speechless, but he understood that she was wrestling with the idea that she'd always been taught that such cultural events as plays and even some films were part of becoming a well-rounded person.

"Sorry," she murmured after a moment.

Rachel smiled and lightly touched her hand. "No need," she said. "It is our way."

"Do you mind if I ask you a question?" Sally squinted up at Rachel.

"Not at all."

"Well, I know that some Catholic nuns wear a covering

on their head—and Muslim women as well. Is there a special meaning to the little hat you wear all the time?"

Rachel smiled. "It is called a 'prayer covering,' Sally, and we wear it as a symbol of our faith."

"But all the time?"

"Sally," Ben warned.

"You never know when you might need to pray," Rachel said, "and how inconvenient it would be to keep putting the cap on and off throughout the day."

"There's the Ringling Museum," Ben said, taking the opportunity to change the subject by pointing to the lavish mansion that the circus owner had built in the early twentieth century. "There was a time, Justin, when John Ringling owned everything you can see here."

"Even that island over there?" Justin asked, his eyes wide.

"Even that. That's Longboat Key, and if you look back toward the bridge, Ringling owned everything from here to there."

"He must have had a ton of money," Justin said.

"He did, and then he lost most of it when the stock market crashed in the late 1920s."

"But he kept the house and that big building next to it?"

Ben chuckled. "John Ringling was a very smart businessman. He and his wife, Mabel, built the original part of that complex to house the huge art collection they had gathered on their many travels throughout Europe. And when he realized that he might have to sell off his mansion and art collection to pay his creditors, he donated everything to the state of Florida."

Sally turned to Rachel. "There's really a neat tour of the house and the grounds. They've got this cool circus museum and a fabulous miniature circus that has its very own building. Can Mennonites go to museums?"

"We can and do."

Sally grinned and turned to Justin. "Let's go there one day. I'll ask Mom to—"

"Do you ever go fishing out here, Dr. Booker?" Justin asked, interrupting Sally and pointedly turning away from her.

"Justin," Rachel said gently, "Sally was speaking."

"Sorry." But he looked out toward the shore, not at Sally.

"Never mind," Sally said. Ben glanced at Rachel.

"Is anyone hungry?" Rachel asked, her voice a shade too bright, her eyes and worried frown focused on her son.

"I'm not feeling so great," Sally said. She walked unsteadily to the far end of the boat and sat alone on the burgundy plastic seat, her arms locked around her bent knees, her back to all of them.

"Maybe we should go back," Rachel said to Ben.

Maybe you should tell your son that he's being a total jerk, Ben thought, but he could see in the worried way Rachel looked at Justin that she knew her son had upset Sally. So Ben nodded and turned the boat around, heading back toward the marina.

"I don't get it," Sally said later, after they had dropped Rachel and Justin off at the cottage. Sally had suddenly decided she was feeling better and persuaded Ben to take her for a hot fudge sundae at their favorite ice cream shop on Main Street. "What is it with that guy? I try to be nice to him like Mom says I should be. I mean he's living in my backyard—like literally twenty yards from our house. What is his problem?" she fumed as the two of them sat outside the ice cream shop eating their sundaes.

"Well, at least you've recovered your appetite," Ben teased as Sally scooped ice cream into her mouth almost without pausing to breathe between bites.

She grinned sheepishly. "It was either pretend not to be hungry or slug the guy," she admitted. "He's gotten involved with the wrong group at school." She shook her head. "Derek Piper and his crew are not the best influence on him. I think Mr. Mortimer is beginning to catch on, and Justin might be in trouble."

"In what way?"

"Derek is such a total bully."

"So is he bullying Justin?"

"Oh no, that's the thing. He's like best buddies with Justin—as long as Justin is willing to do his math homework for him, that is. Justin thinks he's helping Derek, but that's not what's happening. I mean, how can Derek have all the answers right on his homework but still fail the tests?"

"Maybe you should talk to Justin. . ."

Sally rolled her eyes. "Yeah, that'll work. He already thinks I might tell Mortimer what's going on. That's why he wants to stay clear of me."

"Maybe I should talk to his mom, then."

"Not at all a good idea," Sally protested around a mouth filled with ice cream and fudge sauce. "That would just prove to Justin that I'm the rat he already thinks I am. No, please don't say anything, okay? Not to his mom—or mine. Okay?"

She held up both hands, palms out as if wanting to stop him from even thinking about saying something. And that was when he noticed the white spots on her palms.

Ben dropped his spoon and grabbed his niece's hands, holding them closer to the light to examine them, all the while hoping he wasn't seeing what he most feared was there.

"Hey," Sally protested.

"Sally, when did you first notice these spots on your palms?"

She shrugged. "I don't know. Couple of days ago, I guess." She looked at him, tears filling her eyes. "It's not anything serious, is it? I mean, I've been feeling so good and, yeah, I had that virus last week and I'm still a little knocked out from that but Mom had the blood tests run and everything was normal and. . ."

Her naked fear made Ben repress his own terror. "Let's be sure," he said. "How about we make a quick stop at the hospital on the way home, draw some blood, and see what's going on, okay?"

"You think it's GVHD?"

His smile was forced. This kid had spent way too much time in hospitals. She knew all the lingo. GVHD or Graft-Versus-Host Disease was exactly what he was thinking, but at the moment all he wanted was to calm her fears—and his own. Even though it had been months since Sally's transplant, the possibility that her body might yet reject the donor marrow was still there.

"You know me, kid. I don't make guesses when it comes to medicine. Let's run the tests and see what we find, okay?" He pulled out his cell phone and punched in his sister's number and was relieved when Malcolm answered.

169

In as few words as possible he gave Malcolm the news.

"We'll meet you at the hospital," Malcolm said tersely and hung up before Ben could say anything more. Of course, what was there to say? The spots were a symptom. Other than the virus that seemed to have passed there were no other signs. Sally's energy level was fairly normal. Oh, she had seemed tired until she'd suggested going for ice cream, and then she had rallied and admitted that she'd been faking on the boat—or had she?

He resisted the urge to quiz Sally as they drove in silence to the hospital. She seemed small and vulnerable sitting in the passenger seat next to him, her arms wrapped tightly around her chest as if to protect herself from whatever the blood tests might reveal. Ben glanced at her, saw her lips moving and realized that she was praying as tears leaked slowly down her cheeks.

He reached over and cupped her head with his palm. "We can fix this, honey," he promised.

But Ben was far from certain that he would be able to deliver on that promise.

By the time the excursion ended Rachel had begun to wonder if Justin had indeed gotten caught up in wanting so much to connect with a group of boys in his class that he had been drawn into questionable activities. His attitude toward Sally while they were on the boat had alarmed Rachel, and his stubborn refusal to apologize only deepened her worry. She decided that before her meeting with Mr. Mortimer on Monday it was imperative that she learn more about this Derek Piper and his relationship with her son.

"I have an idea," she said when they were back home. "Tomorrow is Saturday. Why don't you invite your friend— Derek—is that his name? Why don't you invite him over here? The two of you could study together for that math test you mentioned, and we could have..."

The look on Justin's face stopped her in midsentence. "What is it? The boy must live in the neighborhood since he rides the same bus with you and Sally."

"He's probably busy with other stuff."

"How will you know if you don't ask?"

Justin turned away from her. She watched as his shoulders sagged. "Please, Mom."

"I don't understand."

Justin turned to face her, his eyes traveling instantly to her prayer covering and then back to the floor. Suddenly it all made sense. He was embarrassed—by her—by who they were.

"I take it your new friends do not know that you are Mennonite. And what if they did? Would that make so much of a difference?"

His head jerked up, and he looked at her with something she could only describe as pity. "Mom, please let it go. Be glad for me that I've made some friends. That was really hard to do, and I don't want to have to start over."

"Are you saying that Derek and the others would not want to be friends with a Mennonite?"

"They wouldn't understand. They don't like different. Look at the way they treat Sally."

"And how do they treat her? Do they roll their eyes as if her comments are stupid as you did on the boat? Do they ignore her as you did in the car tonight? Is this what you have learned from your new friends, Justin?"

"I'm sorry, Mom. Sorry for how I acted tonight with Sally. She's okay, but. . ." He drew himself up to his full height even with her own. "You're the one who put me in that school with all those outsiders. Now you want to ban the only friends I've been able to make?" His eyes challenged hers. Neither of them blinked.

Rachel was on unfamiliar ground. She wished James were here. She wished she could seek counsel from a man—perhaps Ben would know how best to talk to Justin. But it was just the two of them—and she was the parent.

"Do not speak to me in that tone, Justin," she said quietly. "No one has said anything about banning your friends. I have simply asked to meet them. But I can see that you are ashamed of your heritage—your father's heritage." She knew it was a low blow, but it was the truth. She bit her lower lip to stem her own tide of anger. She sucked in a deep breath and continued, "I had a call from Mr. Mortimer today."

Instantly she knew that Justin understood why his teacher had called her. Instantly she realized that what Mr. Mortimer suspected was not only true but that Justin knew that what he was doing was wrong. It was all right there in his eyes that suddenly could not meet hers, in the way his whole body slouched into a defiant posture, and in the way his lips thinned into a hard unyielding line.

Never had there been a more inconvenient time for her pager to go off than that moment, yet it buzzed insistently on the table where she had laid it when they returned from the boat ride. She picked it up and read the message.

"I have to go," she said. Justin turned toward his room, but she stopped him by placing her hand on his shoulder. "Justin?"

He did not look at her, but stood rooted to the spot as if waiting for something. "We will speak of this in the morning. Now it's too late for a bus so please call a taxi for me while I gather my things." Hester had suggested that she invest in a used car, but Rachel was unwilling to spend any more of their meager savings until she could be certain that they were finally settled. She in her job, Justin in a proper Mennonite school, both of them in a small rental house in Pinecraft where the ways of the outside world could not tempt her only child.

Chapter 16

After rushing Sally to the hospital, trying hard all the way not to alarm her, Ben realized he'd failed. As they waited for Sharon and Malcolm to show up, he saw that Sally was shivering and he knew it was from fear—not the temperature.

"I don't want to be sick again," she whispered as he waited with her in one of the small ER examining rooms. A nurse had drawn blood and hand carried the samples to the lab with Ben's instructions to deliver the results directly to him. He felt sick that he seemed incapable of offering Sally any reassurance.

At her insistence, he had promised not to hold back anything. "I want to know what we're fighting," she'd told him, showing far more maturity than most of the adults surrounding her, who were helplessly wringing their hands.

And through it all, Ben had stuck to his promise. First, after her diagnosis and the failure of the first round of chemotherapy, and then again and again as the search for a donor match failed repeatedly he'd told her the truth. Even over the long months that followed the transplant where Sally endured regular testing to be sure that the transplant was a success he had remained totally honest about what she could be facing. Through all those endless weeks and months it had been as if all of them—except Sally—

were holding their collective breath. Only she seemed certain that the fight had been won. Only she dismissed the caution that her parents insisted upon with a disbelieving shake of her head.

She rubbed her eyes, as if trying to change the picture she feared she might see once she opened them again. "Oh great," she muttered. "Skin lesions *and* dry eyes."

Sally knew the signs for chronic Graft-Versus-Host Disease—or GVHD—as well as any of them. It was a risk of transplant, when the patient's body perceived the transplanted cells as foreign. In which case the body would do what the body always did when a foreign invader threatened—her body would begin to reject the healthy cells from the transplant.

When she had reached the one hundredth day after her transplant with no symptoms of the acute form of the disease, she had framed the results of her blood tests—all showing normal levels—and hung it on the wall of her room.

"Party time," she had crowed. Even Sharon had laughed at that.

"Where is she?" Ben heard his sister's voice as she hurried down the corridor.

"In here," Ben called out.

Sharon went immediately to Sally and cradled her against her shoulder.

"Where's Malcolm?" Ben asked.

"Making arrangements to transport her back to Tampa. Don't you think that's the best plan?"

It was, but Ben did not like it since it would mean that he would not be able to oversee Sally's treatment. Still, the transplant team was in Tampa, and they were the ones best qualified to address any complications. Ben worked up a smile for his sister and niece. "Road trip," he said and was rewarded by Sally's half smile.

"Chopper trip more likely, knowing Dad."

The nurse entered the room and handed Ben the lab results without comment. But he only had to look at her face to know he wasn't going to like what they told him.

"The count is high?" Sharon asked, still holding Sally and

rocking her as if she were a toddler.

"It's high," Sally confirmed.

"It's also early in the game," Ben said. "Let's don't jump to conclusions." The nurse was back with a wheelchair.

With a resigned sigh, Sally pulled free of her mother and trudged over to the chair. "To the roof, driver," she instructed wearily as Ben took hold of the chair's handles.

"Your wish is my command, your ladyship," he replied, but his voice cracked in spite of his determination to match Sally's bravery with courage of his own. He glanced at his sister as the elevator carried them to the rooftop landing pad. Tears slid down her cheeks. When they reached the roof, he gestured that she should take charge of Sally's wheelchair. That way Sally would not see her mother crying.

Malcolm was already there, and in the din of the helicopter's engine there were no words. Malcolm insisted on lifting Sally into the helicopter while Ben hugged Sharon. Then Malcolm helped her in to sit beside Sally and climbed in after her. With a nod from Malcolm the hospital aide shut the door and moved away from the perimeter of the huge rotating blades to stand with Ben. The helicopter lifted off and turned north. Even after the noise that had been deafening softened to only a distant buzz, Ben stood staring at the sky.

"Doc?"

The orderly was holding the elevator door for him. Seeing him, Ben realized that for now there was nothing more he could do.

The calls that Rachel got to return to the hospital in the middle of the night had run the gamut. There had been the gang fight that had ended with three boys and one girl badly injured, their mothers huddled in separate corners of the waiting room, eyeing one another angrily as they sobbed or spoke in whispers to their companions. Somehow Rachel had calmed them, revealing that she, like most of them, was a single parent struggling to do the best she could for her child.

Then there had been the night she had arrived to find a

well-dressed couple sitting dry eyed in the family waiting room while their baby was being treated for hiccups that would not stop. They had been on vacation and, since their own pastor was far away, had requested a hospital chaplain. They wanted Rachel to pray with them for their baby.

In short, in the eight weeks since she'd started work at the hospital, Rachel had had to deal with situations she could never have imagined in her role as school nurse back in Ohio. On this night the person in need was a woman about her age who was suffering from terminal brain cancer. "Is her family here?" Rachel asked the nurse as she prepared to enter the room.

"She doesn't have family—or friends from what we've been able to see. When she first came in she was alert enough to ask us to call a couple of people, but they never showed up. Now. . . well, if she makes it through the next hour it would be a miracle. We'll keep trying to reach the next of kin, a cousin in Virginia."

So Rachel entered the room with its machines marking each labored breath for the emaciated and bald woman lying on the bed. She pulled a chair close to the bed and took one of the woman's hands in hers. "Jennifer?" she said softly.

The woman's fingers twitched and then tightened around Rachel's. It was a little like the first time she had extended her finger to Justin when he was first born. After a moment he too had tightened his little hand around that finger and held on.

"I'm right here, Jennifer," Rachel crooned. Realizing that the sound of her voice might be more soothing than the silence that would only exaggerate the sounds of the medical equipment, Rachel began to quote the twenty-third psalm. Pastor Paul had once told her that if all else failed, Psalm Twenty-three should be her fallback plan.

Slowly she delivered the familiar words of the scripture. "The Lord is my shepherd. The Lord is *our* shepherd," she amended, silently praying that God would forgive her editing. "We shall not want. He maketh us to lie down in green pastures; He leadeth us beside the still waters."

Jennifer's dry lips parted into a soft sigh. Without letting go of the woman's hand, Rachel reached for a washcloth, dipped it in the ice water on the side table, and pressed it to Jennifer's lips.

"He restoreth our souls," she continued. "He leadeth us in the paths of righteousness for His name's sake."

Jennifer sucked on the cool cloth, and some of the tension left her body.

Rachel hesitated, but then knowing that Jennifer surely understood that she was dying, she whispered, "Yea, though we walk through the valley of the shadow of death, we will fear no evil."

She took the cloth away, soaked it in the water that was certainly useless for Jennifer to drink, and pressed the cool cloth to the woman's cheek. Then she noticed that Jennifer's lips were moving. Rachel leaned in close and heard Jennifer whisper, "For thou art with us."

It was her use of the plural that made Rachel certain that she had been listening, that she knew Rachel was there with her. In spite of herself, Rachel smiled and let her tears come. "That's right," she whispered. "Thy rod and thy staff they comfort us. Thou preparest a table before us in the presence of our enemies; thou annointest our heads with oil." She moved the cool cloth over Jennifer's bald head and watched as Jennifer's lips formed the next words.

"Our cup runneth over."

Jennifer smiled then, and her breathing seemed even and steady for a moment. And then her fingers holding on to Rachel slackened as the monitor beeped out its death knell.

Rachel bent next to her and whispered the rest. "Surely goodness and mercy have followed you all the days of your life, and you shall dwell in the house of the Lord forever." She kissed Jennifer's temple as the nurse arrived and clicked off the switch.

"Thank you for coming," the nurse said.

"It's my job," Rachel reminded her.

"Maybe, but you go above and beyond—we've all noticed that."

Uncomfortable with the compliment, Rachel smiled. "I have Pastor Paul as my example." She looked down at Jennifer once more. "You reached her cousin?"

"Finally. But Jennifer had already seen to everything. She even asked Pastor Paul to take charge of her memorial service. I'll leave him a message to let him know she's passed. The funeral home will be here tonight, and the cousin said he would arrive tomorrow."

"*Gut.* I'll go now, or shall I wait with her?"

"Not necessary. We've got some paperwork to finalize for the funeral director, and I'll make sure she's laid out properly by the time they get here."

Rachel saw that the nurse was older—sixty at least—and it made sense that she was used to the old-fashioned terms that came with dealing with a dead body. Jennifer was in good hands. "I'll say good night, then."

And farewell, she thought as she looked back at Jennifer one last time.

So Mortimer had called his mom. Justin wondered if he should call Derek and warn him. But then it was late and what if his dad answered? Derek had made a couple of comments about his dad's temper. The two of them had talked about how everything had to be just so with parents and teachers, with adults in general, or they'd go off.

"I hope I don't get to be that way," Derek had moaned once. "They are either weak cowards like my mom or dictators like Dad and Mortimer."

Actually Justin liked Mr. Mortimer. He was a very good teacher, and he had a way of kidding around that reminded Justin of his father. "Dry humor," his grandmother used to call it. But Mr. Mortimer was his teacher, not his friend. Derek was his friend. Derek and Connor and Max. The four of them had formed a tight circle almost from the first day of school. They rode the bus together. They sat together at lunchtime. They passed notes back and forth in class and snickered. And on weekends they sometimes met at the park for a game of hoops or simply to hang out.

Their weekend gatherings were rare because Justin would

often beg off, saying that he had chores, and Sundays were taken up with church stuff. Mainly he wanted to keep Derek and the others from finding out that he was Mennonite—a secret that would be totally exposed the minute any of them caught sight of his mom. Lucky for him it seemed like Derek was also busy. Justin had noticed that his friend always seemed more tense than usual on Mondays, and more than once he had noticed bruises on Derek's arms. Once he'd even come to school with a black eye.

"Mind your own business," Derek had growled when Justin asked about the injury. And he hadn't spoken to Justin the rest of the day. But by the next morning he'd been waiting for Justin to board the bus, his hand out for Justin's math homework so he could compare Justin's work to his own.

Justin wasn't naive enough to believe that Derek had done more than scribble down some numbers—numbers he would change the minute he got hold of Justin's paper. But lately he wasn't even pretending anymore. He grabbed Justin's homework and then bent over a clean sheet of paper, copying the work as fast as he could as the bus rocked from side to side on its way to school.

Sally had warned him that they would get caught eventually. She had this annoying habit of always being right about everything. Derek couldn't stand her, and Justin was beginning to see why. He was fairly sure that she had been the one to tell Mortimer about the math business. And Derek was not going to like that one bit. Justin shuddered to think of the reaction his friend would have to this news. He actually felt a little sorry for Sally.

He stood at the window and looked up toward the Shepherds' house. As usual, it was all lit up. Those folks wasted electricity like nobody he'd ever known. They were nice enough people, Sally's parents. But like Derek said, they had money—piles of it—and money gave people like that the power to do whatever they liked. Nobody would ever dare question why Sally was treated so special by all the teachers.

Justin had reminded Derek that Sally had been really sick— would have maybe even died without the transplant.

"Yeah, right," Derek had sneered. "And how do you think little Sally went to the head of that list? Her daddy bought that transplant for her. Somebody like me—or you—would have been told, 'So sorry, wait your turn.' But not Sally Shepherd."

Derek's disgust for the girl had bordered on outright hatred, and Justin had wrestled with the teachings of his faith about nobody setting himself—or herself in this case—above others. Not that Sally did that. Even Justin had to admit that she tried really hard to be a regular kid, in spite of her family's money and in spite of her sickness. But when he'd hinted at this to Derek, the boy had sneered, "It's an act, you dope." And he had given Justin a slap on the back of his head.

Justin glanced at the clock. It was past ten. He wondered how long his mom would have to stay at the hospital this time. At first when she'd been called back after hours she had asked John or Hester to come stay with him or take him home with them. If they weren't available, she would call the Shepherds. Twice he had spent several endless hours sitting in that enormous house with its white carpeting that made him nervous to even walk on with bare feet.

The Shepherds had been nice enough. Sharon had made popcorn and suggested they all play a board game. "You can do that, right?" she'd asked him.

"Yes ma'am."

But then halfway through the game Sally had said something about being tired and not able to keep her eyes open, and the game had ended. Then while Sharon and Sally went upstairs he was left alone with Malcolm—the Shepherds had insisted that he call them by their first names and his mom had given in. He liked Malcolm well enough but the man talked to him like a father—how was school? What did he think he might want to do for a career someday? That sort of stuff.

When Malcolm asked if Justin thought he might like to follow in his father's footsteps and farm, Justin had lost it. What did any of these people know about his dad? Or his life before he came to Florida for that matter? Things had changed the day his dad was killed, and the ripples of that just kept coming.

It was right after that second visit that he had presented his case to his mother. He was not a baby who needed someone to sit with him. They lived only yards away from the Shepherds, so if anything happened he could either call them or go to the house. In short, he was old enough to stay in the cottage alone when she had to go back to work.

To his amazement, she had agreed. Of course she had given him a huge lecture about trust and laid down all kinds of rules about safety and stuff. She had called him like every fifteen minutes that first time, but after two more times, the only calls had been to let him know when she might be home and to ask if he had finished his homework.

Although he knew it was wrong, he'd taken some pride in his achievement, especially when Derek let slip that his dad watched him all the time and no way would Mr. Piper ever let Derek stay home alone. Justin was well aware that in persuading his mom to let him stay home alone he had scored major points with Derek.

Of course now with this Mortimer thing, that was all about to change. Somehow he had to warn Derek. He was reaching for the phone when it rang.

His mom sounded different—tired and maybe even a little scared. "Justin?"

Exactly who else did she think would answer?

"Hi."

"Everything okay?"

"Fine. You coming home?"

"Just about to leave. Dr. Booker's giving me a ride."

"Okay. Don't worry, Mom. I looked outside and the lights are on up at the Shepherd house, so if—"

"They aren't home, Justin. Sally had to be taken back to Tampa tonight. Her parents went with her. I think they must have left in such a hurry. . ." Her voice trailed off as if she wasn't talking to him anymore.

"Mom?"

"Right here."

"Is Sally going to die?"

"No. Of course not. She'll be fine." But she didn't sound like she believed what she was saying. Then she cleared her throat. "I'll be home soon, okay?"

Justin hung the phone up and went to stand out on the porch. He looked up at the Shepherds' house, focusing in on the window that Sally had pointed out as her room back a few weeks earlier. He couldn't help noticing that it was the only window in the whole back of the house that was dark.

Rachel had been planning to call a taxi when she stepped out of the elevator into the tropical garden, the waterfall silenced for the night. She was on her way to sign out at the security desk when she saw a lone figure sitting bent, nearly double, his head cradled in his hands. If there were an illustration for someone in deep anguish this man was surely it.

Her innate sense of concern for others would not allow her to simply pass by without offering to help. "Sir?" She touched his shoulder lightly, saw that he was wearing the uniform of a physician, and wondered if perhaps this man had been Jennifer's doctor.

But then he'd looked up at her and she saw that it was Ben. Her heart skipped a beat.

"What's happened?" she asked, sliding onto the bench beside him, her palm still resting on his shoulder.

"It's Sally," he began and his voice broke. "I should have seen it, should have known. The signs were all there."

Having already witnessed death that night, Rachel swallowed back her fear and forced her voice to remain calm. "Tell me what happened, Ben. Is Sally all right?"

He shook his head and once again plowed his fingers through his thick hair. "She's. . .her body is rejecting the transplant."

"After all this time?" Rachel didn't know a lot about bone marrow transplants, but she was fairly certain that the longer a patient went without problems the greater the chances for success.

"It's GVHD—chronic."

"Oh." Rachel knew enough to know that the chronic form

of the disease could be far worse than the acute form that came usually within the first hundred days following a transplant and could in most cases be treated successfully. Chronic GVHD could go on for months—even years.

"Her blood tests were always within the normal range," Ben was saying as if going over the data for the hundredth time. "But there were other signs—lately she's complained of something in her eye but it was always when we were at the park or outside and I thought..."

The disease could attack any one or several of the body's systems—skin, eyes, mouth, liver, stomach, or intestines. "You believe it to be ocular, then?"

Ben shrugged. "I'm not going to guess. She's on her way to Tampa. Let the team there make the diagnosis. It's pretty clear that I missed it big-time."

"Sharon and Malcolm must be—"

"They flew up with her." He nodded toward his phone lying next to him. "I was waiting for their call."

"Can I wait with you?"

His gratitude for her offer was reflected in his eyes, but then he shook his head and picked up the phone, perhaps willing the call to come. "That's okay. You should get home. Justin's there alone, right?"

"Yes, but..."

"I'll be fine, Rachel. Thanks."

"Is there anything I can do for Sharon and Malcolm? I mean, at the house?"

"I'll ask when they call and let you know." He stood up, and then he did the oddest thing. He lightly fingered one of the ties of her prayer covering. "Get some rest," he said.

"And you as well. Please tell Sharon that I will pray for Sally."

"Yeah. Thanks."

She was outside dialing the number for the taxi dispatcher when Ben called out to her. "Need a ride?"

"I can call a cab."

"I'll drive you. Sharon called and she wants me to check the house, be sure they locked up, and gather some things she'll need while she's in Tampa with Sally."

"Thank you," Rachel said and walked with him to the parking garage where his was the only car still parked in the area reserved for doctors.

He held the door for her then got in and started the engine. That's when she called Justin to let him know she was on her way home.

"They'll know more tomorrow," Ben said as soon as she hung up. "I expect they'll get her started on the steroid cocktail right away. She's going to hate that. She's already sensitive about her weight and that stuff will make her blow up like the Pillsbury Doughboy." He glanced over at Rachel. "You know that reference? Pillsbury Doughboy?"

"I do. We see the commercials when we watch the news." She studied him for a moment. "Are you going to drive up to Tampa tonight?"

"No. I have patients here that need me. We'll know more tomorrow," he repeated, as if that alone gave him some measure of comfort.

The streets were fairly deserted, and the traffic lights were with them. Added to the fact that Ben drove fast and handled turns as if they were no more than a slight curve in the road, it took less time than usual to reach the Shepherd home.

"Go ahead and park at their house," Rachel said as they approached the turn that would take them to the cottage. "I can walk from there."

He did as she suggested, and she did not wait for him to come around to open her car door. "Thank you for the ride, Ben." She started walking on the path that ran through the gardens connecting the main house to the cottage.

"Thanks," he called out. When she glanced back at him, he added, "For. . .just thanks, okay?"

He looked so lost, standing there alone, the light from the empty house washing over him. She almost retraced her steps. Her instinct was to go to him, hold him as she had longed for someone—man or woman—to hold her after James had died. But Sally hadn't died. There was still the possibility that she would be all right. Rachel thought about the woman she had ministered to earlier and understood that the entire night had been too full of emotional valleys.

Ben would be all right once he received an update on Sally's condition and conferred with his colleagues in Tampa about her treatment. The best thing she could do right now was to go home, hug Justin, and thank God for their many blessings.

Chapter 17

It was almost midnight by the time Ben had found the items Sharon had asked him to bring her; then he turned off the lights and made sure the house was secure—alarm set, garage door that Sharon and Malcolm had left open in their rush to get to the hospital closed. Restless and knowing he would get little sleep tonight, Ben walked around to the back of the house and checked the doors that led into the lanai and the pool. They were locked.

The night was still as beautiful as it had been earlier when they had been out on the bay. Had that only been a few hours ago? It seemed ages. There was a full moon—"Harvest moon," Rachel had called it as they cruised into the marina to return the boat to its slip.

The trip had been something of a disaster with Justin sullen and ornery and Sally withdrawn and depressed. And yet Rachel had found the one thing of beauty to focus on—the moon rising, a large golden ball that put the rest of the Sarasota skyline to shame. She was like that, he realized, always focusing on the good in people, the wonder of her surroundings. Whenever Ben was around her he felt such a sense of peace, as if no matter what happened, in the end everything would be all right.

He looked toward the cottage and saw a single light burning

in the kitchen. He was halfway down the path before he realized that he needed a good strong dose of Rachel's composure—the quality that she wore on the inside the way she wore that silly little hat on the outside.

Sitting at the small kitchen table surrounded by books and papers, she was writing something on a yellow legal pad. She was still dressed in her traditional garb, and Ben suddenly found himself wondering what she might look like with her hair down.

Not wanting to startle her, he made noise as he walked, clearing his throat and scuffling his feet along the crushed-shell path. He tapped at the open screen door, calling her name at the same time. "Rachel? Sorry to bother you," he added when she looked up without the slightest hint of alarm.

"Not at all. Come in. I was going to make some tea. Will you have some?" She busied herself preparing the tea while he took the only other chair at the table. "Is everything all right at the house?"

"It's fine. I just saw your light and. . ." He shrugged, unable to form more words as he fought the combination of exhaustion and fear for Sally that threatened to overwhelm him.

"I know. Sometimes as my minister says, 'The world is too much with us.' "

She set mugs and spoons for each of them and brought sugar and sliced lemon to the table while she waited for the kettle to boil.

Ben considered her white prayer covering and remembered how she had explained to Sally that she wore it all the time because she never knew when she might need to turn to God in prayer. "That works for you?" He pointed to her *kapp*. "The religion thing?"

She reached for the whistling kettle at the same time she glanced at him over her shoulder. "It works for everyone who has faith," she said quietly. She filled a china teapot with the boiling water and carried it to the table. "Do you not have faith, Ben?"

It was a fair question, especially coming from her. After all he'd been the one to bring the whole thing up. "I've kind of let things slide in that department," he said with a half smile and realized that it was the truth. There had been a time. . . .

"Sharon relies heavily on the comforts of prayer and scripture," she said. "More than once I have seen her sitting in the garden, her Bible open next to her."

"Our father was a minister, of the fire and brimstone variety. I struggled with that, and he struggled with me. In the end it was pretty much a standoff. Maybe if we had been able to talk calmly about things but it was his way or the highway." He took a sip of the tea she'd poured for him then added, "I chose the highway and went off to med school. I got distracted with studies, and well, it's been a while since I darkened the door of a church."

The confession made him suddenly shy with her. To this woman a strong faith was everything. He turned his attention to the papers and books spread across the table. "What's all this?"

He knew she was watching him over the rim of her mug. If she had wanted to preach to him, she apparently thought better of it and set her tea on the table. "I have a paper due Tuesday for my certification." She reached for the yellow legal pad. "It's nearly finished—except of course, for the typing of it into the computer." She sighed. "I'm afraid I am not very good at that."

"Ah, but I am." Ben took the pad and flipped through the pages. "Ever since medical documentation went electronic I have become one super typist." He grinned at her. "I'd be happy to type it up for you."

"I could not ask such a thing of you, Ben."

"Why not?"

"You are so busy."

"And you aren't? Let's consider busy. You have your work. . . ."

"As do you," she reminded him.

"Noted, although I seem to see you at the hospital almost as often as I'm there, and you have your course work to earn the required certification."

"That will be finished soon."

"You have Justin."

The shadow that dulled her always clear violet eyes was brief but unmistakable. She sighed. "He was sorry to learn of the return of Sally's illness especially after he had behaved so badly on the boat tonight."

"You're worried about him."

"Ja." She drank her tea, lowering her eyes so that all he could see was the thick fan of black lashes that touched her cheeks. And then he realized that her lashes were wet.

"Rachel?" He reached across the table and covered her hand with his.

"May I ask you a question?" She looked up at him.

"Of course."

"When you were a boy and you and your father were having your differences, how did you find your way?"

"It's not the same thing, Rachel. Justin's father died. You moved here. Justin had no choice but to start over. I had choices with my dad. It's not the same thing at all."

"I know, but..." She shook off the thought. "You did not come here to listen to my worries. Will it help to talk about Sally?"

"It will help if you tell me why you are so worried about Justin. At least I might be able to make some small suggestion for that. I certainly have no power to help Sally."

Rachel smiled and pulled her hand free of his to refill their mugs. "And so we are back to our previous discussion on faith, or rather, your lack of it when it comes to God's power to heal Sally."

Ben lifted his mug in a mock toast. "Touché." He took a swallow and let the warm liquid soothe him. "Talk about Justin. I'm a good listener." He grinned. "Part of the job description of being a doctor."

When she described the call from Justin's teacher, Ben was tempted to shrug it off as boys will be boys. But it was clear to him that she was deeply troubled by the very idea that her son might do anything dishonest—even unknowingly, which Ben very much doubted was the case.

"It's times like these when I miss his father so very much," she admitted. "James would know what to say to Justin—and to the teacher. I have no clue how best to handle this with either of them."

Ben leaned back in his chair. "What do you think is really going on here?"

"I don't know. I have not met any of Justin's new friends, and it's evident to me that Sally doesn't care for them. Oh, she hasn't said anything directly, but on the one occasion when I did mention this Derek boy, it was clear that she had serious reservations about him."

"Is this kid Justin's only friend? I mean, what about other boys he's met, perhaps at church?"

"The population of Pinecraft—at least the population of families that are Old Order like us—is aging, Ben. There are only a few young people living here year-round. Hester Steiner assures me that this will change over the winter, but those children who come to vacation with their parents will be temporary. And then there is the problem of distance. Living here means it is not easy for Justin to spend time with those few children who live in Pinecraft."

In many ways his heart went out to Justin. He well remembered the bullying he'd had to endure when he was around the same age—both at school and at home. Ben could hardly blame the boy for doing whatever it took to avoid that, even if it meant doing another kid's math homework.

"Here's my best advice," he said. "Until you know otherwise I would assume that Justin has helped this other boy because he genuinely thought it was the right thing to do for a friend. When you meet with his teacher I would ask the teacher to relieve Justin of the burden he has taken on to tutor this boy by either tutoring the kid himself or finding some older student to do that."

"You think so?" she said.

"Definitely."

Her smile was so radiant that Ben felt as if he had given her a wonderful gift. "But what do I know?" he said. "Going on instinct here."

"It's the perfect solution," she said. "I stand with Justin without either of us abandoning Derek. Thank you, Ben. I was so worried and I had prayed so hard for some solution and then you stopped by—"

"Whoa." Ben laughed. "Way too much credit here, and I've never been accused of being the answer to anyone's prayers."

"Oh, but you are," she insisted without a glimmer of humor. "At the hospital you are always helping others find their way through their illness—that boy in the shark attack? And Hester told me how very kind you were to Sadie Keller, the girl who accidentally killed her cousin? You must not take your gift for healing others physically and emotionally for granted, Ben."

Uncomfortable with her praise, Ben stood and picked up the yellow pad. "If you're done with this, I'll type it up for you over the weekend and e-mail the file to your work computer on Monday."

"I cannot..."

Instinctively Ben placed his forefinger over her lips. "Yes, you can," he said. "What are friends for?" Reluctantly he pulled his finger away.

"And what can I do for you?" she asked as she walked with him to the porch.

"Be here for me—for us," he whispered huskily as he looked up toward his sister's house and Sally's upstairs bedroom. "It's possible that Sally is facing another long battle—one we may not know the true outcome of for years."

She touched his shoulder, and it was all he could do to restrain himself from turning to her and finding solace in her embrace. "I'll pray for all of you," she replied. "Good night, Ben. Get some rest."

He did not look back as he retraced his steps along the garden path. But he sat in his car for several moments before driving away. He was thinking about Rachel, and he was not seeing her as a coworker or this nice woman who rented his sister's guesthouse. He was thinking about her as a woman that he could be attracted to, a woman he could see spending time with, a beautiful woman.

"A plain woman," he reminded himself firmly before he could carry that thought to the next level. "Get a grip, Booker."

Rachel awoke the following morning to the memory of Ben's light touch on her lips. She lay in her bed as the late-October sun washed over her as she recalled every detail of the time they had spent together the day before. The boat ride. Seeing him so distraught at the hospital. The ride home. The late-night visit. It was as if in a matter of a few hours they had traveled the path from knowing each other through his sister and people at the hospital to becoming truly connected as friends.

And that brought her thoughts back to Justin and his choice of friends. After several weeks in Sarasota she had made many new friends—Pastor Paul, Eileen, some of the others at the hospital, several of the women at church. She had chosen them all, drawn to them because they accepted her—prayer covering and all. So why was it so hard for her to understand that Justin had found similar acceptance with this Derek boy? What had she expected? She was always tied up with work or her courses. They spent practically every Saturday attending to chores. On Sundays they went to church and then spent the rest of the day at Hester's. They needed to broaden their horizons, she decided, if Justin was going to find the right kind of friends.

"Justin?" she called as she got out of bed, twisted her hair into a knot, and padded barefoot to the kitchen to start breakfast. "Time to get up."

"Did somebody come by last night?" Justin asked as he yawned and rubbed his eyes before setting places for each of them at the table.

"Dr. Booker. He needed to talk some."

"About Sally?"

"Actually we talked about when he was a boy and then also about you."

Justin looked at her, fully awake now.

"You told him about Mr. Mortimer calling?"

"I did. He helped me to understand that you have been trying to help a friend who is struggling. He also helped me see that perhaps you had gotten in over your head in trying to tutor Derek. So on Monday I am going to ask Mr. Mortimer to relieve you of that responsibility."

"But Derek. . ."

Rachel sat across from her son and took hold of both of his hands. "Derek needs help, Justin, his teacher's help. Not yours. If he is truly your friend he will understand and accept that."

"But what am I going to tell him when we take the bus?"

"On Monday you will not take the bus. You will go with me early to school and meet with Mr. Mortimer. I will ask Mr. Mortimer to speak with Derek and explain the situation."

Justin groaned. "You don't understand, Mom."

She squeezed his hands, forcing him to focus on what she was saying. "Justin, I am worried about *you*, not Derek. And what I understand is that Mr. Mortimer believes that you have cheated in his class. Such things—right or wrong—can follow you as you move forward in life. We need to resolve this now."

Justin stared at her for a long moment then pulled his hands free of hers and took his breakfast dishes to the sink. "You promised it would be better here," he said petulantly.

"I know, and I will keep that promise, Justin. But you have to give it time."

Her phone rang, and she glanced at the screen. Hester was calling her. Almost always when Hester called it was good news—an invitation for Rachel and Justin to come out to their place for the day or to come with her to the shops in Pinecraft.

"Hi," Rachel said, trying hard to keep her voice from revealing her stress—but failing.

"What's wrong?" Hester asked immediately.

Rachel cleared her throat and forced a light laugh. "Nothing." She would ask forgiveness for the lie as soon as the call ended. "Frog in my throat. How's that?"

"Better." But Hester's tone told her she was still suspicious. "I'm calling to see if you might have time for coffee today."

"Today? Justin and I were going to go downtown to the farmers' market."

"Perfect. John and I will meet you, then Justin can come back here with him while we go for coffee. I have this friend that I think should meet you."

Rachel noticed that Hester didn't say "that I think you should meet." And now she was the one with suspicions. "Why?"

Hester sighed. "The friend is Jeannie Messner—her daughter was the one killed in that horrible car accident last month. She's really struggling and well, I remembered you telling me about that victim offender program that you and Justin went through after James died—vort or something?"

"VORP."

Justin turned around and looked at her, his eyes curious.

"That's it," Hester was saying. "Well, I mean, when you and Justin went through it, the offender was a stranger. In Jeannie's case it's her niece, Sadie, and that girl is like a second daughter to her and her husband—or at least she was until this happened. Rachel, this thing is ripping these two families apart, and I want to do something to help them."

"It's not a simple solution," Rachel warned. "Everyone has to agree to participate—the offender and in the case of a death, all of the victims impacted by that death including the family of the offender. Are you sure they are ready for this?"

"I don't know," Hester moaned. "But what I do know is that this would be a quadruple tragedy if Jeannie and Emma were never able to get past this—and Sadie. I can't begin to imagine what that poor child is going through. She's in jail, you know, or detention as they so eloquently like to call it when it's a child locked up."

"Hold on a minute." Rachel covered the phone and turned to Justin. "How would you feel about—"

"I heard, Mom. Sure. That'll be okay. Maybe John and I can do some fishing."

Justin's willingness to go along with the change in plans without question or protest gave Rachel enormous relief. "Thank you," she mouthed and put the phone back to her ear. "All right. We will meet you at the market. Where?"

"The coffee bus. You can't miss it. It's a red double-decker bus that serves coffee. Half an hour?"

"Forty-five minutes," Rachel bargained. "We need to dress, and the bike trip will take time."

Hester laughed. "At some point we are going to have to find you a good used car."

"Our bikes are fine and the morning is so beautiful. Red bus—we'll find it."

When she ended the call, Justin was already back in his room making his bed and dressing. Rachel dressed, then finished washing the breakfast dishes while Justin got their bikes from the small shed outside the cottage and checked the air pressure in the tires. She picked up the cloth bag she used for shopping and put some money in her pocket.

"God in heaven, please help me keep the promise I made to Justin of a better life," she whispered as she closed the door to the cottage.

As they pedaled out to the main street, she noticed that Justin was staring at the Shepherds' house. "Are you thinking about Sally?" she asked.

Justin shrugged.

"We must pray for her every day until she is home again and on the mend."

"And what if..."

"We will find our way to understanding should that be God's will."

They had stopped to wait for traffic to ease so they could enter the bike lane. Justin looked at her. "Like we did with Dad?"

"Ja. Like we are struggling to do now that your father is not with us," she said. "As every morning and night I ask for God's guidance for both of us. You must do that as well, Justin."

She watched Justin's throat contract as he swallowed. "I miss him so much," he murmured.

"Me too," she admitted. "But sometimes on a morning like this I feel his presence so strongly. Remember how he used to make up those silly songs?"

Justin grinned. "Ja. They were really awful."

"But they made us smile, and the memory of them still does."

Chapter 18

Darcy did a double take as she walked through the farmers' market, intent on finding the ingredients she would need for the fresh vegetable pasta dish she planned to make for Ben that night. He had agreed to come for dinner after she had called to say how sorry she was to hear that Sally was back in the Tampa hospital. She was pretty sure she'd woken him up, poor thing. Of course, that had worked in her favor because he'd been too groggy to refuse her invitation.

Darcy loved to cook. As a teenager she had found refuge from her parents' constant nagging about what they perceived as her lack of ambition and her failure to appreciate the importance of building friendships with "the right people."

"If you're to have any chance at all of getting ahead in this world, then you'd better learn one lesson: It's not so much what you know but who you know," her father had instructed.

She vividly remembered the night she had prepared a five-course gourmet dinner for her parents and six of their friends. That night her parents had glowed with pride as their friends exclaimed over Darcy's cooking. But when she had tested their approval by announcing that she intended to one day open her own restaurant, her parents had smiled tightly.

She had taken their smile for encouragement and gone on to lay out the rest of her plan. "A restaurant where there is nothing on the menu but good healthy food beautifully prepared and served, food that even a truck driver would eat," she exclaimed.

Later that night, her father had come to her room and informed her that if she thought he was going to stand for her throwing her life away as she slung hash in some roadside truck stop she was dead wrong. Her mother had tried to soften the blow by adding that cooking for friends and family was a lovely little hobby. "But it's not a career, dear."

And so cooking had become her way of calming herself from the stresses of achieving the success her parents had expected. Forcing the memory aside, she reached for a bunch of fresh parsley and noticed a man sitting cross-legged on the ground between the herb stand and the next booth. He was strumming a battered guitar.

Since she regularly came to the market, she was well aware that Zeke Shepherd often hung out there, playing for the loose change and occasional dollar bills that people dropped into his open guitar case.

But this man could not be Zeke. In the first place, he was wearing jeans and a freshly laundered plaid shirt—both of which actually fit his lanky frame. Second, the long black hair was a lot shorter. The man strumming the guitar, his face bent low over the instrument, had thick wavy hair that barely covered the tips of his ears. It shone in the sunshine, black as onyx marble. And he was not begging—although Zeke really did not accost people or ask outright for money. The guitar case was nowhere in evidence.

And then as if he felt her staring at him, assessing him the way she might tackle a vexing problem at work, the man looked up and the smile that spread across his burnished face was pure Zeke. "Hey there," he said. "I took your advice." He fingered his hair. "What's next, coach?"

"Very nice," Darcy said primly and turned her attention back to the parsley.

"Ever try this variety?" Zeke asked, moving to his feet and pointing to a curly-leafed parsley. He was standing next to her

197

now, his guitar resting against the support pole of the vendor's stand. He picked up the parsley and sniffed it then sighed. "Heaven," he murmured and held it out to her.

Not knowing what else to do, she leaned in to sniff the fragrance. "Very nice," she said and turned away on the pretense of picking out some other fresh herbs.

"*Very nice* seems to be the slogan you've chosen for today," Zeke teased. "What are you going to make with all these herbs?"

"Spaghetti sauce." Why was she answering him? It would only encourage the man.

"You cook, then?"

Darcy bristled and turned on him in spite of her determination to escape him. "You don't have to sound so shocked."

He grinned. "No worries, Darcy. Simply making conversation."

"Yes, I enjoy cooking. Because of the demands of my work I rarely get to do much of it except on the weekends."

His smiled faded to a frown. "That's the trouble with work, all right—especially working for somebody else. Ever thought about going out on your own?"

She had paid for the herbs and realized that the two of them were moving slowly down the row of vendors—together, him with his guitar slung over his back, her with a cloth bag of fresh produce in her arms. "There isn't a high demand for hospital administrators outside of actual hospitals," she reminded him.

He shrugged. "You could do something else."

As if it were that easy. As if all a person had to do was wish for something and it would be there. "Such as?" She'd meant to deliver the words as a line of dismissal, but the truth was that she was curious about his answer.

"I don't know. You say you love to cook."

This whole conversation was beyond ridiculous. "And speaking of that," Darcy said brightly, "I really do have errands to finish so I can get home. Spaghetti sauce is best simmered slowly."

"No worries." Zeke turned to go but instead of feeling relieved, Darcy felt a tinge of regret. She stood watching him and as if he realized she was still there, he turned. "Hey Darcy, you forgot to give me that second piece of advice," he called out.

Several shoppers turned to look at her—as if they too were waiting. She almost turned and walked away, but then it came to her. Malcolm had worried about Zeke's lifestyle choice for months now. If she could help guide Malcolm's brother to a more traditional lifestyle, then her boss would be in her debt.

"Ditch the flip-flops," she called back.

Zeke grinned and waved as he headed away from her.

The man did have the most engaging smile.

After they all met at the bus, John and Justin loaded the bikes into the van from the co-op, while Hester led the way to her car. "We decided to drive separately. That way the boys can go on back, and then you and I can join them after we meet with Jeannie."

Rachel had to smile at the way Hester lumped Justin and John together as *the boys*. "Tell me about Jeannie," she asked as Hester drove.

"Jeannie is still so fragile and right now that makes her shy away from others, even people she's known all her life. If you wouldn't mind I think it would be best if you didn't know her story. Let's start with three women having coffee and see where things go."

Jeannie was a small woman, dressed in the clothing of the outside world. Her hair was the color of flames that fell in soft curls around her face. She looked as fragile as a porcelain doll.

"Over here," she called when she spotted Hester.

Rachel and Hester dodged traffic as they crossed the busy street to a small café with tables set outside among a garden of potted flowering plants.

"Jeannie Messner, meet another dear friend, Rachel Kaufmann," Hester said.

Over coffee they got better acquainted. Rachel liked Jeannie immediately. But when the conversation came to Rachel's experience with VORP, a shadow of suspicion crossed Jeannie's face. She shot Hester a look.

"Subtle," she murmured as she took a sip of her coffee.

"Okay, tell her," Hester replied with a nod to Rachel.

As Rachel explained the VORP program, Jeannie sat so still and expressionless that Rachel was unsure of how best to proceed. She talked about how James had died and her feelings afterward. When tears welled in Rachel's eyes, Jeannie reached over and squeezed her hand. "I know," she whispered. "I understand."

"Going through the program allowed both Justin and me to talk openly about how much we were hurting to the very person whose action had brought us that pain."

Abruptly, Jeannie stood up. "I'll get refills," she announced. Rachel was relieved to see that she was not leaving—at least not yet. That meant that there was a chance she might consider the idea.

Hester squeezed Rachel's hand. "I think it's working."

But Rachel knew that it would not be that easy. When Jeannie returned, the three of them talked for some time, and finally Rachel offered to act as mediator for the two families.

Jeannie sighed. "Do you really think that you can help us?"

"It depends," Rachel admitted. "Everyone needs to be willing. I'll do my best," she promised. "It will be hard—really hard—for some time, but it will get better." Rachel thought of that same promise that she had given Justin.

Who was she, to go around handing out such assurances as if she had the slightest power to deliver the goods?

Impulsively, Jeannie hugged her, and as Rachel patted the woman's thin shoulders, she squeezed her eyes closed and prayed for the wisdom and guidance to help in whatever way she could.

Driving back from Tampa, Ben's thoughts were consumed with Sally. He'd been reluctant to leave her, but Sharon—upon hearing that Darcy had invited him to a home-cooked meal—had practically pushed him out the door.

"Go. There is not one thing you can do here except sit there looking worried, and frankly that is of no help at all to Sally—or me. So do us a favor and go have dinner. Come back tomorrow full of stories about your evening with Darcy."

But when he thought about who he wanted to talk about his fears for Sally with, it was not Darcy who came to mind. It was Rachel. He glanced at the digital clock on the dashboard. He had time to stop by Sharon's house and check to be sure that everything was okay there. If Rachel was at home he would stop by for a minute to give her the latest update. Plenty of time to do all that and still be at Darcy's by eight.

With his plan in place, he stopped first at his condo where he showered and changed and chose a bottle of wine to take with him to Darcy's. When he arrived at Sharon's house he was disappointed to see no sign of life down at the guesthouse. Instead he found Zeke sitting by the pool, a cup of coffee on the table beside him.

"What's the word?" Zeke asked as if the plan all along had been for Sally's two uncles to meet.

"The diagnosis of ocular GVHD was confirmed."

"In English?"

"She has a chronic condition known as Graft-Versus-Host Disease or GVHD that has settled in her eyes."

Zeke let out a long low whistle. "Is she...I mean, tell me she won't go blind on top of everything else."

"No, although there can be some permanent damage. Right now the doctors in Tampa are running a series of tests."

"And you had no pull to speed up getting the results?"

Ben bristled. "It's the weekend, and I'm not on staff there anyway."

"Sorry, man. I just..." Zeke shook his head and concentrated on his coffee.

"You got a haircut," Ben said, trying not to sound as shocked as he was.

"Seemed like a good idea. Tell me about the GVHD thing."

Ben pulled a chair closer to Zeke's and sat down heavily. "It comes in two forms—acute or chronic. The acute form usually shows up in the first few months following the transplant. It's usually treatable and short lived. Sally had passed that milestone already."

"And the chronic?"

"Shows up later in various parts of the body—eyes, liver, lungs, skin—can be treated successfully. Or the effects can last a lifetime."

"Treatment?"

"Steroids—prednisone, sometimes with cyclosporine, and a whole cocktail of other drugs."

The two men were silent for a long moment. Then Zeke cleared his throat. "I thought she was being tested. I mean, it seemed like she was always going to have blood drawn and stuff."

"That's the thing. Her blood counts were all within normal range until last night, and then they shot through the roof."

"You know that day we all went to watch her game? She was rubbing her eyes a lot that day."

"Yeah. I missed that. Blamed the wind and the dust blowing off the ball field. I thought it was normal."

"We all missed it—Malcolm usually watches the kid like a hawk, and he missed it too."

"Yeah, well, I'm supposed to be the doctor."

"You are the doctor," Zeke said. "You are also human."

They turned at the sound of an approaching vehicle and saw the co-op's van pull up to the guesthouse. Rachel and Justin got out, along with John Steiner. John and Justin unloaded two bikes from the back of the van.

"I think I'll see if I can catch a ride with John," Zeke said. As he headed back inside to leave his mug, he grasped Ben's shoulder. "She's a fighter, our Sally."

That she is, Ben thought as he watched Zeke head down the path. *But just how many times is a twelve-year-old expected to get back up off the mat and fight again?*

He remembered then that Sally had asked him to get her journal from her room. "Do *not* even think about reading it," she'd ordered. So he walked back through the house—a house that felt so very empty now—and on upstairs to Sally's room.

The journal was lying on her desk, a rainbow of ribbons marking her latest entry. It was a surprisingly thick-bound book easily matching the number of pages in the hardcover mystery on the table next to his own bed. Ben resisted the temptation to read the whole thing. Surely if he read it he would have a far better understanding of what exactly it had cost Sally all these long months to keep up the brave and positive outlook she presented daily to the world. But he had promised.

He picked up the journal and the pen next to it and looked around for something he could wrap them in. On her bed was a heart-shaped pillow. He unzipped the outer covering and stuffed the journal and pen inside.

"Ben?"

He hadn't heard Rachel calling or her movement through the house and up the stairs. She stood inside the door.

"Sally wanted her journal," he said, holding up the heart-shaped bundle.

"Is there anything I can do? For Sally or Sharon—or you?"

A half dozen answers to that question raced through his mind, but he shook his head. "Sally's in good hands. Sharon and Malcolm are surrounded by good friends. As for me. . ." He was embarrassed to hear that last come out in a raspy whisper as evidence of his emotional state.

"Zeke told us the basics," she said, taking another step into the room. "He went back with John to tell Hester. He suggested that I might get a better picture of the situation talking directly to you. But that can wait."

Ben felt her calmness filling the space around him. "No, I want to talk about it. I mean, if you have the time."

She sat on the small bench at the foot of Sally's bed. "I have time."

Once Ben started to talk it was as if the floodgates had opened. As Rachel listened he told her about the transplant, the weeks of worry following that, especially because the donor match had not been as strong as they might have hoped. He told her about the endless round of tests and medications. The fear of infection. The boredom of days and weeks and months cooped up in a hospital room or this very room where they sat now as the shadows of evening stretched across the room.

"Then we were well past the one hundred day mark, and the danger of acute GVHD had all but disappeared. Oh, I know there are no absolutes in medicine, but she was doing so well, breaking all records for recovery...."

Rachel's instinct was to lay her hand on Ben's clenched fist, but he stood up suddenly and began to pace. "How could I have missed it?"

"Was Sally not seeing her doctors in Tampa on a regular basis?"

"Sure. But I saw her every day." He paused by the window and stood there, staring out at the growing darkness.

Rachel went to stand with him. "Ben, sometimes God..."

"I place my faith in science," he said flatly.

Rachel closed her eyes and prayed for God to give her the words. "Then you have faith in one of God's creations, and that is a start."

Downstairs a clock chimed and Ben suddenly wheeled around, glancing at his watch and grabbing the bundle with the journal. "I'm late," he said more to himself than to her as he crossed the room.

Rachel followed him down the stairs and out to the lanai. He secured the lock and then started around the house toward his car. He had closed himself off from her—from anything or anyone around.

"Ben?" But there were no words. She could offer little comfort. "I'm here if you ever need to talk."

He placed his hand on her cheek, and she was struck by how smooth his palm was in contrast to James's calloused touch. "That means a great deal to me, Rachel. Thank you." He smiled at her for the first time since she'd come up to Sally's room. "Danke," he murmured then got into his car.

"Give Sally our best," Rachel called out as he drove away. "Tell her..."

But he was gone.

Rachel stood on the driveway for a long moment, her hand touching her cheek, her thoughts on Ben Booker. She did not understand these outsiders. They seemed to go from day to day, checking off items on a list. They valued accomplishment and winning, and they seemed to embrace their individual differences as if this were something to be celebrated. Their lives clamored with the noise of their constant chatter and restless activity.

But was she truly that different? Ever since she'd come to Florida her focus had been on making good at her new job, on getting the certification necessary for her to keep that job. How had she gone from the world she'd grown up in—the Mennonite world that was quieter, simpler, and that revolved around community—to this? At what point had she lost that balance so integral to her faith that allowed everyone to live well and in harmony with their neighbors? Had her brother-in-law been right about her? Had she gotten so caught up in achieving success in her work that she had lost sight of what truly mattered—family, friends, community. . .Justin?

She closed her eyes, allowing the warm moist air of the night to caress her cheek—the way Ben had. Oh, how she wished she could help him find his way home to the faith she felt certain he still carried deep inside him. It was evident that he was a man with much to offer but also a man who struggled with the demands and constraints of the world around him.

Rachel understood that. As a girl she had looked longingly at that outside world, imagining that there she would find true happiness.

This belief that there was something more—something better than the life she'd grown up in—was what had driven her to pester her parents until they had finally agreed that she could attend nursing school. This search for happiness and contentment was why she had sought jobs not in her Mennonite or even the local Amish community after her marriage. Instead she had gone into the public schools to offer her skills.

And she suddenly understood that this was why she had been so drawn to Ben Booker from the moment she'd met him. In him she saw the person she had once been—a person searching in a wilderness. In the short time she had known him she had come to care for him in a way that she had not permitted herself to care for any man since James. With a start she opened her eyes and pressed her hands together.

The disloyalty she felt for James in that moment very nearly overwhelmed her. James had been her first love—her only love. Never had she felt for any other man what she had felt for him. Never—until now.

He was late. The sauce was fine, but the appetizers that Darcy had assembled—bruschetta on toast points—were soggy and inedible. She dumped them into the sink and flipped on the disposal. She had tried calling his cell, then his condo, with no response. She had considered calling the hospital in Tampa. Perhaps Sally had taken a turn for the worst, but if that were true then the last thing Ben needed was a woman who did not understand or accept that he was a physician and always on call when it came to his patients—especially Sally.

She sat down and flipped through a magazine then got up and once again checked the table she'd set on the balcony for the two of them. She'd lit the candles way too early, and now they were burned down to pools of paraffin. She straightened a knife but felt that extinguishing the candles would be to extinguish all hope that he would come.

Just then she heard a car enter the parking area below. She leaned over the balcony and, seeing that it was Ben, resisted the urge to call out to him. Instead she watched as he got out of his car and stood for a long moment, staring out at the man-made lake that her building overlooked. His shoulders were slumped and he looked exhausted.

When he turned toward the entrance, Darcy hurried into her galley kitchen and popped the cork on a bottle of wine then splashed a generous amount into two matching crystal goblets. She checked her makeup and hair in the mirror next to the door and then stepped into the hall to wait for the elevator to deliver Ben. All the while her mind raced with how best to orchestrate the conversation.

She would begin with wine and sympathy for the difficult day he'd endured. She would listen with murmurs of concern while he described the details of Sally's condition. And then at the right moment she would suggest that they enjoy their dinner and speak of other things—at least for tonight—so he could relax a bit before he had to face the hardships of Sally's newest complication the following day.

In a perfect world, he would fall asleep on her sofa, lulled by the wine and the food and the rich chocolate cheesecake that she had prepared for their dessert. In a perfect world, she would cradle his head in her lap, comb his thick hair with her manicured nails. And in a perfect world, sometime in the night he would reach for her and find in her kiss the peace of mind he so clearly needed.

When he stepped off the elevator, he gave her a weary smile and held out a bottle of red wine. "I see you're way ahead of me," he said, nodding toward the two goblets of wine that she held.

"The night is young." She handed him one of the goblets, took the bottle of wine, and waited for him to enter her apartment.

"Sorry I'm so late. Sally asked me to go by the house to get something for her, and Zeke was there so I had to fill him in. Then Rachel Kaufmann stopped by and we got to talking and..." He shrugged. "Sorry."

Darcy's hand tightened on the stem of her wine glass when he mentioned Zeke and then nearly snapped it in two when he said that Rachel had been there as well. "How's Sally doing?" she asked, determined to get things back on plan.

He actually chuckled. "Not at all happy to find herself back in a hospital being pricked and probed, as she likes to call it. We'll know more come Monday." He took a long swallow of his wine. "But let's talk about the incredible smells coming from such a tiny kitchen," he said as he lifted the cover on the sauce. "You've got enough sauce here to feed a third world country," he teased.

Okay, Darcy thought, *skip the preliminaries of wine and sympathy. Moving on.* "I made enough to freeze some—for myself and for you to have at your place. It makes a wonderful base for chili or sloppy joes."

"Impressive." He replaced the lid and picked up the empty wooden salad bowl. "Want me to chop the salad?"

"Sure. You do that while I boil the pasta. You must be famished."

He seemed to consider this, and then he grinned sheepishly. "Not so much. I have to admit that on my way out of the hospital I picked up a turkey sub sandwich that I ate on the road. That was around five. But never fear, I have plenty of room for homemade spaghetti."

"And chocolate cheesecake?"

"Might have to take a rain check on that one." He patted his stomach. "Have to watch the waistline at least a little."

"Yeah, right." She felt herself relax. Even with a late start the evening held promise. They worked together well in the confines of the small kitchen, and it was easy to imagine them making a habit of this, spending their free time together, living together. *Easy, girl, don't get ahead of yourself.*

"I thought we'd eat out on the balcony. It's such a lovely night."

"Works for me." Ben tossed the salad with the dressing she handed him and then filled two side plates with the mixture. "What else, chief?"

Darcy fought the urge to cringe. She didn't want to be someone he thought of as *chief.* She wanted him to think of her in more romantic terms. "I'll dish up the pasta and sauce and take the bread from the warmer and we'll be all set. Why don't you refill our glasses and take the salads out to the table?"

Once they were seated, Darcy raised her glass to his. "To Sally's speedy recovery," she said.

He clinked his glass to hers and took a sip before starting in on his meal. "Rachel Kaufmann offered to pray for Sally," he said as he focused on buttering his bread.

"Well, that's kind of her area, isn't it?" Was it Darcy's imagination or was her tone a bit critical? "I mean, she is part of the spiritual care team."

"How's she doing with that?"

"As far as I can tell there have been no more incidents since the time she invited Zeke Shepherd to play for the children. The supervisor from the certification board seems quite impressed with her work. And as I mentioned before, Paul Cox thinks she's pretty near perfect."

"And what do you think?" Ben's voice was quiet, and he was watching her closely. "Are you going to back Paul's recommendation to make her position permanent once she's certified?"

"Will I have a choice?" Now she knew she sounded peevish. But Rachel Kaufmann had a way of inserting herself into Darcy's private time with Ben, and she seemed capable of doing that without even being on the premises. "Let's not talk about work, okay?"

"Sorry. This sauce is fabulous. What's your secret?"

"Well, I could tell you but then I'd have to shoot you, so best to leave it a secret. After all, if you really like it and know that this is the only place you can get it, then that's all to my advantage."

"Touché." He smiled, but it was evident as the meal continued that he was distracted.

Darcy tried several conversation openers that went nowhere. "You're still in Tampa, aren't you?" she asked after a long silence had stretched between them.

"Maybe. Probably." He smiled and pushed his plate away as he leaned back and stretched his arms high over his head. He was looking out at the stars. "Do you think there's something out there, Darcy? I mean some higher being that's calling the shots?"

Religion was the very last topic of conversation she would have expected from Ben, but it was clear that this was something weighing on him. "I used to," she admitted.

"What happened?"

"Nothing huge. I went off to the university and everything was about getting top grades so I could get into grad school, and by that time going to church had pretty much fallen by the wayside."

"Do you miss it?"

Darcy did what she always did when she found herself asked a question that made her uncomfortable. She turned the tables. "Do you? I mean, your father was a minister, right?"

"Yeah. Pretty hard core at that."

"Meaning?"

"I don't know. He'd preach about a loving God and then

turn around and assure everyone that this same loving God was going to punish all the sinners in terrible and vicious ways. If there was a hurricane or a tornado, that was God's punishment or God's warning. If a famine struck halfway around the world, that was God's message that those people had sinned. If I thought unclean thoughts, God would know and there would be a price. I have to admit that I never really worked out how my feelings for my father affected my overall faith. I mean, the fact is that I do believe, but. . ."

"What brought all this on, Ben?"

He sighed heavily and stood up, moving to the railing of the balcony and continuing to study the night sky. "I don't know. I keep saying that I don't believe—that I'm a man of science. But there's a part of me that still sometimes wishes maybe there was something greater than us out there. Rachel said. . ."

Rachel. Rachel. Rachel. Darcy thought she might actually scream. "Ben, Rachel Kaufmann is a devout Mennonite, and if she has you questioning what *you* believe, perhaps you can understand why I have such doubts about her as an ecumenical spiritual counselor especially for our younger patients."

She knew that her voice sounded shrill and she was talking far too loudly. Still, she couldn't seem to stop. "I don't trust that woman, Ben. It was a mistake to hire her in the first place, and you may as well know that I plan to do everything I can to see that she is replaced at the end of her probationary period."

Ben was staring at her as if she were someone he'd never seen before. To stop her tirade, she picked up her wine glass and drained the last dregs of wine. "Sorry about that," she murmured. "Now I've gone and spoiled our lovely evening." She started stacking their dishes.

"Hey." Ben took the dishes from her and set them back on the table then led her inside to the sofa. "What's going on here?"

She was so tempted to tell him. To finally admit that she was jealous of Rachel. But how ridiculous was that? There was nothing between Ben and Rachel. The very idea that there could be was ludicrous. He admired the woman as he did any other coworker. So what?

"Don't mind me," she said. "The truth is that from the first time we heard that woman's voice on the phone it seemed as if everyone simply accepted her, embraced her as the perfect candidate for the job and a wonderful addition to the entire team. I've never known that kind of instant acceptance, Ben. All my life I have had to fight for everything I've ever achieved."

"So maybe you should stop fighting."

"Give up?"

"Open up," he corrected. "Have a little trust in others."

"Like Rachel," she said flatly.

"Like anyone you come in contact with. Have a little faith in people."

"I thought you didn't believe in faith," she said petulantly.

He hooked his forefinger under her chin to get her to look at him. "I never said I didn't believe, and this is about having faith in *people*, Darcy." He kissed her forehead then and stood up. "It's late, and I want to get an early start back to Tampa tomorrow."

"I could go with you."

"Thanks, but it would be a waste of your time. Sally can't have visitors right now. Maybe after she gets home." He brought the dishes in from the balcony and set them in the sink. "Hate to leave you with all this. . ."

"Go on. You've had a long day—and my meltdown wasn't exactly what you needed."

"Stop that. You have a lot of pressure on you. The occasional meltdown is an occupational hazard. I'm glad I was here." He walked to the door and then paused. "I would ask you"— he looked her in the eye—"to think about how your personal feelings might be influencing your view of Rachel, Darcy. I think she might be a very good addition to the team we're trying to build at Gulf Coast."

Rachel. Always Rachel. Darcy manufactured a smile. "Promise," she said, holding up the three-fingered Girl Scout sign. "Give Sally my best."

When Ben was gone, Darcy stood for a long time looking down the empty hallway toward the elevator. Not a single thing about this evening had gone according to plan. She had totally embarrassed herself and in the process made the serene Rachel look even more saintly.

With a growl of frustration, Darcy walked back inside her condo, slammed the door, and grabbed a fork. She took the cheesecake from the refrigerator, snapped off the springform pan, and carried the whole thing out to the balcony. There she curled herself into the chaise lounge and attacked the cake, shoveling bite after bite into her mouth until she felt as physically sick as she did emotionally wounded.

Chapter 19

W as that your mom?"

Justin jumped when he heard Derek's low voice behind him after he and his mom had left the meeting with Mortimer and she had gone outside to wait for the bus to the hospital.

"Yeah."

"Fat Sally told on us?"

Justin knew he should defend Sally, especially since she was sick again. "No. Mortimer figured it out."

"Yeah, right." Derek smirked. "What's with your mom and that hat? Is she some kind of nun or something?"

So here it was—the moment Justin had dreaded from the very first day. "We're Mennonite," he muttered. "I have to go."

Derek grabbed him by the shoulder and held on. "Whoa, dude. You mean you wear the dorky suspenders and stuff?"

"My mom dresses in the traditional way. Kids don't have to until. . ."

The bell rang, but Derek didn't budge.

"What did you tell Mortimer?"

"Nothing. Like I said, he'd already figured it out. He knows that you've been copying my homework, and he told me not to let you have it anymore. He's going to give you special tutoring during study period."

Derek let out a howl that passed for a laugh. "Yeah, that'll happen. Now listen up, Kaufmann. You got us into this mess—or your little girlfriend did—so somebody pays. If you don't want to be that somebody, then you need to be sure Fat Sally gets the message loud and clear."

"She's back in the hospital."

"Even better. You live at her house, right?"

"Next door." Justin did not like the way Derek was clutching his shoulder and looking at him. His eyes were wild and scary.

"Get me her glove," he ordered.

"Her glove?"

"Her baseball glove, stupid."

"I can't. . . ."

"Here's the deal, Kaufmann. Either you get me that glove or life as you know it is going to change big-time."

He pinched Justin's shoulder hard and then turned and left school.

Justin had seen what Derek did to those he didn't like. Once he had seen Derek actually shove one of the other boys up against a locker and hold him there until the boy nodded and promised to do anything Derek asked. It occurred to Justin that he wasn't really sure exactly how Derek might carry out his threat to make his life miserable, but he had no doubt that it would happen unless he got Sally's baseball glove.

Unexpectedly, his chance to deliver what Derek had demanded came that very night.

"Justin, I need your help," his mom said as they were finishing up their supper. "I spoke with Mrs. Shepherd today and offered to do what I could to prepare the house for Sally to come home."

"She's well again?"

"No. That will take time, but she's on medication that will help her. If all continues to go well, they hope to be home by the end of the week. Mr. Shepherd will return tomorrow. So after supper Zeke is going to meet us to open the house so we can clean it."

"All of it?" Justin glanced toward the multistoried mansion.

"All of it," his mom confirmed. "Zeke will help us, but it's very important to be sure that everything is as clean as possible. Sally is even more susceptible to germs and infection now that she's on these medicines."

Justin chewed his lower lip. It was always fun being with Zeke. Nothing ever seemed to bother him. In fact, Justin thought he might tell the man about Derek's order, but then he remembered that Zeke was Sally's uncle. Telling him would only make things worse.

It was when his mom gave him the chore of gathering the trash from the wastebaskets in all the upstairs rooms that he saw his chance. There on a hook on the back of Sally's door was the baseball glove. He stood for a long time fingering the smooth leather.

He should have asked Derek why he wanted the glove. Maybe he just wanted to scare Sally. Surely that was it. Taking her glove was a warning and once she'd gotten the message then Derek would give it back.

But Sally hadn't done anything.

On the other hand Derek didn't believe that, and now that he knew about Justin being Mennonite he could make life miserable for him. Justin closed his eyes, shutting out the memory of how Derek picked on kids who were different—torturing a boy who wore thick glasses that kept slipping down his nose and another boy that Derek called a *fairy*.

Life since they'd come to Florida had been hard enough. The last thing he needed was Derek turning on him. He would take the glove, and once Sally had gotten the message he would bring it back.

Justin listened in case his mom or Zeke might be coming upstairs. But he could hear them talking as they worked together cleaning out the refrigerator. Carefully, he lifted the glove off the hook and pushed it into the black garbage bag. Then he dumped the paper from Sally's wastebasket on top of it and did the same with the trash from all the other upstairs rooms.

When he got downstairs Zeke had another bag of trash and held out his hand for the one that Justin was carrying. "I'll take these out to the garage," Zeke told Justin's mom. "Then I can do the vacuuming while you change the beds."

"Thank you, Zeke. Justin, you go on with Zeke and start sweeping out the garage."

Justin followed Zeke out to the garage and stood by helplessly as the man heaved the two bags of garbage into one of the bins. *Now what?* He could hardly admit that he'd hidden the glove in the trash. Panic engulfed him. The garbage pickup was the following day. He could offer to put the bins out by the street so Zeke wouldn't have to come back and do that.

But when he made his offer, Zeke said, "No worries. Malcolm will be home tomorrow. He can put them out."

Justin felt sweat breaking out on his forehead. *Think.* "But the bins are dirty and Mom wanted me to sweep out the garage and Mr. Shepherd—"

"All right, dude," Zeke said, laughing and roughing up Justin's hair. "Take the bins out. You folks just go around looking for work to do." The way he said it, Justin knew it was a compliment.

He waited until Zeke went back inside and he heard the vacuum cleaner running over the white carpeting before he rolled the trash bin down to the end of the long driveway. Carefully he positioned it so that it was blocked from the view of the house by a couple of large hibiscus bushes. He checked to be sure that he couldn't be seen from either the street or the house then pulled out first one bag and then the other. He rummaged through them until he felt the glove. With a sigh of relief he pulled it out, hid it under the foliage of the bushes where he could find it and stuff it into his backpack the following morning, and then replaced the garbage bags in the bin.

As he walked back up the driveway he heard a rumble of thunder. What if it rained? What if the glove got soaked?

"Justin?"

His mom was calling for him. He started back for the glove as a car turned into the driveway. *Dr. Booker.* Had he seen anything?

The doctor beeped the horn of his car and stopped next to Justin. "Need a ride?"

"No sir." Justin studied the man closely. Everything about

him seemed normal except for the way he looked so tired, like he hadn't slept in days. "Just putting out the trash. Tell Mom I'm coming."

"Thanks for doing that," Dr. Booker said and drove on around the curve of the driveway.

Another rumble of thunder. Justin searched the trash bin for something he could lay over the glove to protect it. At the very bottom of the bin was an empty plastic shopping bag. He pulled it out, wrapped the glove in it, and replaced the package under the bushes. His hands were shaking. He knew that what he was doing was wrong. Tomorrow he would not give Derek the glove until he knew what his friend intended to do with it.

Feeling a little more certain that he had not yet crossed the line, he headed back up to the house.

Instead of coming directly home as everyone had hoped, Sally was transferred to Gulf Coast Hospital. Her blood counts had dropped slightly, and Sharon and Malcolm wanted to be very sure that Sally was stabilized within normal levels before they brought her home. This latest setback seemed to be the final straw for Sally.

When Rachel entered Sally's hospital room she was shocked to find the girl curled on her side, refusing to interact with anyone. Sally's obvious fury at the unfairness of this latest blow was—as Ben called it—the elephant in the room that no one talked about. Ben had also told Rachel that everyone was at a loss to know what they might do to coax the Sally they knew and loved out of this shell of a girl.

"She admires you so, Rachel," Sharon said as the two women sat together, waiting for Sally to return from yet another round of tests. In the low lighting of the room—kept that way to protect Sally's eyes—Rachel could not really see Sharon's expression, but she heard the weariness and defeat in her voice, saw the exhaustion in the slump of her shoulders. She had refused to leave Sally's side. She slept on a cot next to Sally's bed, and when she ate at all it was to nibble bits from Sally's leftovers. The trays of food that the staff delivered for her went untouched.

Paul had told Rachel that Malcolm was at his wit's end with worry for both his wife and child. She also knew that Ben had stopped by the spiritual care offices earlier that morning to seek Paul's help. "Maybe you can convince Sharon to take a break."

"I expect Rachel would do a better job of that," Paul had replied after calling for Rachel to join the meeting with Ben. "After all, she's a mother with one child. After losing her husband, she certainly has firsthand knowledge of the kind of fear and anxiety that Sharon is facing, that all of you are."

"I could certainly try talking to Sharon."

The way Ben had looked at her then, with such relief and gratitude, she knew she would do more than try. With God's help she would find some way to help Sharon understand that taking care of herself was as critical to Sally's recovery as any medicine might be. "I need to understand the medical situation," she told Ben. "What have they been told about Sally's prognosis—more to the point, what has Sally been told?"

Ben explained that in Tampa, Sally's condition had been treated symptomatically with antibiotics and steroids to strengthen her immune system. "It's the manifestation of the GVHD that needs to be addressed," he explained.

"And she responded well to the treatment?" Paul asked.

"Yes. The team there was even able to take her off the IV administration of her steroids and give them to her orally. That was the turning point for getting her home."

"Sounds like she has a good chance of coming out of this," Paul said. "I know she's been through a great deal, but surely she understands that in the scheme of things. . ."

"She's a twelve-year-old girl," Rachel reminded him. "She is on the brink of becoming a teenager—a young woman. And to girls her age their physical appearance can mean a great deal. Sally has already had to deal with losing her hair and with the weight gain that comes with taking the steroids. She had just begun to see that such physical manifestations of her treatment could be reversed with time. Then this happens and. . ."

"And every time she looks in a mirror—or actually she

doesn't have to look," Ben said. "She knows the steroids have given her the telltale moon face and chipmunk cheeks she had before. Her skin is splotched red and the weight she worked so hard to control will come back and now, on top of all of that, she has to wear the protective glasses." He looked down at his hands. "When I was with her last night, she kept muttering the word 'freak' over and over again."

He did not look up as he choked out the words.

"Let me try to talk to Sharon," Rachel said.

"And Sally?" Ben looked up at her, his face ravaged by days of worry.

"And Sally," she agreed, glancing at Paul for confirmation of the plan. He nodded and stood up. "I have a meeting," he said, laying his hand on Ben's shoulder, "but I'll check on you and the family later."

"Thanks, Paul. Thanks for everything." He followed Paul to the door.

"Ben, Sharon is a woman of strong faith," Rachel reminded him.

"She was," he corrected. "These days? Who knows?" He held the door open for Rachel. "I wouldn't try praying with her if that's what you've got in mind."

"No. At this point, I will pray *for* all of you."

They stepped into the outer office, and Eileen glanced up at them then immediately went back to her work. Ben seemed at a loss as to what he should do next. Rachel looked at the clock. "Do you have rounds now?" she prompted.

"I do." But still he didn't move.

"Come by Sally's room after you finish your rounds," Rachel quietly instructed him as she led the way into the corridor. "If I'm with Sally and Sharon is not, then you'll know that I had some success." It was a poor attempt at lightening the somber mood that pervaded every fiber of his being. But instead of the smile she had hoped for, he touched the sleeve of her dress. "Please be there," he said and then walked quickly down the hall away from her.

Now she had been sitting with Sharon for nearly half an hour. "Please wait with me," she'd said wearily, indicating the only other chair in the small room. "Sally will want to see you."

Given what she'd been told about the girl's demeanor, Rachel doubted that, but she also understood that Sharon hoped that saying the words would make them true. The two women sat in the shadowy room not speaking for a long moment. Rachel closed her eyes and prayed for words that might help break through the wall that surrounded Sharon.

"I had to meet with my son's teacher the other morning," she found herself saying. "Mr. Mortimer?"

Sharon looked up at her but said nothing.

"It seems that Mr. Mortimer thought that Justin had been giving answers to the math homework to a boy named Derek Piper."

"Derek Piper is a bully," Sharon said. "He picks on Sally all the time. But she's tough. She's always been able to hold her own with him. . . ." Her voice trailed off, and then she looked up as if shaking off further thoughts of how Sally might be able to handle Derek in her current condition. "My guess is that Derek is forcing Justin to share the answers. Justin simply doesn't seem like the kind of boy who would willingly cheat."

"Tell me what you know about this boy."

"His family lives on the next block over, behind us. His father owns a couple of car dealerships. He's always bragging about being a self-made man, especially when Malcolm is around. The implication being that Malcolm was handed his money on a silver platter."

Rachel was surprised at Sharon's vehemence but realized that what she had given Sharon by bringing up Derek was a release from the anger and frustration she must have been carrying inside all these long days and nights.

"So, what did Mortimer say?" Sharon asked when her eyes again met Rachel's in the dark room.

Rachel told her about the meeting and her suggestion that the teacher provide tutoring for Derek. That brought a genuine laugh from Sharon.

"Oh yeah. That'll work. Sally tells me that the boy skips more school than he attends."

"But surely his parents. . ."

Sharon sighed. "From what I've observed, Derek comes by his tendency to bully others honestly. His father is a control freak and his mom is a mouse." She stood and got a glass of water for herself and drank it down. It was the most physical action she had taken since Rachel had entered the room. "You should warn Justin to watch his back," she said. "Because if Derek is in trouble with Mortimer then he's in trouble at home, and if that's the case someone will pay."

"But surely if the boy is struggling with his math, his parents..."

"Derek is as smart as any other kid. He's lazy or maybe it's his way of rebelling against his father's strictness." She glanced toward the hallway and then at the wall clock. "What's taking so long?"

"I'm sure things are just backed up in the lab. She'll be back soon."

Sharon started smoothing the covers on Sally's hospital bed. "When Sally tried out for the ball team, she beat out Derek Piper to become the pitcher. He quit the team that same day and for weeks after that he made her life miserable. Then once she was diagnosed, he let up a bit. Of course, she was being homeschooled for most of the time so it all resolved itself." She clutched Sally's pillow to her chest, and her eyes met Rachel's. "We have to protect our children, Rachel. We have to teach them and..."

Her shoulders started to heave as she muffled her sobs in the pillow. Rachel went to her and wrapped her arms around Sharon's too-thin body. "We have to be there for them," Rachel whispered, "and sometimes that means taking care of ourselves so that we have the strength they need to draw upon. You are running on empty, Sharon, and if you have nothing left to give, then what will Sally do?"

"I'm so very tired," Sharon whispered. "And so very, very scared."

"I know." She patted Sharon's back. "But Ben tells me that Sally has already responded well to the antibiotics she received in Tampa, and the steroids will strengthen her immune system. He says it's only a matter of getting her counts stabilized and then she can go home—you can all go home."

Sharon shook her head vehemently. "She's given up. You haven't seen her this way. It's so awful. My little girl is in such pain and I can't help her."

"Yes you can. When Sally comes back you can let her know that you are going home for a while to shower and nap and take care of things like the mail and phone messages." She rubbed Sharon's back and gently added, "Give her normal, Sharon. Let her see that the routine of daily life continues."

Sharon pulled away and stared at Rachel. "You think that will help bring her out of this? I've never seen her come so close to giving up before."

"It can't hurt to take a couple of hours to restore some of your strength so that you're ready to face whatever comes next. It's possible that in refusing to leave her side you've given her the impression that things are much worse than they really are. She's not going to trust what the doctors tell her—they've been wrong before. For the real story she will always look to you."

"And what if she begs me to stay?"

But Sally didn't. In fact, she barely acknowledged her mother's leave-taking or the fact that Rachel remained seated next to her bed. She merely lay there, her eyes open, her body tensed into a fetal position, her fists clenched against her chest.

At first Rachel said nothing, searching her brain for some possible topic that might bring about a breakthrough.

"Sally, do you remember that terrible car accident last month?"

Sally blinked but did not respond.

Rachel pressed on, telling her about the meeting with the accident victim's mother and the request to help. She described the VORP program and her meeting with the dead girl's parents. As she talked, slowly, Sally's body began to relax. She stretched out her legs and unclenched her fingers to pull the sheet over her shoulders. She lay on her back, staring up at the ceiling. All the while Rachel kept talking. The truth was that she was afraid to stop for fear she would break the web of progress that she was weaving.

"The father is going to be the tough one," she continued with a heavy sigh. "He's so very angry and. . ."

There was a sound from the bed. A croak that sounded like "Duh."

Rachel permitted herself a small smile and kept talking. "Exactly. Who wouldn't be furious at such unfairness? I expect that everyone involved is struggling with anger as well as grief—they go hand in hand. But you see, Sally, in our faith, forgiveness is the cornerstone. And these two families need to find their way back to each other because in each other's love and forgiveness they will find the strength they need to go on without this wonderful girl. I just wish. . ."

Sally rolled onto her side and came up on one elbow. "She would have wanted that for them, don't you think?"

"I do," Rachel agreed as she got up to fill a glass with water and hand it to Sally. *Keep it normal,* she reminded herself. "What makes *you* think that she would have wanted that?"

Sally shrugged and sipped the water. "From what you've told me, she loved them, all of them." She took a little more of the water and then flopped back onto the pillow. "But it's so hard," she whispered.

"Ja. Life can be that way."

They were quiet for a moment. Sally closed her eyes, and Rachel thought perhaps she was asleep. But then she murmured, "Did you ever hear the saying that God doesn't give people more than they can handle?"

"I have heard similar words." Rachel wondered where the girl's thoughts might be headed.

"He must think I'm like the strongest person ever," she murmured and closed her eyes again.

Rachel caught the shadow of movement outside, and then she saw Ben silhouetted in the frosted glass panel of the door. Very quietly he turned the handle and stepped inside.

"I can't speak for God," Rachel continued, "but I do know that you are a very strong girl and that you have a good many equally strong people around you helping you find your way through this." She used one of the sterile pads on the side table to wipe away the single tear that trickled from the corner of Sally's closed eyes. "One of them is here now," Rachel whispered. "So I'll leave you to visit with your uncle."

Sally opened her eyes and gave Ben a crooked smile. " 'Bout time you showed up," she said.

"I do have other patients, you know. People who are actually sick instead of malingering," he bantered as he pulled the chair closer. He took Sally's hand, and his voice cracked a little as he added, "And it's way past time that you came back to us, kiddo."

Rachel moved around the end of the bed. "I'll stop by tomorrow if that's okay."

"Rachel?"

"Ja?"

"Danke," Sally murmured.

"Get some rest," Rachel replied. "Both of you."

"Bossy, isn't she?" Rachel heard Ben tell Sally, and then as she stepped into the hall and the door swung closed behind her she heard Sally giggle.

Chapter 20

After Rachel left, Ben sat with Sally until Sharon and Malcolm returned.

"You and Rachel would make a good pair," Sally announced almost as soon as Rachel had said good-bye, promising to stop by again.

"She's Mennonite," he reminded her.

"And?"

"And I'm not."

"Details," she said with a dismissive wave of her hand.

"All right, let's look at this another way. If Rachel and I were to get together you do realize that Justin would be your stepcousin, then?"

"Fine with me."

"Rachel is my friend, honey. Like she's your friend and—"

"She's a better match for you than Darcy is."

"Darcy and I are only friends as well."

Sally let out a bark of a laugh. "Yeah?" She pointed to her eyes shielded by the tinted glasses. "These are rolling right now. As Dad says, 'If you believe she's just a friend, then there's some real estate in the Everglades that I'd like to sell you.'"

"It's true," Ben protested.

"Maybe *you* think that's the deal, but my money is on the fact that Darcy thinks it's a whole lot more."

"You're a kid. What do you know about such things?"

"Apparently more than you do. Men," she sighed dramatically as if he and the rest of the species were a lost cause.

That was the moment Malcolm and Sharon arrived. Ben made his excuses, wanting to give them time to enjoy Sally, whom he could see was tiring fast and would soon be asleep. Sharon followed him into the hallway.

"Thank you, Ben. I don't know how you did it but. . ."

"I didn't. It's Rachel you have to thank. And apparently that goes double for me. It's good to have both my sister and my niece back among the living." He hugged her and then gave her a little shove back toward Sally's room. "Go enjoy your daughter—and do not listen to anything she has to say about Rachel and me."

His sister's laughter followed him down the hall. He was glad to hear that she found the idea of a romantic attachment between Rachel and him as ludicrous as he did.

Or was it really so farfetched? The truth was that he was far more attracted—romantically speaking—to Rachel than he was to Darcy. And under other circumstances—if she weren't Mennonite—he might have asked her out by now. Certainly between the times they had been together at work and then at his sister's house, they had forged a relationship, a friendship.

He found her easy to be with, and once she'd gotten past her initial nerves at starting a new job in a new city where she basically knew no one, she'd seemed at ease with him as well. So, why not ask her out? Why not suggest that they meet for coffee?

He headed down to the spiritual care offices. Eileen was getting ready to leave for the day when he entered.

"Paul's already left," she said.

"Is Rachel in?"

Eileen nodded toward the cubicle next to hers at the same time that Rachel said, "Right here." She stepped around the barrier. "Has something happened to Sally?" she asked.

"No. Thanks to you, Sally is doing a whole lot better—at least emotionally speaking. And so are her parents and uncle."

Eileen was taking her time collecting her purse, lunch bag, and a dog-eared paperback novel. She cast furtive glances from Ben to Rachel as a small smile played over her lips, a smile that Ben saw her bite back as she turned finally and started for the door. "Well, if there's nothing you need, I'll see you both tomorrow."

"Have a good evening," Ben said, holding the door for her.

"Eileen," Rachel said, "remember I won't be in tomorrow. I have to be in Tallahassee for the day."

"That's right. Good luck with that."

"What's in Tallahassee?" Ben asked once Eileen was gone.

"I'm meeting with my supervisor from the certification board. Thank you for typing my paper. I'd like to repay you."

"You already have."

She lifted her eyebrows. "How?"

"Sally."

"Oh, that is my job. Sometimes I think that I gain as much as the patients and families do when there is a breakthrough. Has Sharon come back already?"

Ben smiled. "Yeah. You did wonders getting her to leave for the little time that she did. She had changed clothes, showered. She looked better, and when she saw Sally sitting up..."

"Sally is a fighter. She needed some time to regroup. We all do."

"Even you?"

"Of course I do."

"I don't know. You always seem so composed and calm whatever the situation."

Her cheeks glowed with rising color. "I am not so calm all the time. Ask Justin."

"I'd rather ask you. How about joining me for a cup of coffee before you head home?"

She glanced at the wall clock above Eileen's desk. "Thank you, but I need to be at home. I sent Justin on ahead to start working on the gardens. I want everything to look especially nice when Sally comes home."

"You do know that it won't really matter to her—or any of them. Getting her home is the main thing."

"Ja. But it will matter to me, and it's a way that Justin and I can let them know we are thinking of them."

"Then I'll help." He opened the door and waited. "Ready?"

She didn't move. "I. . .the bus. . ."

"Now, why would anyone stand around on a hot day like this waiting for a bus when she could ride in a convertible?"

"We Mennonites are plain people, Ben. A car is simply a vehicle to get us from one place to another, same as a bus. I would not want others seeing me ride in a convertible car. Something so. . .showy is not our way."

"And yet I seem to recall that you accepted a ride the other night," he reminded her.

She blushed. "That was. . .it was late and Justin was home alone and. . ."

"Got it. Then let's go wait for that bus."

As he paid his fare, Ben realized that he could not remember the last time he'd ridden a city bus. He'd probably been in college at the time. He'd forgotten a lot about the diversity of the riders—each with his or her unique story. In his college days he had enjoyed speculating about each person—who they were, where they were headed, what they were thinking as they stared straight ahead or out the window.

"You know, when I was in med school and used to take the bus between classes and the hospital," he told Rachel as they sat next to each other midway back on the long bus, "I remember having such a deep respect for the people around me. In my mind they were the kind of unsung heroes we barely notice in this country."

"What do you mean?"

"Hardworking folks trying to make it day-to-day. I imagined that in many cases they were coming or going from a job they found unfulfilling but that they worked because they needed the work. I always wondered about their dreams."

"In what way?"

"What did they really want out of this life? What had they once dreamed of achieving?"

She was quiet for a long moment. "And what dreams did

you have in those days, Ben? I mean, why did you wish to be a doctor?"

It had been so long since Ben had thought about those days, those years when his only intent had been to get away from his father's house. The rest had simply fallen into place, and for the first time he realized that he had not chosen medicine at all. "Becoming a doctor was a way out."

"Of what?"

He shrugged and grinned at her as the bus pulled to the curb to discharge and pick up more passengers. "How about you? How did you decide to become a nurse?"

She ducked her head shyly, but he saw that she was smiling. "I'm afraid I was a little rebellious as a girl," she admitted.

"You? I find that impossible to believe."

"It's true. My parents despaired for me, and they could not have been more relieved when James started courting me. They saw him as this steadfast young man who would surely set me on the right path once we married. They didn't even worry that he was older than I was. In their minds that gave him the maturity that I sorely lacked."

"So you married James and then what? How did nursing school fit in?"

"I graduated before James and I married. He thought that having my degree was a good thing because I would be able to serve the community."

Ben stood up as the bus neared their stop. He offered Rachel his hand and noticed that she hesitated a moment before taking it. Once they were off and walking toward his sister's place, he continued the conversation. "So you and James got married and Justin came along. . . ."

A cloud of sadness passed over her features so fleetingly that he thought he must have been seeing things. But she did not look at him as she changed the subject. "You have turned the tables here, Ben. We were talking about you and how you came to be a doctor."

Was she changing the focus back on him because she was still grieving for her late husband so much that the mere mention

229

of his name brought her such sadness? "There was no real plan. I mean, becoming a doctor was never something I consciously thought about. The pieces kind of fell into place and here I am."

"There was a plan," she said. "No one accidentally becomes a doctor." She opened the filigreed wrought iron gate that led to the path next to the driveway then looked back at him. "You may struggle to accept this, but God always has a plan for us."

"What I struggle with, Rachel, is why God's plans seem to include making kids like Sally suffer." He did not wait for her answer but trudged up the path ahead of her, calling out to Justin who was sweeping the flagstone sidewalk.

Rachel went first to the guesthouse to put on an apron and make a pitcher of lemonade. She carried the pitcher and a stack of three glasses out to the gardens and then set to work raking the debris that Ben and Justin had trimmed from some overgrown shrubs into a pile. All the while she was very aware of Ben's nearness. The way he had rolled back his sleeves to expose forearms that were surprisingly tan and muscular for one who worked indoors. The graceful way he moved as he stretched to cut branches that Justin could not reach. The sound of his voice coaching Justin to shape the shrub as he trimmed it.

Not for the first time it struck her that he would be a very good parent, and she wondered again why he had never married. His devotion to Sally was obvious, as was his care and concern for all of his patients. But they were all someone else's children. When a man loved children as much as Ben obviously did, why would he not be anxious to find a wife and raise a family of his own?

She gathered the clippings and deposited them in a rolling cart to be taken to the compost bin hidden behind the shed. She paused to wipe her brow. Justin and Ben were working side by side the way Justin and James had worked back in Ohio.

Ohio. All day she had worried about the meeting with Justin's teacher, knowing that the issue would not even have come up if Justin had been attending the small Mennonite school near their farm. Once again she asked herself if she had made a mistake in coming here. In bringing Justin to this place and exposing him to a world he was unprepared for, had she done what was best for him, or for herself?

It had all seemed so right in the beginning—as if God were leading her to this place, this job, this life. But what if instead she had allowed her grief to rule her decisions, her need to escape the memories of the farm that she and James had shared with his parents? What if instead of facing the future God had set out for her, she had run away and now Justin was paying the price?

"Mom?"

She shielded her eyes from the setting sun. "Ja."

"Are we gonna eat?"

Rachel smiled. Some things did not change, like the appetite of a twelve-year-old boy. "Ja. We will eat."

"Ben too?"

"Ben too."

Darcy was mystified. Ben's car was still parked in its usual spot, and yet he was nowhere to be found in the hospital. She had lingered as long as she could, keeping an eye on the parking garage exit from her office window while she worked on reports for the upcoming board meeting.

The last she'd seen of Ben he'd been on his way to see Sally. She'd actually gone to the children's wing on some excuse but with the sole purpose of running into Ben at the end of the workday, hoping he might suggest they grab a bite to eat together. But that had been well over an hour ago. She picked up the phone and punched in the number for the nurses' station outside Sally's room.

"Is Dr. Booker still with his niece?" she asked.

"He left a while ago. It's just the parents in there now," the voice on the other end assured her. "Do you want me to page him?"

"No, thanks." She hung up and drummed her manicured nails on her desk as she stared out the window at the parking garage. Maybe she'd missed him after all.

With a heavy sigh, she packed her briefcase with the files and reports she still needed to review and hooked the bulging bag over one shoulder. She retrieved her handbag from the drawer of her desk and headed for the parking garage.

Ben's car was still there, so she retraced her steps to the hospital lobby. "Have you seen Dr. Booker tonight?" she asked the security guard sitting at the information desk.

"Yes ma'am. He left a little while ago."

"But his car. . ."

"He took the bus."

The bus?

"He and the new chaplain lady."

"I see." But Darcy didn't see at all. Why would Ben take a bus unless his car had a problem and even then, why not call for a mechanic? And why on earth would he get on a bus with that woman?

"I expect he'll be back directly," the guard continued, clearly wanting to be of help. "His car's here, after all, and Doc Booker does take pride in that car of his."

He grinned at Darcy, and she tried hard to find a smile to offer in return. "Thank you," she murmured and headed outside.

"I'll let him know you were looking for him," the guard called after her.

Darcy walked blindly past the valet parking booth where two employees were busy helping visitors. Without any true destination in mind she walked out to the street and waited for the light to change. She saw the OPEN sign flashing in the family-owned café where she and Ben had shared a few late-night meals of scrambled eggs, toast, and coffee. From the window she would be able to see him return to get his car. It would be the most natural thing in the world for her to call out to him. After all, how many times had he teased her about keeping doctor's hours?

It was after seven, and the café was nearly deserted. She waved to Millie, the owner's wife, who was wiping the counter. "Sit anywhere," the woman said.

Darcy chose a booth near the door with a view of the entrance to the hospital. She took out her laptop and one of the folders.

"Just coffee," she said when Millie offered her a menu.

Only when she heard a bus slow to turn onto the circular drive did she glance up from her work. A few more customers came and went, but Darcy barely noticed them. She was on her third cup of coffee and well aware that she should probably switch to decaffeinated when someone entered the café, started toward a stool at the counter, and then came over to her booth.

"Working pretty late, aren't you?"

The very last person Darcy had expected to see that night was Zeke Shepherd.

Chapter 21

Justin liked the doctor. He reminded him of his dad. Not in the way he looked of course. Except for both having dark hair, the two men didn't look at all alike. His dad's eyes had been so blue that his mom always said it was like looking at the sky on a clear summer day. Ben's eyes were kind of a mix of green and gold. Eyes that looked at you like he was really interested in anything you might have to say. Dad used to look at Justin that way.

Justin missed the talks he and his dad used to have. Talks about how things were going, what Justin thought about stuff, things like that. But that evening working together in the gardens, Ben had seemed really interested in what Justin had to say about school and then about how he was feeling about living in Florida now that he'd been here a couple of months.

"You and your mom are pretty extraordinary people," he'd told Justin. "I mean, picking up and leaving behind everything you've ever known and starting fresh here? That's pretty unusual."

"Starting fresh" was the phrase his mom had used when she was explaining about taking the job in Florida. She hadn't exactly told him that she'd not only have to work but also would have to go to school to get some kind of license. She hadn't exactly mentioned the late nights when she had to return to the hospital.

"It's kind of lonely," Justin had admitted to Ben.

"I'll bet. You making any friends?"

"A couple." Justin didn't really want to talk about Derek Piper. Ever since the thing with Mr. Mortimer and taking Sally's baseball glove, Justin had his doubts about whether or not Derek was really even interested in being his friend. It seemed these days he was only interested in how Sally was doing and when she might get home. And when Justin had asked Derek why he wanted the glove all he would say was that he needed it for a surprise for Sally.

"Sally mentioned a boy called Derek?"

"Yeah." Justin turned away, looking for his mom. "Hey Mom. Are we gonna eat?"

After that Ben had stopped trying to make conversation. Together they cleaned and put away the garden tools and finished adding the clippings to the compost bin. Then they walked back to the guesthouse to wash up and sit down in the little kitchen for supper.

Justin's mom was the best cook he knew, and it looked like Ben thought so too, the way he went back for seconds on almost everything. "You'd better save room for pie," Justin warned him with a shy grin.

"There's pie?"

"There's always pie, right, Mom?"

"Your favorite—banana cream."

"See?" Justin said, nudging Ben's elbow. "Told you."

It was nice having three people at the table, like it used to be when they lived on the farm. He wished they could go back to those times, but all that had changed.

"You should have told me sooner," Ben teased. "I wouldn't have stuffed myself."

Justin got up and helped clear the table while his mom cut pieces of pie for the three of them. To his surprise Ben helped as well. His dad had never done that. In fact, none of the men in his family had done that. Justin had kind of assumed that once he was married with his own place he would no longer help with those kinds of chores either. He glanced at his mom, who looked like she was as surprised as he was to see Ben scraping the food remains off plates into the garbage.

"I'll take care of that, Ben. You come have your pie and some coffee."

She refilled Justin's milk glass before pouring coffee for Ben and herself.

Ben sat down and put his napkin on his lap then waited.

"We only pray at the start of the meal," Justin advised in a low tone, remembering how Ben had started to pass the rolls to him before the blessing had been said earlier.

"Got it," Ben whispered back. "I was waiting for your mom to sit down."

Justin set his glass of milk aside and waited as well. Ben winked at him.

"Don't you like it—the pie?" Mom said. It seemed pretty important to his mom that Ben like her pie.

"Haven't tried it yet," he replied. "Justin and I were waiting for you."

It had been a long time since Justin had seen his mom smile the way she did just then. It was the kind of smile she used to have whenever his dad teased her about something or paid her a compliment. It was a smile that made her look really pretty, and Justin realized that he wasn't the only one who liked having the doctor around.

After supper, Rachel washed the dishes while Ben helped Justin with a science assignment he'd been struggling to understand. Watching the two of them, their heads bent low over the work, Rachel felt the pangs of the loneliness that had become her constant companion ever since James's death.

In the two years that had passed there had been some healing of the gaping wound his absence had left in her life. After the first anniversary, she had finally begun to accept that her life— and Justin's—must go forward. James would want that for both of them. And she found that she could see a clear path for Justin. In time—God willing—he would find his true calling; he would meet a girl who would turn his thoughts to marriage and family, and the cycle of life would continue.

For Rachel, finding her way into a future that would not include James had been far more difficult. Lately Hester had implied that there were one or two men in Pinecraft that Rachel might enjoy meeting. Rachel had not been fooled by her friend's transparent hints at matchmaking. But she had protested that between work and school and Justin she had as much as she could handle. "Perhaps once I get my certificate and know that the job is secure," she'd told her friend.

She folded the dish towel and wandered out to the screened porch where she stared up at a sky filled with stars. Sometimes at night after Justin was asleep she would stand at the windows and wonder what God's plan might be for her. In taking James so suddenly there had to have been a lesson. She had thought that God's plan had led her here to Florida, but things did not seem to be falling into place the way she had hoped. Not for Justin— and not for her.

Earlier that week she had received her second warning from Darcy via Mark Boynton. Mark had called her to his office in Human Resources and closed the door. When he took his seat behind his desk, he did not look at her but focused instead on a file—her file.

"Is there a problem, Mark?"

He cleared his throat. "Earlier this week you were working with a family, a boy about your son's age whose father had just died."

"The Wilson family. Yes, such a sad case."

"You were speaking with the boy in the hallway outside his father's room, and you were overheard to tell him that with the passing of his father he was now the man of the family." All of this Mark delivered in a flat, impersonal tone without once looking up from the file.

"That was not. . ." Rachel bit her lip to stop herself from saying more. In her faith, a person did not try to argue or defend when accused. Doing so was seen as arrogant, as putting one's self before the good of the community. But surely this was different.

These were outsiders who did not practice such things.

"Did you say this to that boy, Rachel?" Mark had looked at her then, his eyes pleading with her to deny the charge.

"What I said was that when my son's father died, several well-meaning people had said such words to him, but they were not true. Justin was not the man of the family, and neither is the Wilson boy. They are both still children, to be protected and comforted and—"

"I thought it must be something like that, but it may be too late. It's already part of your file. There's really nothing I can do about it. You can appeal it to the powers that be, but frankly I would just leave it alone." Mark had stood and offered her a handshake then, indicating that the meeting was over. "Look, you didn't hear this from me, but be careful, okay? Darcy seems to be trying to build a case for letting you go at the end of your probation."

"Why would anyone go to such lengths to. . ."

Mark shrugged. "Welcome to the ways of corporate America, honey. I'll try explaining things, but don't hold your breath. Now, I really have said too much already. Just be careful, okay?"

Later that day when Rachel had offered to drop off some mail for Eileen on her way home for the night, she had passed by Mark's office. Inside Darcy Meekins was standing, her hands braced on Mark's desk as she leaned toward him and made her point. She couldn't hear what they were saying, but Mark had glanced up and seen Rachel. Their eyes had locked for an instant, and she was positive that his look held pity.

Strike two, she thought with a sigh.

She was so lost in her thoughts and worries that she was unaware that Ben had come out onto the porch, leaving Justin to finish his homework at the kitchen table. "You're very quiet," he said.

"A little tired," she admitted. "You must be exhausted. Seeing patients all day long and worrying about Sally."

Ben shrugged.

"I will pray for her."

A silence stretched between them. "You really believe that

prayer can make a difference, don't you?" Ben asked.

"Ja."

"Even though your husband. . ."

"God did not kill my husband, Ben." The two of them were standing side by side, neither looking at the other, and yet she felt a connection that could not be ignored. "Your father was a minister?"

"He was."

"And yet you question the very idea of faith in things unseen, in a higher power?"

Ben sighed. "When I was growing up, my father painted a picture of God as angry and vengeful. His sermons dwelled on the punishment awaiting those who did not follow the precise teachings of the scriptures. I remember one time I had read a news article about children starving in Africa because of a terrible famine."

"Did you ask him about that?"

"I did. He told me that clearly the people in that land had sinned and turned away from God. To him this was another version of the plague God had sent to the firstborn of every household in the time of Moses."

Rachel had no words to respond to such an idea.

"Once I decided to be a doctor, my plan was to go wherever children were suffering and do what I could to make their lives better."

"And you have done that."

Ben laughed. "Not so much. It's true that I treat sick and injured children, but I do it right here in the safety of America, in the luxury of a medical center where I have everything I need to succeed at my fingertips. I go home at night in my fancy sports car to my high-rise condo overlooking a bay filled with yachts. I open a bottle of wine that costs more than some of those people in Africa make in a year. I am—in short—a fraud, Rachel."

"It's not too late for you to follow your dream, Ben. Perhaps God. . ."

"What about your dreams, Rachel?"

She knew that she should take a step away from him, and

yet she stayed where she was. "We are a simple people, Ben. We accept the path God has chosen for us. I went to nursing school, I married James, we had Justin, and then James was killed, and I brought Justin here."

"Why?"

"Because I needed to provide for our son. I needed to find a place where he could find his way without his father. And my husband's brother took over as head of household and made it clear that if we left, we would not be welcomed back."

"Have you ever considered that maybe you are running from the memories of the life you thought you would have with your husband?"

Was she?

"No. I know people sometimes think that moving away will make a difference, but grief dwells inside you. It cannot be healed by something as simple as a change of location."

"Then how is it healed?"

"Time. Prayer. Watching Justin grow. Making sure he is safe and well." The conversation was disturbing on a number of levels. They were standing too close. His voice was too soft. It was too dark, and far too intimate. Finally, she stepped away. "Perhaps you should think about going to church again...," she said, grasping at anything that might break the mood that held them in its web. Then she covered her mouth with her fingers. "I'm sorry. That was..."

"I do pray sometimes," he said and smiled. "Most times it surprises me to realize that's what I'm doing, but it comes mostly when I've run out of solutions. See. Maybe we aren't as different as you think."

Gently, he tugged her hand away from her lips and kissed the tips of her fingers. "Good night, Rachel. Thank you—for everything you've done today."

Darcy and Zeke had been sitting across from each other in the worn vinyl booth of the diner for nearly two hours. They had talked about everything from the fact that the current owners of the diner were ready to retire to whether or not Darcy's downing three cups of coffee in less than an hour could be labeled an addiction.

She had no idea how it had happened. She certainly had had no intention of inviting Zeke to join her or of spending the time she should have been concentrating on her work trying to follow his casual leap from one subject to another. But here she was—all thoughts of Ben Booker gone—as she tried not to give in to her growing attraction to this impossibly charming man.

Only when she heard the definitive roar of Ben's sports car speeding out of the hospital parking garage and on down the street did she glance out the window.

"He's a good guy—Ben Booker, but he's not for you," Zeke said as he too watched the flash of the blue convertible pass by.

"And you are the authority on this because. . . ?" Darcy challenged.

Zeke shrugged. "You're both wound too tight. You both think you've climbed the mountain, but now that you're at the top, you're not all that thrilled with the view."

"Interesting theory coming from a man who has pretty much laid down at the bottom of the mountain. How's that plan to get back into life coming along?" Darcy meant for her sarcasm to sting him, but Zeke simply grinned.

"No worries. Got the haircut, updated the wardrobe. . . ." He pointed to the freshly pressed cotton shirt he was wearing. "I'd say I'm on a roll."

"Job? Career? Future?"

"Got a job at the packinghouse that gives me enough to live on while I do what I really love—play guitar and write my songs. And as for the future? Who knows? The one thing I know for sure is that anybody thinking she has the least bit of control is fooling herself."

His dark eyes met hers and held them.

"You don't want a family?" she challenged.

"I do indeed but first I have to find me a wife."

She laughed in spite of herself. "You've got everything mapped out, don't you?"

241

"That would be the way you operate. You like to have a step-by-step plan, and that's probably a good thing in business, but in life. . .in love? Not so much."

"For a man who—"

"You're tired, Darcy. Tired of the fight. That's something I know about. When I got back from my first tour of duty it seemed like everything had changed. I wasn't the same person. I'd seen too much of the way things really were over there. I came back and went to work for Malcolm, but more than a couple of months before, I had signed on for another tour."

"And the second time you came back?" Darcy was fascinated in spite of her determination not to be.

"I didn't. I took some time off and hung out in Europe, then signed up for number three."

The expression that crossed his face in that moment was so filled with pain and sadness that Darcy found she could not look away. Instead she reached across the table and covered his hand with hers. "It must have been. . ." Her words trailed off.

"Nothing had changed," he said, as his dark eyes clouded over with memories. "Nothing. In all that time. I had joined up after 9/11 because I thought I could make a difference. But it was the wrong fight, Darcy, for all the wrong reasons, and in that situation all you can do is tread water until you can pull yourself out."

"So you came home and surrendered?"

His smile was one of pity. "You might think that. I prefer to think of these last years as a kind of strategic retreat, a time to regroup. As the Paul Simon song goes, 'Make a new plan, Stan.' "

"And that plan is. . . ?"

He glanced around the café. "I'm thinking of buying this place."

She couldn't help herself. She burst out laughing. "With what?" An image of the loose change accumulating in his guitar case at the farmers' market flashed through her mind.

He grinned. "I'm a Shepherd, remember? There's this little trust fund my dad left me. Wanna come be the chef when I get this place up and running?"

"Yeah. Right."

"Think about it." He got up then and laid some bills on the table to cover the cost of her coffee.

"You don't have to—"

"Ah Darcy, let a guy do the right thing, okay?" He cupped her cheek gently, waved to Millie, and sauntered out.

Darcy watched out the window, and as he passed by, he grinned and blew her a kiss. She put a hand to her cheek and realized she was blushing.

Chapter 22

Justin had begun to dread school. He'd made a huge mistake taking up with Derek and his group. Now that Derek had turned on him, he had no friends and whenever he approached Derek and the others they would turn around and walk away. He'd begun to live for Fridays when he knew he would have at least the weekend to stop trying to figure out what Derek planned to do with Sally's baseball glove.

He never should have taken it. If his mom knew—if she ever found out... Every night he prayed hard for a miracle, for some way that he could get the glove and return it to Sally's room before she got home from the hospital. He'd seen it hanging in Derek's locker where Derek had put it when Justin delivered it to him. If he could just get it back.

Oh, how he wished his mom had never taken this job, had never decided to move onto the Shepherds' property, had never left their little community in Ohio. No, that part wasn't true. He didn't miss Ohio all that much, especially living with his uncle. The truth was that there was lots about Florida that he liked—the weather and the beach and the fishing with John and Zeke. The weekends were great when he and his mom spent their time in Pinecraft shopping and visiting and going to church. A couple of times they'd attended programs at the bigger church on the edge of Pinecraft, and he'd even met some kids his age there— Mennonite kids like him. Being in Pinecraft was like being in a whole other world. He wished they could live there all the time.

Whatever came of this business with Derek and the baseball glove, it was up to him to fix it. He decided to talk to Derek and try to convince him once again that Sally had had nothing to do with Mortimer catching them cheating. What he knew for sure was that the conversation needed to take place when Max and Connor weren't around. With Derek it was all about looking good in front of the others.

So when Justin's mom got a call from the hospital right after breakfast that Saturday, Justin saw his chance. He assured her that he would take care of his chores, and then he asked her permission to take his bike and ride over to the park. What he left out was that Derek's house was on the way to the park.

As soon as his mom had boarded the bus, Justin mounted his bike and took off. He would have plenty of time to handle his chores later, but right now the important thing was to catch Derek at home.

He'd never actually been to Derek's house, just ridden by the long driveway guarded by an impressive pair of black metal gates that opened only when Derek—or his parents—entered some secret code. It occurred to him now that his first problem was going to be getting past those gates. He decided the best thing to do would be to wait across the street and hope that Derek would come out.

He leaned his bike on a patch of grass and then sat down on the curb to wait. No more than five minutes later the gates slowly swung open. A minute later a car came toward him, a woman driving. She saw him waiting there and frowned. "Are you lost?" she asked, her voice high and tight when she rolled the window down.

"No ma'am. I'm a friend of Derek's. Is he home?"

She glanced at the rearview mirror and then back at Justin. "Do we know you?"

"Well, no—I mean you never met me exactly. I'm Justin

Kaufmann. My mom and I live. . ."

Her smile was one of pure relief. "Oh, you're the boy who has helped Derek with his math assignments."

"Yes ma'am." Justin was confused. His mom didn't know what had happened? He knew that Mr. Mortimer had met with Derek. Surely he'd also asked to see his parents like he had asked to see Justin's mom.

"Go on through," she said with a wave toward the gates. "Derek is having his breakfast on the terrace. Tell our cook that I said to prepare anything you want—pancakes, eggs—she makes wonderful waffles." She glanced both ways and then turned onto the street. The car window glided silently closed, and Derek's mom waved as she drove away. Justin mounted his bike and got through the gates as they started to swing shut.

It was pretty clear that Justin was the last person Derek expected to see that morning.

"How did you get in here?" he snarled.

"Your mom. . ."

Derek rolled his eyes and attacked the stack of pancakes in front of him. "So what do you want?"

Suddenly Justin had no words. He should have thought this through more thoroughly, practiced what he would say, how he would make his case. "It's about Sally Shepherd," he blurted.

A slow smile spread across Derek's face as he leaned back and fixed his gaze on Justin. "What about her?" He pinned Justin with a glare. "Is she home? Why didn't you tell me she was coming home today?"

"She was supposed to come home a few days ago, but now she's in the hospital where my mom works. Something about her blood counts not being right." He was hoping that Derek might feel some tiny bit of sympathy "She's coming home for Thanksgiving if everything goes okay and I was thinking maybe. . ."

"You were thinking about letting her off the hook for what she did to us?"

"No. Yes. I mean. . ."

"Spit it out, Kaufmann. I haven't got all day."

"I want you to give me back the glove."

246

Derek made a show of looking around as if searching for something. "Gee, now let me think. Her glove?"

"It's in your locker. I want you to give it back to me Monday so I can return it."

"And I would do this because?"

"It's me you should be blaming for getting in trouble with Mortimer. Sally had nothing to do with it."

"Right." Derek stood up and moved around the glass-topped table to tower over Justin. "Let's get something straight here, freak. What I do or don't do to Sally Shepherd or her precious glove is no longer any of your business. You need to think about what I'm going to do to you."

He walked past Justin, picked up Justin's bike, and casually tossed it into the deep end of the swimming pool that took up most of the backyard. Then he turned and walked into the house without another word.

Now that Rachel had entertained the first hint of a romantic thought about Ben Booker, she could not seem to get the man out of her mind. Of course, the more time that passed without James the more the idea that someday she might love again lingered there. In addition to Hester pointing out the eligible men Rachel's age living in Pinecraft, John had teased her about one older man in their congregation who seemed to have his eye on her.

But how shocked would her friends be to discover that the man she felt drawn to was Ben Booker?

It was impossible of course, and the sheer impossibility of the match made it all the more difficult to turn her thoughts elsewhere. He was not of her faith. He was not of *any* faith, really, although she had been touched to hear him admit that he did pray.

She had seen him with his patients and their parents. She could never forget the hours he'd spent checking up on the boy whose arm had been nearly severed by the shark, sitting with him in the days following the surgery and stopping by to encourage the teen as he struggled through weeks of rehabilitation. And that was only one example of his devotion to his work. Surely, in spite of the fact that he did not seem to be a churchgoing man, he was ministering to their emotional and spiritual needs as much as she or anyone else was.

But daydreaming about a future with Ben Booker was pure folly. Even taking the issue of religion out of the discussion altogether, a man of the world like that in love with a plain woman like her? It was—as she'd once heard Sally say—beyond ridiculous.

Determined to put aside any fantasy of what it might be like to love Ben, Rachel turned her attention to other matters. She spent hours working to finish the course work for her state certification. She identified and then tried to avoid those places at the hospital where she was most likely to see Ben. She timed her visits to Sally and her parents when she knew he was otherwise occupied. Twice when she saw his car parked in his sister's driveway, she had suggested to Justin that they take a bike ride down to Pinecraft for ice cream and see if any new rental listings had been posted on the bulletin board outside the post office.

Out of sight, out of mind became her guidepost.

She certainly had plenty to keep her busy. The pressure she placed on herself to excel increased as she neared the completion of the requirements for earning her certification. Pastor Paul had given her high praise for the work she had done, and Eileen talked as if it was a foregone conclusion that by Christmas Rachel would be a permanent member of the staff. The supervisor sent by the certification board in Tallahassee to observe her work had been equally reassuring.

But getting her license was only one step in the process. There was still the job review, and Mark Boynton had told her that although he had tried explaining her side of things to Darcy, the second perceived offense was still included in her record. "Unfortunately, no one but the boy heard the entire conversation," he told her. The review was set for the Monday following the Thanksgiving holiday.

Because Hester and John were planning to be away for that weekend visiting relatives near Orlando, Rachel was planning a quiet day with Justin. But Sharon Shepherd wouldn't hear of it.

"If you have no other plans," Sharon said, "Sally comes home that Wednesday and she's so looking forward to the day. I know that she would be so happy if you and Justin could come." Sharon smiled and squeezed Rachel's hand. "Surely you know by now that our Sally considers you one of the people she is most thankful for meeting this last year."

It was difficult to refuse after that. Rachel admitted that she and Justin had no special plans for the day, and Sharon clapped her hands together with delight. "Then you'll come. It's going to be such a wonderful celebration—a celebration of true thanksgiving." She sighed.

"You will allow me to bake the pies?" Rachel asked.

"Absolutely. Malcolm loves your pies, and so does Ben."

Of course, Ben would be there. And Zeke. Suddenly Rachel was having second thoughts about the whole idea. But it had been so long since Rachel had seen Sharon looking so happy. How could she disappoint her?

"Malcolm's mom makes a wonderful sweet potato casserole," she gushed. "Our dad—mine and Ben's—won't be able to come, but I have all my mom's best recipes. Sage and pecan stuffing, acorn squash soup, and the most wonderful molded cranberry salad." She ticked off each item on her manicured fingernails. "I thought I would invite Darcy Meekins as well. Ben's been seeing her and well. . ." She smiled mischievously. "Malcolm tells me not to interfere, but I so want my big brother to be happy."

So Darcy would be invited. Rachel felt her stomach lurch.

"We dine at four but don't stand on ceremony," Sharon continued. "Come anytime after one and don't make the pies ahead of time. It's all such fun with the women together in the kitchen cooking and the men watching their football games and the house is alive with. . .well, life." She sighed happily, and then her eyes welled with tears. "Oh Rachel, was it only a few weeks ago that everything looked so bleak?"

Apparently the question was a rhetorical one because Sharon

gave Rachel a quick hug and then hurried away. Rachel remained standing outside the children's chapel, her mind cluttered with everything she needed to accomplish in the next few days. Surely God was taking a hand in making sure that she was kept so busy that she would have little time to think about Ben. And yet somehow thoughts of him were never far from her mind.

Darcy was nervous, and excited. If Sharon Shepherd had invited her for Thanksgiving dinner then surely Ben had approved. Things between them had gotten pretty awkward over the last couple of weeks. Understandably he'd been preoccupied with Sally's recovery, and the few times they had run into each other at the hospital there had been little time for more than a few words. Sitting down together for a family dinner would be the perfect solution for easing them back into the kind of relationship Darcy had imagined them building.

Imagined.

That was the crux of it. She had to admit that she had fantasized about a future with Ben, envisioning the two of them doing everything together. But she could not get past the reality that some of those encounters at work could have turned into a quick lunch or cup of coffee. There had been time for Ben to ask if she wanted to go for a pizza after work. There had been time to suggest a light supper by the bay or watching an old movie to give him some distance from worrying about his niece and his sister. But it had not happened.

So when Darcy parked her car on the circular drive in front of the Shepherds' home and saw Ben's sports car, she had to wonder what the next several hours might hold for her—for them. She opened her trunk to retrieve the bags of fresh herbs and vegetables that she'd brought at Sharon's urging.

"You must be quite the gourmet cook," Sharon had gushed when she'd called to invite Darcy for the day.

Darcy's heart had raced with pleasure at the very idea that Ben might have mentioned the meal she'd prepared for him.

"Zeke says that you're a regular at the market. I love going there, but I never know quite what to do with all those beautiful herbs and veggies," Sharon continued. "Come early and prepare your veggie casserole here. It's a huge kitchen. Maybe you can give me some pointers."

So it had been Zeke who had mentioned her flair for cooking—not Ben. Well, she would simply have to try harder to impress Ben with her culinary skills. Zeke was wrong about her being wound too tight. She knew how to relax and have fun. The man needed to stop playing the amateur shrink and open his eyes to the idea that she had ever so much more to bring to a relationship than he imagined.

She frowned. Not that she gave two cents for what Zeke Shepherd might think of her. It was Ben she was out to impress. She rang the bell even though the front door was open.

"Come on in," Malcolm called as he came toward her. "Need some help?" He held open the screen door to let her pass then took the shopping bags from her. He smiled and tilted his head for her to follow. "Sharon? Reinforcements," he called as he led the way toward the kitchen.

In the background Darcy could hear the sounds of a college football game, and then Ben's shout as his team scored a touchdown.

"Who's playing?" she asked Malcolm, suddenly much preferring to be in the family room with its big-screen television—and Ben.

"Florida State and Florida." Malcolm set the bags on the island counter and grinned at her as another roar—this one more like a groan—erupted from the family room. "Oops, sounds like somebody's team messed up. Glad you could make it, Darcy," he said as he left.

Darcy smiled and turned to greet Sharon and Sally as well as Malcolm's mother, Angie. And one person it had never occurred to her would be there—Rachel Kaufmann.

Rachel couldn't help but notice that Justin had seemed more than a little nervous about sharing Thanksgiving dinner with the Shepherds. When they were still at the guest cottage, he kept glancing outside, up toward the Shepherds' house. "It's just dinner," she told him, assuming that was the cause of his jitters.

"I know," he mumbled. "So Sally came home yesterday?"

"That's right. She was discharged right after lunch."

"She'll be there, then?"

"Well of course she will, Justin. She lives there. What is going on in that head of yours?" She playfully ruffled his hair hoping for a smile.

But none came. Thankfully the moment they arrived at the Shepherds', Zeke took Justin in hand. "You like football?"

Justin shrugged and Zeke grinned. "Me neither, but it's part of the script for today."

For the first time all morning Justin showed some real interest in what the day might bring. "I don't understand."

" 'Tis a day of rituals dating back decades," Zeke announced. "No worries. I'll help you through it. For starters, your mom and all other females are banished to the kitchen while we men. . ." He actually puffed out his chest and pounded it so that Justin laughed. "We men take up our places in the man cave with the ginormous television and watch a bunch of college kids run up and down a field trying their best to give each other concussions."

Rachel frowned. "I don't know if—"

"It's a show," Zeke assured her. "Now from time to time you ladies in the kitchen are going to hear the men do any or all of the following—cheer, shout, groan, possibly cry out as if in pain. You must ignore all of it because it's part—"

"—of the script," Justin said, grinning from ear to ear.

"That's right. So, Rachel, you run along and bake those pies while Justin and I. . ."

Just then Sally came down the stairs. She was much thinner than she'd been a few weeks earlier, but her blood levels had been normal for more than a week now and the special eyedrops, tinted glasses, and regimen of medications prescribed to treat her GVHD and rebuild her immune system seemed to be working. Still, she was frowning.

"Mom," she called out and then seemed to notice that Rachel,

Justin, and Zeke were standing in the hall next to the stairway. "I can't find my glove."

"You don't need your glove today," Sharon called back. "Come here. I need some help."

"That's right," Zeke said as he relieved Justin of the basket of supplies he was carrying and passed them along to Sally. "Women in the kitchen and men. . ." He wrapped his arm around Justin's shoulder.

"Got it," Sally said with a roll of her eyes. "But if Florida State gets ready to score. . ."

"No worries. I'll send my minion here to fetch you. Now scoot."

Rachel liked Zeke so much. Hester had confided to her that lately Zeke's interest in settling into a more orthodox lifestyle had been on the rise. "I think he might be falling in love," she'd whispered. "Why else would he have this sudden interest in how he looks and what he wears?"

It was true. The Zeke that Rachel had met when she first came to Florida was far different—at least in appearance—from the man leading Justin off to watch the game. This current Zeke was dressed in jeans that fit him without the benefit of the piece of rope that doubled as a belt he'd worn when she'd first met him. He was also wearing a solid blue shirt, sleeves rolled back to his elbows, and what looked to Rachel like new sandals.

"I'm really glad you came today, Rachel," Sally was saying as she led the way to the kitchen. "Mom wasn't sure you could do this—I mean, that maybe it wouldn't be right, you know, because of your religion."

"Thanksgiving is a lovely tradition, Sally. Dinner with friends and family all pausing to consider the many blessings God has given them," Rachel assured her. "How could there be anything wrong with that?"

Sally grinned. "Can I help you make the pies?"

"I'd love it."

By the time Darcy Meekins arrived, Rachel was up to her wrists in flour and dough, a wisp of her hair having worked its way loose from her tight bun and tickling her nose as she showed Sally how to roll out the crusts for the pies. By contrast

Darcy looked like a magazine cover model. She was wearing a sleeveless print sundress, her hair pulled back but loose around her shoulders, and her makeup so perfect that it was like she wasn't wearing any at all.

"Darcy, why don't you set up over here?" Sharon directed, pointing to a clear area of the large granite-topped island that dominated the room.

From the family room came a rising chant of, "Food! Food! Food!" Rachel blushed when she realized Justin's voice was a part of the chant.

Malcolm carried several empty soda cans into the kitchen. "Halftime," he commented as he took the cans out to the recycle bin and then headed back to the family room with a fresh supply of soda.

Sharon removed two large platters—one loaded with fresh vegetables and a container of dip and the other piled high with a variety of cheeses and deli meats—from the double-door refrigerator and handed one to her mother-in-law, Angie. "Come on, Mom, let's go feed the animals. Sally, bring those crackers and napkins."

Suddenly Rachel and Darcy were alone. The kitchen was so quiet that Rachel could hear the pan of water that Angie had set to boil for cooking the yams bubbling away. At the same moment she and Darcy reached to turn down the flame. Rachel smiled and stepped away. Darcy set the flame and turned back to chopping the herbs for her casserole.

"It seems you've become quite close to the Shepherds," Darcy said after a moment. "Almost like family."

"They have been very kind to Justin and me. Everyone has been so very kind, and patient."

"Everyone meaning Ben?"

Rachel paused in mixing the apples with cinnamon, dried cherries, nuts, and brown sugar. "Ben is also our friend, yes."

Darcy did not look at her, but Rachel could not miss the way her chopping knife seemed to come down on the bunch of chives with extra force. "Do you think this is a good idea, Rachel? I mean, your close association with the president of the hospital board and his family? Well, it could be seen as something of a conflict of interest in terms of your position at the hospital."

She was as surprised as Darcy apparently was by the comment given the expression on her face. Rachel closed her eyes for a moment, sending up a prayer for guidance. Then Rachel's next words were, "And yet you also work at the hospital and are also very close with the Shepherds—and with Dr. Booker."

Blessedly that was the moment when Sharon, Angie, and Sally returned. They were laughing, bringing with them all the joy that had filled the house earlier. Rachel turned her attention back to Sally. "Shall we do plain pecan for the second pie or perhaps chocolate pecan?"

"Oh, definitely chocolate," Sally said.

Darcy picked up a tray filled with chopped vegetables and turned to Sharon. "Did you say there was a grill outside? I have more than we'll need for the casserole, so why don't I grill the rest?"

"Lovely," Sharon said. "Let me turn it on for you."

"You know after we eat dinner and clean everything up," Sally said, "then we make Christmas cookies, right, Grams?"

Rachel saw Angie frown slightly before changing her expression to a loving smile. "Well, perhaps tonight—since you've only been home. . ."

"Oh Grammie, I've been lying in bed for like an eon. We always make cookies. And I'll bet Rachel has a bazillion recipes for cookies, don't you?"

"Your grandmother is right to worry, Sally. You mustn't overdo it," Rachel said. "Perhaps you could come to the guesthouse on another day and we could bake some together."

"One batch tonight," Sally bartered.

Angie and Rachel exchanged a look. "One batch," Angie agreed. "One batch of sugar cookie dough that we will freeze and decorate when you are stronger."

Sally sighed. "Grams drives a hard bargain," she admitted, and all three of them were laughing when Sharon and Darcy returned from grilling the vegetables.

"I'll take these into the family room." Darcy held up the tray of grilled vegetables.

Rachel had gotten so accustomed to Darcy's disapproval that when the woman glanced at her with something that Rachel could only label as envy, she was stunned. Surely Darcy with all of her success and beauty could not possibly be jealous of Rachel. Her heart went out to Darcy. Seeing her here out of the hospital where she was so clearly in charge made Rachel realize that there was far more to Darcy Meekins than she had thought. Was there any reason why she and Darcy could not find something in common beyond their roles at the hospital?

Until now, Rachel had followed Eileen's advice and simply ignored Darcy's evident concerns when it came to whether or not Rachel was up to the job. That had been a mistake, she decided. Starting here and now she intended to take the first step toward changing that.

So when they were all at dinner and Angie raised the topic of the Keller and Messner families and how difficult the coming holidays would be for them, it was Justin who gave her the opening she'd been seeking.

"Mom's counseling them," Justin blurted, and Darcy's head shot up, her eyes pinning Rachel. "It's a program that Mom and I went through after Dad died. It helps," he added, seemingly oblivious to the adult dynamics surrounding him.

Darcy was staring hard at Rachel while Malcolm's eyebrows had lifted with interest. Everyone seemed to be waiting for her to say something.

"After my husband died, Justin and I were fortunate enough to take part in a counseling program that allowed us to face the man responsible for his death, work through our grief—and anger—and begin to move on."

"I remember seeing something about that on your résumé," Malcolm said. "You got some kind of license to counsel?"

Darcy was focusing all of her attention on her food, but Rachel was determined not to give up on finding some way to connect with this woman. "That's right. I've been thinking about seeing if you and I might talk about possibly bringing some form of the VORP program to Gulf Coast, Darcy." She could have just as easily made the statement to Malcolm as head of the board, but she focused on Darcy as she continued to explain the concept.

"It has some potential," Malcolm jumped in.

"It would certainly be unique to Gulf Coast—Memorial has nothing like that," Ben added, glancing at Darcy. "It could be a positive marketing tool."

"You've been trained as a mediator for this program?" Darcy asked Rachel.

Rachel nodded, her heart hammering. Darcy actually seemed interested. "If you have some time on Monday, I could. . ."

The front doorbell chimed.

"Got it," Malcolm said, placing his napkin on his chair as he went to answer the door. Conversation around the table turned to speculation about who the visitor might be. He returned a moment later with a large gift-wrapped package that he handed to Sally. "Seems you have a secret admirer, kiddo."

"Dad," she groaned, but she took the package and eagerly tore off the gold foil bow and ribbon.

"Who brought it?" Sharon asked.

Malcolm shrugged. "It was sitting there—nobody in sight."

"No card?" Angie asked, examining the wrapping paper that Sally had now cast aside.

Sally pried open what looked like a large hatbox and fished through the layers of tissue paper.

Suddenly her face twisted into a grimace of such pain and shock that both her parents as well as Ben and Zeke were immediately on their feet.

"Give me that," Ben ordered when Sally withdrew a shaking hand from the box.

He dumped the contents onto the floor, and there was a collective gasp as everyone saw Sally's baseball glove, the leather scorched black from a fire and sliced into strips.

Sally was shaking as she stood and stared at her ruined glove. "How. . .who. . . ? It was in my room. It's always in my room."

Justin made a noise as if he might be choking and squirmed uncomfortably in the chair next to Rachel. She glanced at him and so did Sally.

"It was you, wasn't it? Uncle Zeke told me that you and your mom helped him clean the house. You took my glove."

Justin seemed incapable of meeting her glare, and now everyone around the table was looking at him.

"Why?" Sally demanded, her fists clenched at her sides. "What did I ever do to you but try to be your friend?"

And then she ran from the room, Sharon and Malcolm and her grandmother following her up the stairs. Those left behind heard the slam of a door and then silence.

Part Three

But it is good for me to draw near to God. . .
PSALM 73:28

Chapter 23

All through the long hours that followed the dinner at the Shepherds' Justin tried to figure out some way—any way—that he might explain himself. He had not denied Sally's accusation. How could he? It was the truth.

Instead while Sally and her parents and grandmother were upstairs, Zeke and Darcy began clearing the table and then stayed in the kitchen leaving him, his mom, and Ben at the table.

"Please give me a moment with my son," his mom had said, her voice so soft it was not much more than a whisper.

Ben had folded his arms across his chest and leaned back in his chair. "I'm not going anywhere until you explain what's going on here, Justin."

That was when his mom stood up. "Then I think it's best if we leave. Please thank Sharon and Malcolm for the dinner."

"Don't you want to know. . ."

"What I know is that Justin was sitting right here next to me when that box was delivered. If there is more to it, then I trust my son to tell me himself, but right now it is best for everyone if we leave."

Justin had followed her through the kitchen where Zeke and Darcy were busy loading the dishwasher and covering leftovers.

Neither of them had looked at him as his mom retrieved the basket she'd used to bring the pie ingredients and then left without a word through the back door.

The minute they were inside the guesthouse, she set down the basket and turned to him. "Did you steal that glove, Justin?"

"Not exactly," he hedged.

"Did you take it with Sally's permission?"

"No, but. . ."

"Then you stole it." She sighed as if she needed to get rid of all the air inside her lungs and start fresh. "Why?"

Guilt welled up in him, but instead of feeling ashamed all he felt was angry. "It's your fault," he told her. "If you hadn't gone to that meeting with Mr. Mortimer. . ."

"Do not speak to me in that way, Justin." He had never seen his mother look at him the way she had in that moment. Her mouth had tightened so much that her lips had almost disappeared. "What does our meeting with your teacher have anything to do with—"

"Derek saw you, okay? He saw the way you dress and he put it together. He was already mad because he'd been caught cheating and then he was mad all over again because he'd been hanging around somebody like me without even knowing it."

"What's wrong with someone like you?"

"We're different. . .weird."

"We are different. And if living our lives according to centuries of the faith is weird, then so be it." The heavy silence that fell between them was worse than if his mom had started to shout at him. All he could hear was the ticking of the clock on the fireplace mantel.

"Justin, I am trying to understand this. Tell me why you took Sally's glove."

"Derek threatened me."

"How?"

The question stumped Justin completely. There had been nothing specific. "He said he would make my life miserable."

"How?"

Justin's shoulders slumped. "I don't know," he admitted. "It's what he does. Everybody knows it. I was afraid."

"Oh Justin, why did you not come to me?"

The full force of his anger and disappointment hit him like a fist. He stared at her. "Right. When exactly was I supposed to do that, Mom? You are always gone or busy or thinking about somebody else—Sally, the Keller girl, some kid at the hospital." His voice was shaking and his fists were clenched. "You promised," he shouted, and then stormed off to his room and slammed the door.

Almost immediately he regretted his actions. Never in his life had he spoken to either of his parents that way. If his dad had still been alive Justin had no doubt that he would be in for a paddling. He waited for the door to open, for his mom to confront him— to punish him as he deserved.

Instead after a long while he heard the murmur of her voice and realized she was talking to someone on the telephone. A few minutes later he saw her walking back up to the Shepherds' house, her pace slow like it had been the day they buried his dad.

Ben had helped Zeke and Darcy finish clearing the table, and still there had been no sign of Sally or Sharon or Malcolm. Angie had come downstairs to report that Sally was resting and it was probably best if everyone else left. She had picked up Sally's glove with two fingers and handed it to Zeke. "Get rid of this thing, son, and then please take me home. I'm suddenly too exhausted to drive myself."

To Ben's surprise Darcy had offered to follow Angie and Zeke in her car so that she could give Zeke a ride back. Once they all left, Ben was alone in the spacious downstairs of his sister's house.

He wandered from room to room, window to window, pausing to look out toward the guesthouse. He wondered what Rachel was saying to her son. Would she punish the boy or, like so many parents that Ben had encountered in his practice, insist that her child had done no wrong? That he was in fact the victim of the bully Derek Piper. For Ben had no doubt that it was the

Piper kid who was behind this whole business.

From the day that Sally had beaten him for the position of pitcher on the team, he had set out to get his revenge. He was a first-class bully. Of course, he had learned from the best. Ben recalled Malcolm's tales of Derek's father terrorizing weaker students—including Zeke—when the two of them had been in high school together.

He considered going over to the Piper house and confronting Derek. But what good would that do? He glanced out the window. It was dusk now, and he saw Rachel coming through the gardens on her way up to the house. He thought about how he'd wanted this day to go—how he had planned to find some time when the two of them could talk, how he had wanted to tell her that his feelings for her were complicated but undeniable.

Moving out to the lanai, he stood in the shadows and waited for her. The last rays of the sun cast her features in shadow, but he did not need to see her face to know that she was as filled with misery as he was. His anger had dissipated. Now in its place he felt only sadness and regret for what the day might have been.

He opened the side door for her. "Rachel," he said.

"Is Darcy still here?" she asked.

It was the very last thing he had expected. "No. She went with Zeke to drive Angie home."

Rachel nodded, her eyes downcast. "Then I would like to speak with Sharon and Malcolm if they are available."

"They are with Sally. If you've come to apologize for what Justin—"

"My son will seek their forgiveness," she said.

"Then what? You certainly have nothing to apologize for, and right now the last thing they need—"

"I have come to let your sister know that Justin and I will be moving out on Saturday, and I wanted to offer my resignation to Darcy and Malcolm."

"You're giving up and going back to Ohio?"

"If we need to, Justin and I can stay with Hester and John until I can determine what is best. In the meantime I will enroll Justin in the Mennonite school in Pinecraft."

"You've decided all of this in the last hour?"

She looked at him then. A half smile played across her lips. "I have made many mistakes since coming here. Most of all I have placed my only child in a position where he was so afraid—and felt so alone—that he has lost his way. We both have."

Suddenly the understanding that she planned to simply walk out of his life—out of all their lives—hit him. And as angry as he was with Justin for whatever part he'd played in the horrid prank, the idea that he might never have contact with Rachel again was unthinkable.

"Don't you think you're overreacting here?" He seemed incapable of keeping the anger from his voice.

Her eyes flashed, but she did not raise her voice in response. "I am doing what is best for my son."

"And what about you? What about us? Rachel, I have feelings for you that go beyond...that could grow into..."

She placed her fingers on his lips, silencing him. "It has been an emotional day for everyone, Ben. Please don't speak of things that are impossible. It only makes this more difficult." She turned then and started back down the path. "If you would please tell Sharon and Malcolm why I stopped by," she said as she walked away. "Thank you, Ben." She stopped and looked back at him. "For everything."

It took him less than a second to realize that somehow he had to stop her. As she walked away he ran to catch up with her, caught her arm, and spun her so that she was close enough to kiss. "Don't you realize that I am falling in love with you, Rachel?"

She did not try to pull away from him. Instead she pushed a lock of his hair back from his forehead. "I know that feeling as well, but we are the adults here, Ben. It is not our wants and needs that are at stake here. Justin..."

"Justin is twelve. He'll get over this."

"When I moved him from the only home he's ever known to here, I made a promise to my son, and I will honor that promise. As for you and...as for us..." Her fingers lingered, curled around the lock of his hair. He pulled her closer.

"Tell me why this has to be impossible," he said.

"You know why as well as I do, Ben. You place most of your faith in facts—what you can see and prove. I am a woman whose whole life is rooted in faith. Tell me how that can work?" She pulled away then. "The mistake I made in taking the position at the hospital was to put my need to escape a life that I hardly recognized anymore ahead of everything else. I thrust Justin into a world that was so very different from the one he knows. I only pray that I can remedy that so that in a couple of years when his time comes to be baptized and take his place as a member of the church, he will have found his way again."

Ben was fresh out of arguments. The light from Sally's bedroom window spilled across the lawn. Rachel was right of course. In fact, she had proven her case so well that he could find no fault with it. "For a woman who makes decisions on faith, you sure can come up with a convincing argument."

He had hoped to make her smile. Instead she looked up at the stars. "I wish you happiness, Ben, or if not happiness at least peace—contentment."

The light in Sally's room went out, and a moment later Ben heard Sharon and Malcolm talking quietly as they came downstairs. Rachel had also heard them, and in her hesitation he saw that she was considering going back inside the house to meet with them.

"Let me tell them," Ben said. "It'll be best that way."

Rachel nodded and stood on her toes to kiss his cheek. Without another word, she walked back toward the guesthouse, the thorns of the rosebushes tugging at her ankle-length skirt as she went.

A thin stream of light shone from under Justin's door. Rachel knocked and then entered the small bedroom. Justin was sitting against the headboard of the single bed, still wearing his best clothes.

"Are you hungry?"

He shook his head, watching her closely, no doubt trying to figure out what might be coming next. She sat on the side of the bed and took his hand between both of hers.

"Pray with me, Justin." She closed her eyes and poured all of her energy into entreating God to help them both find their way. On her way up to the Shepherds' house she had been so certain of her plan. She had called Hester and told her the whole story, and her friend had agreed that if necessary she and Justin could come stay with them until they could rent a cottage in Pinecraft.

"But leaving your job when you're so close to getting your license?" Hester had protested.

"I'll finish the work I need for certification, Hester. But my job and studies are the two things that have taken me away from Justin when he needed me most. I can find work, and I've saved enough to cover our other needs until then."

Together they had come up with a plan that would work for getting Justin to and from the Mennonite school while Rachel looked for steady work and a house to rent in Pinecraft. After she hung up, Rachel had stood for a long moment, the phone still in her hand. How she would miss the hospital and Eileen and Pastor Paul and especially the children and their parents.

She had fallen into the trap of thinking of her needs and ambitions, and it was time to remedy that. The temptation to feel sorry for herself in having to give up all she had worked so hard to achieve was all the impetus she needed to head for the Shepherds' house immediately and make sure they knew that she and Justin would vacate the guesthouse by Saturday.

But when she had run into Ben she had come so very close to changing her mind. The very suggestion that he might have feelings for her that went beyond mere friendship had almost been her undoing. But surely his declaration had arisen from his desperation to stop her from leaving the hospital. Ben could not love her—he barely knew her. She had no doubt that he truly believed that his feelings for her went beyond simple friendship, but what he felt for her was not love. And what she felt for him— what had been growing inside her these last weeks—that was only more evidence of how she had gotten so caught up in the ways of these outsiders that she had lost her way. With God's forgiveness and guidance there was still time to put such feelings to rest and concentrate on building the life she'd promised Justin they would find in Florida. The simple life that did not stray beyond the teachings of their faith.

So she bowed her head and closed her eyes and thanked God for pulling her back from the precipice of her selfishness. Oh, she had told herself that the hours she had given to work and study had been for Justin. But the truth was that she had enjoyed the work, the camaraderie with her coworkers, the knowledge that she could make a difference in the lives of patients and their families.

"*Pride goeth before destruction, and an haughty spirit before a fall,*" she thought. But it was Justin who had suffered the fall. She opened her eyes and looked up at Justin, cupping his cheek tenderly. She realized that she was crying and that his eyes were filled with tears that he was fighting hard to hold back.

"I'm so sorry, Mom," he said, his voice husky with emotion. "For the way I talked to you before. For what I did to Sally, for. . ."

"I forgive you and, knowing Sally, in time she will as well. But you must think of how best to seek her forgiveness, Justin. Whatever part you had in this business, you wronged her."

"I know." His voice choked and he looked away. "Dad would be so ashamed of me," he whispered.

"He would be disappointed in both of us, but he would know that in the end we will make this right."

Justin looked at her with such trust and hope that her heart overflowed with love for him. "Justin, I have thought about what you said, and you are right. When we left Ohio I made you a promise, a promise I have not kept."

"You've really tried," Justin protested. "I know you have."

"Tried and failed. I got all caught up in their world, Justin, never pausing to consider what really mattered—you. I have come to understand that the path I chose is not the path that God had for us."

"I don't want to go back to Ohio."

Rachel smiled. "Good. Neither do I. So for now here is what we will do. . . ."

As she explained her plan, Justin's eyes cleared and she saw in the place of his tears a look of hope that was a welcome relief from the furtive glances filled with doubt that he'd given her these last weeks. Seeing that gave her the courage to believe that she was finally making the right decision. And it was at that moment that she heard the familiar roar of Ben's sports car driving away.

"Well, that was certainly an interesting day," Darcy said after she and Zeke had taken his mom home. She was driving Zeke back to his sister's so he could pick up the van from the fruit co-op that he'd driven there earlier. Ever since they'd said good night to Zeke's mom he'd not said a word. "I'm sure Sally will rally, but I don't know.... It's just so hard."

"It's hard to fathom the damage a bully can do," Zeke said as he stared out the side window.

"Well, I certainly would never have thought that Rachel's son..."

"He's not the bully," Zeke defended. "He's collateral damage. That other kid—Derek—he's the bully."

"And yet Justin took Sally's glove and gave it to him, making it possible for him to..."

"He was afraid."

Darcy glanced at him. "Of what? The guy was after Sally, not him. Besides, Justin looks like he could hold his own."

"That's how bullies work. They find a person's weak spot and then they work that angle. In Justin's case my guess is that Derek discovered that he was Mennonite."

"So?"

"Different—especially *that* different—doesn't play all that well when you're twelve. And if Derek knew that Justin would never fight back—that in his religion..."

"You're going pretty light on the kid."

There was a moment's pause, and then very quietly she heard Zeke say, "Maybe it's because at that age I *was* that kid."

"You? That's pretty hard to believe. From what Malcolm tells me you earned pretty much every medal for bravery that exists in the military."

"I wasn't twelve then, and I was proving a point." He stretched

269

and yawned and then turned his full attention on her, that lazy grin that she was coming to like spreading across his face. "Let's talk about you. I mean, talk about somebody who goes through life trying to prove herself."

"I do not," she protested. "If holding myself and others to high standards qualifies me as a bully. . ."

"Whoa, who said anything about you being a bully?"

"That was the topic," she shot back, her hands tightening around the steering wheel.

Zeke reached over and pulled one hand free and held it, weaving his fingers through hers. "Hey, it's been a strange and upsetting day. I don't know about you, but on Thanksgiving I want dessert. How about we stop at the café for some of Millie's pie?"

"It's Thanksgiving," she pointed out. "The café's probably closed."

"Is the hospital open?"

"Of course, but. . ."

"Then Millie and Al are open. Let's go."

She glanced at him. He was still holding her hand, and she realized she had no desire to pull away.

Chapter 24

Ben did what he always did when he was at a loss to make sense of his personal life—he buried himself in work. If he could only get through the last two weeks that Rachel would be at the hospital then maybe he could move forward. To that end he arranged his schedule so that he was making rounds well before she arrived in the morning and checking in on patients that he needed to see more than once during the day later in the evening, after he knew she had gone home.

With Hester's help it had taken her only two days after they moved out of the guesthouse to rent a small cottage on the banks of Phillippi Creek in Pinecraft and move there with Justin. He had actually driven through the small Amish/Mennonite community one night after Eileen had, unsolicited, offered this bit of news. There had been any number of people out on the main and side streets that made up the neighborhood, but he had not seen Rachel.

"Oh good," he muttered to himself as he turned around and headed back to his condo, "you're very close to becoming a stalker, Booker."

Sharon had reported that Rachel and Justin had moved out without a word, although there had been notes of apology and appreciation from both of them left on the guesthouse's kitchen table. In the envelope that Justin had left for Sally there had been two crisp twenty-dollar bills and a note that read:

Sally,

I made a big mistake that first day at school. I chose the wrong friend and I'm sorry for that. I know a new glove can't replace your other one but in case you decide to buy a new one, I want you to have this money I earned helping out at the co-op. If it's not enough, let me know. Mom says that if I ask for forgiveness and you give it then this is all behind us, but she doesn't understand that that's our way and might not be yours. I don't expect you to forgive me, but please know that I am very, very sorry for hurting you and if I could have a do-over, I would choose you to be my friend.

Justin

Typical for her, Sharon seemed inclined to forgive Justin, as did Sally. In fact it was Sally who had instructed Ben to "let it go."

"Derek Piper is a creep," she'd told him. "That's not exactly news, and if you want to know the truth I feel really bad that Justin and his mom moved out. He took a stupid baseball glove, not a kidney."

Ben had smiled at that. Leave it to Sally to find the pony in a barn filled with manure. He wished he could be as pragmatic in facing the fact that Rachel was leaving the hospital to find her place once again with her own people. It was impossible not to admire the strength it had taken her to put her son's happiness ahead of her own.

A week to the day after the Thanksgiving debacle, Ben rounded a corner on his way to the physicians' locker room to change for the night and saw her coming toward him. She moved with the unselfconscious grace of a dancer and, as always, her loveliness emanated from the inner calm with which she seemed to face whatever life might throw at her. Once she left her position in the spiritual care unit, she was going to be hard to replace.

She was talking to someone on her cell phone, her smile evidence of the good news she was hearing. She had not yet noticed him, and Ben savored the moment that he had to observe her. Then she glanced up and their gazes connected. Her features softened into a smile as she ended the call.

"Hello," she said, and he was reminded of that very first day when she'd stepped off that bus and into his life.

"Good news?" he asked, nodding toward the phone she held.

Her smile widened and her eyes sparkled. "Amazing news. My friend Hester tells me that Zeke Shepherd has bought the café across the street from the hospital."

It was such an unexpected bit of news that Ben laughed. "Zeke?"

"Apparently he has this trust fund left to him by his father and, well, he has decided to put it to use."

"Good for him."

She studied him closely for a moment. "You look tired, Ben."

"Just finishing up for the day. How about you? You're here later than usual."

"Paul and his wife are celebrating their anniversary so I offered to be on call in his place."

"Eileen told me you moved to Pinecraft. How's Justin doing in his new school?"

"He is settling in—we both are."

"Seems to be a lot of that going around these days—you, now Zeke making these big life changes." He was incapable of keeping a note of bitterness from creeping into his voice.

"And you, Ben? Are you. . .well?"

Instinctively he knew that she'd deliberately avoided asking if he was happy. He met her eyes directly. "I miss you."

"Me too," she admitted. "And Sharon and Sally. It's been. . . harder than I thought it would be."

"Then stay—at least in the job. In time we can find our way. I mean, if we're just to be friends so be it, but to give up everything?"

She glanced at her pager as if willing it to interrupt this conversation she clearly did not want to have. Ben pressed his point by taking her hand. "Stay," he pleaded.

"I have promised Justin. . ."

"You promised Justin that you would make a life for him that was better than life without his father back on the farm. Why can't you give him that and have a life for yourself as well?"

Slowly she withdrew her hand. "I have to go," she said and hurried away down the corridor to the elevator, where the door was about to close.

By the time the elevator had come to a stop and the doors slid open to reveal the tropical gardens of the atrium in the lobby, Rachel had managed to get her breathing back to normal. The encounter with Ben had been unexpected, and at first—because of the news she'd been able to share about Zeke—she had thought she could keep the encounter light and unemotional.

Over the last several days she had seen him only twice, and neither time had he been aware of her presence. The first time, he'd been sitting with a family, talking quietly to them, reassuring them that their child—the victim of a terrible fall—would be all right. The second was when she had been waiting for the bus to take her home to Pinecraft and she'd seen him drive out of the parking lot, Darcy Meekins at his side.

In the first instance her admiration and respect for the way he cared for his patients and their families had almost overwhelmed her. In the second she had felt the cruel and relentless undertow of pure unadulterated jealousy.

What was the matter with her? Didn't she want Ben to be happy? If she cared for him, wasn't that what she should wish for him? But when he'd asked her to stay on, promised her that if friendship was all there could be, then that would be enough, she had known in her heart that it would never be enough for her. She was in love with him.

"Rachel?"

She looked up to find Darcy Meekins standing before her.

"Hello, Darcy. You're here late."

"The board meets tonight. Do you have a minute to talk?"

"Of course." Darcy had taken the news of Rachel's resignation in stride, showing neither surprise nor regret. Rather she had turned the entire matter over to Mark Boynton, instructing him to post an ad for Rachel's replacement and to work with Paul Cox to set Rachel's schedule for the time she had left. Rachel could not help but be surprised that Darcy would have any reason—or inclination—to speak with her now.

She followed the hospital administrator to a bench near the atrium's waterfall.

"I heard you were still in the hospital. I was about to have you paged."

"Is there a problem?"

"We are having some difficulty attracting appropriate candidates for your position. I need to report our progress to the board tonight and, given Mark's report, they are not going to be pleased with what I have to tell them. I was wondering if you might consider staying on."

The very last thing Rachel could ever have imagined was that Darcy Meekins—the woman who had seemed to dedicate her days to getting Rachel out of the hospital—would be asking her to reconsider.

"It seems to me," Darcy continued, "that your reasons for leaving had to do with being overwhelmed with the combination of work and the prep for the certification."

"I would not say that I was overwhelmed," Rachel replied. "There were other concerns, but the main reason that I am leaving is because my son needs me."

"Yes, and that includes needing you to have some way of supporting the two of you. What better care could you possibly offer the boy than to have a secure job with benefits?"

Rachel fought a smile. For Darcy such matters were so clear. "Justin needs my time, my presence. If I take a position where I can build my schedule around his, then I can meet all of his needs."

Darcy frowned. "I really don't understand you, Rachel." She seemed genuinely mystified.

"My needs are simple enough," Rachel explained. "It was when I allowed those needs to become more complicated that I lost my way."

"And what about the children here? Paul cannot do this alone. As the hospital gets busier, he will have to divide his time..."

Rachel understood that Darcy was less concerned about the children—or even Paul—than she was about making a good impression to the board. Admittedly the offer was tempting. Now that she had earned her certification she found that she had a lot more time to call her own—hers and Justin's. There would be no more trips to Tallahassee and no more long nights of study.

And with Paul's approval, Eileen and Mark had worked out a schedule for her that made sure she was home when Justin finished school for the day. And she could not deny that a few more weeks of the wages she received at the hospital would go a long way toward establishing a nest egg that she and Justin might need down the road. But it was too late. She had made her choice, and she was certain that it was the right one.

"I am sorry for your difficulties, Darcy."

"Stay until the end of the year, then."

"That's really not possible. My son and I have the opportunity to travel to Central America in two weeks. Our church is sponsoring a relief mission to help rebuild a remote village that was destroyed by last Tuesday's earthquake."

She stood up and offered Darcy a handshake. Shuffling her stack of files from one arm to the other, Darcy stood as well. She clutched her files to her chest instead of accepting Rachel's offer to shake hands. "As I said before, I don't understand you," she said.

Rachel smiled. "Then at last we have something in common, for I don't understand you either, but I know that you are a good person, dedicated to your work. I genuinely admire you and I thank you for the opportunity you and the others have given me here. But I need to focus on my son for now. It really is that simple. So I'll say good night, Darcy."

Outside, she stood for a moment enjoying the cool dry night. The sky was filled with stars, the fronds of the tall, thin palm trees silhouetted by the light of a half moon. As she walked to the bus stop she checked her pager to be sure there were no more emergencies she needed to address before she left for the night. Justin was on an overnight camping trip with the youth group from the church, part of the preparation for the mission trip. Once there he and the other young people would help rebuild housing and a school while she helped out in the mobile medical unit that the Mennonite Disaster Service had set up in the village.

Her heart welled with pleasure when she thought about how excited Justin had been when she'd agreed that joining the mission trip was the perfect way for them to celebrate Christmas. Hester and John were going as well as several other adults and young people from the congregation. They would leave two days after she completed her work at the hospital and return on New Year's Eve.

Across the street, Rachel saw the lights on in the café. She decided to treat herself to a cup of coffee before heading home. Inside the café, she was mildly surprised to see Zeke sitting at the counter. She congratulated him on buying the business, and then she had an idea.

"Have you got a minute to talk?"

"For you? Anytime." He patted the stool beside him then reached across the counter to retrieve a clean mug and the pot of coffee brewing there. "Regular or decaf?"

"Decaf."

He filled her mug and refilled his own and then swiveled on his stool to face her. "So, what's up?"

She knew that he was aware of the missions trip, so she told him that she and Justin were going. Hester and John had asked him to manage the co-op while they were gone. "But once we return I'm going to need a job."

"Go on."

"Well, I don't know what you have in mind for this place, but I was thinking that maybe if you needed somebody to wait tables. . ."

Zeke frowned. "Wait tables? You? Why would you give up nursing to wait tables here?"

"Right now I need uncomplicated, Zeke. You of all people must understand that."

"But when Darcy was in here earlier she said she was going to ask you to stay."

"She did. I turned her down."

Zeke grinned. "Bet that blew her mind."

"She'll find somebody."

Zeke covered her hand with his. "I get it, Rachel. Sometimes you simply need to sit on the sidelines awhile. It's just that I'll be keeping the waitstaff that's here now."

"Oh." Rachel sipped her coffee to hide her disappointment.

Zeke also focused on drinking his coffee. The silence that stretched between them threatened to ruin the good mood Rachel had brought with her into the café. Zeke drummed his fingers on the counter. "Now if you'd be interested in handling the baking—pies, cakes, breads—that position is wide open. And I could probably use a busboy—evenings and weekends—if you think Justin might be interested."

Rachel smiled. "I'll ask him."

"And the baking?"

"Count me in."

After Rachel turned down her offer, Darcy remained seated in the atrium for several long minutes. What was it with that woman? Who in their right mind walked away from a sure thing—with benefits, not to mention the opportunity to someday take charge of the entire spiritual care department? Maybe if Darcy had offered her the two weeks for the mission trip. . .

She sighed heavily and went to wait for the elevator. The board meeting was scheduled to begin in ten minutes and she still had to figure out how to put the best possible spin on her report. Rachel Kaufmann's leaving wasn't the only bad news she had to deliver tonight. Of even more concern would be the fact that the patient census for the quarter had not lived up to projections.

She wished Zeke Shepherd was going to be at this meeting rather than his brother Malcolm. Zeke had a way of looking at things that helped calm her. Admittedly at first his "no worries" philosophy had driven her to distraction. But ever since

Thanksgiving when they'd shared pie at the café and stayed there talking well into the morning, she had realized that Zeke Shepherd was the one person she didn't have to impress or prove herself to. He liked her. He'd said as much when he kissed her lightly on the lips as she'd dropped him off to pick up the co-op's van early that Friday morning. And she had carried the memory of that kiss with her now for an entire week.

The elevator doors slid open, and Ben stepped out. "Hi." He held the door for her. "You look like you're running off to something. Don't you ever take a break from this place?"

"Board meeting," she replied as she stepped onto the elevator.

"How about I meet you, say, in an hour at the café?"

"Can't. I promised. . .I have another. . ." The elevator doors slid shut. Now why hadn't she simply said that she was meeting Zeke at the café once the board meeting ended? And why not invite Ben to join them?

Because it's not Ben you want to be with. It's Zeke.

Chapter 25

This is going to be the best Christmas ever," Justin exclaimed as he pressed close to the window of the plane that was carrying the relief team to Costa Rica.

Rachel could not disagree. For the first time since leaving the farm in Ohio she finally felt some certainty that she was traveling the path that God had set for her and Justin. In only a matter of days after they moved to Pinecraft and he had enrolled in the Mennonite school there, Justin's whole outlook had changed.

She could actually see signs of the talkative, inquisitive boy he'd been before his father died. Suddenly he was interested in everything about life in Florida. And the few other boys and girls living in the community seemed to accept him into their circle without question.

Going on the trip had been Justin's idea. He'd argued that the ten days of relief that they would provide for the devastated inhabitants of the mountain village of Kingstown was the perfect way to spend Christmas.

And Rachel had agreed. This trip was more than a chance for her to spend time with Justin. It was also exactly what she had needed to let go of any regrets she had held about leaving her job at the hospital.

Once they arrived at the main airport in San Jose they transferred to a much smaller plane for the last leg of their journey to reach the devastated village.

"Mom, look," Justin said in an awed whisper. Everyone on the plane grew silent as they all looked out the tiny windows and saw for the first time the havoc left in the wake of the earthquake. Whole villages were underwater. Piles of rubble that had once been buildings dotted the landscape. Here and there a decapitated palm tree stood sentry over the devastation. A couple of small boats moved slowly over the water that probably had not been there before.

"Search parties from the government," Pastor Detlef—Hester's father—guessed. "Hopefully they've found everyone by now."

There was more dry land but no less destruction as their plane approached a short runway surrounded on all sides by trucks and a couple of other small planes. The tower that had served the airport was tilted at an odd angle, and if there had been a terminal, it was gone.

As the plane landed and taxied, every member of the team prayed silently, and once it stopped the band of rescue workers gathered their belongings and filed off in silence. They were ready to get to work.

After a short but harrowing ride in the canvas-covered back of a military truck to what was left of the village they had come to help, Rachel was pressed into service almost immediately in the large tent that served as a hospital for the area. She soon learned that there were no doctors, only Mary Palmer, a nurse practitioner from the area who had taken charge.

"Where do you need me?" Rachel asked, sliding the straps of her backpack from her shoulders and glancing around at the cots filled with patients.

"Everywhere," Mary said wearily. "You're both trained nurses?" she asked, including Hester in her question.

"Yes," they said as one.

"Good. Why don't the two of you start triaging those folks waiting out there?" She nodded toward a small gathering of children and adults huddled together as if it were below freezing instead of almost eighty degrees outside.

"We don't speak Spanish," Hester admitted.

"Fortunately, most of them speak enough English to understand and be understood. If you need help, there's an interpreter—Juan Carlos. Just shout out for him if you need him."

John and the other men took charge of the teen volunteers and headed off to assess the damage to the school that had once been the largest and most stable building in the village. An engineer had told them that if they could repair the roof on the school, they would be able to provide better shelter for the wounded and displaced. Once that was accomplished they could go to work repairing other buildings that could be used to shelter the earthquake victims. Hester's father, Pastor Detlef, had assured the engineer that there was much that could be accomplished in the ten days they had. The engineer had looked skeptical but then he'd apparently never seen what a group of Mennonite relief workers could accomplish in short order.

As Rachel and Hester checked each person for injuries, they tried to gather each person's medical information. With the help of Juan Carlos they came to understand that these people were not all from this village. Many of them had found their way here from the surrounding area after the initial earthquake had hit. Some of the children had no idea where their parents or siblings were. Others pointed toward the filled beds of the hospital tent when asked about their parents. It was all so very heartbreaking.

After several long hours, someone brought them prepackaged food rations and bottles of fresh water. "Water's going to be the main problem," Hester mused as she held a plastic water bottle for a little girl who was too traumatized to hold the bottle herself.

"Why do you say that?"

"If they run out of clean water then they'll use what's available. Contaminated water means disease—likely cholera. Those trucks at the airport were loaded with cases of water. Why aren't they distributing it?" She directed this question to Mary.

"Because," Mary said, as she joined them, "the local government is in a turf war with the powers that be in another, less damaged village down the road as to which of them gets the water and other supplies. It's an oft-told tale—supplies pour in from all over the place and then they sit." She shook her head and then turned her attention to Rachel. "If you think you can handle things here I could use some help from Hester on the ward." She indicated the larger hospital tent.

"Yes. I can manage," Rachel assured her.

The setting sun brought little relief from the humidity. Rachel wiped sweat from her forehead and looked around to face a woman of indeterminate age dressed only in a thin shift, her hair matted and tangled, her face a mask of dirt marked with scrapes and cuts.

"*Hola,*" Rachel said, using one of the few words she'd picked up from listening to Juan.

"My son is still there," the woman said, pointing toward a pile of rubble several yards down the road where Rachel could see men in uniform working alongside some of the locals. Her English was perfect.

"The men are searching," Rachel said. "They will find him."

Vehemently the woman shook her head. "They are not looking where he is. They sent me away. They believe he is dead, but I know he is not."

"How do you know?"

"God has already taken the boy's father. He would not take my son as well and leave me alone."

In the gathering darkness, Rachel saw that the men were returning to the tents where the volunteers would stay while they were here.

"They are giving up," the woman said angrily. "We must do something!"

Rachel had no idea why this woman had chosen her to champion her cause, but she understood that she could offer her no comfort unless she at least tried. She followed the woman toward the men.

They were filthy with caked dust, streaked with rivulets of sweat, and so weary that they stumbled over the rubble that passed for a road. They carried their tools over their bent shoulders or hanging from limp fingers. When Rachel told them the woman's story, they looked at her with sympathy but offered no hope.

"We'll start again at daybreak," the soldier in charge told the mother.

"You are looking in the wrong place," the woman argued.

The man—Hispanic in features but American by his accent—met her gaze. Rachel saw him struggle to hold his temper. "It may seem that way from where you're standing but trust me, we need to get to him in a way that doesn't risk having the whole hillside cave in on top of him." He nodded to Rachel and then walked on toward the kerosene light coming from the hospital tent. Meanwhile the woman walked on down the road in the direction of the rubble.

Justin had come alongside Rachel, and he placed his hand on hers. "Mom?"

She looked at him and knew in an instant why the woman had come to her. Perhaps she had seen Rachel sending Justin off with the others to start work on the school. Perhaps not. But somehow she had known that Rachel was a mother and that only a mother would understand that she could not—would not—abandon her son until he was found.

It was tradition that Ben spent the Sunday before Christmas with his sister and her family. But this year, as a marker of how well Sally's recovery was going, they decided to drive north to spend Christmas Day with Sally's grandfather.

"You should come," Sharon said as they sat by the pool early one morning watching Sally swim laps before the sun could become a factor.

The last time Ben had seen his father had been when his mom had died. On that occasion, his father had greeted him with, "Her last wish was to see you. You should have come sooner." It did not matter to him that Ben had been halfway around the world attending a medical conference when the call came—not from his father, but from Sharon. It did not matter that his mom had slipped into a coma as soon as she was brought to the hospital after the stroke and never regained consciousness.

Ben glanced at Sharon, but her eyes were hidden behind large black sunglasses. "You're never going to stop trying to mend that particular fence, are you?" Ben said.

She lifted her sunglasses for a moment and pinned him with her startling blue eyes. "All I'm saying is that it would do you good to get away. I gave up on trying to get you and Dad to play nice a long time ago." She let the sunglasses drop back into place and returned to watching Sally. "But I will say this," she added, this time without looking at him. "I will say that you have allowed this feud with Dad to impact everything about your life—and not in a good way."

Ben could have protested her logic, but Sharon was on a roll and it was evident that she did not expect him to debate with her. She needed to say her piece.

"Here's the thing, Ben. I get it that you and Dad have always been on different pages when it comes to religion, but you're as guilty as he ever was of wanting things your own way."

"Dad is—"

"A man, Ben. Just like you. He figured out how to make this life work for him and Mom. He did what he thought was best for you and me and everyone in his congregation. But he can be wrong. There can be another way. Grow up already, and stop blaming him for your restlessness and failure to find your true calling."

"I'm a doctor," he reminded her. "It's what I set out to be and I got there."

"I seem to recall that your original plan was to go to med school and then use your skills to minister—yes, *minister*—to those less fortunate, those who could not afford to pay or get insurance. What happened to that?"

"Why are you suddenly so mad at me?"

Sharon sighed and stared out toward the pool where Sally was swimming laps. "Because the one lesson I have learned in everything we've been through with Sally is that life is short and we don't get too many do-overs."

Ben reached over and took his sister's hand. "Hey, Sally's going to make it."

She turned to him and covered his hand with hers. "I know that. We're not talking about Sally here, Ben. We're talking about you."

"I am fine."

"Right. And I'm Lady Gaga." She stood up and laid her sunglasses on the chaise then walked toward the pool's deep end. "Clock's ticking, big brother." Then she pinched her fingers to her nose and bellowed, "Cannonball!" as she jumped into the water.

As the spray from the pool splashed over him, Ben's phone began vibrating on the small round table next to him. He checked caller identification and saw that it was the hospital calling. "Gotta go," he shouted over the noise of Sharon and Sally laughing and splashing each other. "Hospital emergency. I'll be back later."

When he got to the hospital and walked through the atrium, waving to the security guard and then taking the elevator to the children's wing, he realized he was hoping to see Rachel.

But Rachel wasn't there. If a counselor had been called, it would be Paul Cox waiting with the family—or the new guy they had shifted over from social services to fill in. Ben couldn't remember his name—only that he wasn't Rachel.

At her farewell party, Rachel had told him about the trip that she and Justin would be taking over the holidays. "Our church is sponsoring a youth mission to help victims of the earthquake in Central America."

"You're leaving again?" He had blurted out the words, and

he'd made no attempt to censor his assumption that she was running away.

The flash of anger that passed over her face was gone in an instant, and she'd smiled at him. "It's only for ten days, Ben. It was Justin's idea for us to go."

But after the party—after she had boarded the bus for Pinecraft, refusing his offer of a ride home—it had struck him why the idea of Rachel at the site of an earthquake was so unsettling for him. It wasn't safe there. Some of the aftershocks had been pretty powerful, and there had been widespread flooding. The feeling that had washed over him as he'd watched the bus leave the hospital had been similar to the helpless not-again feeling he'd had when he'd first spotted Sally's GVHD symptoms.

"Dr. Booker?" Ben turned at the sound of the nurse's voice. Somehow he had left the elevator, made his way to the station, and this nurse had handed him the patient's chart.

"Sorry." He focused all of his attention on the facts laid out before him—a girl of seven had been stung by a jellyfish and had had an allergic reaction to the venom. Ben gave the nurse a series of orders and then went in to examine the child and reassure the parents.

By the time he had gotten the child stabilized and out of danger, it was well past dinnertime. He was bone weary. He called Sharon and made his apologies, spoke with Sally and teased her about the gift he had for her, that she would have to wait until she returned from her trip to open it, and then he headed for home.

Home. Who was he kidding? This sterile place with its rooms filled with furniture picked out by some designer had no more feeling of being a home than a hotel room. There was not a single personal item in the place—artsy glass vases where there should have been framed family photos. And an impressive set of leather-bound books chosen for their ability to accent the décor instead of the dog-eared oft-read novels that had once lined the bookshelves of his room when he was a boy.

Twinkling Christmas lights from a neighbor's balcony were

reflected in the floor-to-ceiling windows. They were the closest thing he had to having any decorations for the season. He flipped through the mail and found two Christmas cards from college friends. Each featured a photo of the family dressed for the season and smiling at the camera.

He didn't send cards. He didn't have a family. He was a doctor, and it dawned on him that this had become his entire identity. Suddenly the need for human contact was overwhelming. He called the only person he could think of that was unlikely to be busy with family or the festivities. He called Darcy.

"Ben?" She was definitely surprised to hear from him.

"Yeah. Look, I just finished up a tough case and I thought maybe if you're up for it, we could grab a late supper."

There was a long pause, and he became aware of background noises—music, laughter. "But it sounds like you've got something going, so..."

"No, wait. I'm at the café—with Zeke and some people. We're helping Zeke paint the place. Come help us. There's plenty of food...."

"Another time. I'm pretty beat." *And the last thing I want right now is a party.* "Give Zeke my best."

"Sure. Merry Christmas, Ben."

"Yeah. Merry Christmas."

He hung up and paced the rooms of his condo—the spacious, mostly unused rooms. Then he picked up his keys and left. Outside, he walked along the bay then up Main Street to Pineapple on his way to Burns Court. He was thinking maybe a movie would clear his mind, and the theater there always offered something of interest. But as he walked past one of the large old churches that dotted the streets of downtown Sarasota, he heard music—not the usual organ/choir music he might have expected but the sounds of the season's carols rendered by a jazz group.

He stood on the sidewalk for a moment listening then stepped inside. A woman smiled at him and handed him a program then pointed out a seat on the very end of the last pew in the church's chapel. The place was lit by candlelight, and a trio of jazz musicians were seated on a small platform at the front of the room. It took less than a minute for Ben to be drawn into the unique beauty of their rendition of "O Come All Ye Faithful."

How long had it been since he'd sung the familiar words? And yet he found himself thinking them as he closed his eyes and listened. The carol took him back to the Christmases of his youth. The services at his father's church. The nativity story acted out by the children—he had played Joseph to Sharon's Mary for three years running. The packed house for his father's annual midnight service on Christmas Eve—the one sermon, Ben realized, he had always looked forward to hearing.

This service was when his father spoke only of God's love for all humankind, where he exhorted those blessed with more to share their blessings with those less fortunate. And always after that service ended and the last member of the congregation had gone, Ben and Sharon and their parents had not gone home—they had gone instead to a local shelter where they had personally delivered the congregation's generous donations of coats and sweaters and blankets and food to those in need.

Ben opened his eyes and tried to swallow around the lump that had formed in his throat. He hadn't thought about those days in a very long time, not since the day he'd left home for college, left home for good. He thought about what Sharon had said to him earlier that day. Their father wasn't any more perfect than any other human being. But he had done what he thought was best for his family—and his congregation.

After the concert, instead of heading for the theater, Ben walked down the mostly deserted streets until he reached the bay. There he sat on a park bench and took out his phone.

It rang for some time, and he was about to hang up when he heard his father's sleep-filled, raspy voice. "Pastor Booker here."

"Dad?"

The silence that stretched across the miles separating them was a fragile thread, one that Ben was suddenly afraid might snap if he didn't say something. "I was thinking—if it's okay with you—that I might drive up with Sharon and Malcolm and Sally. Maybe stay with you for a few days."

Silence—the silence that screamed with all the hurt that had never been spoken between Ben and his father. Then finally, "That would be fine, son. Really fine."

Chapter 26

On their second day in the village, much-needed supplies of water and food and medical supplies were delivered. Cooking over open fires, the earthquake victims prepared the food while the teams of soldiers and volunteers continued their work. By sundown the Mennonites had made a good start on repairing the school so that at least part of it was again roofed, and plans were made to move the most seriously injured there.

"We just got word that there's a medical team on the way," Mary told Hester and Rachel as the three of them sat on toppled stone walls eating their supper. "Let's hope there's a doctor in the mix."

"Too late for her," Hester said with a nod toward the woman whose son had been buried in the rubble.

"It wasn't the original quake that buried her son," Mary told them. "It was an aftershock yesterday before you got here. The boy was out there helping in the search. The ground shifted and. . ." She shrugged.

"So he's been buried how long?" Rachel asked, her eyes on the mother whose vigil for her son was unceasing even as the woman halfheartedly picked at her supper.

"A day and a half now." Mary scraped the last of her food onto her fork. "Going without food or water for that long? You do the math," she said somberly as she headed back to work.

"You okay?" Hester asked Rachel once they were alone.

"I feel so sad for her." Rachel watched the woman who was now fingering the beads of her rosary, her eyes closed, her lips moving.

"Well, clearly she has not yet given up hope."

Rachel looked over to where Justin was part of a lively group of nationals and volunteers kicking a soccer ball around in a circle. She was so very blessed to have him in her life. Her heart went out to the woman praying for her child. "I'll be back," she told Hester, and taking two cookies from a package, she picked her way across the rubble.

"My name is Rachel," she said after waiting respectfully for the woman to finish her prayers.

"Isabel," the woman replied, accepting the cookie that Rachel handed her and taking a bite.

"My son's name is Justin." Rachel nodded toward the group of young people.

"Raoul," the woman replied with a glance toward the pile of rocks and stones.

"I'm so sorry for your loss—your husband…" The two women ate their cookies while Rachel tried to come up with some topic that might offer the woman a reprieve. "Your English is perfect."

Isabel shrugged. "My husband is…*was* American. I met him when I was in graduate school. He was a professor in California. Raoul was born there, but every year over the Christmas holidays we come here to see my family. He died in the aftershock that followed the original quake."

Rachel was almost afraid to ask the next question. "And the rest of your family?"

"Safe. They had gone to San Jose for the day. But Raoul had a stomachache—it takes him some time to adjust to the change in diet—so we stayed here. I had left for church when the earthquake struck. I turned back and saw my son running toward me yelling for me to go back to the church."

"And your husband?"

"Stayed behind to check on the neighbors to make sure everyone was out." She fingered her rosary and murmured, "Everyone got out except for him."

Rachel let the silence and the darkness wrap around them until she heard Isabel release a shuddering sigh. "When I awoke, Raoul had gone with the soldiers and men of the village the next day to search. He was there when they brought out my husband's body. It was so very hard for him."

"How old is he?"

"Ten." She stared at the rock pile that had killed her husband and now held her son. "He kept going back there as if it might not be true. Then yesterday there was a strong aftershock and the shifting. . ." She buried her face in her hands, the rosary dangling from her fingers.

Rachel wrapped her arm around Isabel's shoulders. "You need to rest."

Isabel pulled away with a vehemence that was surprising. "No. I will not leave him. As long as there is a chance, I will not leave him out here alone."

"Then I will watch with you—we can spell each other."

"Your son. . ."

". . .has the comfort of friends. He knows where I am. He understands."

"*Gracias.*"

Hester sent John to deliver blankets for them to rest on as well as several small bottles of water. He also handed Rachel her Bible and a flashlight. "Justin asked me to bring you these."

The two women settled in for the night's vigil. "One of the other women in your group told me that your husband died suddenly too," Isabel said.

"It was two years ago, but I well remember the immediate shock of not having him there—of having to come to grips with the idea that he would not be there again."

They sat in silence for a long moment, Isabel resting her chin on her bent knees. "And after two years is it. . .better?"

Rachel had to think about that. "I still miss him—I expect that a part of me always will. I especially miss what we shared together in raising our son."

Isabel glanced at her. "But?"

"But I am a woman of faith as you are. So I know that God has a plan for our lives, Isabel."

"I only hope. . ." Isabel's voice broke and she shook her head vehemently then surrendered to the tears.

Rachel held her until her sobs finally dwindled to shuddering sighs. "You will make it, Isabel. If you hold fast to your faith, you can get through this. But you need to get some rest."

Promising Isabel that she would wake her in two hours— sooner if anything happened—Rachel settled against a tree and opened her Bible. But she did not turn on the flashlight. Instead she ran her fingers lightly over the pages, praying silently for Raoul and Isabel and thanking God for giving her and Justin this opportunity to serve others.

The two hours passed, but Isabel was sleeping so soundly that Rachel could not bring herself to wake her. Instead she focused her attention on the blackness of the night sky, the sheer vastness of it like the boundless sea. How could anyone doubt God's existence?

It did not surprise her in the least that her query brought thoughts of Ben to mind. She couldn't help but think that some-how if he could find his way back to God he would be a happier man. She tried to imagine Ben in this place, and she smiled as she envisioned the way his lighthearted teasing would comfort the children. He was so very good with children. Not for the first time she thought about what a good father he would make. And perhaps it was the quietness of the night, the starless sky, or her own weariness, but she found herself envisioning him as Justin's father, as the father of children that he and she might have together.

"I love him, heavenly Father," she whispered. "I love him as I first loved James. He fills my thoughts and my dreams, and I don't know what to do."

Beside her, Isabel stirred. "What time is it?"

"Almost four," Rachel confessed. "You were sleeping so soundly."

"Well, I am awake now, and it is you who must rest." She stretched and sat up.

She was right of course. Rachel had come here as part of a relief team, and what relief could she offer if she were exhausted? She curled onto her side and closed her eyes. The last thing she remembered hearing was the rhythmic clicking of Isabel's rosary beads.

It had been two long years since Justin had felt so sure that everything was going to work out for him and his mom after all. Coming on the youth mission had been exactly what he needed to get past the disaster of Sally's ruined glove and his part in it. Being in a place where he could do things that actually helped other people gave Justin a sense of purpose. Somehow every time he made an injured kid laugh or brought water to another patient he felt like he was making amends for hurting Sally. He knew that he wasn't supposed to take pride in things he did, but he and the others were making a real difference for these people—and doing that made him feel closer to his dad.

They had already managed to repair the school building as well as a few of the less damaged homes and shops in the village. The youth volunteers spent their free time in the evenings with kids their age from the village, learning a few Spanish words, singing songs, and trading stories. Justin was telling one of the older kids about moving to Florida when he heard a cry go up from the rock pile where they all knew a boy was still buried. Just about everybody took off running to see what was happening.

As everyone crowded together at the base of the pile of rubble, Justin saw one of the soldiers carefully roll back a boulder. The heavy rock tumbled down toward them, causing everything in its path to shift and resettle. The onlookers jumped out of its way. It was almost like they were all holding their breath until the boulder came to a stop.

"There," he heard the boy's mother say, her voice high pitched and excited. "Can you see him?" She switched to Spanish, edging closer to the opening that the soldier had exposed. "Raoul!" she cried out. The sound echoed in the silence of the crowd.

Justin edged closer to his mom. "What's going on?"

"The soldier came this morning with a dog specially trained to search for any signs of someone still buried beneath the rocks," Hester told him. "We think the dog may have located Raoul."

"Is he alive?"

His mom wrapped her arm around Justin's shoulder. "We don't know yet. Pray that he is."

"I see him," the soldier yelled.

"Can you reach him?" another man shouted in Spanish, gesturing as he made his way across the rubble, trying hard not to disturb the loose rock.

The soldier shook his head.

The crowd groaned.

The boy's mother lay on her stomach as she edged closer and closer to the small opening. "Raoul," she said, her voice husky now, like she might cry.

The men worked together through the long, hot afternoon, but it seemed everything that they tried only caused the ground to shift and the opening they had made to get smaller.

Around suppertime, a truck rolled into the village and most of the people went to unload the supplies. "Go help the others," Justin's mom said, urging him away from the scene playing out on the rock pile. "Go on," she said, turning him toward the truck and giving him a little push.

"Mom? Is Raoul going to make it?"

"We must pray that he will," she said.

But Justin wasn't sure prayer was going to work in this case.

Rachel found herself wishing Ben was with them. He would know what to do, she was certain of it. Somehow he would find a way to reach the boy, treat him, and bring him to the surface. But Ben was not there.

Instead, Mary introduced Rachel and Hester to the new arrivals—three medical students. "I was filling them in on the situation out there." Mary jerked her head in the general direction of the rubble pile.

"The mother has great faith even now," Rachel said. She saw how the medical students followed her gaze up to the place where the boy had been buried now for almost two days. The mother still lay on her stomach staring down at her son.

"What's keeping them from bringing the boy up?" one student asked.

"The opening is very narrow, and the terrain surrounding it is still so unstable," Rachel told him. "They do not want to try anything until they are certain that they will not cause another cave-in. Soon it will be dark and they will stop for the night—but his mother will stay with him."

"We have lights," another of the students said, more to himself than to Rachel.

"Let's go," the third added as he took the knapsack that held his medical supplies and a large LED lantern from the truck. "If they can't get him out, then maybe we can figure out how to get a man down there. If by some miracle he is still alive, then he's got to be badly dehydrated."

Rachel followed the group to where the rescuers stood helplessly off to the side as the woman repeated her son's name over and over again, her voice now no more than a whisper.

After consulting with the rescue team, using Juan Carlos as their interpreter, one of the medical students edged his way carefully toward the opening. "You're the nurse?"

Rachel nodded.

"Come with me."

With every step, a trickle of pebbles tumbled down the slope. The young man would freeze waiting for everything to settle before pressing on. At the base of the pile, Rachel saw the workers setting up more lights and focusing the beams on the path that she and the medical student must take to reach the opening. Isabel sat up, watching them come.

"I cannot see him," she said. "It's so dark."

At last, Rachel and the young doctor made it to the opening and sat down. "Then let's throw a little light down there, okay?" He tied a rope to a thin but powerful flashlight and slowly lowered it into the crevice. The rescuers had not been kidding when they said the opening was impossibly narrow. There was no way that any of the men could make it down there.

"Raoul?" Isabel called. "The doctor is here now. Just hang on a little longer. The doctor will save you."

"I can't see anything," the doctor admitted. He scooted to one side. "You try."

Rachel settled herself between him and Isabel then lay prone as she edged her way over the lip of the crevice. The light swung like a pendulum as the med student lowered it as far as the rope allowed. She could see the boy. He was on his back, one leg straight and the other at an angle. His hands, white with the dust of the rubble that surrounded him, were resting against his chest. He wore a dark T-shirt and shorts.

Rubbing sweat from her own eyes, Rachel studied the boy, searching for signs of life that she prayed she might find. And then she thought she saw the slightest twitch of the boy's eyelids and lips. Surely it was a mirage, a longing for the boy to have made it when there was almost no possibility that he could have. *Please.*

She waited, forcing her breathing to steady. Then, seeing no more signs of life, she considered how best to break the news to Isabel. Suddenly one of the boy's hands moved toward his face— less than an inch—but this was no mirage. *He's alive,* she thought incredulously. Never in her life had she witnessed a miracle. Yet this child had been lying at the bottom of this pit with no food or water for two days now, the extent of his injuries—especially the internal ones—unknown and still he was alive. She shouted the news to those gathered above her.

She sat up, felt Isabel grasp her shoulder, and then carefully lowered as much of her upper body as possible into the opening for a closer look. Now the boy's hand was thrown across his eyes, so there was no doubt that he was alive.

"Raoul, lie still. We're going to get you out," she promised and closed her eyes tight for a moment as she sent up a prayer of thanksgiving. The odds against getting this child to the surface in time were still astronomical. It would take hours—perhaps days. *Please. He's made it this far. Don't let us fail him now.*

She felt a hand on her back and turned her head to find Isabel and the med student both leaning in close. "He's really alive?"

Rachel nodded as she pulled herself back to the edge and faced Isabel. "Your son is alive," she told her, "but he is very weak. We need to get him medical attention and fluids as soon as possible."

Isabel nodded, her tears flowing freely now, her smile radiant even in the darkness that surrounded them. She leaned closer to the opening, her hand extended as if to touch her son so many feet below her. "We are coming, Raoul. I promise you. . .we will come."

"Do you think we can get to him in time?" the medical student asked Rachel.

"We must. Isabel has given her son her promise, and we mothers do not make promises we cannot keep."

By morning the trio of medical students had rigged up tubing by which they could send down a trickle of water for Raoul, but even in the rare moments when he was conscious the boy was too weak and disoriented to follow their instructions. An engineer was studying the area, trying to decide the best way to get to the boy without causing the rubble around him to collapse. And at the base of the earthquake-created hill, everyone else gathered to pray and sing, hoping to keep up the spirits of the rescuers as well as provide comfort for Raoul and Isabel.

Rachel could not stop thinking about the boy. The place where he lay was not so very deep. There was a jagged piece of concrete jutting out from a wall of rubble that prevented them from getting all the way down to where he lay. One of the medical students had actually climbed down to the thin ledge, but his report was not good. He had been unable to reach Raoul, and unless they could get past the barrier...

Rachel closed her eyes. *There has got to be an answer,* she prayed. *Show us the way.*

Two rescuers walked past her on their way back to their trucks to gather more supplies. "If we had a kid—a skinny kid..."

"You can't ask any kid to go down there," his companion argued. "What if the whole thing caves in? Then we've lost two kids, devastated two families."

Rachel opened her eyes, pressing her palms down the front of her apron. Suddenly she stared down at her hands, stilling them on her body—her thin-as-a-boy's body. Could she make it past the barrier? And if she could, wasn't she the next best person to reach Raoul first? To administer the emergency care he so badly needed? To check him for injuries not readily evident from their vantage point at the top of the hole that held him?

"Justin!" She beckoned for her son to join her in the tent the staff used as their sleeping quarters. Inside the tent she pulled out a pair of her son's jeans and a shirt. "Sit there," she said, indicating the cot next to his. "I need to talk to you while I change." She pulled closed the curtain that hung between cots to give herself a little privacy and began laying out her plan while she changed into Justin's clothes.

"But Mom, it's dangerous. Let me go."

Rachel's heart swelled with love for him. She pulled back the curtain, her change of dress causing his eyes to widen in surprise. "You are such a brave young man."

"You look—different." He glanced toward the top of her head and then to the starched white prayer covering lying on the cot.

"Ja." She knelt next to him and took his hands in hers. "I have asked a great deal of you since your father died, Justin."

"But..."

She pulled him close and stroked his hair as she continued,

"And if you had not asked to come—to be a part of this youth mission, then just think. . . We would not have been here."

"And you would not be doing this," Justin argued.

"Time is wasting, Justin. Tell me you understand why I need to try."

He sighed. "Because like Raoul's mom or Sally's, you can't stand seeing any kid in trouble. It's a mom thing." His voice dripped with resignation. He straightened and faced her squarely. "But I'm going to be there and if there's any chance at all that. . ."

"I'll be tethered to a rope—they'll pull me out if anything starts to go wrong," she said.

"Promise?"

"Promise." She waited. If he begged her not to go she wouldn't. Justin had already lost one parent, and he was right to be concerned about the possible danger. "If you don't want. . ."

"Maybe this is why we came here, Mom. Do you think maybe this is why God sent us here?"

She had never loved her child more than she did in that moment. "I don't know. What does your heart tell you?"

"Go," he said as he wrapped his arms around her and held on. "Please come back safe, okay?"

To Rachel's relief, Hester and the others from their church had gone to get their lunches in the mess tent when she made her way up to the opening on the rock pile. It was going to be a lot easier to convince the rescue team that she was the perfect candidate to go and get the boy than it would ever be to convince her friends.

And sure enough, they had already rigged her to the necessary climbing apparatus and begun to lower her into the hole when she heard Pastor Detlef's stern voice. "Bring her out of there—now."

She found her footing on the cleft of concrete and looked up. "It's okay, Pastor. I'm here. Now what?"

On a separate rope, the medical team lowered down a canvas bag that they had packed with emergency medical supplies and water. Lying flat on her stomach, she lowered the bag past the jagged edges of her fragile platform and down to where Raoul lay. He was so still, and there had been almost no sign that he was still alive for hours now.

"Okay," she reported, feeling the dust fill her lungs. "Going now." She paused for a moment to gather her wits and heard the faint strains of a favorite Christmas carol sung in harmony. She smiled. It was Christmas Eve. Surely God would be with them on this of all days.

She was halfway between Raoul below her and the ledge above when the rope caught on one of the jagged edges. For an instant she was left dangling, swinging back and forth the way the flashlight had the night before. She was surrounded by the ominous sound of rock coming loose. Instinctively she covered her head with her arms as a trickle of stones and dust pelted her from above.

"That's it," she heard one of the medical students say. "This is too dangerous."

Rachel swung her body over toward the place where the rope was caught, freed it, and landed with a thud inches from Raoul's inert body. "I'm here," she called up and immediately opened her bag and took out what she needed to check the boy's vitals.

In an instant she was lost in her work, oblivious to her surroundings, focused only on calling out her findings, checking Raoul for injuries, and assessing his status. Using one of the clips from her climbing apparatus, she was able to hang a bag of fluids and get an IV started. He groaned a little when she poked him with the needle. She thought it was the most wonderful sound she had ever heard.

He was alive and with God's help, he was going to make it. She pulled out a thin but strong nylon sheet the engineer had given her. "Once he's got that first bag of fluids in him, then we can move him. Wrap him in this and then hitch the ropes to him like so," he'd instructed her as they'd lowered her into the hole. "Hopefully we can get him through the crevice and past the concrete barrier. Once we accomplish that he'll be home free, and we'll send down the rope for you, okay?"

Rachel set the drip on the IV and then squatted against the rough wall to wait. Above her, she could hear Isabel praying the beads of her rosary.

She sat for a long moment, watching the fluid slowly drip down the tubing. And she thought about Ben. Where was he spending this Christmas Eve? Would anything about the season touch him, bring back memories of what his faith must have meant to him once? Sharon had told her how as a teenager Ben had been a real leader—at school and in the summer camp they had attended. "But not in our father's church," she had admitted sadly. "He and Dad never seemed to be on the same page."

Finally, the IV bag was empty. Rachel pushed herself to her feet and unhooked the tubing, leaving the port so that once Raoul was brought to the surface he could continue to receive the vital fluids.

"Call the others. I'm getting him ready for the ascent," she said.

It took the rescuers nearly half an hour to maneuver Raoul's wrapped and upright body to safety. Then a shout of victory echoed around the opening and funneled down into the hole where she waited her turn to be brought up. She smiled and thanked God for this blessing. Then she heard another sound, nothing so soothing or consoling as the hymn singing or the shouts of celebration. No, this sound was a sharp crack followed by silence followed by a scattering of stones and dust falling from above.

Rachel turned to face the wall and covered her head with her arms when she heard a loud thundering noise that seemed to be coming directly at her. Seconds later she felt the scrape of something sharp and hard brush her shoulder and then land with a heavy thud inches from where she crouched. She waited an instant, aware that above her the celebration had gone silent, and now there were voices calling out for her as the hole around and above her filled with dust and falling debris.

In the sudden shadowy confines, she realized that if she hadn't moved to where she now was, the heavy concrete slab that had broken loose and fallen would have landed right on her.

"Mom!" she heard Justin shriek.

"Rachel!" Hester sounded every bit as panicked.

Her throat was filled with dust and her bag with its bottled water and other supplies was buried beneath the huge piece of concrete. She coughed and tugged on the dangling rope. "Right here," she croaked.

"Get her out of there *now*," she heard Pastor Detlef order for the second time.

This time she hoped the others would listen to him.

$$\sim\!\!\gtrless\quad Chapter\ 27\quad\lessgtr\!\!\sim$$

Justin had never in his life prayed as hard as he did that afternoon. He squeezed his eyes closed and kept them that way, allowing his ears to tell him what was happening with the rescue. A shout of joy from the rescue workers told him that the boy was alive.

"Thank you, God," he murmured aloud. "Now please please please bring them both out of there alive."

Was he asking for too much?

He felt Hester's comforting hand on his shoulder, and then he heard another cry of relief from those gathered on the hillside. Opening his eyes, he saw rescue workers grab hold of the boy as he reached the opening. They carefully put him on a stretcher they'd had waiting, and two workers carried the stretcher down the hillside toward the medical tent.

But where was his mom?

Justin broke free of Hester's grasp and started up the hill. "Mom?"

He heard a distant rumble like thunder, but it wasn't coming from the sky. It was coming from the ground. Around him small avalanches of stones trickled down the hillside. "Mom!" he shouted and ran for the place where Pastor Detlef and others were leaning over the opening.

"Get back, Justin," John Steiner ordered.

He looked worried and scared. "Is Mom..."

"She's okay," John said. "We have to figure out how to get her out of there."

A thousand thoughts raced through Justin's mind. What if they couldn't get her out? What if she was trapped like the boy had been? What if they were too late?

"Mom?" he shouted and was grateful when everybody else stopped talking for a minute.

"I'm okay, Justin. Do what John tells you, okay? John and Hester will take care of you, okay?"

He tried to make sense of her words. Why would she say something like that? "Mom? You promised," he shouted, and then he broke down in the tears he'd forced back ever since he'd watched her head up that hillside.

"You promised," he sobbed as Hester wrapped him in her embrace.

Rachel thought her heart might actually break when she heard Justin calling out to her. It was hard not to cry out to God to stop her son's suffering. But instead she closed her eyes and prayed the prayer she had known from childhood on. *Thy will be done.*

And after a moment she felt such a sense of peace wash over her. In spite of the fact that she was pretty certain that she had a broken arm and perhaps other injuries, she felt sure that whatever her fate might be, it was what would be best for Justin. She would keep her promise of giving him a better life.

Hester and John would take Justin if she didn't make it out of here. Hester had told her as much once when they'd been talking about how hard things were for Justin without James.

"Thank You, God, for bringing Hester back into my life," she murmured and then coughed because her throat and mouth were filled with the dust that continued to fall all around her. If this was to be her death then she was at peace because Justin would have a good life with Hester and John.

Suddenly she felt the rope she was holding grow taut, and

her will to survive and care for Justin herself kicked into high gear. "I can climb the wall if you pull," she called up to the men above her. It would be difficult with only one working arm, but she was determined to do it.

She planted her feet against the wall and squeezed her body past the barrier above. She felt the sharp rock rip her clothing and into her skin, but she was not going to let that stop her.

"Pull," she called, and then she closed her eyes against the sudden brightness of the sun as she realized that she had finally reached the top.

She held out her good arm to John, wincing as pain shot through her other arm. "Thank you," she whispered as John and another man pulled her the rest of the way out and helped her to a stretcher,

"Mom!"

Never in all her life had she heard a sound more sweet than Justin's voice.

"Right here," she answered, and as he buried his face against her chest, she cradled his head. "Right here as long as you need me," she said.

On Christmas Day everyone stopped working to celebrate. Together they all sang carols and Pastor Detlef along with the local priest led services.

A few days later Justin and his mom and the others were at the San Jose airport. It all seemed like a world away from the little village as they waited for the plane that would take them back to Sarasota.

"Mom?"

"Right here," she said, and patted his knee.

"I've been thinking. I mean, do you really want to bake pies and stuff for Zeke's café?"

"I like to bake and he needs help."

"I know but, well, I mean lots of people can bake and lots of people need jobs."

"I need a job, Justin. We have rent to pay and food to buy and—"

"But what about the kids at the hospital?"

"They have Pastor Paul."

"They need you, Mom."

Her eyes flickered away as if she wasn't quite sure how to answer him. He decided to press his case. "And that's not all. They need you—not just those sick kids but Pastor Paul—and Dr. Booker."

Now she was staring hard at him. "Why would you say that—about Dr. Booker?"

Justin sighed. "Come on, Mom. I may be twelve, but it's pretty clear even to a kid like me that he likes you—a lot. And you like him. I mean, he makes you happy—the way Dad used to."

"Dr. Booker is a good friend. . . ."

"He's more than that. I overheard Hester saying that he's in love with you." Instantly he realized that he might have gone too far. Hester—who was seated on the aisle across from them— rolled her eyes and then shrugged when Justin's mom looked at her.

"Well, he is," she said and turned back to her knitting.

"So, I mean. . .people get married again after someone dies, don't they?"

"Yes, but. . ."

"So if you went back to work at the hospital and you and Dr. Booker spent time together, maybe. . ." For the first time since his father's death Justin found himself excited about the future—more than excited, he felt certain about the future. "It could work," he said hopefully.

"I'll think about it."

It had been a long time since Ben had spent any real time with his father. When he'd gone home for his mom's funeral, there had always been people around and he hadn't stayed long. But being back in his childhood home with Sharon and her family made things easier somehow. For one thing, his father doted on Sally, and from all evidence the feeling was mutual.

The man he watched with Sally was not at all the man he remembered parenting him.

"You doing okay with the change in hospitals, son?" his dad asked one day as the two of them sat at the kitchen table eating lunch. Sharon and Malcolm had taken Sally shopping, and for the first time Ben found himself alone with his father.

"Yeah. It's good."

"Maybe now you'll think about settling down—raising a family?"

"I think about it."

"Good, because you'd make a good parent—not like me. You've got more patience than I did—and you're not as scared."

It was an odd thing for him to say, and for a minute Ben was at a loss for words. Uncomfortable with the situation, he laughed. "You? Scared?"

His father pinned him with those ice-blue eyes that so often had seemed to expect more than Ben could give. "Scared," he repeated, and Ben realized that those eyes weren't nearly as cold and penetrating as he'd remembered them.

"Of what?"

"Failing."

"You were the senior minister of one of the largest churches in the state," Ben reminded him.

His father waved his hand impatiently. "Not at my work. At home—right here. With you and your sister."

Ben was speechless. "I never knew," he said. "I mean, Dad, you were always so. . ."

"I know." He turned away and stared out the window. "I'm sorry, son. I really thought that I needed to be that way if you were going to be stronger than I was. But I see now that in many ways I still failed you."

"How can you say that? I have a successful practice, friends—a good life."

"And I'm proud of you, but I want more for you than a career. I want you to have faith. I want you to have a wife and family. I want so much for you, son." His father stood up and took his dishes to the sink. "Those things are the keys, son. I was never able to make you see that." He stood at the sink with his back to Ben, letting the water run.

When Ben saw the older man's shoulders start to shake, he went to him and placed his hand on his father's back, noticing for the first time how old and frail he'd grown in these last years. "You didn't fail me, Dad. If anything, I failed you."

"I wanted so much for you kids. . . ."

"We have it, Dad. Look around you. Sally alone is reason enough for you to believe that you and Mom did everything. . ."

"I miss her so much," he blubbered. "She was the rock in this house."

Ben was desperate to say anything that might give his father some comfort. "I was thinking maybe, if you feel up to it, we might all go for midnight services tonight. Remember how much Mom loved that?"

His father sniffed back the last of his tears and nodded. "I haven't been able to go since she passed."

"We'll go together—all of us—exactly like we did when you were in the pulpit."

And to his astonishment his father turned and gripped him in a bear hug. "I love you, son. Sally tells me I don't say that enough so I'll say it twice. I love you, and I couldn't be more proud of the way you've turned out."

Out of the mouths of babes, Ben thought as he returned his father's embrace. "Love you too, Dad."

And he realized that he truly did.

On New Year's Eve Rachel got a call from the hospital. It was so good to be back. She thanked God every day for the blessing of her work. She finished counseling the couple whose son was going into surgery and was escorting them to the waiting room when she saw Ben waiting for her.

"Do you have a minute?" he asked.

She nodded and said a few last words to the couple then returned to the chapel. Ben closed the door and leaned against it. "Hi. You're back."

"I am."

"To stay?"

"It was Justin's idea." She moved around the room, straightening the cushions and putting away some materials in the small closet. "Eileen tells me that you went to visit your father over the holidays."

"I did."

"How did that go?"

"We made our peace—found our way."

"I'm glad for you—and your father."

"I told him about you. He'd like to meet you, and Justin of course."

"You should invite him here for a visit."

She felt shy with him and was well aware that their conversation was stiff and uncomfortable.

"How's your arm?"

She glanced down at the cast. "It'll heal." She had run out of things to do and started to open the door.

But he took her hand between his to stop her from going. She did not pull away—or look up. "I missed you."

"I'm happy to be back here with everyone."

"Not working with you—although I missed that. I missed *you*, Rachel."

She pulled her hand free of his and placed her palm against his cheek. "I missed you as well."

He smiled. "Ever hear of the song lyrics, 'What are you doing New Year's Eve?' "

"Is that a question?"

"It's an invitation—to spend some time with me—to welcome in the New Year together."

"I promised Justin. . . ," she murmured then shook her head.

"What? You promised Justin what?"

"Oh Ben, he misses his father and he has built up this idea— this fantasy—about you and me."

Ben covered her hand still resting lightly against his cheek and pulled it away so that he could kiss her palm. "Then it would seem that Justin and I are on the same page. I love you, Rachel. The one thing I realized when I saw my father was that I had allowed too much time to pass—lost too many chances to build memories with him—to know the man he is and the man he helped me become in spite of what I once thought. And then when I heard about you in that hole and realized that I might have lost you forever. . ."

Her eyes glistened with tears, but she was smiling. It was a little like seeing a rainbow through the clouds. "So?" he pressed. "You—me—Justin? A New Year and a new beginning?"

"Yes," she whispered as she stood on tiptoe and kissed him gently.

Ben drew her closer and deepened their kiss. "I love you, Rachel," he said. "I don't know how we're going to work things out, but that's a fact."

She pulled a little away and stroked his hair away from his forehead. "And we both know that facts are very important to you, Dr. Booker. But I'm curious. Facts must be provable. How do you intend to prove this one?"

He smiled. "I've learned that there are some things it seems even a doctor has to accept—on faith."

Epilogue

A lot of stuff changed after Justin and his mom got home from Costa Rica. She went back to work at the hospital and seemed happier than he'd seen her in a long time. Dr. Booker—Ben—started coming around just about every day. He even started attending services at the bigger Mennonite church where Justin had joined the youth group and made several new friends.

Then one day his mom asked him how he would feel if they both started going to that church regularly. She had made some friends there, the couple whose daughter had been killed in the car accident, for one. Next thing Justin knew, it was him, his mom, and Ben going there together just about every Sunday—unless Ben had to be at the hospital or his mom got a call.

After church, they would head over to Hester and John's place for a big lunch. Then one day Ben suggested they stop by his sister's house—Sally's house. That was pretty awkward at first, but then they were all sitting around the swimming pool and all of a sudden Sally pushed him in.

He came up sputtering and saw that everybody was laughing—even his mom had a smile on her face.

"That's for not trusting me to be your one true friend when you first got here," Sally said.

Justin had made his way to the side of the pool where she was standing, hands on her hips, looking pretty healthy for a kid that had been through everything she'd been through. He squinted up at her. "Hey, I apologized for that," he reminded her. "I put it in writing."

She grinned and squatted down to offer him a hand so he could get out of the pool. "Okay, so now we're friends?"

"Not quite," Justin said, taking her hand and pulling her into the water. He waited until she came to the surface, sputtering the way he had, with all the adults laughing at them. "*Now* we're friends."

But the most amazing change of all was the day that Ben asked him to go fishing with him.

"You mean just you and me?"

"Yeah. I've got something I want to talk over with you."

Justin wasn't sure where this conversation was headed so he simply shrugged. "Okay."

On the way to the park at the south end of Lido Key Ben asked him all about the trip to Costa Rica. While they staked out a spot on the pass that led from the bay to the Gulf and set up their equipment, Ben continued to praise Justin for the courage he had shown in deciding to join the mission.

"I'd do it again," Justin told him.

"Maybe next time I could go with you," Ben said.

"Sure."

They fished for a while in silence. A great blue heron stood a few feet to Justin's right, keeping an eye out for any possibility of snaring a baitfish. A motorboat came by, and the people on it waved like they were in a parade or something. And Justin was aware that Ben kept glancing over at him—like he had something to say but wasn't sure how to say it. Finally, he cleared his throat and slowly reeled in his line.

"Justin? What would you think about the idea that maybe your mom and I—I mean one day—might get married?"

Justin felt a grin start to spread across his face. "For real? Like we'd be a real family and everything?"

He liked the way Ben laughed. It was a sound that came

from somewhere deep inside him. He liked it even better when Ben reached over and ruffled his hair, the way his dad used to do when he was pleased with something Justin had done or said.

Justin thought about the promise his mom had made him when they'd left Ohio—the promise he had thrown back at her on a couple of occasions. If his mom and Ben got married they'd be a family again. "Did you ask her yet?"

"Sort of. But not officially. First I wanted to ask you how you'd feel about it."

Justin was suddenly cautious about saying too much before he had a chance to talk to his mom about how she felt. "I'm pretty sure she'll say yes."

"What do *you* say?"

"I guess it could work."

Ben offered him a handshake—an actual grown-up handshake—and Justin accepted. "We're going to be okay," Ben said as he cast his line far out into the water. He was smiling.

Justin couldn't seem to control the grin of pure joy that spread across his face. "Yeah."

Just like his mom had promised.

Discussion Questions

1. What is Rachel's promise to Justin?

2. Why does she feel such a promise is needed?

3. How does she try to keep her promise in the early days after she and Justin arrive in Florida?

4. Twelve-year-old Justin and twelve-year-old Sally are struggling with different challenges—how does each face those challenges and deal with them as the story progresses?

5. What are your impressions of Darcy Meekins and how her story develops?

6. What role does faith play in the romance between Rachel and Ben—how does it keep them apart and how does it bring them together?

7. How does Rachel's daring rescue of the boy trapped underground change her relationship with Justin?

8. Almost all of the main adult characters are struggling with the choices they are making for themselves in terms of their careers and their personal lives—how do each of them (Rachel, Ben, Darcy and Zeke) meet those challenges?

9. One of the underlying themes of the book is the impact bullying can have. Other than Derek, who else in the story might be identified as a bully in certain situations and what are those situations?

10. Does Rachel truly live up to the promise she made to Justin after his father died and she decided to move them to Florida? If so, how, and if not, why not?

ANNA SCHMIDT is the author of over twenty works of fiction. Among her many honors, Anna is the recipient of *Romantic Times'* Reviewer's Choice Award and a finalist for the RITA award for romantic fiction. She enjoys gardening and collecting seashells at her winter home in Florida.

If you enjoyed *A Mother's Promise*
be sure to read

A STRANGER'S GIFT

A horrific hurricane has devastated the area of Sarasota, Florida. Enter Hester Detlef, a field director for the Mennonite Disaster Service, who has dedicated her life to helping others. Will this Old Order Mennonite find love amid the debris? Having refused to evacuate his cluster of beach cottages at the onset of the hurricane, former Amish man John Hafner now finds himself homeless, jobless, faithless, and badly injured. Will his limited patience for a Mennonite do-gooder keep him from accepting the help he so desperately needs? Or will Hester find a way to restore his faith, love, and livelihood?

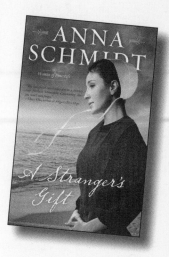

A SISTER'S FORGIVENESS

Sisters Emma and Jeannie are best friends, as are their teenage daughters Sadie and Tessa. But when a tragic accident results in Tessa's death—and Sadie is to blame— both families reel from grief and loss. Can they find a way from heartbreak to forgiveness?

Available wherever Christian books are sold.

Due . 9/29.

Life holds no guarantees. . . .

Recently widowed, Rachel Kaufmann has moved to Pinecraft, Florida, with her teenage son, Justin, to take a job as chaplain at a local hospital. But despite Rachel's best intentions for a fresh start, she is struggling to maintain her traditional Mennonite values with the demands of her new job. Worse, Justin is struggling, too, and regains control by becoming a bully—the complete opposite of the boy he was back in Ohio.

From the moment Dr. Ben Booker meets Rachel Kaufmann, he is attracted to her vulnerability, although he understands that she does a good job of masking that fragility by focusing on the pain of others. Ben knows that spirit in a younger version—his niece, Sally, who has battled a debilitating illness for most of her life. But when Sally opens up about a new kid teasing her at school—and the bully turns out to be Justin—Ben is torn between protecting his niece and his growing feelings for Rachel.

How will God turn potential disaster into paradise for them all?

ANNA SCHMIDT, who lives in Wisconsin, is an award-winning author of over

U.S. $12.99

ISBN 978-1-61626-236-5

51299

9 781616 262365

FICT / Fiction / Christian / Romance